Missing and Exploited

Kim Baysinger

Missing
and
Exploited

Ken Baysinger

To order additional copies of this book, contact:
Xlibris
1-888-795-4274
www.Xlibris.com
Orders@Xlibris.com
748944

Dedicated to
Elizabeth Smart, Jaycee Dugard, Michelle
Knight, Amanda Berry, Gina DeJesus, Colleen
Stan, and so many others whose fate is unknown.

24-Hour HOTLINE
1-800-THE-LOST (1-800-843-5678)

If you think you have seen a missing child, contact
the National Center for Missing & Exploited
Children 24-hours a day, 7 days a week.

Report Child Sexual Exploitation

25% of the author's first-year royalties from the
sale of this novel will be donated to the National
Center for Missing and Exploited Children.

Chapter 1

oes Groundhog Day really deserve holiday status? An overgrown rodent pokes his head out of his underground den and does or does not see his shadow, resulting in the same thing every year—it's still six weeks to the first day of spring. Honestly, I find it hard to get excited about that. But that doesn't mean that I don't *like* Groundhog Day. It is, as Winston Churchill might have said, not the end of winter, nor is it the beginning of the end, but rather it is the end of the beginning, for it is the time when the daylight hours become noticeably longer each day.

Winter in Western Oregon is made tolerable by the existence of ski slopes. How Oregonians who don't ski manage to survive the weeks and months of dreary, gray weather is something I cannot comprehend, though one must admire them for their rugged persistence. I ski. Cold rain at home means fresh snow on Mt. Hood, and as long as I can look forward to my next trip to the mountain, I can endure the crappy weather.

But I wasn't skiing on this particular day because I was planning to watch Super Bowl XLVIII (Why couldn't they just say 48?) featuring the Seahawks and their former archnemesis, the Broncos. I'd already read everything of interest in the Sunday newspaper, and the kickoff was still hours away. Together with my extra special friend, Kim Stayton, I was frittering away the afternoon doing meaningless things that would neither pay the bills nor enrich my life.

I was watching a comic video that someone had posted on Facebook, when an ancient Studebaker pickup pulled into the parking space in front of my Canemah home/office. To say "ancient Studebaker" is actually redundant, since even the newest Studebaker is fifty years old. This particular specimen was at least a decade older than that.

Studebaker pickups had always looked kind of stunted to me, like they were *meant* to be real pickups but had suffered some sort of misfortune during gestation that prevented them from achieving full development.

I met Giles Svensen at the door and welcomed him inside. Giles was a fisherman, and I'd occasionally see him in his boat out on the river. I first met him after hitting a submerged log that destroyed my propeller and left me drifting helplessly without power. He towed me back to my dock where we got properly acquainted over a couple of beers.

Giles Svensen is a Studebaker collector. He has a big warehouse about three miles upriver from my place, where he stores tree or four dozen Studebakers. His cars are not restored, though it is his intention to begin restoration as soon as he can find the time. Still, the crudely painted sign on the door of the old warehouse building proudly proclaims, "Studebaker Museum," and if anybody stops in, Giles will gladly give a free tour.

"I was wondering if you could help me check out a story I heard a few days ago," Giles said.

"Give me some more information," I coached.

"A guy told me that he heard about a brand-new '64 Studebaker Avanti that is in an abandoned garage somewhere upriver," he explained. "The story is that the big Christmas Flood in 1964 washed away the driveway and left the garage stranded on a newly formed island. The owner had died shortly before the flood, and his heirs were out of state. They knew nothing about the garage or the car in it when they sold off the estate."

"If the car still exists, I think it would still belong to the heirs," I pointed out.

"Well, that's where the story gets interesting. Some people stumbled across the garage while they were floating down the river on a rubber raft. They got inside and looked over the car. It was under some kind of a cloth cover, so it wasn't even dusty. It had about fifty miles on the odometer, and there were no license plates on it. They thought it was an interesting discovery, so they wrote down the VIN. When they checked it out, the state had no record of it. Through a Studebaker collectors' club, the guy was able to track the VIN to the name of the dealer in Salem that sold it but couldn't find anyone who ever worked there, or any other records."

"Still, it has to belong to someone," I said.

"Yeah, but whoever owns it obviously doesn't know it or care about it, otherwise it wouldn't be there. Anyway, the DMV says that you can get a rebuilder's title for it."

"But first you have to find it." I could see where this was leading.

"Right. I thought maybe you'd be able to help figure out where it is. If we could locate it, then I'd be in a position to see if I can do anything with it."

Having listened quietly throughout the discussion, Kim finally spoke up. "That sounds a bit like the old 'Death Car' myth."

Svensen looked at her with a puzzled expression on his face. "Death Car?"

Making a belated introduction, I said, "Giles, this is Kim Stayton. You may have met her out on the river. She runs the sheriff's marine unit."

"Well, I run the marine unit boat," Kim corrected. "Sheriff Jamieson runs the marine unit."

"I thought I recognized you from someplace," Svensen said. "So what's this Death Car business?"

"It's an old urban legend. It's been around for years—decades, really. It's usually a Corvette, but it's always some highly desired car, almost new, on the back lot at a dealer, for sale for $100. The only thing is someone died in the car and wasn't found for several days. The car's been cleaned up, but nobody's figured out how to get rid of the smell."

Giles said, "I never heard that story."

"Were you raised in a monastery?" I asked with a smile.

He laughed. "I guess so because I never heard of it."

"Look it up on Snopes," I suggested.

"I'll do that," he said. "Anyway, maybe you could find out if the Avanti story is real."

"I still owe you for that tow-in. I'll poke around a little bit for you. How can I get in touch with the guy who told you the story?"

"His name is Tom Vilkas. I don't have a phone number or anything, but you can find him just about any Friday or Saturday night at the Wichita Pub up on Molalla Avenue."

After Svensen left, I went to my computer, which is a lot closer than the Wichita Pub, and found a phone number for a Thomas Vilkas on Leland Road.

"My name is Corrigan. I'm a private investigator," I said when he answered. "Are you acquainted with Giles Svensen?"

"No," he said and then quickly corrected himself. "Well, I know a guy named Giles. I don't know his last name."

"He says that he was talking with you at the Wichita Pub a few days ago."

"Yeah, okay, I know who you're talking about. What about him?"

"I understand that you told him about an old car in a garage by the river."

"Sure, we talked about that."

"Well, if you know Giles at all, you know that he's a Studebaker fanatic, so the story about an abandoned Avanti was bound to get his attention. He's asked me to help track it down, so I thought I'd start with you."

"I told Giles everything I know about it. Some people floating down the Willamette from Salem found an old garage with the car inside. I heard the

3

story—oh, gosh, about twenty-five years ago, and I spent some time trying to find the garage. I didn't have a boat, though, so I didn't have much luck."

"Did you know the people who found the car?"

"No, I heard the story from a friend of theirs. He said that he'd done some research into the legalities of recovering an abandoned old car, but like me, he didn't own a boat."

So there it was. The story came from a friend of a friend. It's always that way with the urban myths—tantalizing secondhand information. And if you ever manage to track down the friend of the friend, he'll tell you that he heard the story from a friend. You can never trace the story to its source.

"Who was it that told you the story?" I asked despite my feeling that the whole pursuit was pointless.

"I don't remember his name," Tom said, "but he was an engineer at a company I worked for when I was in high school."

"What company is that?"

"They manufacture dental equipment—Adec."

"In Newberg?" I asked.

"Yeah, in high school we had a work-study program, and I worked in the engineering department there for a couple of semesters."

"But you can't remember the name of the guy who told the story?"

"Oh hell no. That was a long time ago."

It was a dead end. Taking it any further would be a complete waste of time. Besides, it was approaching time for the football game, which the Seahawks won decisively.

February 3 Monday

Chapter 2

On the feeling that my ten-minute conversation with Tom Vilkas did not begin to pay back Giles Svensen for the time and fuel he'd spent towing my boat, I put in a call to the dental equipment company.

I asked the receptionist, "Can you tell me if there is anybody in the engineering department who was working there in about 1990?"

"There are several," she said. "Would you like to talk with one of the managers?"

"It doesn't have to be a manager—just someone who's been there that long."

She put the call through, and I found myself talking with an engineer named Pat Marlier. I went through my standard introduction and asked if he remembered Tom Vilkas.

"Sure, I remember him. What would you like to know?"

"What can you tell me about him?" I asked. The more you know about a witness, the better you'll be able to evaluate his story.

Pat chuckled. "Tom was a bullshitter. He was just a kid, but he could tell a story. And he was a wheeler-dealer too."

"What do you mean by that?"

"Well, like one time he came in and said that he was selling a bunch of plywood for a friend. His story was that the guy had been planning to build greenhouses and bought a couple of units of plywood, and then decided to go join a fishing crew in Alaska. It was a weird story—I mean, why would you buy plywood for greenhouses? They're made of glass, right?"

"That's what I'd use," I said, playing along.

"Anyway, some of the guys in the department were working on building projects, so they were interested in the plywood. Tom sold it to them at about half the retail price. Months later, it came out that Tom's brother worked in a lumber yard and was suspected of stealing truckloads of lumber. I think I heard that he actually went to jail for it. Anyway, that's what I mean about Vilkas being a bullshitter and a wheeler-dealer."

"Did you ever hear him talk about an old car abandoned alongside the Willamette River?"

Pat laughed. "Sure. For about a month, that was *all* he talked about. But I don't think much of it was actually true."

"Vilkas said that someone at Adec originally told him about the car. Do you know who that might have been?"

"Sure. Want his phone number?"

A few minutes later, I found myself talking with someone named Ken.

"I never expected *that* story to find its way back to me." Ken laughed. "It's hard to believe that Vilkas is still telling it."

I asked, "Is there any truth to it?"

"Well, as they say in the movies, it is based on actual events. Have time for an amusing story?"

"Sure. Go ahead."

"Okay. I do a lot of whitewater rafting. Way back when I first started rafting, I told stories of my adventures to anyone who was interested or too polite to tell me to give it a rest. Well, one couple got all excited and wanted to give rafting a try.

"So they went out and spent about thirty dollars on a little vinyl raft, knowing that it wasn't any good for whitewater, but then all they wanted to do was drift on smooth, easy water. For their first float trip, they drove to Salem, probably thinking, 'It's only forty-five minutes away.' With some sandwiches and a few drinks, they set out for their afternoon float to Wilsonville—a distance of nearly fifty miles on the river.

"They floated lazily down the river, somehow not noticing that it took half an hour just to get out of sight of the launch ramp. After an hour or two, they decided they'd better start paddling downstream. Three hours later, they were sincerely wishing they had brought more food and drink. By the time some shade started to reach the river, they were thirsty, hungry, and thoroughly burned, although they didn't know how thoroughly until later that night.

"With no idea where they were but certain that the Wilsonville bridges would come into view 'around the next bend,' they paddled downstream into the evening. When it began getting dark, they finally decided that they'd better find a place to get off the river. They spotted a fisherman on shore and paddled over to ask where they were. They were at a greenway access park eleven miles downstream from Salem. Now, that's a very long distance to float when there's no discernible current, but they were still thirty-nine miles short of their destination.

"About then, a state cop appeared and told them that he was just about to lock the gate for the night. They asked him if he could take them to Wilsonville, but he said he wasn't allowed to give rides to civilians. The fisherman offered to take them as far as Newberg, so they hurriedly squeezed the air out of their raft and stuffed it into the guy's trunk. He let them out on the St. Paul highway and wished them luck. After walking for an hour in the dark, with their rolled up raft, they managed to hitch a ride to Wilsonville. They got out where Wilsonville Road goes under the freeway and then made their way down to the river at the old Boone's Ferry landing.

"When they got there, they realized that their car was on the other side of the river—an easy mistake. So they blew up the raft—by mouth because the pump was in their car in Salem. Then they discovered that they'd left the paddles in the car that had taken them to Wilsonville. So paddling with their hands, they were unable to compensate for the gentle current that pushed them downstream as they crossed the river.

"Eventually reaching shore about two hundred yards below the boat ramp, they waded along the shore through mud, branches, and slime, back upstream toward the marina. Along the way, an overhanging blackberry vine snagged the raft and ripped a hole in it, so by the time they got to the boat ramp, it was mostly deflated. They were so discouraged and disgusted by then that they stuffed the raft into a trash barrel. It was a half-hour before midnight on a Sunday, so even the fast-food restaurants were closed. Despite being painfully hungry, they drove to Salem to get their other car.

"When they got there, they remembered that they had put the keys to it in a little side pouch in the raft they had ditched. There was nothing to do but drive all the way back to Wilsonville and go dumpster diving. Arriving home in Portland about 2:30 a.m., they took cold showers and sprayed each other with Solarcaine. The next morning they had to go to work.

"They actually admitted to all of this rather than saying that they had been mugged by hippies who tied them up in the sun and stole their raft. That would have been my story, if I'd done something like that!"

"But what about the Studebaker?" I asked.

"Somewhere during the float, they went ashore to take a leak and found a garage with an old Studebaker inside. That's the *true* part of the story that I told Vilkas," he concluded.

"So there *really is* a car?"

"Yeah, but when I told the story to Vilkas, I modified a few details," Ken admitted.

"Such as . . ."

"Okay, here's the thing. Vilkas was a compulsive liar. He made up stories all the time, sometimes for no reason. Over lunch one day, I was talking about his stories with a friend, and we decided to put one over on Vilkas. So we took the story I just told and embellished it to appeal to the kid."

"Embellished it in what way?"

"Mainly, we turned the car into a 'brand-new' '64 Avanti with a 400-horsepower supercharged engine. It was actually just an old Studebaker from about 1950. But we knew Vilkas wouldn't be interested unless it was something fast, so that's what we made it. And then we added a whole bunch of detail about serial numbers, conversations with DMV, and collectors' clubs—all made-up. But Vilkas took the bait, and spent weeks trying to track down the location."

"And twenty-five years later, he still believes it," I observed.

"That's great." Ken chuckled. "What's more fun than running a con on a con man?"

When I phoned Giles Svensen and relayed the tale to him, he was obviously disappointed to learn that there was no a pristine Avanti waiting for him, but he was still interested in the 1950s Studebaker.

"Some of the old bullet-nose Studebakers are worth good money. If it's a Starlight Coupe, in restorable condition, it would be worth going after."

"Well, the guy who told the story to Vilkas doesn't know what model the car is. Or for that matter, if it's even still there."

"I wonder if the garage would be visible from the river," Giles mused.

A thought occurred to me.

"I know someone who probably would know," I said. "Have you ever met Captain Alan?"

"You mean the old guy with the tugboat?"

"That's right. If anybody knows what's visible from the river, it'd be Captain Alan."

"Well, maybe you can ask him about it sometime," Giles concluded.

Chapter 3

I was in the kitchen taking a taste of my legendary spaghetti sauce when I heard Kim come in through the front door. Peering around the corner, I saw her flop tiredly into the armchair that she usually leaves for me. It was a clear sign that she'd had a rough day.

"Get caught in the rain?" I asked, doing my best to sound sympathetic.

She ignored my question. "I need to move into investigations. I'm tired of being involved in the front end of these cases and then not being able to do anything about them."

Kim had worked on the Sheriff's Office Marine Unit for nearly fifteen years, so maybe it shouldn't have surprised me to hear her say that she was tired of it, but it did.

"So you want to join HVCU?" That's the Homicide and Violent Crimes Unit, the part of the sheriff's office that does all the investigations.

"I'm just sick of feeling helpless every time we find another dead girl," Kim said.

I noticed that she had tears in her eyes and seemed on the verge of crying, something that she almost never did. I sat down on the ottoman in front of her and reached for her hand, but she was having none of it.

"What happened out there today?"

She wiped her eyes with the back of her hand and said, "We were just out doing routine safety stops. There weren't many boats out today. We probably shouldn't have even bothered going out. We were just about to pack it in for the day when—you know the homeless camp up by Wattles Corner?"

I nodded. For many years, there had been a semipermanent encampment above the riverbank just downstream from the unfinished mansion abandoned by Mark Wattles, who made millions with his nationwide chain of video stores before the movie rental business shifted to cable and the internet.

"We were coming downstream when an old guy came running out of the trees waving his arms and shouting. We couldn't hear what he was saying, but it was obvious that he wanted to talk to us. I figured that one of the residents must have had a heart attack or something, so I told Sammy to get the first aid kit and defibrillator.

"I beached the boat, and the old guy grabbed the bow line. He was acting pretty excited and shaken up, and it took a minute to get him calmed down enough so I could understand him. 'There's bones up there, and they're human,' was what he finally managed to say."

"So Sammy and I followed him up a path that leads from the camp to the railroad and highway. There's an overgrown branch off the main trail, going in the general direction of that Studebaker guy's warehouse. We went about fifty feet up that way and came to where the old man had flipped over a piece of roofing metal. Sure enough, there were bones.

"The old man said he'd been scavenging materials to use in the camp. He said that he had to move some rocks off the metal before he could pick it up. I called in HVCU and hung around until they got there."

"This is hardly the first time you've found human remains. What is it about this case that upsets you?" I asked.

Barely above a whisper, she said, "It was just a girl. Or maybe a young woman. I'm not entirely sure. She'd been there a while—I'd guess five years—but some of her clothing was still recognizable. And the hair. Long, brown hair. Corrigan, why can't we stop people from doing this kind of thing?"

"You sure it wasn't an accident? I remember one of the homeless men got hit by a train up there a few years ago."

"Sure," she said sharply. "Maybe she had an accident, and maybe she buried herself out in the mud!"

I raised my hands. "Sorry, I didn't have—"

"Someone took her out there—probably made her walk to her own grave, because it was too far from the road for anyone to carry her—and then killed her and covered her body with an old piece of sheet metal. What kind of ruthless bastard does that? It just makes me feel so—so helpless!"

A flood of questions entered my mind. "How do you know how old she was?"

Kim looked at me. "I saw the skull, okay? The cranial sutures in the skull were not fused. That means she was probably under twenty. Definitely under twenty-five, and definitely female, based on the size of the mastoid process and the shape of the pelvis."

Her matter-of-fact tone of voice was so far out of character that it felt like she was talking to a stranger. This was hardly the first time she'd worked a homicide scene. I was surprised by her knowledge of forensic pathology, but I wondered what was so different about this case that would cause this unexpected reaction.

"Any clue who she might have been?"

"Yeah! Lots of clues. She was a defenseless little girl. She was someone who should have lived to have a family and watch her own children grow up. And God knows what happened to her before he killed her."

Kim got up tiredly and went to the kitchen, where she got a glass and poured herself a generous drink of Kentucky bourbon.

"That girl has parents who have been looking for her for all the time she's been lying under that piece of sheet metal. Maybe she has a husband. And children. They're all living in pain and uncertainty because she's gone and they don't know why."

She slumped back into the armchair and took a gulp of bourbon before picking up the TV remote and switching on the news. The way she riveted her eyes to the screen told me that she didn't have anything more to say. The brief news coverage of the discovery contained far less information than Kim had provided. The sheriff's office spokesman, Cal Westfall, said that there would be a review of all recent missing person reports.

"Missing person reports," Kim said bitterly. "A girl's whole life is reduced to a useless piece of paper."

I desperately wanted to say something to take the edge off Kim's obvious distress, but for the life of me, I couldn't think of anything to say. Instead, I turned off the heat under the spaghetti sauce and poured some bourbon for myself. We sat quietly through the remainder of the newscast.

"Can we go get ice cream?" Kim finally asked. "I think I want a banana split sundae."

Chapter 4

I hadn't completely forgotten about Giles and his interest in the old Studebaker, but there clearly was no urgency in the quest either, so I'd set it aside. After all, Captain Alan doesn't have a phone. In fact, he is about as close to being a homeless person as you can be, short of living out of a shopping cart. Most of the year he lives aboard his old tugboat *Misty Rose*, but this time of year, he was more likely to be found at Lumpy's Tavern in Dundee, about thirty miles upriver from my place.

I wasn't thinking about any of that as Kim and I drove through Dundee on our way to the coast, where we were going to spend the weekend and maybe forget about the body by the homeless camp. But I spotted Alan's old pickup parked at Lumpy's, made a quick U-turn, and stopped to have a chat. And a beer. You can't have a chat in a tavern without having a beer.

"Hey, Corrigan," Captain Alan hollered when he spotted me. "You're a bit outside your jurisdiction."

I wasn't sure if the second comment was meant for me or Kim.

"We were just driving by when I saw your truck," I explained.

"And you couldn't resist stopping to buy me a beer," he finished for me. Alan isn't one to pass up the possibility of a free drink.

He was engaged in a pool game with a couple of rough-looking local drunks, so Kim and I settled at a nearby table and ordered drinks—beers for Alan and me and a Perrier for Kim. The waitress didn't know what a Perrier was, so Kim settled for a glass of soda water from the bar.

We made small talk while the other guys were shooting, but they were pretty lousy pool players. Our conversation was broken into short segments until the game came to a merciful end when one of the drunks suddenly made a mad dash toward the restroom. He came up short, barfed on the floor, and was escorted outside by a disgruntled bartender.

"You're pretty familiar with the stretch of river downstream from Salem," I said rhetorically when I finally had Alan's full attention.

"I don't go that far as often as I used to, but I know it pretty well. What would you like to know?"

"There's a story about a concrete block garage on an island, somewhere about five or ten miles down from Salem. Does that ring a bell?"

"That'd probably be the old Coffman farm. During the big flood, the river cut a new channel and cut off access to that building. I haven't seen it for years—the blackberries swallowed it up. But I imagine it's still there."

"Have you ever looked inside it?"

"Oh hell no. Like I said, it's been covered in blackberries for decades. Someone once told me that there was something inside it—old farm machinery or some such thing," Alan said.

"I heard that it was an old Studebaker," I said, hoping to jog his memory.

"Yeah, it could be that. Like I said, I never looked."

"Would you be able to find the place?" I asked.

"Not sure I could get to it on shore, but it'd be easy to find from the river."

"I know a guy who'd really like to know what's in that garage. Would you be willing to go upriver sometime and show us where it is?"

Alan paused, and I could see that he was doing some mental arithmetic. He finally said, "River's running pretty strong right now. It'd probably take twenty or thirty gallons of fuel to go up there with *Misty Rose*."

"Here's another idea," I said. "The guy who wants to see the place has a little jet sled. He could launch it in Salem and avoid the long upriver run. Would you be willing to come along and show us where the garage is?"

"When did you plan to do it?" he asked.

I picked up my phone and found Giles Svensen's number. After kicking it around for a few minutes, we reached a tentative agreement to make the trip the following weekend, contingent on decent weather.

"Bring your fishing rig," Giles suggested. "There ought to be some Chinook still running, if the water stays clear."

"I guess I'm going fishing," I told Kim as we left Lumpy's.

"Fish on!" Giles hollered as he pulled hard on his fishing rod.

We had unexpectedly nice weather for our fishing trip, and both the steelhead and salmon were running. We were working our way downstream from the boat landing in West Salem, stopping at promising fishing holes along the way to find the long-lost Studebaker. The fish that Giles finally reeled in was a thirteen-inch pikeminnow, what we used to call a squawfish before political correctness overran even the language of fishermen. Or should that be "fisherpeople"?

Giles killed the predatory fish and tossed the carcass back into the river to feed the crawdads—or crawparents. Giles and I were sharing a thermos of black coffee while Alan drank from a pocket flask. At eight in the morning, I'd like to think that the flask contained orange juice, but I knew better. Still, it was a pleasant time, and we were all hoping to tie into a thirty-pound Chinook.

We were idling downstream between fishing holes when Alan pointed toward a brush-covered bit of high ground separated from the right bank by a deep gully.

"That ought to be it," he said. "The old Coffman farmhouse used to be on that rise where the oak trees are."

Following Alan's instructions, Giles maneuvered his boat into a pool at the lower end of the island and beached it on the gravel shore. After tying up, the three of us made our way up the embankment onto the top of the island, which was covered with dormant blackberry vines. We poked around until we found what looked like an animal trail—actually more like a tunnel than a trail—through the brambles.

Duckwalking under the canopy of blackberry brambles, we were about thirty feet in when we spotted the old cinderblock garage. Wielding a pruning tool that he'd brought along, Giles clipped furiously at the brambles, his excitement growing as he approached the building.

"Sonofagoddamnbitchhellmotherbearshit!" Alan complained as he pulled a particularly aggressive blackberry vine away from his forearm, leaving a trail of torn skin and bleeding punctures.

"There's Band-Aids in my tackle box," Giles offered.

Alan grumbled, "I ain't gonna bleed to death. Let's just keep going."

Five minutes later, we were peering through a broken window into the old garage at what Giles identified as a 1951 Studebaker Champion supporting the partially collapsed roof on its dented and rusting hood.

"What do you think, Giles? Do you see anything in there worth salvaging?" I asked.

"I don't know," he said sadly. "There might be some parts."

"Looks pretty bad," Alan said unnecessarily while Giles carefully climbed through the window.

"I want to see if there's anything good inside," he said.

When he tugged on the driver's door handle, it broke off in his hand. Not exactly a promising sign. But the backdoor unlatched, and Giles tugged it open. The rusty hinges protested loudly, and we were instantly greeted by the combined aromas of rat urine, moldy upholstery, and a decomposing possum that lay on the backseat.

Retreating from the swarm of flies that rose off the possum carcass, Giles tried to slam the door shut, an action that sent a fresh wave of odor in the direction of the window where Alan and I stood. Trying to escape the stench, we dodged away as Giles threw himself headfirst through the opening and landed in a tangle of thorny vines.

"Holy shit!" he exclaimed.

Alan started laughing, and I couldn't help joining in. What started out as a treasure hunt had ended as a championship goat rodeo. After escaping the blackberry tunnel, we scrambled down to the boat, gasping for fresh air and laughing at ourselves.

The only redeeming factor in the whole adventure was that on our way back up to Salem, we made a few more fishing stops, where both Giles and Alan managed to land nice salmon. Because he didn't have a good way to cook it onboard *Misty Rose*, Alan tossed his fish to me. Later, when I showed the fish to Kim, I could honestly say that I had caught it.

"I think I'm going to tell Tom Vilkas that we found the Avanti, all right, but couldn't figure out a good way to get it off the island," Giles said on our way back. "It'll serve him right if he goes on the same wild-goose chase we did!"

We trailered the boat and then drove back to Dundee to drop off Alan at his barge on the Yamhill River outside of town. Then we took the back roads across French Prairie to Aurora and Highway 99E, which took us back to the bright green house that Giles owns, across the highway from the big old warehouse where he keeps his Studebaker collection.

After we backed the boat into the warehouse, Giles offered a tour, and under the circumstances, I could hardly turn him down. The nearest car was one of the most peculiar-looking vehicles ever built. It was a Studebaker. That much was evident at a glance. But it *wasn't* a Studebaker. The lettering across its protruding front end, which looked like the mouth of a giant catfish, spelled out Packard.

"That's a 1958 Packard—the last year for the brand," Giles explained. "People called it the Ubangi Packard. It was a Studebaker Hawk with that fish mouth bolted on in a lame attempt to conceal its true heritage. It was a sad end to a once-great car company.

"The next car over is a 1957 Golden Hawk 400. It's the best and rarest Studebaker I have here. It has a supercharged 289 V-8 that produces 275 horsepower. That was almost unheard of in production cars of that era."

We walked down between the rows of old cars, and Giles had a story for each one. The collection was mostly post–World War II cars, but there were a few relics from the 1930s, when the Studebaker Company had barely survived bankruptcy. The story of the Studebaker Company is one of slow, agonizing death. The 1964 Avanti was the last gasp of the dying company, and I could see why Giles wanted one to round out the collection.

"Did I tell you that I have a chance to buy this place?" Giles asked as we concluded the tour and walked back outside.

"I thought you already owned it."

"No, I'm just leasing the building. The property is owned by Ted Birkenfield. Maybe you know him. He's a hard money lender. The old owner kept borrowing against the property until he couldn't make the payments. Birkenfield foreclosed about four years ago, but it's taken this long to get a clear title. Now he'd like to sell the whole shebang to me."

"Well, that ought to work out well for you," I commented.

"Yeah, maybe. We haven't come to terms on a price. He wants more than it's worth and says that he has another buyer—someone who wants to put a big marijuana farm in the warehouse. I think he's just trying to bluff me into paying too much. But I still have most of three years on my lease, so if there really is another buyer, he'd have to buy out my lease before he could do anything with the building, and that isn't going to happen."

I thanked Giles for the tour. I wished him luck with the purchase without asking where he'd come up with the money. It wouldn't be from selling museum tours, I was sure of that. Maybe he was one of those guys with hidden wealth in old stocks and bonds.

Chapter 5

Martha Hoskins nearly jumped out of her chair as she exclaimed, "Would you look at this! They *bought the timer* that was used to start the fire that destroyed their store."

Martha is my assistant. No, actually she's my partner. After working as my assistant for a year and a half, she got her own license and earned the promotion to partner. She has good investigative instincts and is a quick learner and a hard worker. She still has the appearance of a holdover from the era of the Grateful Dead and the old Oregon Country Fair with her long straight hair and preference for floor-length dresses. But it serves her well. People tend to underestimate her.

I looked at the sheet of paper that she handed me. It was a copy of an invoice for the purchase of a VM-136 adjustable interval timer module from an online store called Apogee Kits. We knew from the fire marshal's investigation that this was the timer used to trigger an incendiary device that started the fire that destroyed the furniture store owned by our clients.

"Where on earth did you get that?" I asked in amazement.

Martha said, "Their accountant gave it to me. It was in a packet of information that I requested relating to the ownership of the store."

"I don't get it. How does this relate to ownership documents?"

"It was part of their tax return for last year. The owners included it in their application to refinance the store. They got the loan two weeks before the fire."

"Wait a minute. Are you telling me that they tried to deduct the timer as a business expense?"

"That's right. Do you believe that? They bought a timer to burn down their store and then deducted the cost from their taxes!"

I groaned. "Can we bill them before we give them the result of our investigation?"

"Oh crap. I hadn't thought about that! Why in hell did they hire us? Did they really think we wouldn't find anything?"

"That's exactly what they were thinking. Hiring us was just a show, meant to convince the authorities—or the news media—or the public—that they sincerely wanted the case solved."

"So what do we do now?"

"Well, we could slip this invoice to the fire marshal and pretend we never saw it. Then we could write a report saying that we were unable to solve the case and submit it to them along with a billing statement."

"Is that ethical?"

"It's more ethical than burning down your own store and then hiring us to bolster their claim of innocence."

Martha and I looked at each other for about ten seconds.

I sighed. "But we won't do it. We'll just turn in the evidence and eat the loss. We can write it off *our* taxes."

Changing the subject, Martha asked, "Hey, did you see the newspaper article about the body Kim found?"

More than a month had passed since the discovery of the human remains up by the homeless camp, and the investigators still had been unable to identify the victim. All that they had been able to determine in their five-week investigation was that the victim had been female, sixteen to twenty-five years old, Caucasian, about five three or five four, and had been dead about three to five years.

What took the investigators a month to figure out, Kim had told me the day she found the remains. But it was still a touchy subject with her, and I could feel a latent emotional storm lying close beneath her outward coolness. And coolness it was. She wouldn't even talk about the case. Except for what she told me that first day, everything I knew about it had come from news reports.

"The paper didn't say anything we didn't already know," I said to Martha.

"What about the list of missing women?"

The article included a list of women of the right age who had gone missing between 2008 and 2012 in the western United States. More than half had been eliminated because they were the wrong height or race. Of those remaining, many were listed as prostitutes.

"Kim was pretty adamant that the victim wasn't a hooker."

"How could she know that?"

"It was the clothes. The victim wasn't dressed like a hooker."

"Maybe she wasn't on the job at the time," Martha suggested.

———

"Yeah, maybe. But when prostitutes go missing, it's nearly always when they're working."

"That'll leave a pretty short list. It shouldn't take very long to screen them."

"Right. I'm sure they already have a DNA profile for the victim, so they'll be comparing that with relatives of the missing women. I'd say the chances are pretty good that they'll find a match."

The sound of footsteps on the back porch interrupted the conversation, and I looked through the kitchen to see my neighbor Bud Tiernan motioning for me to join him outside.

"What's up?" I asked.

"I was wondering if you had a suggestion on what color I should paint my house."

It seemed like an odd thing to ask. "Paint it whatever color you like."

"No, I mean, what color do you think Martha would like?" he whispered.

"Ah. Let me think about that. Can I get you a beer?"

Giving Bud a beer would buy me a few extra moments to ponder the question. For more than a year, Bud had been doing a top-to-bottom renovation of the tiny cabin he occupied across the alley from my place. It was a pay-as-you-go project financed by his social security checks, so progress was necessarily slow, but the exterior paint would finally finish it.

For years, before he started collecting social security, Bud had lived in squalor in his dilapidated shack behind his son's cottage. It was no secret that he was smitten with Martha, and that was what was behind his interest in knowing what color she might like.

"Okay, I'm no expert, but here's what I think," I said after we'd opened our beers and walked over to his cabin. "You don't want girly colors. She won't buy that. Keep it manly—maybe earth tones or a combination of gray tones."

"Really? You don't think she'd like pastels or something like that?"

"Definitely not. I don't think Martha was ever the Barbie-doll type. If you want to add a touch of color and feminine appeal, do it with flowers. Put planters at the sides of the porch for petunias or mums."

"I never thought of that," Bud admitted.

"Dress the place up with some landscaping bark—you know, just to make it look finished."

Bud continued the conversation long enough to hit me up for another beer. I excused myself on the legitimate grounds that I had to get back to work.

Chapter 6

I have long believed that hobbies are a form of mental illness. If you need proof of that, just look at the game of golf. My personal manifestation of this truth is the 110-foot schooner that I keep moored at a dock in West Linn. Built in England in 1885, she was originally a fishing vessel named *Chrisholm*. Over the course of her 124-year life prior to my purchase, the ship had gone through a succession of owners, each with a different vision for her.

A diesel propulsion engine was added in the 1930s, and that saved *Chrisholm* from the fate that befell most other ships of her age and purpose when it became economically impossible for a sailing vessel to compete with motor vessels. But the masts and rigging were retained, so she still had the option of sailing without power, and she still had the stately look of her original design.

After the Second World War, a movie studio bought the ship and used her for two decades as a movie prop, and she starred in at least fifteen films. *Chrisholm* then went to Cabo San Lucas, where she ran sunset cruises for tourists until the lousy economy drove the owners to bankruptcy.

When I bought her on a reckless whim in the bankruptcy auction, she was still largely the same as she had been at the time of her last Hollywood role, for which she had been superficially refitted to represent the personal yacht of Prince Rainier III of Monaco. On her sunset cruises in Cabo, all the passengers stayed out on deck, so there had never been a need to modify the interior spaces.

By the time I bought her, whatever elegance she once had as a make-believe luxury yacht had long since worn off, but I got the notion that I could live aboard her while restoring her to prime sailing condition. I renamed her *Annabel Lee* and went to work.

I figured it would take a year to get her to a point where I could move aboard. That was five years ago. Now, with the plumbing, electrical, and heating systems all upgraded to modern standards, I was engaged in refurbishing the interior woodwork. This was where I ran headlong into the superficiality of the work done by the movie studio.

Most of the cabinetry consisted of only the doors and drawer fronts. The actual cabinetry wasn't there. The elegant-looking paneling was actually cheap plywood with paper-thin plastic veneer. So starting in what had been the crew quarters up forward, I went in and stripped out the Hollywood façade and set out to rebuild her to actually be what she had been pretending to be for the last fifty years.

Since the first of the year, I'd bought a table saw and a full set of cabinet-making tools and set up a woodshop in the main salon, using some of the proceeds from my successful lawsuit against the IRS. I had accumulated a tall pile of oak and walnut lumber and was stockpiling hardware and wood finishing supplies. I was pretty sure that if I were to go for a week without making a trip to Home Depot, my picture would show up on milk cartons.

The final step in tearing out the fake interior from the forward cabins was hauling armloads of scrap up to the parking lot where a dumpster was parked. It was midafternoon when I paused on deck to take a break. I pulled a sandwich and a beer out of my ice chest and took a seat on the roof of the main salon.

I noticed that the missed call light was flashing on my phone, so I checked and found that Kim had called, probably during one of my trips to the dumpster. I called her back, and she told me that she wouldn't be over that evening. Her mother was coming to town for a surprise visit.

All her visits were surprise visits. I'd always considered Vera Lyons to be a bit of a space cadet. She had a twenty-two-foot motor home, and she spent most of her time traveling the country, stopping at various points of interest, and staying until she'd seen everything there was to see.

"Is she in town now?" I asked.

"She called from Eugene. She'll be here in a couple of hours."

"What's she been up to lately?"

"Are you ready for this? She's just finished a raft trip in Grand Canyon," Kim said.

"A raft trip? Your mother?"

"That's what she says. Ten days."

"You *mother* has been camping out?" I asked, incredulous at the mere thought of it.

"That's what she says," Kim repeated. "The guides did all the cooking, but she had to put up her own tent."

"Did they let her take her knitting along?"

"My mother doesn't knit, and you know it."

"Well, it'll be interesting to hear her trip report. Why don't we take her out to dinner and let her tell us all about it?"

"Oh, I don't know . . ."

"Nothing fancy—we'll just go for Chinese. And I'll buy."

"You know what you're getting into," she cautioned.

"Oh, she won't eat so much I can't afford it."

"That's not what I meant, smartass."

"I'm a grown-up. I can handle it."

"Okay then. Let me give you Mom's phone number in case you need to call her."

I couldn't imagine why I'd need to call her, but I scribbled the number on the only thing handy—a scrap of oak wainscoting.

"Hey, I gotta go talk to some people about life preservers," she said suddenly. "I'll talk to you later."

She clicked off without waiting for a response, no doubt in hot pursuit of a boatload of kids without lifejackets or something of the sort.

"You did *what*?" Kim exclaimed.

Vera Lyons repeated, "I chased a whole pack of coyotes away from our food! They came around in the night and were going to steal our breakfast, so I got a big spoon and a tin pot, and I banged on the pot until the coyotes left."

"But, Mom, where were the guides?" Kim asked.

"Oh, I don't know," Vera said. "I just didn't want those coyotes to eat my bacon!"

"That was dangerous! Coyotes are wild animals," Kim scolded.

Vera looked at Kim and said, "So am I, sweetheart. So am I."

We were having dinner at New Hing's Chinese restaurant on Main Street, and Vera was telling us all about her raft trip.

"We rode on great big rubber rafts with motors, and we went through *huge* rapids. And we stopped at some of the most amazing places."

She scrolled through the photos on her camera until she came to a group showing people jumping off a small waterfall, twenty feet into a crystal clear pool of water.

"They call this Elves Chasm," she explained. "We hiked way up from the bottom of the canyon, and then the guides showed us where to climb through the rocks to get to the top of the falls. Oh, that was a scary jump!"

"Well, it serves you right," Kim said. "You have no business doing things like that at your age!"

"Poop!" Vera said defiantly. "I did it because it looked like fun. And it *was* fun, so I did it again!"

"Take that!" I teased Kim.

"The scenery was so beautiful!" Vera exclaimed. "And we went hiking every day. We camped on the beaches next to the river, and the guides cooked meals that you just wouldn't believe!"

"Sounds like you had a good time," I commented.

"Oh, everything about it was *wonderful!*" she exclaimed. After a pause, she added, "Except for one thing. We had to crap in a bucket! Can you believe that? They made us crap in a damned bucket!"

Kim looked like she was ready to burst, so I asked, "How did you like the guides?"

"Oh, they were hot!" Vera confided with a wink. "Bare chested, all tanned and sweaty, broad shoulders and big muscles—I was ready to do some tepee creeping, if you know what I mean."

"Mother!" Kim exclaimed.

Vera patted her arm and said, "Don't worry about me, dear. I always carry a condominium in my fanny pack."

"You never know when you're going to need a condominium," I commented with a straight face.

Vera said, "You got that right."

"Enough!" Kim said. "I don't want to hear any more of this!"

Changing the subject, I asked, "Where are you going next?"

"I'm going to go to Seattle and have dinner in the Space Needle," she said. "And then maybe I'll go see Grand Coulee Dam. I've never seen Grand Coulee Dam."

"When do you plan to leave?" Kim asked.

"Oh, I'm leaving first thing in the morning. My Triple-A Tourbook says that they give tours of the brewery in Olympia, and they give out free samples."

"Uh, how old is your Tourbook?" Kim asked.

Vera pondered for a moment and finally said, "Well, it might be a few years old. Why?"

"Because the Olympia Brewery was shut down about ten years ago," Kim told her.

Looking disappointed, Vera just said, "Oh."

"But there are some good wineries in eastern Washington," I said, "and they have tasting rooms."

"Now, that's a good idea," Vera said, happy again.

After dinner, Kim took Vera to her condo for the night, and I went back home.

Chapter 7

When I answered the phone, Giles Svensen asked, "Hey, Corrigan, you got time to come up here? I have something I'd like to show you."

"Did you add another Studebaker to your collection?"

"No. Nothing like that. It's just something I found, and I don't know what to make of it."

Well, that was sufficiently mysterious to get my interest, so instead of heading down to do some more work on *Annabel Lee*, I drove the other way, to Svensen's old warehouse. I found Giles standing on a large concrete slab about a hundred feet from his old warehouse building, surveying a large pile of debris from the demolition of the building that had been taken down a few years before.

"I've been trying to get this place cleaned up," he told me.

"I guess this means that you bought it from Birkenfield," I speculated.

"Yep. He let me have it at my price as long as he didn't have to do the cleanup."

I looked at the big scrap heap and said, "I never could figure out why they tore down this building. It didn't look like it was in bad shape or anything."

"Meth. The last people who leased the building were meth cooks. They came down here with half a dozen old travel trailers that they lived in and had a big meth lab in the building. After they got raided, the owner was supposed to do a major cleanup."

"Yeah, I remember when it was raided. Did they ever catch the guys?"

"No, they must have been warned, because they all took off just before the raid. After that, what with the contamination and all, the owner couldn't rent the building. He borrowed a bunch of money from Birkenfield to have the place cleaned up, but then he tore the building down instead and sold whatever was salvageable for recycling. And now I have to clean up the mess."

"So what is it that you want to show me?" I asked.

He led me around to a stack of heavy timber beams, most of which were split or too short to be of any value. He climbed to the top of the stack and pointed at one of the beams. At first I didn't see anything, but moving closer, I was able to make out letters scratched deeply into the old wood: BRITTANY HARLAN 9-11-01. It meant nothing to me.

I shrugged. "So what about it?"

"Brittany Harlan," Giles said emphatically. "Don't you remember Brittany Harlan?"

"No. Should I?"

"Where were you in the late eighties?"

"Moscow, Idaho. I was still in college. So enlighten me."

"Brittany Harlan was a little girl—about six or seven years old. She was kidnapped while selling Girl Scout cookies and never seen again. And now here's her name and a date more than a dozen years later."

"My first reaction is that it's a hoax. The choice of nine eleven as the date is just too contrived. Someone climbed up here just like we did and carved her name."

"Yeah, probably. But what if it's real?"

"The thing to do is call the cops. Let them decide."

I knew that advice disappointed Giles because everyone wants to be the one who finds the clue that solves an old mystery. Still, I found myself doing some mental arithmetic. If Brittany Harlan had been seven in 1989, then she'd have been about twenty in 2001 and close to thirty in 2010—too old to be the girl Kim had found a quarter mile away. Probably.

"You really think it's a hoax?" Giles asked.

"The cops will be able to determine that," I told him while my mind took off on a tangent of its own, organizing the steps I'd take if the case were mine:

1. Study the scratchings.
2. Take photos.
3. Learn about the Brittany Harlan kidnapping.
4. Look for Brittany Harlan sighting reports.
5. Figure out what part of the building the beam came from.
6. Track down the building's tenants.

After step two, each successive step depended upon finding something that warranted pushing forward. I pulled out my phone and snapped a couple of pictures of the name scratched in the old wood. At one end of the timber, I tested the hardness of the wood by trying to carve something with my pocket knife. I'll admit that my knife wasn't exactly razor sharp, but still I was surprised at how difficult it was to cut into the aged wood.

The prankster had to be pretty determined to carve the whole name plus the date. But then again, it wasn't actually carved. It was scratched. I pulled out a little folding 10X magnifier that I habitually carry in the watch pocket of my Levi's. When was the last time *anyone* carried a watch in that pocket?

As I studied the scratchings under magnification, something caught my eye. There were tiny bits of what appeared to be glass embedded in the wood as though the prankster had scratched the lettering with a broken Coke bottle. I quickly corrected myself. Coke bottles were plastic by the time this scratching was supposed to have been done. But the point was whether or not a prankster would resort to using broken glass.

I suppose a prankster might if he really wanted to make his work look authentic. The alternative to that might be that it actually *was* authentic. So I went back and reconsidered the time line. If Giles was off by a couple of years on Brittany's age, if the medical examiner was off by a couple of years in his estimate of when Kim's victim had been killed, and if the estimate of the victim's age at the time of death was off by a couple of years, then maybe. Just maybe.

All of that was a huge stretch. I knew that. But I also knew I couldn't ignore it. Not given the way Kim had reacted to the discovery of the body, with a depression from which she still had not completely recovered. I simply didn't have a choice.

"Before you call the cops," I told Giles, "let me go home and get some proper equipment to photograph this. Once the cops take it, I won't have another chance."

An hour later, I was back with my digital Nikon and a microscope adapted for photomicrography. I brought my portable generator so that I could set up high-intensity lighting, and I used a set of colored filters to get photos at different frequencies within the visible light spectrum. All of this had to be done without actually touching the timber or the scratchings.

Next, I got out my measuring tape. The beam was thirteen and a half feet in length, sixteen inches wide, and six inches thick. The tightness of the grain told me that it had been cut from old growth timber, and the dimensions hinted that it had been milled before the days of mass-produced lumber.

As I loaded my equipment back into my Yukon, I told Giles to go ahead and phone the Canby police. They undoubtedly would call Washington County's authorities since that's where Brittany Harlan was kidnapped. I didn't have the same kind of working relationship with Washington County that I had with Clackamas County, so I could assume that official channels would be closed to me.

Having already taken half a day away from my work on *Annabel Lee,* I stopped at home only long enough to put away the gear I'd used out at Svensen's place. And then I headed off to Home Depot.

April 14 Monday

Chapter 8

My first question of the day for Martha was, "Do you know anything about a girl named Brittany Harlan?"

"I remember that she was kidnapped and never found. Why do you ask?"

"It happened while I was still in college. I don't remember hearing anything about it."

"Sometimes there are news stories commemorating the anniversary of the kidnapping. I remember a couple of years ago it got put on a list for the new cold-case team to investigate, but as far as I know, they never found anything."

The truth is, I don't spend much time reading local crime reports unless I'm somehow involved. With half a dozen gang shootings every week, it's too much to keep up with. Not to mention, after a point it's just boring.

After my compulsory pilgrimage to Home Depot on Saturday, I'd managed to avoid thinking about Brittany Harlan for the rest of the weekend, which was a practical necessity if I wanted to stay focused on the task at hand—building two staterooms where the old crew quarters had been. Each stateroom would have a private head, for which I'd already installed the plumbing.

"So what makes you ask about Brittany Harlan?" Martha asked.

"You know the guy with the Studebaker museum down the highway? He called me Saturday because he found her name scratched in an old piece of wood. He thought it might mean something, but I think it's probably the work of pranksters."

I showed her the snapshots I'd taken with my phone.

"That's pretty close to where Kim found the body, isn't it? Do you think it could be connected?"

"I doubt it. Like I said, it's probably just a sick hoax. But Giles called the Canby police and told them about it, so they'll figure it out. But I'm going to catch up on the case so that I'm not the only person in Oregon who doesn't know about it."

"Want any help?"

"No, one of us has to make some money, and today it's your turn."

Martha went to work on the preliminary investigation for our newest client. The Dakota Mutual Insurance investigation would require her to learn all about repetitive motion injuries.

After being contacted by Dakota Mutual, I had done some Internet searches on the subject. As I read all about tendonitis and bursitis, my joints started to ache. Then when I read about carpal tunnel syndrome, my wrists stiffened up and started to hurt. Just when I was beginning to feel arthritis flaring up in my fingers, I decided to give the case to Martha, no doubt saving myself from total paralysis.

"What on earth is a ganglion cyst?" Martha asked. "Isn't that some kind of growth?"

I said, "Yes, but there's more to this case than that. There's a Dr. Steve Gaston in Tacoma who has billed Dakota Mutual for treating sixty-three patients with ganglion cysts. He claims they're caused by repetitive motion in the workplace. His patients are everything from hairdressers to graphic designers."

"Graphic designers?"

"Yeah. He says it's from pushing the computer mouse."

"If it's that common, why don't we all know about it?"

"That's the same question I had."

I'd already spent several hours roaming the Internet in search of a connection between ganglion cysts and repetitive-motion injuries. It turned out that this doctor in Tacoma was the only one in the world who had made the connection and was trying to bill the workers' compensation insurance companies.

Even though there was absolutely no medical evidence that ganglion cysts were caused by repetitive motion, this doctor had been helping patients file workers' comp claims that add up to staggering amounts of money. The insurance companies paid off, apparently because they didn't know any more about ganglion cysts than I did.

But how could a single doctor find sixty-three patients, all insured by Dakota Mutual, with the same relatively obscure affliction? The odds were astronomical.

"There must be twenty different companies selling workers' comp insurance in the state of Washington. Unless Dr. Gaston treats only Dakota Mutual patients—which is extremely unlikely—it's reasonable to guess that he's been billing all the others too," I speculated.

"That could be hundreds of claims," Martha agreed.

"My instincts tell me that Dr. Gaston has found something that isn't in the insurance companies' handbooks and is taking advantage of their confusion. He gets paid by the insurance companies, and the people who file the claims get some paid time off work—and maybe a kickback from the doctor too."

"So how do we prove that it's fraud?"

"Well, we'll start by getting all the information Dakota Mutual can give us about the claims. They undoubtedly have medical experts who assess the validity of all workers' comp claims. My guess is that this thing just flew in under their radar."

"But still, there can't possibly be *hundreds* of people all going to this one doctor with the same ailment."

"Let's just see what Dakota Mutual has to say. If they think it's bogus and want us to prove it, maybe you'll be going to Tacoma with a sore wrist."

"No way. I'm a lousy actress."

"Well, first things first. Learn everything you can about repetitive motion injuries in general and ganglion cysts in particular. Look for statistics relating to the occurrences of these things. Is it one in a thousand or one in a hundred thousand? Then run that probability against the recent workers' comp claims. I think you can make a statistical case for fraud. If Dakota Mutual agrees, then we've got a case."

"Ten-four, boss."

The phenomenon I had come to think of as "the Martha Machine" took over at that point. Once she started on a project, her focus was so intense that she could be shaken loose only by some natural catastrophe. Actually, that hadn't been proven because we hadn't *had* a natural catastrophe, but no human intervention had ever been enough to break her concentration.

So while Martha did our work, I set out to see what I could learn about Brittany Harlan.

Giles Svensen was wrong. Brittany Harlan wasn't selling Girl Scout cookies. She was a Bluebird, and she was selling Camp Fire Girl mints—a small point but one of major importance to the girls in the competing organizations. Brittany had vanished on March 6, 1989, thirty years to the day after the disappearance of Candice Rogers in Spokane, who had also been selling Camp Fire Girl mints.

Largely because of the Candy Rogers case, by 1989 Camp Fire Girls had long since stopped allowing the girls to go door to door without adult supervision. Brittany Harlan wasn't going door to door. She was with two other girls at a table by the entrance to the Fred Meyer store in Beaverton. She was last seen talking to a man so ordinary in appearance that witnesses were unable to give a useful description. And then she was gone.

There were no AMBER Alerts then. The abduction of Amber Haggerman, which would spark the creation of the AMBER Alert system, was still seven years in the future. The adult in charge of the girls called 911 as soon as she noticed that seven-year-old Brittany was gone, but there was no way to lock down the shopping center, which was located at the intersection of three major highways. By the time a BOLO or APB was issued, the abductor could have been twenty miles away in any direction. It was a hopeless gesture.

Nevertheless, hundreds of witnesses reported having seen a child matching Brittany's description in hundreds of different locations over the weeks following her disappearance. Investigating agencies were overwhelmed by the sheer volume of witness reports. Somewhere among the reports, there may well have been someone who actually saw Brittany Harlan. But if so, it was lost among all the false leads.

The most commonly circulated photos of Brittany showed a smiling girl with curly blond hair holding a black kitten. Kim's victim had had long, dark-brown hair. But I knew that many girls who are blonde in childhood grow up with brown hair.

There I was again. Measuring Brittany Harlan against Kim's unidentified victim. The more I thought about it, the less outlandish the possibility appeared to be—Brittany's name scratched on an old beam less than a quarter mile from where Kim's victim was found. But the apparent age difference of at least ten years argued strongly against it.

And that was where I hit the wall.

My dilemma was that I didn't dare bring up the subject with Kim, but at the same time, I knew what the consequences would be if I didn't. I knew that, for whatever reason, the case of the unidentified girl found at the homeless camp was somehow connected directly to Kim's heart, and on that basis, I could not keep from her something that might bear on the case. But I also knew that telling her about Brittany Harlan would tear open whatever wound caused her such pain.

The more I learned about Brittany Harlan, the less I believed that Kim's victim could be her. But I simply had to tell her what I knew.

"Kim, I have to show you something."

"You're not going to flash me, are you?" she joked. That was the last glimpse I'd get for a long time of the Kim I'd known for five years.

"I will if you want, but that's not it. A few days ago, Giles Svensen called me out to his place to see something."

"Another rusty old car?"

"No. It was this."

I handed her my phone with the photo of the scratching on the old timber. She stared at it for a strangely long time.

"Why didn't you tell me about this?" she demanded.

"I didn't know anything about Brittany Harlan until I looked it up on the Internet today."

"Don't hand me that. You knew what this was, or you wouldn't have taken the picture!"

"I took the picture because—"

"You should have told me!" I saw the tears forming.

"I don't think it's connected—"

"What the hell do you know about it?"

She strode out the front door to her Explorer, got in, and sped away, spraying gravel and causing the tires to screech when she hit the asphalt on Water Street. And then she was gone.

Chapter 9

For the third morning in a row, I scanned the newspaper looking for any mention of Giles Svensen's discovery. It was odd that something relating to the mystery of Brittany Harlan's disappearance didn't make the news. The only thing I could conclude from that was that the Canby police had determined that the scratching on the beam was a hoax and thus not worth mentioning to the media.

"Sure, they came out here and looked at it," Giles told me in answer to my question.

"So what did they do?"

"They scratched their heads and said that it had to be a hoax, and then they left."

"What kind of investigation did they do?"

"None at all. They spent about one minute looking at it, and that was it."

"They didn't even take the beam?"

"Nope. It's still out there."

Surely, I thought, they must know something that I didn't that allowed them to so easily dismiss the scratchings as a hoax. They wouldn't simply turn their backs on something that might relate to a high-profile unsolved mystery. Would they?

"I think we should get that beam out of the weather," I told Giles.

"It's pretty damned heavy," he said.

"What'll it take to move it?"

"Well, I figure that I'm going to have to hire someone with a front loader to clean this place up. I can't think of any other good way to move it."

"When'll that be?"

"Maybe next week. First I need to get some drop boxes out here to put all the trash in."

"Do you have something to cover that beam with?"

"I'll find something. But you know that thing has been exposed to the weather for years."

"Yeah, I know. It's just that I'd hate to have to explain why we didn't cover something that we thought might be important evidence."

"No problem. I'll cover it. And I'll give you a call when I'm ready to move it inside."

I wanted to talk with someone who could explain the lack of interest by the Canby police, but I didn't know anyone there. Under other circumstances, I'd have asked Kim if she'd heard anything around the sheriff's office; but I could hardly approach that subject again.

During the course of my investigation of the "Girl in the Carpet" case the previous year, I'd become good friends with HVCU detective Michael Wheeler. I decided to see if he'd share any information that would shed some light on what was happening with Canby PD.

"What's up, Corrigan?" Wheeler asked. "I haven't heard from you for a while."

"I was wondering if you could tell me if you guys had been contacted by Canby PD about the Brittany Harlan case."

"Brittany Harlan? You mean the missing kid from Beaverton? That was almost thirty years ago. What does Canby PD have to do with it?"

"A few days ago, a property owner outside Canby found Brittany's name carved in a beam from a building that was torn down a few years ago. He called Canby PD about it, but they apparently dismissed it as a hoax. I was just wondering if they consulted the sheriff's office about it."

"Not that I heard. What's your interest in it?"

"The place where the beam was found is just a quarter mile from where Kim Stayton found the bones last month. It seemed an unlikely coincidence."

"The Harlan girl was only six or seven years old. How could that be related to the vic from the homeless camp?"

I realized that I hadn't given Wheeler enough information, so I took a few minutes to give him the full story about Giles Svensen's discovery.

"According to Svensen, Canby PD just glanced at the beam and dismissed it as a hoax," I said.

"So? It probably *is* a hoax. Come on, Corrigan. Nine eleven? Really?"

"Yeah, I know. But someone put a lot of effort into scratching that name and date into a piece of wood that would probably never be seen by anybody."

"Okay, I'll play along for a moment. Suppose Brittany Harlan really did scratch her name on the beam twelve years after she was kidnapped. And suppose she was still alive ten years later when the homeless girl died. She'd have been over thirty years old, and that's ten years too old. Those aren't Brittany Harlan's bones."

"But if—"

"Forget it, Corrigan. That girl was homeless. She lived in the camp."

"Did someone out there say that?"

"No, but would you expect them to?"

"So what makes you say she was homeless?"

"The teeth. She'd apparently never been to a dentist. No fillings. But she definitely needed some work. There were signs of decay in several molars and her upper incisors. They think that if she could have afforded a dentist, she'd certainly have had that work done."

That was new information to me, and it was pretty conclusive.

"Cause of death?" I asked.

"Don't know. There was nothing obvious. No broken bones. No bullet wounds. No knife marks on the bones. Cause and manner are on the books as unknown, and that's probably the way it'll stay."

"And no idea who she was?"

"She could be a runaway from Philadelphia or an orphan from Atlanta. Unless someone in the homeless camp spills it, it's not likely that we'll ever know."

He was probably right. On the other hand, I could have pointed out that the old building at Svensen's place was torn down at just about the same time Kim's victim died. I couldn't quite let that go.

After storming out on Monday night, Kim finally returned late Wednesday afternoon. I saw her take her patrol boat into the canal to the sheriff's dock, and half an hour later, she parked in her usual place next to my back porch. She didn't say a word about what happened on Monday. But it wasn't as though nothing had happened. The tension was so powerful that neither of us dared to say anything.

The uncomfortable silence underscored the depth of Kim's emotional connection to the mystery of the girl at the homeless camp. I wanted to talk with her about the apparently coincidental timing of her victim's death and the demolition of the building where Brittany's name was found, but I could hardly ignore the way she'd reacted when I showed her the picture of the beam.

Still, on the theory that nothing I could say would do more harm than this tense standoff, I decided to open the discussion.

I held my breath, and I asked, "Do you think there could be a connection between your case and Brittany Harlan?"

Kim stared out the window and sighed. "Of course, there's a connection. They were both little girls whose lives were taken away from them."

"Sure, but what I mean is that if—"

She snapped, "I don't want to talk about this, okay?"

It *wasn't* okay. We spent the rest of the evening in a silent standoff.

Chapter 10

I left Martha alone in her work for Dakota Mutual while I pondered for the hundredth time what I could or should do about the girl at the homeless camp. Except for Kim's puzzling reaction, it probably would have been easy to walk away from it. In all likelihood, it was just what it appeared to be—a homeless girl who died of disease or malnutrition and a prankster with a twisted sense of humor.

But my mind wouldn't let me leave it alone. The first thing I had to do was separate the homeless girl's case from the Brittany Harlan mystery, even though their physical proximity implied a connection. The sheriff's office was still at least nominally investigating Kim's victim, so I decided to focus on Brittany Harlan. I'd already mapped out a basic action plan, and with the photography I did a week earlier, I had taken the first steps toward an investigation.

I'd already downloaded the photos from my camera, so I sat down at my computer to take a close look at them. Under the 250X magnification of the photomicrographs, I could see that the letters had been gouged into the wood by repeated strokes of a sharp edge.

The letters were about two inches tall, but the strokes that formed them were no more than a quarter-inch long. It had taken hundreds of such strokes to dig each letter into the wood. The many particles of glass embedded in the scratches hinted at the difficulty of the task.

And one other thing caught my eye. In several places in and around the scratching, I thought I could see small blood smears. It was difficult to tell for sure because the smears were nearly the same color as the dark-brown wood. But it didn't take a lot of imagination to see that it would be hard to use a piece of broken glass to carve the letters without cutting your fingers.

I had to question why any prankster would go to that much trouble. Or was I completely misjudging the difficulty of the task? I decided that the only way to know for sure would be to go out to Svensen's place and try scratching letters into one of the timbers. That would also give me the opportunity to take a close look at those brown stains, which I hadn't even noticed the first time I'd looked at the carving.

After confirming that Giles was there, I picked up the cheap plastic tackle box that Kim irreverently calls my junior investigator's CSI kit, which contains the things I need to make a superficial examination of a potential crime scene, hopefully without compromising any evidence present. I picked a Corona bottle from the recycle tub and put it in the back of my Yukon along with the tackle box.

Giles met me at the gate and let me through. I parked next to the stack of old timbers and noted the blue tarp covering the one with Brittany's name on it. I got out my stuff and selected a timber that was down at ground level. I put an old shop towel over the Corona bottle and whacked it with a lug wrench.

From the fragments of broken glass, I selected one from the mouth of the bottle because it had what looked like a pretty good place to grip. Then I sat down and started scratching. It wasn't as difficult as I'd expected. It took fifteen minutes to dig a pretty good replica of Brittany's *B*. At that rate, it would take about four and a half hours to complete the job. A prankster might do that.

But it wouldn't explain the blood—if that's what the stains were. I needed to test that, so I got my tackle box and climbed to the top of the timber pile. I untied the cords that held the tarp over the timber where Brittany's name was carved and drew the tarp aside. Using a magnifying glass, I located a small stain about half an inch below the carving.

The Kastle-Meyer procedure is an old-fashioned but effective test for the presence of blood. Its advantage over the Luminol test is that it does not degrade the sample. I used an eyedropper to dampen the tip of a sterile cotton swab with distilled water. After blotting excess water from the swab, I pressed it against the rust-colored spot on the wood, allowing time for some of the material in the spot to dissolve and transfer to the swab.

Next, I applied a drop of phenolphthalein reagent to the swab. I held my breath for five seconds, waiting to see if the swab turned pink. If it did, the test would have been invalid because it would indicate the presence of contaminating chemicals such as copper or nickel salts.

When no color appeared, I applied a drop of hydrogen peroxide solution, and within a few seconds, the swab turned bright pink. The phenolphthalein test is not 100 percent conclusive, but it did indicate a high likelihood that the spot contained hemoglobin, meaning that there was a high probability that the brown stain was blood.

That opened up all kinds of possibilities. It was likely that a good lab could develop a DNA profile from the blood on the timber. Even if there were no samples that might contain Brittany's DNA left from the original investigation, a profile still could be compared with DNA from a member of Brittany's family. That could settle it.

But I was not the right person to take the sample for testing. There are experts who know how to take samples that can't be dismissed by a clever defense attorney like Johnny Cochran. I wasn't ready to spend the kind of money it would take to have that done, so I went back to where I started—trying to replicate the Brittany Harlan carvings.

This time I selected a small fragment of glass that was sharp on all edges and set out to carve an *R* next to the *B*. It proved to be much more difficult without the smooth edge to grip. I had to scratch much more lightly, and it took many more strokes to dig into the wood. And despite the fact that I was genuinely trying to avoid cutting myself, I found my fingers bleeding from two or three little nicks in my skin. It took an entire hour to carve that *R*.

When I studied my *B* and *R* under magnification, the difference in their appearances was remarkable. The *B*, carved with deep, decisive strokes, looked completely different from the *R* with its careful, shallow strokes. And it was the *R* that more closely resembled the original carvings. Based on the time it took me to carve one letter, it meant that someone had spent about twenty hours doing the original.

With the smooth, easy-to-hold piece of glass, the job might have been done in three or four hours. I could possibly envision the prankster being stuck out there with no better form of entertainment sitting down and carving Brittany's name. Maybe he was with a buddy who went down to the river to do some fishing and left the bored prankster with nothing to do. But if it took twenty hours to do it, that scenario was out the window.

I won't say that I was convinced that the carving was real, but my skepticism was definitely softening. I packed up my stuff and headed back to the office. I spent the rest of the day searching the Internet for everything I could find on the Brittany Harlan disappearance. I compiled a list of every name associated with the 1989 investigation. This included the parents and other adults who were with Brittany on the day she was abducted, witnesses, investigators, and even a few suspects.

In many ways, it reminded me of what I'd found two years earlier when I was looking into the disappearance of another girl—Jessie Devonshire—who had vanished, apparently without a trace. In both cases, there were many reported sightings, all of which had been investigated and none of which produced anything of use to the investigation.

Brittany had been featured on two episodes of John Walsh's *America's Most Wanted*, but all the leads generated had also led to dead ends. Since

1989, whenever the remains of a child were found anywhere in the western states, they were screened for any possible connection to Brittany Harlan. That too produced nothing.

A cold case task force had been created by the Washington County Sheriff's Office in 2003, and the Brittany Harlan abduction was one of their first undertakings. After going over everything in the case file, they were forced to concede that there was nothing there to investigate any further.

When the file was put back in storage, a small newspaper article quoted the deputy in charge of the cold-case investigation as saying, "Of all the cases on our list, this is the one I'd most like to solve. It's one of those cases that just haunt you forever."

I located the deputy's phone number and left a voice message. Half an hour later, I found myself talking with the deputy's widow. He had died two years ago—a fatal heart attack at age fifty-four. I went back to the news reports looking for the name of someone else I could call. But by then, I'd had time to reflect on how little I actually had.

What I really needed to do was get the DNA profile from the blood on the timber. But that could cost me about ten grand, and unless the profile actually solved the mystery, there was no way I would ever recover the cost. Did it make good sense to gamble that much against such a small possibility of any return?

It all hinged on whether or not I believed that Brittany could have been alive in 2001, more than twelve years after her abduction. I remembered the recent case of Ariel Castro, who had held three young women captive for over ten years in his Cleveland home before one of them escaped and sounded the alarm. So I knew it *could* happen, but it still seemed a remote possibility.

When I searched the Internet, however, I was surprised to find a handful of other cases of long-term captivity involving young girls. There was a 1977 case where a victim abducted in Red Bluff, California, was held for seven years, a 1996 case where a Pittsburgh girl was held for ten years, and a 1991 abduction in South Lake Tahoe where the victim was held for *eighteen* years.

The most perplexing case I came across involved a young woman found naked in a park in Salt Lake City during the summer of 2010. She didn't remember where or when she was abducted, and the only name she knew was Sassy, which was what her captor had called her. She had a vague memory of being with other kids in kindergarten or preschool, but she didn't remember ever going to first grade. Police estimated her age to be around twenty, which meant that she probably had been held for about fifteen years. Four years later, her identity was still unknown.

I read a recent newspaper article with morbid fascination.

Salt Lake City Mystery Girl, Three Years Later

By Lynette Friend
The Utah Spokesman

SALT LAKE CITY — She was nearly dead when she was found naked, dehydrated, and hypothermic on a bench in Pioneer Park in downtown Salt Lake City on August 7, 2010. Rushed by ambulance to the Salt Lake Regional Medical Center, she hovered near death for six days before opening her eyes and asking where she was. The story she told was so baffling that authorities at first believed that it couldn't possibly be true.

Her name, she said, was Sassy. It was the only name she could remember ever being called. She didn't know how old she was, but medical experts estimated her age to be between 18 and 22 years. She had no memory of how she got to Pioneer Park, and she couldn't tell where she had lived. And that's where her story went from bizarre to incredible.

Sassy told of a life in a tiny windowless cell, where the only person she ever saw was a man who insisted that she call him "Papa."

Sassy's drawing of the cell where she was held

Her cell contained a bed, a toilet, and a sink. There was also a table and chair, and a TV-VCR unit on a shelf in the corner. Heat came from a vent high on the wall above the door. Day and night were determined by when the ceiling light and TV were turned on and off from some remote location. When the power was off, no light penetrated the cell.

Twice a day "Papa" would bring food—in the morning, a single-serving package of Honey Nut Cheerios

and a half-pint carton of milk, and in the evening, a Banquet frozen dinner, freshly microwaved. Her only utensil was a fragile plastic spoon.

Then there were the *other* visits—and the things she doesn't like to talk about, when "Papa" came to her cell and forced her to do the unspeakable. This went on for perhaps fifteen years.

Sassy knows how to read, and since she was found in the park she has learned how to write. She says that she learned to read from watching *Sesame Street* on television. "Papa" had given her a stack of video cassettes filled with *Sesame Street*. For a long time, probably several years, that was the only entertainment she had. Later, "Papa" brought her books to read and porn videos, which he made her watch while he was there.

The first time Sassy learned anything about the outside world was, in her words, "the day the airplanes crashed into the buildings," when "Papa" connected her TV to a cable featuring one channel—CNN. He told her that it was a special privilege and often reminded her that he would disconnect the cable if she didn't behave as he commanded.

For the past three years, authorities have attempted to figure out Sassy's true identity. Under hypnosis, the young woman has recalled a few fragments of her life before the cell. She has vague memories of Mommy and Daddy but can't remember who they were or where they lived. In one session, she described a room with other children, where there were stuffed animals and blocks.

Police artists have spent hundreds of hours with Sassy attempting to develop a likeness of her captor, but the efforts have thus far produced no leads. He is a middle-aged Caucasian, is about five-eight to five-ten, with a medium build, brown eyes, and brown hair. He usually has short facial hair but not long

enough to be considered a beard.

Authorities have worked their way through long lists of missing children, attempting to determine Sassy's true identity. They have few clues. When she was first found, fiber evidence was recovered from her hair, but it is of no value until they find something to compare it with. A specialist in linguistics has found traces of a Canadian or Upper Midwestern accent in Sassy's speech, although it is not known if this came from her early childhood or from her captor.

As far as where her cell was located, the only thing that is known is that a busy railroad ran nearby. Sassy has estimated that about twenty trains a day went by, close enough for her to hear the rumble and feel the building shake. The cell is speculated to have been constructed as a storm cellar or perhaps as a 1960s bomb shelter.

Today, Sassy is living in a shelter for abused women, where she is preparing for a

life on her own. She has given herself a new name and is learning job skills that will enable her to support herself. But the emotional scars run deep. She is distrustful of strangers, and she is shy to the point of being reclusive.

She receives counseling and support from the shelter's staff psychologists, who say that Sassy is remarkably strong and expected to make a full recovery. But authorities fear that she may never know who she really is.

The level of depravity in a case like this was almost beyond my imagination. And the problem with undertaking an investigation of this kind is that it can turn into a crusade, something that sucks up all your time and energy while the chances of producing a solution are almost nil. It was as true of Brittany as it was of "Sassy." Did I really want to go down that road?

Lying awake late in the night, while Kim slept next to me, I couldn't get my mind to shut off and let me sleep. If Brittany Harlan really had carved her name on that timber, it meant that she had been held prisoner in the old building that had been torn down. There were two things I could investigate.

The first nagging question was from which part of the building that timber had come. If it had been part of the roof structure, twenty or thirty feet above the floor level, then the name was probably carved after the building was demolished, meaning that the carving was a hoax.

And then came the question of who had occupied that building in 2001. It was possible that Giles Svensen could help with both questions.

April 18 Friday

Chapter 11

Kim woke up in a bad mood. I didn't wake up at all because I hadn't ever really gotten to sleep. I cooked up some bacon and eggs for breakfast while Kim showered, but even that failed to start any kind of conversation. Instead, we ate in uncomfortable silence, leading me to wonder if she had seen my scribbled notes from the previous day's Internet searches. I resolved to avoid leaving anything related to this investigation out where she might find it.

And I hated myself for thinking that I had to hide my work from Kim.

Martha came in, so we talked for a few minutes about her insurance fraud case.

"But how do I fake a ganglion cyst?" she asked when I again suggested that she go visit Dr. Gaston in Tacoma.

"I think I read somewhere that they can occur without a visible lump— I'm not sure, so you'd better check that out before you try it. I guess plan B would be to develop arthritis or carpal tunnel syndrome."

Martha groaned. "I don't know how to fake that stuff."

"I'll bet you can find a video on YouTube," I suggested.

She grunted.

"To make this sting work, you'll have to get Dakota Mutual to help you get set up as an employee of a company that has workers' comp insurance in Washington. I don't think Dr. Gaston will take the bait if you reveal that you are a private investigator."

"They're already working on that. I'm going to use Mom's address in Seattle. She's getting me a prepaid cell phone with a 206 area code."

"Sounds like you're way ahead of me on this."

"Just doing what you taught me, boss."

"Then I'll just get out of your way," I concluded.

I picked up my phone and punched in the number for Giles Svensen. When he answered, I asked, "How long have you lived down there?"

"My wife and I bought the place about thirty years ago. 1983 to be exact."

"So how much do you know about the comings and goings on the property across the highway?"

"Eh. I'm not a snoopy neighbor, but I've seen some things," he demurred.

"Do you have some free time? I'd like to drive down there and talk to you about that place."

So in the middle of the afternoon, I put a few beers into a little six-pack cooler and headed down to see Giles. I saw the big sliding door on the warehouse building open, so I pulled into the parking lot and found Giles connecting a battery charger to one of his Studebakers.

"I've taken the batteries out of most of 'em because they'll just go dead and corrode the battery platforms. But this one—I start the engine from time to time. I just like to hear the sound of it, ya know?"

I couldn't deny that the old flathead six had a sound all its own, but to me it wasn't a sound to get nostalgic about.

"They don't make 'em like that anymore," I said absently.

"Now they're all choked up with smog controls and computers. You can't even *see* the engines anymore, let alone hear them."

He switched the battery charger on and led me over to the small office at the corner of the warehouse. There were no chairs, so I sat on an old metal desk with a peeling Formica top. Giles accepted the beer I offered and leaned against the door jamb.

I pulled out a tiny digital voice recorder and held it up for Giles to see. He nodded, so I switched it on and pressed the record button. Its memory was a lot better than mine.

"How much do you know about the history of this property?" I asked.

He shrugged. "You can't live across the street from a place for thirty years without hearing things and seeing things."

"So what's the story?"

"Well, there's about four acres to it altogether. It starts up there at the old homesite—the old man's house burnt down in 1991, and everything went to his grandson. By all accounts, the grandson wasn't much good. He's the one who rang up all the debt and got foreclosed on."

I pointed at a faded old sign next to the highway, advertising Walters Marine Service – Engine Repair, Welding, and Fiberglass Work.

"So was Walter the grandfather?"

"No, no. The grandfather was Charles Roy. I heard somewhere that his family owned this property since the 1920s. It used to be a cedar mill. They'd float the logs down the river and tie 'em up in the eddy down there.

I suppose there must have been a crane to lift the logs out of the river. My understanding is that the original mill was here as far back as the 1890s."

"This building looks old—but not *that* old," I observed.

"Hardly. When Charles Roy took over the operation from his old man in about 1940, he decided to modernize. In the old days, the mill just produced dimensional lumber. But Charlie saw good money to be made in cedar shingles. That's when he put up this building. He moved the mill operation over here and set up the old building for making shingles."

"The old building—you mean the one that was torn down." I motioned toward the slab where the pile of timbers was stacked.

"Right. That building went way back. Some people say it was built when the railroad first came through in the 1870s. Not sure if that's true, but you can tell by some of the old timbers that it was all old-growth lumber."

"Yeah, I could see that in the beams you showed me."

"Anyway, they'd get the logs into this building, where they'd strip the bark and decide which ones would go for lumber and which would go for shingles. They'd take the ones for shingles and cut 'em into two-foot lengths. Then they'd haul them over to the other building, where they'd split 'em into shingles, dry 'em, and treat 'em with preservative."

"How long did that go on?"

"Not sure exactly. Old Charlie had a son who died in Vietnam. I think that kind of took the heart out of him, ya know? Then in the late seventies, the environmentalists put an end to logging, so Charlie shut down the mill."

"So that must be when they opened the boatyard," I speculated.

"Almost. That actually came a few years later. When he shut down the mill, old Charlie turned everything—including his bank accounts, I guess—over to his ne'er-do-well grandson, Douglas Roy. Well, young Douglas burned through whatever money the old man had, and all he had to show for it was an old houseboat—one of the ones they used to rent on Lake Billy Chinook.

"That was about the time I bought my place across the highway. Our front window looks right out over this property, so we had a front-row seat. We could tell that Douglas was having a hard time because more than once, the power company shut off their electricity. So that's when he leased the buildings to Harvey Walters. The boat repair shop was in the other building, and he sublet this one for boat and RV storage."

"I remember seeing the other building from the highway as I drove by, but I never paid any particular attention to it."

"I was never inside it—never had any reason to be. But it looked like a pretty good building. It never made sense why they tore it down rather than just cleaning it up."

"As I recall, it was a pretty tall building," I commented.

"Yeah, the main bay was probably twenty-five or thirty feet tall inside. There was a gantry crane on tracks that ran the length of the building. That was probably put in by Charlie. That part was all steel, of course, but the building itself was wood."

"Hmm. I remember it as being a metal building."

"Sheet metal was added on later, but the building was originally all wood and concrete."

A thought occurred to me. "Would you have any photographs of the building?"

Giles rubbed his forehead. "I never deliberately took any pictures of the building, but it probably shows up in pictures of other things—sunsets or things like that. The wife took a lot of pictures."

"Would it be difficult to find the ones that show the building?"

"Not really. I'd just have to look through some photo albums."

"I'd like to see some photos of the building if it isn't too much trouble."

"I'll take a look and see what I can find."

Looking back at the sign up by the highway, I asked, "How long did the boat business last?"

"Yeah, well, the boat business never really caught on, but they scraped by all through the nineties. Then in 2003, the warehouse building was damaged by a fire, so they couldn't rent it out anymore, and they couldn't afford to fix it either.

"Now, up to that time, I'd kept my cars in an old hangar at the Aurora airport, but those guys kept jacking up the rent. So when I saw the warehouse sitting empty, I asked Douglas Roy about taking over the lease from the boat business. He said he'd let me do that if I'd repair the fire damage. Well, that got me a place for my cars, and it helped keep the boat business afloat for a while too. But they finally folded up for good in 2007 when the economy started going to crap.

"That's when Douglas leased the boat repair building to that bunch of druggers. They brought in their little travel trailers and lived on-site. Really messed the place up. It wasn't until later that we found out that they were making meth."

"And you said that they never caught the guys," I said. "Any idea who they were?"

"Not a clue. I stayed as far away from them as I could and just prayed that they'd stay away from my cars."

"So let me get the time lines straight," I said. "The boat works occupied the building from the mideighties until 2007, and then the meth cooks were there until . . ."

"They were only there about a year. Don't remember exactly when they got busted. But that's when the DEQ slapped a quarantine on the building, requiring a certified cleanup before it could be occupied again. I don't know how much the cleanup was going to cost, but it wasn't cheap. Douglas got a big loan from Ted Birkenfield to finance the job, but then he never did it. And he never paid back the money, so Birkenfield foreclosed."

"I take it Charles Roy was gone by then."

Giles pointed over to the riverbank, where a steel framework was visible among the blackberry brambles.

"There used to be a double-wide sitting on that frame. It burned down in '91. We watched it go. Man, it went up like nuke! By the time the fire department got here, there was nothing to do but break out the hot dogs and marshmallows. That was the end of the house and old Charlie too."

"Are you saying that Charles Roy died when the house burned down?"

"Well, there was kind of a flap about that. The medical examiner determined that he'd been dead for some time before the fire—maybe weeks. Douglas was living on his little houseboat down there in the cove, and he claimed he didn't know anything about it. Nobody ever proved otherwise, so he inherited the place."

"Where is Douglas now?"

"No idea. He tore down the building and sold off all the steel, and nobody's seen him since. That's why it took four years for Birkenfield to foreclose on him. It all had to be done in absentia as they say."

"What're *you* going to do with the property?"

"Well, of course, the only thing I want is the warehouse, and now I own it. After I finish cleaning up the rest, I may sell off the part by the river. There's a guy who wants to put in a houseboat moorage and floatplane base."

"When do you plan on doing the cleanup?" I asked, indicating the piles of timbers and debris on the old building site.

"Good question. I have some guys coming out to look at the old lumber, to see if anything there is salvageable. If I can get some money out of that, maybe I'll be able to afford to hire someone to come in with some machines to clean up the rest."

"I have a line on a couple of equipment operators who might be able to do the job for you," I suggested. "Their mom is one of my neighbors. They work in construction, but they take on an occasional freelance job."

Back at my office, I slumped into my chair, feeling the full effect of my lost night's sleep. I plugged a headset into my recorder and played back the recording of my conversation with Giles, scribbling two pages of notes on a yellow pad.

A spring storm moved in during the afternoon with a period of blustery wind accompanied by driving rain that lasted into the evening. I had fallen asleep on the couch in front of the television and didn't hear Kim come in.

Chapter 12

I woke up at 6:40, and through the front window, I watched a southbound Amtrak Cascade train roll past. For a few disorienting moments, I wasn't sure if it was evening or morning. The dull gray sky gave no hint whether the light was coming from the west or the east. But my brain managed to put it together. In the evening, the Cascade trains always have at least a few passengers. In the morning, the southbound train is always empty. It was morning.

Unwilling to resign myself too quickly to the idea of getting up, I lay there contemplating how I'd spend my day. If the weather had been decent, Kim would be going out on river patrol, and I could try to get something done on my Brittany Harlan investigation. But with the crappy weather, she'd probably stay home.

"Yeow!"

DC, my big yellow tomcat, possessed a sixth sense regarding when I woke up. To my knowledge, I hadn't made a sound or a movement, but somehow he knew I was awake, and he let me know that he was done standing guard on the front porch. He had successfully defended us through the night, and now he wanted in.

I struggled to my feet and let him inside. Instead of showing the slightest trace of gratitude, DC lumbered past me and into the kitchen.

"Yeow!"

Of course. Yesterday's crunchies were *old*. He needed *new* crunchies. I got a scoop of fresh cat food and put it into his bowl.

"Anything else?" I asked.

He ignored me, so I excused myself to go take a shower and shave. Kim was still asleep, or pretending to be, when I finished, so I decided to go down to *Annabel Lee* and immerse myself in the woodworking project. Normally, this would be a relaxing and rejuvenating activity, but on this rainy morning, I simply couldn't shake the hollow feeling regarding Kim's silence.

We hadn't spoken more than ten words since Wednesday. And that kind of silence is insidious. I should have turned around and gone home. Maybe it would have made a difference but probably not. At least, that's what I would tell myself over and over in the succeeding days and weeks.

While I carefully trimmed and fitted each piece of hardwood into the irregular shapes of the ship's hull, my mind wandered back and forth between what might have happened to Brittany Harlan and what was happening between Kim and me. There was some kind of connection that I couldn't see, and I kept coming back to the conclusion that things wouldn't be right between us until I knew who the homeless camp victim was and how her death related to Brittany.

After about six hours' work, I was getting hungry. I decided to call it quits and go see if I could somehow break through to Kim. I put things away, cleaned up a bit, and used an air hose to blow the sawdust out of my hair. When I got home, the first thing I noticed was that Kim's marine unit Explorer was not in the driveway where it had been when I left in the morning.

So much for talking. The rain had stopped in the middle of the day, so I figured she'd gone out on river patrol after all. I was about to go inside when I spotted a boat racing downriver toward my dock. It was a silver-and-gray Sanger ski boat that belonged to a guy I knew as Slalom Jim.

Jim was a tournament skier in his younger days, and he still could ski circles around me and just about anybody else on the river. But he was way out of his usual stomping grounds. His riverfront property is in Newberg, twenty-five miles upstream, and it is rare to see him all the way down here. I walked down to say hi as he pulled in and tied up.

"You have a gas-powered water pump, don't you?" he asked without preamble.

"Yeah. It's just a little one, but it runs. What's up?"

"Like to borrow it for a while. Captain Alan's tugboat sank, and we're trying to raise it. We have one pump, but it can't move quite enough water. We think with two pumps, we'll be able to refloat her."

"What happened? Did he hit something?"

"Nothing that dramatic. He let someone else use it yesterday, and the guy didn't pump grease into the shaft seal first. Burned up the seal, so when he parked it, it was leaking so fast the bilge pump couldn't keep up."

"Where'd this happen?"

"You know where Pete's Place is?"

I did. It was a mile or so upstream from my place, where a small houseboat was tied to a concrete pylon where there used to be a crane for lifting logs out of the river and transferring them to rail cars. There was a faded old wooden sign on the pylon proclaiming it to be Pete's Place.

I went up to my garage and grabbed the pump, some hose, and a can of fuel, already mixed for the pump's little two-stroke engine. We raced upstream to Pete's Place, where Alan and someone I didn't know—presumably Pete—stood on the deck of the houseboat looking into the water alongside.

The pilothouse was all that showed of *Misty Rose*, which was resting in water about seven feet deep. Atop the pilothouse was a water pump a lot bigger than mine, and a suction hose was routed through the open window down into the depths of the bilges.

I asked Jim what the plan was, and he said, "Well, Alan has already gone down and stuffed rags and towels into as many openings as he could find. When we had the pump running, it would take the water level down, but it doesn't move quite enough water. We're hoping that the two pumps together can do the trick."

It took a few minutes to get my little pump set up next to the larger one, and then Alan jumped into the cold water and pushed the suction hose through the pilothouse window. He went inside, ducked underwater, and dragged the hose out of sight down into the engine room. When he came back out, he closed the door and spent the next few minutes packing rags around it.

We fired up the two pumps, and in a few seconds, we had two healthy streams of water shooting over the side of the sunken vessel. Through the window, we could all see the water level in the pilothouse start to go down.

"I think it's gonna work!" Alan shouted over the roar of the pumps. "We never got it down that far the first time."

There was still water gushing through the gaps around the pilothouse door, so Alan went back into the water to stuff more rags into the leaks. After twenty minutes, we noticed some movement as the stern of the vessel started to rise.

Misty Rose started to heel over toward the houseboat, and Alan immediately jumped into the water. He hooked a cable hoist to a deck cleat and handed it up to Pete, who attached it to the houseboat deck. Alan started working the handle as fast as he could until he had the tugboat back on even keel. All the while, the pumps continued shooting fat jets of water away from the pilothouse.

Alan had to stay in the water, shifting his weight from side to side to keep *Misty Rose* from rolling onto her side until her deck finally broke the surface and the swamped vessel gradually became stabilized. By this time, Alan was able to go back into the pilothouse and reposition the suction hoses into the deepest parts of the bilges.

Once the deck was above water, the amount of inflow was greatly reduced, and it didn't take long before the pumps started sucking air. Alan disappeared below deck with a grease gun, which he used to repack the shaft seal and slow the inflow to a drizzle.

With the pumps finally quiet, we could finally carry on a conversation.

"What's next?" I asked.

"First thing to do will be to pull the batteries out and see if river water got inside. I think they might be okay because the bilge pump was still running," Alan said. "Then I'll have to see what happened with the engine. Course it wasn't running when it went under, so it probably didn't get much water into the cylinders. Anyway, that's what I'm hoping."

"Will she stay afloat now?" Pete asked.

"Not without the bilge pump. If I had a battery charger, I could hook it up to a battery and let the pump run off of that."

"How about this?" Jim pulled a little twelve-amp charger from under one of the seats in his boat.

"That'll do it. Got a place to plug it in?" Alan asked Pete.

Once we were sure that everything was secure, Jim started his engine to shuttle me and my pump back to my dock. Alan asked if he could go along.

"I need to go to Mike's place and borrow some dry clothes," he explained.

Mike Mohler was Captain Alan's brother, who lived in Canemah just a couple of blocks up the hill from my place.

As we approached my dock, Alan turned and asked, "I don't suppose you could drive me out to Dundee to get my pickup. Mike doesn't drive anymore."

I wasn't enthusiastic about spending two hours doing that, but I knew Alan wasn't the kind of guy who would forget a favor. One way or another, he'd pay me back for my trouble. Half an hour later, Alan returned in dry clothes, so we took off for Dundee, forty miles away. Slalom Jim had already sped back upstream in his ski boat to beat the darkness.

As we went past Giles Svensen's place on our way toward Canby, I commented on his recent purchase of the property.

"I used to know the old owner," Alan said. "Charles Roy. I went to school with his son, Dale. We were on the wrestling team together. Dale got killed in 'Nam in 1969."

"You ever spend any time down there at the mill?"

"Oh sure. Dale and me used to get into the old man's booze and go down to the river and drink 'til we couldn't walk. Then we'd smoke some weed and pass out."

"Did you go to Vietnam?" I asked.

"Nope. First job I had out of high school was working in a marine salvage yard in Portland. I knew how to use a cutting torch, so they put me to work cutting up an old navy destroyer. I was having a grand old time, torching everything in sight. Nobody warned me not to burn the galvanized stuff, so when I found an old water tank, I started cutting it apart. Before long, I was enveloped in yellow smoke."

"Zinc oxide?"

"Damn near killed me. I didn't realize anything was wrong until I'd developed what the old-timers called galvie flu. My lungs were permanently damaged, so I couldn't pass the draft physical. Dale passed and got himself killed, and I failed, and here I am. Go figure."

"Crap," was all I could think to say.

It was after dark when I finally got back home. DC was camped out on the back porch, and there were no lights on inside. That was odd. Kim certainly should have been off the river and home by then. I went inside, where my first order of business was to feed DC, who made it clear that being left outside all day was not what he'd had in mind. For the record, if he'd been left *inside* all day, he'd have complained just as much about that. He *is* a cat, after all.

Walking into my bedroom after dark was always a gamble. There was no wall switch for the lights, so I had to walk across the room to switch on the lamp on the nightstand. Invariably that meant stumbling over, stepping on, or kicking one or two pairs of Kim's shoes, which never seemed to find their way into the closet. But not this time.

It didn't register immediately. For a brief moment, I was pleased that Kim had decided to do something nice and put away the shoes that I occasionally griped about. And then a wave of dread swept in, and I suddenly felt nauseous. One glance into the closet confirmed my worst fear. Kim was gone. Not just gone. Moved out.

April 20 Sunday

Chapter 13

I tried again to phone Kim but got no answer. This time, I didn't bother with voice mail. I'd already left three messages since finding the empty closet the night before. How in hell had this happened?

Unable to get up the enthusiasm to go down to work on *Annabel Lee*, I switched on a basketball game. The Trailblazers squeezed past the Rockets in double overtime to take the first game of their playoff series. But even that didn't do anything to change my outlook. I was tempted to hammer down some booze and anesthetize myself into oblivion as I might have done twenty years ago, but those days were long past.

It wasn't that I was more mature. It was just that I didn't want to pay the inevitable price. Besides, I had to *do* something. I had to find a way to *fix* it. I had to make it right. Through my mind, I played a hundred different speeches that I'd deliver to Kim if I just had the chance, all of them accepting full blame for whatever was bothering her. But that was the problem. I didn't *know* what was bothering her.

And that's what led me back to my desk, where the yellow pad with my notes from Friday still lay face down next to my computer monitors. I opened a new spreadsheet on my computer and started copying dates and events, building a database to which I added a few things I'd learned from Captain Alan the day before.

I then sorted the data based on the entries in the date column to make a chronological list of everything I knew about Svensen's property and the old mill. To this I added what I knew about Brittany Harlan and the girl Kim had found, whom I nicknamed Sunny, to give a small sense of brightness to her sad, short life.

1890   The cedar mill begins operation.

1920   The Roy family buys the business.

1940   Charles Roy takes over the family business and expands the cedar mill operation into the manufacture of cedar shingles.

1969   Dale Roy is killed in Vietnam.

1980   Charles Roy closes mill due to old age and decreasing availability of cedar logs.

Douglas Roy (Dale's son?) comes to live with his grandfather.

1983   Svensen buys the house across the highway from the mill property.

1984   Douglas Roy moves into the houseboat.

1986   Harvey Walters leases the buildings and opens his boat repair company.

1989   Brittany Harlan, age 7, disappears from Beaverton.

1991   Charles Roy dies; fire destroys his old house.

2001   Brittany's name is scratched on beam (if authentic).

2003   Warehouse building is damaged by fire.

2004   Svensen leases the warehouse building for his Studebaker collection.

2007   Boat repair business goes bankrupt and shuts down.

Building is leased to meth cooks

2008   The meth operation gets busted, leaving the building contaminated and unusable.

Douglas Roy borrows money for environmental cleanup but spends it on other things.

2009   Approximate year of Sunny's death (plus or minus a year?).

Ted Birkenfield begins foreclosure proceedings against Douglas Roy.

2010   Douglas Roy demolishes the old building and vanishes.

2014   Sunny's body is found at the homeless camp.

Svensen buys the property and finds the beam with "Brittany Harlan 9-11-01" scratched in it.

Sometimes, when you lay things out in chronological order, it reveals relationships between seemingly unrelated events. But not this time. There simply wasn't enough data. The only thing that was clear was that Harvey Walters occupied the old building at the time Brittany Harlan was abducted and was still there when her name was carved into the beam. Assuming, of course, that the carving was authentic—and I guess I *was* assuming that.

What's more, with a little stretching of the time line on Sunny's death, Walters may have been there when that happened too. It was well within the range of possibility.

I recognized the wheezing rattle of Giles Svensen's Studebaker on Water Street, approaching my place. I went out onto the front porch and watched him park the old pickup. When he got out, Giles was carrying a manila envelope.

"Cup of coffee?" I asked.

"No thanks," he said. "I can't stay. I'm on my way to a swap meet."

"Buying or selling?"

"Just looking . . . Well, unless I find something really good."

"Photographs?" I asked, indicating the envelope.

"Yeah, there's half a dozen different shots. Hope there's something there that'll do you some good."

After he left, I took the envelope inside and emptied it onto my desk. Glancing through the photos, there was one shot that showed the boat repair building particularly well. It was a picture taken from inside the warehouse, showing the damage done by the fire, but in the background was an unobstructed view of the other building.

I made high-resolution scans of all six photos and then returned them to their envelope. In Photoshop, I opened the best photo and cropped out most everything but the building, which sat at a forty-five-degree angle to the focal plane, showing the north and east facades.

The north façade was dominated by a tall sliding door hanging from a track on a steel framework. Just as I had remembered it, the building had barn-red sheet metal siding and a galvanized-steel roof. The ground floor windows on the east façade were covered with weathered plywood. Off to the side, there was a pair of trashy-looking travel trailers, which I guessed belonged to the meth heads.

I could see nothing in the photo, however, that helped identify where Brittany Harlan's beam might have been in the structure. Not that I'd expected to be that lucky. The best I hoped for was to concoct a floor plan that would help me guess at the structural elements. If I could do that, then I might be able to guess where the beam had fit into the building's structure.

I made a copy of the cropped photo and zoomed in on the north façade. With the image perspective tool, I expanded the far edge of the building until the east and west corners were the same height. This produced what would appear as a straight-on shot of the north façade.

The challenge at this point was to establish the proper height-width proportion. I studied the photo in search of anything of known dimensions that would give me the scale. A four-by-eight-foot sheet of plywood would be ideal, but that was too much to hope for.

There was a man door to the right of the large sliding door. In a typical industrial building, a man door would be thirty-six inches wide and eighty inches tall. I zoomed in on the door and adjusted the image proportions until the width of the doorway was 45 percent of its height. Then I zoomed back to show the entire north side of the building. It was exactly what I needed.

I went through the same steps on the east façade. Since I didn't have a man door to help establish the proportion scale, I counted the number of ribs in the siding above the thirty-six-inch doorway on the north façade. There were six, meaning that the ribs were spaced at six-inch intervals, so there would be twenty ribs in a ten-foot section of wall. With that, I adjusted the proportions.

I now had accurate representations of the north and east elevations of the boat repair building. I calculated the wall height to be twenty-seven feet. The ridge of the hip roof structure ran north and south, with an estimated height of forty feet. Given the age of the structure, I could assume that its trusses were built on-site.

Glancing at the notes I'd made when I photographed Brittany's timber, I quickly concluded that its dimensions meant that the only way it could have fit into the roof framing would have been as a vertical or diagonal brace. One by one, I opened the photos of the beam and zoomed in on the area with the carving, looking closely at the stains that I had determined to be blood.

One stain in particular caught my attention. Most of the stains appeared to be blood smears, but this particular one, directly below the *r* in *Harlan*, appeared to be a drip that had flowed at right angles to the beam. That meant that the timber had been horizontal, so I concluded that it was very unlikely that it had been part of the roof framing. It was too short to have been a horizontal part of a truss.

From that, I deduced that the timber had been part of an interior structure—a ceiling rafter. And from its dimensions, I knew it was intended to carry a substantial load. But that was as far as logic could take me. What I really needed was somebody who had been inside the building and could tell me what had been there.

April

Monday 21

Chapter 14

Martha had a batch of e-mail messages from Dakota Mutual regarding the investigation of Dr. Gaston. They agreed to explore the possibility of helping with a sting.

"Only thing is, there's no way I can fake a ganglion cyst."

"Yeah, but if you get in with some other complaint, maybe you'll be able to see what their scam is."

"I suppose so. But it's the ganglion cyst that is the basis of their scam."

At that moment, Bud came up the steps onto the front porch.

"What's that about a ganglion?" he asked as he opened the screen door.

I don't like sharing information about investigations with anybody. Not that I didn't trust Bud. It just isn't good to have group conversations about things we're doing.

So I answered with a noncommittal question, "What's up, Bud?"

"I have a ganglion cyst," he said, pulling up his left sleeve. "Bugs the hell out of me. I can't even wear a wristwatch."

Sure enough, there was a lump about the size of a pea on Bud's wrist.

"How long have you had that?" Martha asked.

"Long time. Now that I have Medicare, maybe I can get something done about it."

Martha and I looked at each other. She had the same thought I had. I waved her off from saying anything about it.

To change the subject, I asked Bud, "What gets you up so early?" It was barely 9:00 a.m.

"Oh, the flooring guys ran me out. They're doing the bathroom and kitchen, and they're taking up the whole place. I just came over to see if you'd mind if I look for night crawlers in your tomato bed. Then I can go fishing 'til they're done."

"Sure, Bud. Go ahead. But if you catch a big salmon, I get half."

He knew I was kidding but said, "Sure, no problem. Thanks."

"What do you think?" I asked Martha after Bud left.

"Oh my god. It's hard to get my mind around Bud as an undercover operative."

"I know what you mean. But think about it. He has the real thing. All we'd have to do is set him up with a fake employer."

Martha added, "Yeah, and he'll also need to use Mom's address on fake ID."

It appeared that Martha was warming to the idea.

"No need to make a hasty decision," I said. "Just give it some thought. If it seems doable, fly it by the guys at Dakota Mutual."

I turned my thoughts back to the Brittany Harlan investigation. Until or unless I could conjure up a floor plan, there wasn't much I could do with the carving except assume that it was authentic. Turning to the theory that the cases of Brittany and Sunny were related, there was a natural implication that Sunny would have been abducted in a manner similar to the way Brittany was, though maybe as much as ten years later.

I went to the website for the Center for Missing and Exploited Children. After poking around for a few minutes, I found a state-by-state search utility. I searched for children who had gone missing between 1986 and 2000. What was surprising was that there actually were more missing boys than missing girls. I hadn't expected that.

In order to focus my search and produce a manageable number of hits, I had to make a number of assumptions about my hypothetical kidnapper based on the profiles of my one *probable* victim, Brittany, and my one *suspected* victim, Sunny. Most obviously, both were girls.

So I started with the assumption that my kidnapper was interested only in girls, simply as a means of limiting the search. If it didn't pan out, I could go back later and change the parameters, but for the moment, I searched only for girls.

Second, he abducted Brittany when she was seven years old. That's young enough to be compliant and easily tricked but old enough to require no special care. Assuming that my perp was abducting girls to groom into future sex slaves, he probably wouldn't want infants or toddlers. They require far too much attention. Nor would he want teenagers because they would be more resistant to both the abduction and the subsequent psychological manipulation.

And last, my kidnapper didn't travel very far. Brittany had been abducted from a store that was only about twenty-five miles from where she was held captive. That might mean he was working alone, so the risks associated with transporting an abducted girl multiplied enormously in relation to the distances involved. I limited my search to girls taken from within a fifty-mile radius of Svensen's warehouse.

As I screened the names of missing children, I excluded those who were listed as probably having been taken by a family member in a custody dispute. The crime involving Brittany Harlan was clearly something other than a custody dispute, and I assumed the same to be true of Sunny. After two hours, I had a list of ten names which I listed arranged alphabetically:

> *Evelyn Curtin, Portland OR, 1992, age 5*
> *Arianna Durkee, Vancouver WA, 1987, age 6*
> *Brittany Harlan, Beaverton, 1989, age 7*
> *Makayla Imbler, Woodburn OR, 1996, age 5*
> *Lisa Jewell, Portland OR, 1998, age 6*
> *Caroline Lowell, Portland OR, 1990, age 6*
> *Alyssa Marquam, Beacon Rock WA, 1993, age 5*
> *Lacey McCredie, Gresham OR 1995, age 5*
> *Megan Moro, Salem OR, 1996, age 5*
> *Audrey Sheridan, Tigard OR, 1991, age 7*

Almost any one of these missing girls could have been Sunny. And then there was the horrifying possibility that *all of them* had been victims of the same twisted predator—ten girls in a thirteen-year period, all within fifty miles.

"I think you're imagining things, Corrigan," Michael Wheeler said when I phoned him about my list. "There's nothing statistically unusual about that number of abductions in your eight-thousand-square-mile area over a fifteen-year period."

"I know that," I admitted, "but the question remains. Is there anything you can share with me about any of these cases?"

"I think you know the answer to that. None of those are Clackamas County cases. We won't have any files on any of them."

"Yeah, I was just hoping that maybe something had come across your desk that might help."

"I have nothing for you. Sorry."

It was what I'd expected. But I had to give it a try. I'd feel pretty foolish if, after spending weeks investing a missing girl, I were to learn that the sheriff's office had quietly solved the case ten years ago. With no shortcuts coming my way, I made a file folder for each case and arranged them chronologically based on when the girls were abducted.

Then I went to Google to see what I could find out about each of the girls.

The first file was for Arianna Durkee. She vanished on July 4, 1987, during the Independence Day fireworks show. The family had arrived early at Fort Vancouver Park and spread a blanket on the lawn. They had snacks and a cooler filled with beverages, including beer and wine. That would become a point of contention during the investigation since alcohol was prohibited in the park.

Six-year-old Arianna had at first been energetic and excited, but during the long wait for darkness, she became cranky. Her parents attempted without success to get her to go to sleep. They were on the verge of packing up and leaving when the first fireworks were launched. With the explosion of colorful sparks, Arianna became enthralled.

While music played over the loudspeaker system, Arianna danced about happily. Nobody saw her go. But suddenly she was gone. In the crowded confusion, the darkness, and the ongoing fireworks display, the girl's father searched frantically for Arianna while the mother stayed with their other child, eight-year-old Garrett.

In the days before everyone carried a cell phone, it was twenty minutes before someone called the police to report that a child was missing. It was impossible to conduct an effective search. Some witnesses reported seeing a man carrying a child, but none had seen any behavior to suggest that there was anything wrong.

The second file was for Brittany Harlan. Into her file I put every piece of information I had found in the nine days since Giles showed me the name scratched in the beam, including my photographs, notes on my experiments carving with broken pieces of glass, and everything I knew about the old cedar mill. I started a list of people to track down and interview. This list would include family members, witnesses, investigators, and suspects.

The abduction of Caroline Lowell was frightening in its brazenness. Caroline was kidnapped on May 22, 1990. She was sitting in a shopping cart while her mother, Charlotte Lowell, waited at the meat counter in an Albertson supermarket. Nobody saw the man walk up and wheel the shopping cart away. Mrs. Lowell received her package of steaks and turned to put it into her cart, but it was gone.

Four different witnesses saw a man pushing the cart through the store with the child in the seat. The cart was found abandoned in a narrow aisle near the check stands. A clerk saw a man carrying Caroline from the store. The descriptions of the kidnapper were remarkably consistent and, at the same time, remarkably unremarkable.

I noted the two similarities with the Brittany Harlan abduction. Both girls were taken from supermarkets, and in both cases, the witnesses had described an abductor as being so ordinary in appearance that the descriptions were worthless.

"So I guess I'll see you tomorrow afternoon," I heard Martha saying.

"Hmm?" I asked.

"I just said I'll see you tomorrow afternoon. Remember? I'm going to Vancouver in the morning to see your friend about the electronics."

I looked at the clock and was surprised to see that it was after five. I'd been so absorbed in my research that I had completely lost track of time. After Martha left, I heated up some Chinese food left over from the day before. I didn't actually have much of an appetite and ended up throwing most of the food away.

Too weary to go back to work, I switched on television. One of the Bruce Willis *Die Hard* movies was on, and I didn't have the energy to change channels. I went into a zombielike state, neither alive nor dead, not even hearing John McClane's witty lines for the inept terrorists who were determined to do him in.

Chapter 15

I felt better after a long shower in the morning. Following a quick breakfast, I resumed my Google searches for information about the missing girls.

Audrey Sheridan was seven years old when she disappeared from her school in Tigard, Oregon, on February 19, 1991. There were conflicting stories about exactly when she was last seen. The girl's mother insisted that she had walked Audrey to her classroom and watched her go inside. The first grade teacher, who was in the classroom at the time, denied having seen Audrey at all that morning.

As a matter of course, the school phoned Audrey's mother when the girl was reported absent. But that was nearly two hours after she was last seen. A third grader had reported seeing a man leading a little girl down the sidewalk away from the school first thing in the morning.

There had been several sightings that the authorities investigated, but nothing developed from them.

On June 17, 1992, Evelyn Curtin was dragged into a blue minivan as she walked down the sidewalk toward her friend's house in southeast Portland. The van sped away before any of the witnesses could get a license number or even an accurate description.

Three witnesses saw the abduction. One said the van was a Toyota, one said it was a Dodge Caravan, and the other said it was a Chevy Astro. Even though police were on the scene within minutes, the van and the girl were never found.

Alyssa Marquam was a five-year-old from Michigan, on vacation with her family, when she vanished from Beacon Rock State Park in the Columbia Gorge on August 16, 1993. Alyssa had been playing with three older siblings while her parents set up for a picnic dinner.

The older children said that Alyssa had gotten tired and sat on a bench to rest. The next time they looked in that direction, she was gone. Two witnesses reported seeing a man walking toward the parking lot holding the hand of a little girl. The man was described as average height and maybe a bit overweight.

The next file was for Lacey McCredie, abducted on April 1, 1995. She had been playing in the fenced yard of her family home in Gresham, Oregon, when she vanished. In the absence of any witnesses or evidence, the authorities had focused their investigation on the girl's mother, who insisted that she had left the child alone for only as long as it took to go inside and use the bathroom.

Despite hours of interrogation, Lacey's mother never changed her story. Possibly because of news reports quoting the authorities' suspicions about the mother, there was only a handful of reported sightings following the girl's disappearance. And this only served to deepen suspicions. When Lacey's mother took her own life a few months later, it was accepted as an admission of guilt even though the case remained officially unsolved.

On April 10, 1996, Makayla Imbler vanished while with her mother in the Walmart store in Woodburn. She was three days short of her fifth birthday. Her mother was trying on shoes when she saw a man leading Makayla toward the door. She shouted and ran after them, but barefooted, she was unable to catch up.

Once outside, the man scooped up the girl and ran out into the parking lot. Two witnesses saw a man put a girl into a small motor home and then speed out of the parking lot. They noted that the vehicle had Oregon plates, but they were not able to get the number.

Megan Moro was abducted from a Burger King restaurant along Interstate 5 in Salem on August 3, 1996. She had gone to the restroom, accompanied by her older sister, who reported that a lady had approached them and said that their mother wanted them outside. The older girl objected that she had to pee, so the lady had left her behind, taking only Megan.

The girl's parents launched a search as soon as the sister told her story. A witness reported seeing a woman and little girl get into an old gray van driven by a male subject who was described as looking like a homeless person.

The last file was for Lisa Jewell, who was six years old when she was taken on June 26, 1998. She was with her aunt at the Lloyd Center ice arena in Portland. The aunt had been teaching Lisa to skate, but when the child became tired, she left her on a bench at the edge of the ice.

There was a great disparity in the statements about how long Lisa was left alone. The aunt said it was only a few seconds, but other witnesses said it had been half an hour. Witnesses saw a middle-aged woman talking with Lisa, and a few minutes later, she was gone.

The aunt took the time to get her skates off before raising the alarm. She later explained that she figured Lisa had simply gone to the bathroom, so she wasn't greatly concerned. Witnesses saw a lady carrying a girl wearing skates in the underground parking lot but didn't see where they went.

I was leaning back in my chair and staring at the ceiling, trying to decide what to do next, when I heard a knock at my backdoor. I got up and found Captain Alan standing on my porch with a half case of Miller Genuine Draft.

"This don't hardly pay you back for the ride out to Dundee, but I know it's the kind you drink," Alan explained.

I waved that off. "Have time to put some of this to good use?"

"They're not expecting me in the office today," he said.

I put the half case into the refrigerator and got out a couple of cans that were already cold. I handed one to Alan, and then I grabbed a third can on a hunch. We walked through the house and out onto the front porch, where we pulled up a couple of chairs.

"Been down to *Misty Rose* today?" I asked as we snapped our beers open.

"Spent the last two days getting water out of the transmission and engine. Drained the crankcase, pulled the plugs. Really, there wasn't that much in there, but it's a pain in the ass getting it out. Then I had to pump out about thirty gallons of contaminated fuel."

"I *thought* I heard voices out here," said a voice from the alley.

"Hey, Bud. Want to join us?" I held up the extra beer that I'd brought out for exactly this contingency. Bud's hearing was as good as ever.

"Heard your tugboat sank," Bud said to Alan.

"It's happened before. She'll be okay once I get everything dried out. I'll have her running in a day or two."

I let the conversation take its own course for the next few minutes while Alan explained all the things he'd have to do in order to get the boat running again. The hollow sound that Bud's can made when he put it down told me that it was time to go get some fresh beers. My can was still nearly full, so I got only two.

"You mentioned that you went to school with Dale Roy," I said to Alan, finally getting to what I wanted to talk with him about.

"Oh yeah. We raised a lot of hell together."

"I'm interested in what you can tell me about the property where the mill used to be."

"What would you like to know?"

"Anything at all. I'm especially interested in the building that was torn down. You know anything about it?"

He shrugged. "It was used as a meth lab. They said it was polluted with chemicals. That's why they tore it down."

"Did you ever go inside it?"

"Oh sure. Lots of times, back in the fifties and sixties when I was hanging out with Dale."

"Do you think you could draw a sketch of the floor plan?"

"I'm no artist. It'd be pretty rough."

"That's okay. I just want to get a sense of what it was like and what was inside."

"What the hell for?" Bud asked.

It was stupid of me not to have anticipated the question. I should have been ready with an answer. So while I thought something up, I used the excuse of a bathroom break, and while inside, I got a pencil and pad for Alan, along with prints of my edited photos of the building.

"There's a guy who wants to build a floatplane base up there, and he needs a building. Someone at the county told him that it would be easier to get a building permit if he passed it off as a renovation of the old building instead of a whole new one—something to do with grandfathering."

It was a complete fabrication, of course, but it was good enough for Bud—and Alan too, for that matter. He started by studying my photos. At my urging, he made notes and explained various features and their purposes.

His observation skills were far better than I'd dared hope for. When he finished marking up the exterior images, he turned a fresh page and started laying out a floor plan, which identified key spaces within the structure.

"Out here in the middle, there was a big open space with overhead cranes. One weekend, we took Dale's '53 Bel Air in there, pulled out the old six-cylinder engine, and dropped a 327 in its place. Dale's old man was pissed because he didn't want him driving a hot-rod. He said we were going to have to switch back, but he never made us do it." Alan chuckled.

I pointed to a big square Alan had drawn near the side of the main bay.

"That's the hydraulic pit. There was a big hydraulic ram in there for the splitter that made the cedar into shingles. The hydraulic pump was right next to the pit."

He drew a box with an X inside. "That's the pump housing."

Outside what was the west side of the building, he drew a long rectangular box.

"That was the oldest part of the building. It was built in the 1870s. During railroad construction, it was used for equipment and supplies. Sometime after the railroad was finished, the main building was added on."

With his finger, he traced the outline of the concrete slab on his sketch.

"It ended up looking like the old building was an addition to the newer one, but actually, it was the other way around. The west wall of the *big* building was actually the east wall of the *old* one. There were doors going into the original part, but I never went in there. The old man told us that they used to use chemicals in there to treat the shingles, and it was permanently contaminated."

"What's this in the corner?" I asked.

"Oh, that's where the tunnel came up."

"Tunnel?"

"Yeah. There was a tunnel that went down to the riverbank. The old man said that it was dug back in the 1880s after they were done building the railroad. At that time, the property belonged to a San Francisco outfit that had provided laborers for railroad construction. Mostly, they were Chinese. The company would pay for the workers' passage from China, and then the Chinamen would have to work it off. Of course, the company always overcharged for the boat ride and underpaid for the work, so the workers were almost like slaves."

"What was the tunnel for?"

"The old man said that they converted the old storage building into a dormitory and used the tunnel to smuggle Chinamen in and out of the place by boat. After the railroad was finished, there was a bunch of 'em still around, so the company rented 'em out to logging companies, mills, or whoever else wanted cheap labor. But they had to do it on the sly because the local workers didn't take kindly to losing their jobs to Chinamen."

I shook my head, recalling that this was the same period of time when thirty-four Chinese gold miners were gunned down by a gang of rustlers in Wallowa County on the other side of the state.

"Dale and me used to play in those tunnels. It was great fun."

"Tunnels? More than one?"

"Well, there was one that went down to the river and another that went over where the house was. It came up next to the house, and it was used as a potato cellar for years."

Bud farted loudly and said, "Well, I guess I'll just have to leave it at that."

He got up and shuffled back toward his place, carrying the half-finished beer.

"Yeah, I gotta get going too," Alan said.

"I wonder if you could come out to Svensen's place with me and show me where some of this stuff was," I said as he got up.

"When're you thinking?"

"I don't know—maybe tomorrow or the next day."

"Sure. I can do that."

"How do I get hold of you?"

"Oh, I expect I'll be up at Pete's Place or over at Mike's. Looks like I ain't gonna have much drinking money for a while."

"Traffic was horrible!" Martha complained when she returned from Vancouver.

"So basically normal," I said.

"If we hire Bud, maybe we can send *him* on errands like this."

"Did you find anything worthwhile?"

Her face brightened.

"You were right. That guy has *everything*."

My old friend Jerry Midland runs a pawnshop in Vancouver, just north of the Columbia River. In the back room, he has a shop where he spends his spare time building highly specialized electronic devices for all kinds of surveillance, and he stocks a full inventory of off-the-shelf items as well.

During the Mendelson-Devonshire investigation, Jerry had helped me with some devices that had proven critical to solving the case. I'd sent Martha over there to see if he had anything that would help in the Dakota Mutual case. If we were going to carry off a sting in Dr. Gaston's office, we'd need to do some covert recording.

If Martha had been the operative, she could have simply carried my miniature digital audio recorder in her purse. But now we were considering sending Bud as the operative, and I didn't think we'd be able to convince him to carry a purse.

"I found two things of interest. The first is an audio recorder designed to look like a hearing aid—one of those ones that go behind the ear."

"That could work with Bud," I commented.

"But then Jerry showed me this."

From her purse, she removed a small bag. She showed me a man's wristwatch packaged in that bombproof plastic stuff that you have to cut away with industrial shears. I was not impressed.

"Bud said he can't wear a wristwatch because of his ganglion cyst."

"He can wear it on his other wrist," Martha said impatiently.

"And then he'll know what time it is."

Martha made a face.

"Yes, he'll know what time it is. And he'll record a high-resolution video of everything that happens."

She handed me the wristwatch, and then I was able to read what was printed on the cardboard backing inside the package: "Brickhouse Security Waterproof Spy Watch."

"Spy Watch? Is this real, or is it a kid's toy?"

"Two hours recording time, 640-by-480 resolution video. Audio too. It's perfect."

"I'm afraid to ask what it cost."

"I'd love to tell you that it was under fifty bucks," Martha said.

I groaned.

"But sales tax took it up to fifty-three."

"You can't even buy a decent watch for fifty-three dollars."

"So? Do you care if it doesn't keep perfect time?"

"I guess we'll need to have a talk with Bud, then."

"Ten-four, boss."

April
Wednesday 23

Chapter 16

While waiting for her computer to boot up, Martha asked, "Hey, what's the story on Kim? I haven't seen her around here all week."

I mumbled, "She hasn't *been* around here all week."

"There something wrong?"

"Yes."

"You want to talk about it?"

"No."

"You know, sometimes it helps, just to talk to someone."

"Martha, you know me. I don't spill my guts about this kind of thing, okay? That doesn't mean I don't have feelings. It just means that I choose to keep them to myself."

"But you two have always been so *happy* together. You're *perfect* for each other—everyone can *see* that!"

I made no comment.

"This has something to do with that girl up by the homeless camp, doesn't it."

It wasn't a question. It was a statement.

"I'm calling the girl Sunny. She deserves to have a name."

"Okay, boss, but what does Sunny have to do with Kim being gone?"

I still remained silent, pretending to focus on my computer screen.

"And that other girl too—Brittany Harlan. That's why you're investigating them, isn't it?"

She wasn't going to give it up until I said something.

"I'm trying to determine if the Brittany Harlan carving is real. If it is, then it might be connected with Sunny. But right now, the only connection is geographical. Sunny was found four hundred yards from where the Brittany Harlan carving was found."

"Can we get a client—someone to pay for the investigation?"

I sighed. "Maybe. If we can establish with any certainty that Brittany could have been alive in 2001, then we might get her family interested. But at this point, I don't even know where they are, let alone whether they could afford to pay for an investigation."

"So you're just going to do it out of love?"

"Martha, anything I do on this case is on my own dime, all right?"

"Corrigan, you're hurting my feelings. We're partners. If you take on a pro bono job, I'm perfectly happy to absorb my share in the split. That's what it *means* to be partners."

I sighed. "Not this time. If I have to pay for DNA, it could be ten grand. I won't let you pay for that. It isn't your problem, and it isn't your case."

The look that flashed over Martha's face was unlike anything I'd ever seen from her. And the firmness in her voice was unlike anything I'd ever heard from her.

"Sorry, boss. That's not how it's going to be. We are in this thing together. You've done some pretty big favors for me, and you're not going to prevent me from paying some of that back now!"

Rather than surrender, I said, "I haven't spent any money yet, so there's nothing to split. We can talk about it when or if it comes to that."

"There's nothing to talk about. I want to see this thing solved as much as you do."

I had no answer, so I just raised my hands—not in a gesture of surrender but more of a "this conversation is over" gesture.

Martha had the final word. "We'll get her back, boss."

I drove across the railroad tracks on a gravel driveway that led to a rough parking area next to the river at Pete's Place, where Captain Alan's old pickup was parked. As I walked down the plank onto Pete's houseboat, there was a sudden roar, and a cloud of smoke and steam rose from the dual exhaust stacks on *Misty Rose*. The sound of the engine was matched by the cheer from the pilothouse.

Alan ran the engine at about 3,000 rpm for a couple of minutes and then gradually pulled back the throttle as the engine temperature rose. After perhaps five minutes, the engine was idling smoothly at 800 rpm, and the exhaust was clear. As water evaporated off the engine and the surrounding surfaces, clouds of vapor condensed in the cool air and rose up through the pilothouse.

"How about *that*?" Captain Alan asked when he saw me.

"Sounds pretty good," I said.

"It *ought* to, what with all the money I've poured into it."

"When do you think she'll be ready to sail?"

Alan glanced at his watch.

"About three minutes."

"Oh really! I thought you had a bunch more to do first."

"There's a bunch more to do, for sure, but she's ready to go right now. Want to come along?"

I had serious misgivings about leaving the security of the moorage to take the untested vessel out onto the open river, where an ounce of water in the fuel tank could bring a sudden end to the merriment.

"Sure," I said in spite of myself.

I untied the lines that secured *Misty Rose* to Pete's houseboat and stepped aboard. Alan stepped on the pedal shifting the transmission into forward, and the thirty-six-inch propeller started turning. We pulled out toward the deep water, where Alan eased the throttle lever forward and turned upstream.

Chugging along at a comfortable speed of about eight knots, with billows of steam still streaming up through the pilothouse and out the windows, we ran against the spring current toward the Rock Islands. The current was swift through the narrows, and Alan pushed the throttle wide open to maintain headway. With a mighty roar and a trail of fuel-rich black exhaust, *Misty Rose* beat her way through the fast water.

In the broad pool above Rock Islands, Alan turned *Misty Rose* in circles, testing the steering and sloshing the remaining puddles of water in the bilges down toward the pump intakes. When he pulled the overhead cord, the air horn made a gurgling sound and shot a blast of water over the foredeck before finding its voice. With the steam still rising up from below deck, the pilothouse became a sauna.

"How much fuel did you take aboard?" I asked looking at the fuel gauge, where the needle rested firmly on the peg next to the letter *E*.

"We put ten gallons in. That ought to get us to the gas dock at Wilsonville."

"Will it be open this early in the season?"

"I sure hope so."

So did I.

It took forty-five minutes to get to Wilsonville, where the gas dock was indeed open. By then, things below deck had dried out enough to ease the sauna conditions topside. When Alan pulled alongside, I stepped onto the dock with a tie-up line.

"Hope she restarts," he said when he shut off the engine.

"I'd like to hear a bit more confidence," I said.

Alan put in two hundred dollars' worth of gasoline—about fifty gallons. The engine started easily, and the fuel gauge rose to a quarter tank. Running with the current, we moved at a good pace with the engine at idle speed. As we made the big turn at Wattles Corner, I spotted the homeless camp on the right bank.

"Say, do you have time to stop at Svensen's place? Maybe you could give me that tour of the old building site like we talked about."

"Sure, why not?"

We looped around the downstream tip of a long, narrow island near the right bank and then ran upstream into the sheltered cove. Alan brought us alongside a rusting old barge that had been tied to shore there for as long as I could remember. I scrambled onto the barge and secured a dock line. There was a crude gangplank leading to shore, where a well-beaten fishermen's path led up onto the flat.

I pulled out my phone and called Giles to let him know that we were there, and a few minutes later, he joined us near the concrete slab where the building had been.

"Not much left," Alan observed.

"Let's walk around the slab, and you can tell us what you remember about the building," I suggested.

We approached from the north side, and Alan pointed out the small porch where the man door had been. To its left, he pointed to the gap in the footing where the big garage door was.

"The door was nearly always open—at least in the old days. It was twelve or fourteen feet tall."

Pointing toward the east side of the building, he said, "There was a foreman's office over there and a bathroom in the far corner. In between was a place they used for a lunchroom. Last time I was in here was when Walters had his boat shop. The whole place was filled with junk. I mean, that guy couldn't throw anything away. Boat parts everywhere."

That was of special interest to me because the boat works had been in operation throughout the period when Brittany Harlan might have been held there.

"Can you describe the rooms?"

He led us over to the east side of the slab and pointed at the stained concrete, where faint lines showed where interior walls had once been.

"The rooms over here were just regular height. There was kind of a mezzanine up on top. In the old days, that's where the mill workers took their lunch breaks. The room down here was a repair shop where they'd fix any machinery that broke down. See how the floor's all soaked in oil?"

When we got to the south end of the slab, Alan pointed out the garage door opening, identical in size and straight in line with the one on the other end of the building. In the corner next to it, Alan pointed at the cut-off stubs of anchor bolts in the concrete.

"There used to be an air compressor there—huge thing with a two-hundred-gallon tank. The stairway up to the mezzanine went right past the drive belts. If anyone had ever put an arm past the stair railing, that thing would have torn him to shreds."

As we walked toward the southwest corner, we had to make our way around the pile of timbers that included the one with Brittany's name on it. Partially obscured under the heap was a square pit.

"That's where the hydraulic splitter was. Dale's old man thought it was a pretty dangerous place, and he ordered us to stay away from it."

I peered into the hole and could see some greasy machinery that I was unable to identify. The pit seemed to be partially filled with dirt. Turning from that, Alan pointed toward the corner of the slab.

"There was a big enclosed hydraulic pump over here. That's what powered the splitter."

There was a black stain on the concrete and four imprints where the machinery had been anchored in the slab. Alan led us over to the western edge of the slab.

"This wall was actually part of the old original building."

Pointing down at the footing, he explained, "You can see the difference in the concrete. The older foundation is different. There was a big door at each end, where they'd roll carts full of shingles through for treatment."

Pointing across the overgrown rectangle that was about fourteen feet wide and fifty feet long, Alan called our attention to the crumbling top of a concrete wall, barely visible at ground level.

"That's what's left of the old foundation. Dale told me once that this place was used as a dormitory for the illegal Chinese laborers back before the mill was built. That's why the tunnel came up to it."

"What did Harvey Walters do with this part of the building?"

"Nothing, as far as I know. What I remember is a bunch of boat molds and stuff leaning against that wall, blocking the doors. So I guess if he used it for anything, it would have been storage."

"You mentioned some tunnels," I reminded Alan.

"Yeah. They came up over at the northwest corner of the building, kind of off the end of the original building. There was a little vestibule where the steps came up, and a door led into the building. It was always locked because the old man didn't want people going in there. But the guys who ran the mill had keys. There was an iron door at the bottom of the stairs, and I guess that went under the old original building."

That corner of the slab was covered in perhaps a foot of dirt, all overgrown in blackberries and brush, so there was no evidence of the tunnels to be seen.

"Maybe it's still open over by the house," Alan suggested.

We walked northward on a trail that was increasingly overgrown as we approached the steel beams that used to support the double-wide where Charles Roy had lived. Alan tramped down the blackberry brambles in an area a few yards from the steel framework.

"Before they brought in the double-wide in the late sixties, there was a farmhouse here. The tunnel used to come up into the old house. After they tore it down, the tunnel was all that was left, but they kept it for a potato cellar.

"Here it is!" he finally said. "Looks like it's been filled in, but this is the place."

There was a depression in the ground about ten feet across and a couple of feet deep. I could see nothing to indicate that it had ever been the entrance to a tunnel.

"You sure this is it?" I asked.

Looking mildly offended, Alan said, "This is it. When the old man would go on one of his rampages, Dale and me would duck down in there and bar the door. That'd piss him off even more, and we'd have to hide out all night sometimes."

"Did you say that the tunnels went down to the river?"

"The other one did. This one went over and joined into it right next to the shake mill. Kind of in that vestibule place I told you about."

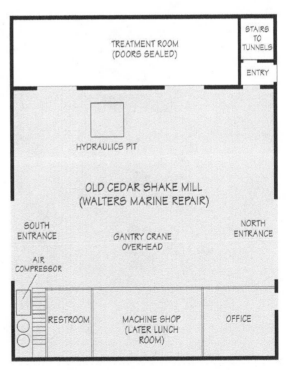

"Where'd the tunnel come out down below?"

"I doubt we can get there now. It'd be in that mess of blackberries, and you'd have to be a rodent to get through there."

Back home, I made a scale drawing of the floor plan that Alan had drawn on Tuesday, and then I added lines and notes regarding everything he'd shown me while we walked the site. I thought about how the new information related to the timber with Brittany's carving. I recalled that it had measured thirteen and a half feet in length.

There were two places on the updated floor plan where a beam of that length might have fit into the structure: the machine shop/lunchroom on the east side of the building or the older original structure on the west side. I asked myself where a prison cell capable of keeping Brittany Harlan for at least twelve years could have been concealed there.

The conclusion was obvious: the old railroad shed. It was outside the main building. Access to it was blocked off except to the person who held the key to the iron doors. And from 1986 to 2003, that would have been Harvey Walters.

April 24 Thursday

Chapter 17

Bud declared, "Check it out."

He gestured toward the potted geraniums arranged next to his porch and the small beds of marigolds and mums planted between the sidewalk and the foundation of his cottage.

"That looks good!"

"It's just like you suggested." He lowered his voice and asked, "Do you think Martha will like it?"

"I'm sure she will," I assured him.

"Should I bring her here and show her?"

"You're pushing me outside my area of expertise, Bud. I'm not the guy to hand out advice on this kind of stuff."

"Yeah, but—"

"Can you cook?"

He shrugged. I took that to mean no.

"Okay, then, go get some Chinese takeout and invite Martha to dinner at your place. She'll see the flowers, and she'll also see what you've done inside."

"Oh. Well, maybe I should get some furniture before I do that."

"Yeah, that'd be a good idea."

"That's gonna cost some money," he said thoughtfully.

"How much furniture do you need?"

"Well, I have a pretty good TV set."

"That's all?"

"I have a mattress, but it's just on the floor."

"Okay, bare minimum, you need a bedroom set, a living room set, and a dining set. Doesn't have to be extravagant, but it has to be nice. And you need some window coverings."

Bud looked crestfallen. "Damn! It'll take a couple of months to buy all that stuff with my social security checks."

"Cash-flow issues, huh?" I commiserated.

"Yeah, that's what it is. Cash-flow issues."

"Maybe I could help you with that."

"Like a loan?" he asked brightly.

"I had something else in mind."

His face clouded. "Like what?"

"A payroll advance, maybe."

"Huh? What payroll?"

"I have a job that I think you could help with."

"You mean like working on your ship? Something like that?"

"I was thinking you might be able to help with an investigation that Martha is doing. You interested?"

"An investigation? Yeah, sure! I watch all of those CSI shows on TV. I know a lot about that stuff."

"Well, you wouldn't actually be doing any investigating. It'd be more like acting."

Bud struck a pose and recited, "Tomorrow and tomorrow and tomorrow creeps in its petty pace from day to day 'til the last syllable of recorded time—"

"This won't be Shakespeare," I interrupted. "We're trying to see if a doctor is fraudulently billing workers' compensation insurance, and you are uniquely qualified to help with that."

"I don't know very much about insurance."

"The fraud involves ganglion cysts."

Bud looked at his wrist, and his face brightened with new understanding.

"Here's the deal," I explained. "We'll set you up with a fake identity and a fake employer. You'll go to this doctor for treatment of the ganglion cyst. We suspect that he'll then pump you for information about your job, and you'll just need to play along."

"What's the guy's scam?"

"He'll treat the problem. But then he'll pad the bill to the insurance company. And he might offer you a kickback if you file for extra benefits under workers' comp. Pain and suffering, extended disability, stuff like that. All you'll need to do is sign, and he'll take care of the rest."

"Will he really give me money?"

"We think he'll offer it. But you won't get to keep it."

"Oh."

"But *we'll* pay you. It'll be $300 a day plus your expenses. It'll probably take at least three days and a trip to Tacoma."

"When's all this going to happen?"

"It'll take a couple of weeks to get everything set up. Then we'll make an appointment with the doctor. In the meantime, you'll work with Martha perfecting your role. Your acting's going to have to be pretty good."

"So I'll be working with Martha?" he asked brightly.

"That's right. This is her investigation."

"Oh man, this is going to work out great! I'll probably need to have that furniture first though, so that we can, you know, pur-*fect* my role."

"Here's an idea for you. Instead of getting takeout, invite Martha to help you pick out furniture down on Main Street, and when you're done, you can go across the street to New Hing's and have dinner."

"Cool! That's a great plan."

Later I talked with Martha about my conversation with Bud. "You'll have to be the one to judge whether or not he's a good-enough actor to pull it off."

"I think you underestimate Bud sometimes," she said. "He's actually a pretty smart man."

"You're probably right. It's just that I've seen him when he was at rock bottom, when he had nothing, couldn't get a job, and picked up cans by the highway to earn beer money."

"He's not the only one who was hurt by the recession, you know."

"No, he certainly isn't. Anyway, here's the deal. He wants you to help him pick out some furniture that he'll pay for with what he earns from doing the Dakota Mutual job. You know what the budget is for that job, so you know what the budget is for the furniture."

"Oh, I get it. So I'm the chaperone."

"No, that's not it. Bud's not going to break the bank—his place won't hold enough furniture to do that. But he really wants your decorating advice."

"Hmmph. Okay, I can go with that. When's all this going to happen?"

I shrugged. "When Bud asks, I guess."

April

Saturday 26

Chapter 18

I stood with Giles Svensen next to the heap of timbers from the old building and watched the F-350 dually tow a flatbed trailer down from Highway 99 into the parking area next to the Studebaker Museum. The name on the side of the pickup said Marsden Equipment Rentals, and on the trailer sat a dirt-stained yellow backhoe with front loader.

"You want to unload it here?" shouted the pickup's driver.

"Yeah, anyplace is fine. Our operator is on the way," replied Giles.

The driver looked irritated. "He was supposed to be here. I need to get back to the yard. I have another delivery to make. I thought your operator would be here."

"He'll be here. He had some engine trouble and had to get a ride, that's all."

The driver paced back and forth, glancing frequently at his watch.

"I don't have time to wait around here for your guy. I'll just unload it myself," the driver announced after a couple of minutes.

He walked to the rear end of the trailer and started releasing the tie-down chains from the front end of the machine.

"No problem," Giles told him.

The driver paused to gripe, "They always do this to me—schedule things so tight that I don't have any slack. And then they complain if I'm a minute late. They're too cheap to buy another trailer, so I have to drive all over creation and make multiple deliveries."

My thought was "If your job bothers you that much, maybe you should look for another." But I didn't say anything.

He threw the tie-downs aside and climbed onto the backhoe. The diesel engine fired up with a puff of black smoke, and after a few seconds, the driver raised the front scoop a foot off the trailer bed.

"Wait! You need to—"

I was too late. The driver shifted into gear and stepped on the throttle. The front of the backhoe flew skyward, pitching the driver out of his seat, against the back of the cab. Fortunately, as he fell backward, his desperately flailing hand grabbed the shift lever, pulling the machine out of gear. The engine raced, and the front of the backhoe crashed back down onto the trailer.

"—unhitch the rear tie-downs," I finished.

The engine went quiet—I'm not sure if it stalled or if the driver shut it down. He sat, half in the seat and half out, rubbing his forehead and shouting a litany of foul language that set new standards for creativity in cursing. A blue BMW came down the drive and pulled up next to the trailer. Kevin Beatty got out of the passenger side and evaluated the situation.

"Better get those rear tie-downs before you try to drive it off the trailer," he suggested.

He was not prepared for the stream of obscenities that came from the driver.

Kevin's mom got out of the BMW and walked over to where Giles and I stood in diplomatic silence.

"Something going on here that I don't know about?" she asked.

"No, just a little lesson in focus," Giles said.

"Giles, this is Kaylin Beatty," I said. "She's the real estate broker I told you about. She's also Kevin's mom."

While Kevin took over the unloading of the backhoe, Giles talked with Kaylin about his plan to divide the property and sell off the part he didn't need.

"Is this all one tax lot?" Kaylin asked.

"Yeah, why?"

Kaylin explained, "The zoning here is for a five-acre minimum, so the county probably can't let you divide it."

She paused. "But there might be a way around it. As I recall, this place was at one time platted for a town site."

"That's right. The town was never built though," Giles said.

"Okay, so what you can do, if there is a copy of the original plat on record, is file for a lot-line reaffirmation and then a lot-line adjustment. That'll accomplish the same thing as the subdivision but with different terminology so that it complies with land-use law."

"I don't know what you just said, but I agree. Your son know what he's doing with that machine?"

"He's been running equipment for about ten years now. He knows his stuff."

Once the backhoe was unloaded, the rental company driver swung his rig in a wide circle and headed back toward the highway and his next delivery. Kevin climbed off the machine and came over and joined our conversation.

"Giles, meet Lucky," I said. "Tell him what you need."

"First thing is to move that heap of timbers. Corrigan has some special instructions for the one on top—the one with the blue tarp over it. The rest go on the trailer."

He gestured toward a tandem-axle car hauler parked a few yards from the lumber pile. A pair of twenty-yard drop boxes stood just beyond the trailer.

I said, "We need to handle that one timber pretty carefully. It needs to go up into the warehouse."

"Once all the timbers are on the trailer, then we'll see how much of this junk we can get into the drop boxes."

While Kevin removed the front scoop and rigged a pair of slings on the arms, Giles and I walked with Kaylin up toward the warehouse.

"So why do you call him Lucky?" Giles asked me.

I looked at Kaylin, and she chuckled.

"When Kevin was in seventh grade, he was talking about a couple of the girls in his class. He kept referring to them as hoes, like 'This ho did this, and that ho did that.' I didn't think it was appropriate, so I asked him what he calls the boys who go with those girls. Without missing a beat, he said, 'Oh, I call 'em *lucky*!' And that's been his nickname ever since."

On that note, Kaylin took her leave and walked back to her car. Kevin got Brittany's timber safely stored in the warehouse and then, with Giles supervising, went to work clearing the piles of dirt and junk from the concrete slab. I got out a hundred-foot measuring tape and took down the dimensions of the mill building slab and the old foundation of the original building. But mostly, I just stayed out of the way.

Looking off to the south, I saw a wide graveled drive curving away from the building site, down toward the river's edge. The drive ended at a level place covered with heaps of trash and junk. Some of it was obviously debris from the boat works, but it also appeared that people had been bringing trailer-loads of household trash and dumping it there.

Another pair of drop boxes had been deposited next to the dump site. I wondered if all that trash would fit in just two dumpsters. Maybe Lucky would be able to compact it.

While walking back up the drive, I spotted a footpath that branched off into the brush and trees to the south. It occurred to me that the trail appeared to go in the direction of the homeless camp upstream. Curious, I took off up the trail.

Even though we'd had several days of nice weather, the trail was still muddy and slick. It appeared to be a well-beaten path, but I was not able to determine for sure whether it was an animal trail or a human trail. But given the proximity of the homeless camp, I guessed that it was the latter.

I passed a couple of places where other paths branched off from the main trail, both heading down toward the river. Could be a fishermen's trail, I thought. And then I came to a flat area with a patch of bare earth in the middle, surrounded by trampled brush. A few scraps of yellow plastic ribbon still hung from the branches of a vine maple: CRIME SCENE DO NOT CROSS.

This was where Sunny was found. Looking around, I noted how well screened the site was. The surrounding foliage was so thick that it was impossible to see more than about thirty feet in any direction. It seemed like the kind of place a methodical killer might choose to conceal his victim.

Following the trail past the burial site, I went perhaps twenty yards when the path intersected a much more heavily traveled trail. To my right, toward the river, I could see the tents of the homeless camp. To my left, the trail led toward the railroad tracks and the highway. I wondered how people living so close to a decomposing body could have failed to notice the smell.

This made me reconsider my earlier evaluation of the dump site. Maybe the killer wasn't as astute as I'd at first concluded. All of this seemed to support the theory that the girl had been a resident of the homeless camp. And yet Kim hadn't believed that.

"Who the hell are you?"

The loud challenge startled me, and for a second I froze. When I turned, I saw a smallish man with bad teeth carrying a red plastic gasoline container.

"I just walked up the trail," I said.

"You a cop or something?"

"Or something," I said. "I'm not a cop."

"You come to see where the body was?"

I pointed back down the trail. "Was that the place?"

"Yeah. I was the one found it."

"How'd that happen?" I asked.

"There was a big piece of metal on the ground. I turned it over, and there it was. I heard the sheriff boat, so I ran down and waved them in."

"Have you lived here a long time?"

"Yeah. Long time. There's worse places to live."

"They say the girl was killed about five years ago," I said.

"Yeah. I heard that."

"Were you living here then?"

"I didn't have nothing to do with it."

"The body wasn't buried. I was wondering why you didn't smell it."

"I told the cops."

"Told 'em what?"

"There was a pair of deer that got hit by a train. Middle of the summer. Stunk to high heaven."

"Are you saying that's when the body was dumped here?"

"How the hell should I know? I'm just saying that if it was, we wouldn't a known the difference."

It was possible.

"You ever walk down that trail?"

"Yeah, sometimes."

"Ever see anything down there?"

"Like what?"

"I don't know. Anything that might relate to the dead girl?"

"Shit. I told you. I don't know nothing about it."

I wasn't going to get anything from him. I made some kind of comment to end the conversation and turned back down the path. On my way back to Giles's place, I explored the two side paths I'd seen on my way up. They led not to the river but to a clearing of about half an acre. Although the plot was not currently in cultivation, it was obvious that a crop had been grown there in the past.

A few scraggly marijuana plants growing wild in the clearing did a lot to explain why there was a trail between Giles's place and the homeless camp. It also explained why the homeless man was so reluctant to talk about it. I couldn't ignore the possibility that a pot farm could have something to do with Sunny's death.

But neither could I ignore the fact that the walk from the boat repair building to the dump site had taken only about ten minutes.

April 27 Sunday

Chapter 19

Eight days. That's how long Kim had been gone. If anybody at the sheriff's office knew where she was, they weren't talking. All they'd say was that she had taken a leave of absence. I made several trips up to her condo but saw no sign that she'd been there. The only thing I could do to keep my mind off Kim was try to solve the mystery that lay behind her departure.

Nothing I'd found at Svensen's place had provided the definitive connection I sought between Sunny's death and the Brittany Harlan carving. While I was pretty sure that I'd be able to establish that Brittany's beam came from the old chemical treatment room, the trail to Sunny's grave didn't prove any kind of a connection. If anything, it offered a viable *alternative* to that connection—the possibility that the death was related to the pot farm.

I got out the floor plan I had drawn and stared at it. I again tried to envision exactly how Brittany's beam fit into the structure. It almost *had* to be a ceiling rafter. That was the only place where a horizontal structural element would have been accessible for her to scratch her name in it.

What's more, the fourteen-foot width of the 1860s foundation coincided nicely with the length of Brittany's beam. The only thing about it that bothered me was the beam's six-by-sixteen inch cross-section. That was way beyond the structural need for a thirteen-foot span. I had to assume that the structure had been seriously overbuilt.

Working with the theory that Brittany and perhaps Sunny had been held in some part of the old chemical-treatment room, the big question had to be how that could have been kept secret from the workers in the main building. Access to the room was controlled by Harvey Walters. He had the key to one door and, according to Alan, had kept the other doors blocked by boat molds.

But that didn't explain why nobody had ever heard her. One might reasonably assume that she would have tried to shout or hammer on the walls in an effort to get somebody's attention. So why hadn't anyone heard her? Machinery noise, railroad noise, and highway noise would obscure whatever sounds Brittany could make, but there *had to have been* periods when all of those things were silent.

Would it have been possible for Walters to construct some kind of soundproof room inside the old structure? I'd seen the sound-absorbing materials used in recording studios, and they are reputed to be pretty effective. But those materials are not durable and could easily be torn down by anybody in the room.

Looking at it from the other direction, if Brittany *had* been there in 2001, it meant that Walters had somehow solved the soundproofing issue. What's more, if Walters was responsible for Sunny's death in 2007, then he had almost certainly killed Brittany as well. With his business failing and eviction looming, he'd have seen the need to do something with his captives. I closed my eyes. All of this was speculation. There was still no proof.

The answers to all my questions lay in finding Harvey Walters. A quick name search came up with forty people by that name nationwide but none at all in Oregon. The man I was looking for had opened the boat repair business in 1986. One could reasonably guess that he had to be at least thirty years old at that time to have the financial wherewithal to open a business. That would make him at least sixty-seven years old now.

Even allowing for the remote possibility that a wealthy relative had bankrolled the business, it was unlikely that he was younger than sixty-five. Filtering my search for only those over sixty-five shortened the list by only a few. It figures. When was the last time somebody named a boy Harvey? Answer: about sixty years ago.

Next I went to the Oregon Secretary of State's website and found the Corporation Division page. There I searched for Walters Marine Service and found a registration in that name dated in 1986, renewed annually until 2006. At the end of that year, the registration had expired.

The business was registered to Harvey C. Walters, DOB June 29, 1941. The address given was in the 1600 block on Van Buren Street in Oregon City. With this information, I did a search of property ownership records. Walters had lost the Van Buren house to foreclosure in February 2007.

I was unable to find him in any of the sex offender databases or, for that matter, in any other criminal database. So either he was clean, or he was clever enough to avoid getting caught. And if he was that clever, he might have anticipated that some kind of evidence at the Highway 99 site might lead to him. If so, his only recourse would be to establish a new identity.

Still, I tried doing various Google searches involving Harvey Walters and boat repair, but I came up empty. I tried pairing the name with *fiberglass, welding, boat parts,* and anything else that might be related to the things he did while occupying the old mill building. No luck. When I removed the first name, I did come up with a few hits. But one by one, I eliminated them as being related to my suspect.

But with or without a new identity, what would a bankrupt sixty-six-year-old man do for a living? Under the circumstances, it seemed unlikely that he'd have been able to squirrel away enough money for a new start, and precious few jobs were available to people his age.

One possibility occurred to me. Maybe he went to live in a homeless camp. It was a fleeting thought. Far more likely, he'd be drawing Social Security and living with a relative. And yet . . .

"First thing you need to do is fill out the paperwork."

I handed Bud a W-4 and I-9. He put down his beer and accepted them with a look of disappointment.

"I thought maybe I could work, like, you know, under the table."

"Can't take that risk, Bud. The IRS still has me under their microscope."

"Well . . . Okay, I guess it doesn't matter—unless it changes my Social Security eligibility."

"I'm putting you down as part time, temporary. We'll make sure to keep your income below the threshold."

"I guess that'll be all right. So tell me what you want me to do."

I explained, "I need you to infiltrate a homeless camp and see what you can find out about the other people there—present and past."

"People who live on the streets generally don't talk much."

"Not to outsiders. That's why I need you to get on the inside."

"When?"

I looked at Bud. In the old days, he'd often go for a week or more without shaving. But since Martha came to work for me, he rarely went for longer than a weekend. The two days' growth that he was currently sporting was a good start.

"Maybe a couple of days from now. It'll take that long to get ready."

"How long's this gonna take?"

"I don't know. We'll have to play that by ear. I hope it'll just be a couple of days."

Bud drained his beer and looked at me expectantly.

"Somebody'll have to take care of Pedro," he called to me as I went to the refrigerator.

Pedro is Bud's Chihuahua.

He looked pleased when I said, "I'm sure Martha will be able to do that."

"I'll need some stuff."

"Yeah, starting with some convincingly worn and dirty clothes. I saw you working under Red Harper's truck yesterday."

"I put a new rear seal in his transmission. It was leaking all over the place."

"The clothes you had on . . ."

"They're pretty bad. That was a dirty mess."

"That sounds perfect. I've been working on finding a tent and sleeping bag. A backpack too."

"I have a sleeping bag."

"Good. Kaylin says she can get an old tent from one of her sons."

Bud leaned back in his chair and gave that some deep thought. "Okay, what is it that you want to know?" he finally asked.

"I'm looking for a man named Harvey Walters. He used to own a boat repair business up by the homeless camp. I have reason to believe that he might have moved into the camp after his business went broke. That was about seven years ago."

"In the homeless community, seven years is a *long* time," Bud said.

"I know, but I talked with one old guy who's been there at least that long. If you can get him talking, maybe he'll know about Walters."

I handed Bud a printout of a 2011 news report. A man named John Greenhorn, from Klamath Falls, had been struck and killed by a freight train while walking the tracks near the homeless camp. The article dwelt on the tragedy of the homeless vet and gave some good background information, including the fact that he had been staying at the camp.

"This might help you get into the camp," I explained. "You can tell a story about how you met 'Old Johnny' in a camp outside Roseburg a few years back—before 2011, obviously. Think up a couple of funny stories but keep it all within the information in the news story. I'll give you some booze that you can pass around, and maybe we can get Red to let you have some of that 'medical' marijuana he grows."

The sudden brightness in Bud's eyes made me wonder how much of the booze and pot would actually make it to the homeless camp residents.

———

"This will be good practice for the undercover work we talked about the other day."

"Sounds good. I'd better get started. I'll need to work up a good sweat. I can't go in there smelling like Irish Spring," Bud said.

I hadn't detected any trace of Irish Spring in Bud's aroma, but there was no point in mentioning that.

"There's one other thing," I said. "A young woman's body was found by the homeless camp a few weeks ago. They think she died about five to seven years ago. The investigators think that she might have been living in the camp, but nobody there will talk to the cops about it."

"You think this Walters guy had something to do with that?"

Bud sometimes surprised me with his quick intelligence.

April
Monday 28

Chapter 20

Martha exclaimed, "Into a homeless camp—but that could be dangerous!"

"I think Bud can take care of himself."

"But if someone out there killed that girl—"

"He knows how to talk with the people up there. Some of them are vets. He can swap war stories with them."

"But what if they don't buy his act? He could be in serious trouble."

I didn't think Bud would have to do too much acting. He had more experience at being homeless than he would ever admit to Martha.

"I'm giving him a prepaid cell phone. He's going to sew it into the lining of his sleeping bag. If he needs help, he can call us. Or the cops. He'll be fine."

As though our talking about him had somehow conjured him up, Bud materialized on the front porch with DC.

"Your cat spent the night in my place, sharing Pedro's bed—and his food."

"Great," I said. "Then I won't have to feed him."

I noted that Bud was dressed in the greasy clothes he'd worn under Red's pickup.

"I was wondering if I might use your chainsaw. There're some logs down on the beach that I'd like to cut up for firewood. That way, I can work up a pretty good sweat—and get these clothes appropriately fragrant."

"You're welcome to use the chainsaw, but I was thinking you might want to postpone the camping trip."

"What for? I thought you needed the information."

"I do, but have you heard the weather forecast?"

Bud shrugged. "I heard it's going to rain."

"It's going to rain *a lot*," I clarified.

"Oh, that won't bother me. Not as long as I can get my tent set up before it starts. It isn't supposed to blow in until tomorrow afternoon, so it'll be okay."

"Well, feel free to change your mind. They say it's going to be a wet one."

Bud followed me out to my garage to get the saw.

He explained, "Crappy weather might actually help. When folks are forced to huddle together under a shelter, they get bored just looking at each other—so they naturally start talking."

I couldn't disagree with his logic, so while Bud went to work on the firewood, I went back to work on Harvey Walters. I'd already figured out that Walters hadn't done much with computers. There were no tracks of him or his business on the Internet. When I ran out of ideas for new Google searches, I went to the kitchen and found a respectable pinot noir from Australia.

I offered it to Kaylin Beatty and asked if she had time to do some magic on her real estate websites. She invited me in and led me to the back room that served as her office.

"Okay, here it is," Kaylin said. "Harvey Walters's house on Van Buren was foreclosed on February 13, 2007. He owed $127,550. The bank sold it for $135,000. That means it was probably in pretty bad shape. Doesn't look like Walters made any effort to sell out before the foreclosure—at least not with a Realtor."

"Does he own any other property?"

Kaylin did a quick search of the tax rolls. "Nothing in Oregon," she finally said.

"Can you tell me if any of his neighbors are still around?"

"Maybe. If they're renting, I can't do much. But I can tell you if the people who owned the properties in 2007 still do. Would that help?"

"Sure. If it gives me a few people to talk with, that'll be a start."

When she was finished, I had names and addresses for three people on Walters's block who had been there before 2007. Back at the office, Martha volunteered to go up to Van Buren Street and talk with the people.

"I'll tell them I'm an investigator working for Dakota Mutual—which is true—and I'm trying to locate Harvey Walters and that he might be owed some money on an insurance settlement. And that's true too. He *might* be owed some money."

"That's good," I agreed. "People always like to help others come into money. I guess they might be hoping that they'll get a piece of the action. Anyway, things you're looking for are names of family members, personal history, vehicles, and anything else that might lead us to him."

"I'm on it, boss."

As Martha headed out the front door, there as a knock at my backdoor. Seeing Captain Alan through the glass, I waved him inside.

"Hey, Corrigan, I have a favor to ask."

Without waiting for an answer, he continued, "If you don't mind, I'd like to tie up *Misty Rose* at your dock for a few days while I finish working on her."

"That's no problem. How much more do you have left to do?"

"It's mainly just electrical shit. So far, everything works once it's dried out, but I'm still blowing heaters on the radios and navigation. I want to make sure they're good and dry before I hook 'em up. So that's the other thing. I'll need to hook up to your electricity."

"That's fine. When do you want to bring her down?"

"If you can give me a ride up to Pete's Place, I'll do it now."

During the short drive up to Pete's, Alan told me the rest of the story.

"Pete's cheap-ass landlord says I'm using too much electricity and is threatening to throw him out if I don't get *Misty Rose* out of there."

"Who *is* the landlord?" I asked.

"I don't know his name. He's a reclusive bastard. He's been bitching at Pete about having too many visitors. Too much traffic, he says. And too much noise."

"Maybe I should reconsider having you at my place if you're going to cause all that trouble."

"But *you're* the only one besides me who's been there. The guy's just a crazy damned hermit."

I dropped off Alan and returned home. I was waiting on my dock when he pulled in. Bud killed the chainsaw when he saw that I was carrying my little ice chest. Sometimes I think about loading it up with cream sodas just to see what he'd do. But that would be cruel.

Once we had *Misty Rose* tied up and connected to shore power, we pulled up chairs and took a break. I noted that Bud had achieved remarkable success with his aroma enhancement and moved my chair upwind.

I recalled that Captain Alan had mentioned that he'd had some work done at Walters Boat Repair, so I asked him what he knew about Harvey Walters.

"Well, I knew him—same as I know everyone else who works on boats. He was a pretty good mechanic but a lousy welder."

"What kind of a guy was he?"

"He never tried to cheat me or run up a bill on me even when I was stranded there with my transmission all jammed up. He could have made me pay for a complete overhaul, but instead, he took parts out of an old gearbox he had in the shop and just charged me for labor."

"Maybe that's why he went broke," I suggested.

Alan shrugged. "He was kind of a strange duck."

"How's that?"

"Oh, I don't know. He was one of those guys who never seems to know how to keep up his side of a conversation—like he never learned how to bullshit with the guys."

In my mind, an image took shape of an insecure man who'd never learned how to communicate with other people. This was precisely the kind of personality that might feel the need to keep a sex slave or two.

"Any idea where he went after he shut down the boat repair?"

"I heard he had a brother somewhere—out at the coast, I think."

"And you think he went there?"

"Nope. I don't have any idea where he went. I just brought that up as a possibility."

Late that afternoon, Bud showed up with his backpack and fishing rod, ready to become a homeless person. He certainly looked and smelled the part.

"You understand that there's a good chance that somebody will go through your stuff," I reminded him.

"Yeah, I know. All they'll find is some of Red's pot and my dirty socks."

"Okay. And you have the phone. All you need to do is press the Send button. If your number shows up on my phone, I'll be there in ten minutes."

"Got it. But you're worrying too much. This is just a little campout, like when I was a Boy Scout."

"Some of the people out there might be a bit rougher than your scouting friends."

"Guess you never saw my scout troop."

I drove Bud up the highway to a turnout on the hillside above the homeless camp. As he shouldered his backpack, I handed him a large black plastic bag containing an assortment of empty cans and bottles.

"This might help establish your credentials."

"It might buy me dinner."

We shook hands, and he shuffled down the trail from the turnout.

April
Tuesday 29

Chapter 21

In the morning, Martha told me, "Okay, I canvassed the whole neighborhood where Harvey Walters used to live, and I talked with about a dozen people who remembered him. Everyone said that he kept to himself and didn't cause any trouble."

"That's what neighbors *always* say when someone is found to be a heinous criminal," I pointed out.

"They had some negative things to say as well. He didn't do much yard work and didn't take care of his house, but then, that's what I'd expect from someone about to be foreclosed on."

"Did you find out *anything* worthwhile?"

"Bits and pieces. Maybe we can put them together to make something. Three different people said that Walters had a younger brother who sometimes visited and stayed for weeks at a time. They said he drove an old Chevy pickup that had extensive body rust and Oregon plates."

"Captain Alan said he thought Walters had a brother who lived out at the coast somewhere. That could explain the rusted-out pickup."

"There's more. One of the neighbors said that the brother was a commercial crabber. He said that he saw crab rings in the back of the pickup. And he said he thought that the brother had brought his boat up from the coast for Harvey to repair."

"Must have been a pretty major repair."

"Why do you say that?"

"Distance. It's a long way to tow a boat. You wouldn't do it for something as simple as a tune-up."

"That might explain why he stayed around for a long time."

"Did the witness actually see the boat?"

"Yeah. But at first he couldn't remember much about it. When I pressed him, he was able to recall that it was an open boat with low sides and a small crane or hoist in the front."

"The crane would be for lifting crab pots. I wonder how many places there are where a guy could use a small boat for commercial crabbing."

"Who said it was a small boat?"

"It had to be. Otherwise he wouldn't have been able to tow it with a pickup," I explained.

"Okay, that makes sense.

"And it doesn't sound like the kind of boat he could use on the open water—more like something a crabber would use in the estuaries. We ought to be able to get a list of places where people use boats like that. And then we can find a list of commercial crabbers who work those places."

"It was nearly ten years ago," Martha reminded me.

"You said the brother was younger than Harvey. He might still be in business."

"Okay, I guess we're going to have to learn about crabbing."

"There can't be that many places that support commercial harvest. We might see if Oregon Fish and Wildlife can give us a list."

Martha nodded. "There was something else. The lady who lived next door to Walters struck me as a bit of a busybody. She said that when the two brothers got together, they'd often stay out all night and come home drunk."

"Praise the lord for busybodies. They give people like us a lot of useful information."

"You thinking what I'm thinking?" she asked.

"That they had more than just boat repair going on up there? We can't ignore the possibility."

"That's pretty twisted."

"This whole thing is pretty twisted."

I heard DC on the front porch rattling the screen door, so I got up and let him in. His fur was dripping, and he left muddy tracks across the floor to the corner next to the heat duct, where he plopped down and glowered at me—his way of letting me know that he wasn't happy that I had permitted the weather conditions that resulted in his soaking.

The rain had started shortly after dawn, ushered in by a blustery warm south wind. There is, of course, nothing unusual about rain in the Willamette Valley. For six months of the year, rain showers soak the region and hydrate the greenery for which Western Oregon is famous.

But this was not an ordinary Willamette Valley rain shower. It was a sustained cloudburst. For two hours, the rain had been falling in waves of raindrops so big as to defy the laws of physics, rattling on the roof and overflowing the gutters. The phenomenon is known to locals as the Pineapple Express, a tropical storm that somehow gets misdirected into the Pacific Northwest.

Reading my mind, Martha said, "They say it's going to rain like this for the rest of the week."

"I don't think that's possible." I scoffed. "It may rain for the rest of the week but not like this. This kind of thing won't last more than a few hours. Then it'll slack off."

By that evening, my words had been proven definitively wrong. The rain did not slack off. It poured unrelentingly all morning and all afternoon. The five o'clock news was filled with reports of storm drains overwhelmed by the rain, flooded streets, and rising water in all the rivers and streams up and down the Willamette Valley.

Martha shook the water from her umbrella before coming into the office the next morning. The rain had continued without a break all throughout the night, and the river out front was noticeably higher than it had been the evening before when my dock and Captain Alan's tugboat had been concealed from view beyond and below the railroad grade.

But looking across the railroad tracks now, we could see the lights in the pilothouse on *Misty Rose*, which was floating perhaps six feet higher than the day before. The surface of the river was littered with driftwood, and the water was tinted brown with silt.

"Hey, is Captain Alan living onboard his tugboat now?" Martha asked.

"I guess so. I saw him carrying some groceries down there last night," I said.

"Wow. It seems like a really poor time to move aboard a boat."

"Well, you know Alan. He doesn't demand much in the way of creature comforts beyond what comes in bottles."

"But still, that's got to be a miserable way to live."

"For you and me, maybe, but it suits Alan."

"Actually, I didn't know the boat even had a galley and head," Martha observed.

"Well . . . the 'galley' consists of a two-burner propane stove on a shelf in the pilothouse. As for sanitation, I'm pretty sure he uses the HIOTR system."

"The *what* system?"

"HIOTR. Hang it over the rail," I explained.

"Oh my god. I didn't need to hear that!"

"Yeah, it violates half a dozen different laws, but he somehow gets away with it."

Changing the subject, Martha said, "I wonder how Bud is doing. I hope he's found a way to stay out of the rain."

"We talked about the weather before he went in. He knew the rain was coming and didn't see it as a problem."

"I hope he's right."

"I know what you mean. But he has the phone. He can call us and bail out whenever he wants to. And remember why he's there. We need to know if Harvey Walters is living there—or was when Sunny was killed."

Martha sighed. "I know. I just wish there was a better way."

I nodded. I'd been working on that, using the information she'd gotten from the neighbors. After a few Web searches that failed to produce anything, I landed on the Oregon Department of Fish and Wildlife website. There I found a list of popular places for crabbing.

I found thirteen estuaries listed as prime habitat for Dungeness crabs. If Harvey's brother was a commercial crabber, it probably would have been at one of those places. I spent the next couple of hours attempting to find commercial crabbing operations on the many websites that had business directories listed by location.

It was a slow, tedious process because there was no guarantee that Walters would have used his own name for the business. Taking each town located near one of the thirteen estuaries, I first made a list of all the commercial crabbers. Then I had to search for business licenses for each company and look for anyone named Walters among the principals.

With every fruitless search, the whole process seemed less viable in its concept. Realistically, what were the chances of finding Harvey Walters this way? And yet I didn't have any other way to go, so I kept at it, all day and into the night.

The rain just kept coming.

Chapter 22

I awoke to the sound of a police siren screaming by on Highway 99. It was 12:25 a.m., and I had been asleep for little more than an hour. Before I could doze off again, two more cop cars raced by, briefly illuminating the neighborhood with flashing red and blue lights. I could hear other sirens in the distance, so I knew something big had happened.

Most often, this kind of activity indicated that there had been a car wreck on the highway. The number of responding vehicles told me that this must have been a big one. It was easy to guess that the rain had played a part in it since it was still pouring down. Getting back to sleep at this point was no longer an option, so I went to the kitchen and poured a glass of orange juice.

While getting dressed, I switched on the radio to see if there was anything on the news. There were many reports of local flooding, power outages, and road closures due to high water. The weather forecast promised that the "worst of it" was over and that drier weather was coming. I was just finishing my orange juice when I heard something about the closure of Highway 99 between Canby and Oregon City.

Surprisingly, it wasn't due to a car wreck. It was due to a mudslide. The report was that a hillside had let go and blocked the entire highway, both north and south. That would make life interesting for the many commuters who travel Highway 99 every day.

I heard the muffled sound of my phone ringing and quickly determined that it was still in the pocket of the jacket I'd worn down to my dock the previous evening to check on the rising river. The ringing stopped before I could pull my jacket out of the closet, unzip the inside pocket, and pull the phone out. The number on the missed-call list was Bud's. I touched the callback button.

"Jesus, I'm glad to hear you," Bud gasped. He sounded like he'd just run a hundred-yard sprint. Before I could say anything, he continued, "I need help up here. There was a train wreck—a bad one! I can't move. I think a boxcar landed on my tent."

"All right, listen. I'll get up there as quick as I can. You call 911, okay?"

I started making a mental list of things I'd need. I pulled out a set of heavy-duty rain gear and waterproof work boots. In the garage, I rounded up a couple of hydraulic jacks, flashlights, a first aid kit, and a backpack to carry it all in. All of this stuff went into the back of my Yukon, and then I started out to the highway.

Not knowing where the highway was blocked, I could only hope that the mudslide was somewhere south of the homeless camp. The thought crossed my mind that the mudslide might be what *caused* the train wreck. As I approached the intersection of South End Road and Highway 99, I saw a row of flares across the road and several Oregon State Police cars blocking the southbound lanes.

"You can't go past here," the officer informed me when I rolled down the window.

"I just need to go a quarter mile—" I started.

He interrupted, "Can't do it. I can't let anyone go past here."

"If I park here, can I walk up there?"

"No way. You'll just have to turn back."

"But a friend of mine is pinned under a boxcar," I said urgently.

"How do you know that?" the officer asked with a puzzled expression.

"He phoned me. Said when the train derailed, it came right down on top of him."

"Listen. I just heard on the radio that there's a train wreck up there someplace. But our people are working on it. Best thing you can do is just stay out of the way and let the professionals handle it."

It was futile trying to talk my way past the roadblock. All I could do was go back home and hope that a rescue team would find Bud and pull him out from under the train wreck. Once back in my garage, I pulled out my phone and called Bud.

"How're ya doing?" I asked.

"Not so good. It's kinda hard to breathe with this boxcar sitting on my back."

"They told me that there are rescue teams looking for you."

"I haven't heard anyone. It's a real mess here. I can feel water rising up beneath me, and I'm starting to worry about drowning."

"Listen, Bud. You need to conserve your phone's battery. We could socialize all night, but all we'd do is use up the battery. I have an idea about getting up there, so I have to go now. But call me if anything changes."

"Yeah, okay. I'm not going anywhere."

I hurried down to *Misty Rose* and banged on the pilothouse window while shouting to wake up Captain Alan.

"Do you think you'd be able to get us up to where the homeless people camp—up there past Giles Svensen's place?"

Alan rubbed his face and stared out at the river.

"She's running pretty hard," he observed.

"But can you do it?"

"Probably. I mean, it'll all come down to how things are at the narrows. What's this all about, anyway?"

"Old Bud got caught in a train wreck up there. The highway is blocked, so this is the only way we can get there."

"We can give it a try. I don't know if I have enough fuel though."

"Warm up the engine. I'll go up and bring down all the gas I can find."

Over the next fifteen minutes, I made half a dozen trips between my garage and *Misty Rose*, carrying about ten gallons of gas, plus a pair of shovels, a chainsaw, and the backpack from the Yukon. Alan joined me on the last trip, helping me lug my Honda generator along with extension cords and work lights.

"I wish we had more fuel," Alan said. "I can't guarantee that there's enough onboard to get us there against this current."

"Let's go up to Big Dan's place. He probably has some gas," I suggested.

Big Dan is a commercial diver who lives a block upriver from my place. He is a former Navy SEAL and is probably the toughest man I've ever met. He keeps a work barge at his place, and I knew there was a large fuel tank onboard. What I didn't know was whether it contained gasoline or diesel—or anything at all, for that matter.

I pounded on the door, hoping that Big Dan didn't wake up grouchy. He was known to have a substantial collection of firearms, which I knew he was willing to use. He answered the door so quickly, I had to guess he'd heard me coming.

"You selling tickets to the policeman's ball or what?" he asked.

"Want to join a rescue mission? There's a train wreck upriver, and Bud Tiernan is tangled up in it. The highway's closed, so Captain Alan is going to try to get there with his tugboat."

Dan whistled. "The river's running pretty fast."

"He thinks he can make it. Thing is he's hoping you have some gas. He's not sure he has enough to get there."

"Well, let's get to it then. I'll get my stuff and meet you down at the barge."

"We're already there," I said.

"I'm right behind you."

Big Dan's pump could move ten gallons a minute, so five minutes later, we had added fifty gallons of gas to *Misty Rose*. It was impossible not to worry about the condition of the old tugboat despite Alan's assurances that everything was working "like new." Everything, that is, except the electronics.

As we started upstream, Alan tried to keep us out of the fastest part of the current. Usually the slower current was along one shore or the other. The trick was that finding the slowest current sometimes involved crossing from one side of the river to the other, and that meant passing through the fastest current along the way. On more than one occasion, I felt the current grab the thirty-three-foot tugboat and push it backward downstream. It was impossible to forget that Willamette Falls was only a short distance in that direction.

With the searchlight atop the pilothouse pointing the way, we labored against the current. The first mile took fifteen minutes. That was good news, actually. At that rate, we'd get to the homeless camp in less than forty-five minutes.

Another fifteen minutes brought us within sight of the Rock Islands, where the river is divided by three islands into four roughly parallel channels. The main channel is very deep in its narrowest part, so it is actually capable of handling a lot of water. But immediately downstream from the islands, there is a basalt ridge that extends clear across the river, creating a kind of underwater dam.

At summer flows, there is a slot about eight feet deep that allows safe passage over the submerged ridge. But at extreme water levels, the ridge holds back so much of the flow that a huge water slide forms with a visible slope and freakishly fast current. What none of us knew was whether *Misty Rose* would be able to climb over that obstacle.

"Well, here goes nothing," Alan said as he switched on the GPS navigator.

After a few seconds, the LED screen lit up, showing a detailed representation of what lay under the surface of the water. Shining the spotlight at the center of the main channel, we could see a set of standing waves about three feet tall, where the fast water in the shallow chute met the slower water in the pool below.

"I'm going to try to steer just to the left of that chute!" Alan shouted. "It's touchy because there's some really shallow water over there."

"How shallow is it?" I asked, not really wanting to hear the answer.

"That's hard to say. I'm guessing it's deep enough."

The closer we got to the narrows, the more the current fought our advance. Alan pushed the throttle lever as far as it would go. I looked at the gauges. Oil pressure was good. Alternator voltage was good. Engine temperature was at 225 and rising. That was what worried me. That and the 6,500 rpm, which was a thousand over the red line.

But we were still making headway. If the engine or gearbox didn't fly to pieces or burn up, we just might make it. I don't know how long I held my breath, watching the flames from the exhaust stacks illuminate the after deck. Several times, our forward motion stopped momentarily, as though an invisible surge of water had come at us. Then we'd lunge a few feet forward, the steel deck quivering under our feet.

With excruciating slowness, we lumbered forward while we strained to hear any sound that might warn us of impending engine failure or a collision with bedrock. Glancing down into the engine room, I saw a sudden burst of flames as Alan's mattress was ignited by the red-hot exhaust manifold. I ducked below and threw the mattress aside, where Big Dan blasted it with a fire extinguisher.

The abrupt change in the engine pitch told me that either we'd overheated and the pistons were seizing up, or we'd made our way above the fast water. Dan and I bolted topside to see which but knew the answer before we got there. The engine was still running. We'd made it.

During the next few minutes, I was able to catch my breath despite the way the twisting current pushed the boat back and forth in unpredictable directions. While Alan wrestled with steering the boat, Dan and I dragged the still-smoldering mattress from the engine room and threw it over the side, where it quickly vanished in our wake.

Just above the Rock Islands, there is another area of shallow bedrock, which creates an obstacle similar to—if less extreme than—the one we'd just navigated. To our right, the high water had covered the basalt ridges that stand a couple of feet high at normal water levels, their locations revealed by erratic waves and swirling current. As below, the main chute was too fast for *Misty Rose*, forcing us to the left, where a broad eddy swirled above the islands.

I knew from years of boating through this area that several massive boulders lay underwater, and they were too far from shore to get an accurate fix on their position. We were completely reliant on the GPS chartplotter to show us where they were. I silently prayed that the calibration of the instrument had not been affected by its recent submersion.

The roar of the engine deepened as Alan again advanced the throttle lever, and we crept slowly forward. We crossed an eddy line, and the boat was twisted violently to starboard. Alan spun the wheel to the left to keep from broaching. Now in the main current, we hovered, making no headway at all and with no more power to give.

"I'm going to ease her to the right!" Alan shouted.

"But the rocks," I cautioned.

"I think we're clear, but we gotta take the chance in any case. We have nowhere else to go."

As often happens in high water, the main current was higher than the surrounding slower water, so we actually went downhill as Alan eased us to the right. I gritted my teeth in anticipation of the collision with bedrock. In an instant, *Misty Rose* sprang free of the current and accelerated forward. As Alan pulled back the throttle lever, we all breathed silent thanks to our deities of choice.

The final mile was easy. We worked our way past Parrot Creek, where we could see the state police roadblock on Highway 99 and then past Giles Svensen's place.

"Holy shit!" Alan exclaimed when the searchlight revealed an enormous tangle of shattered trees and underbrush floating directly toward us.

He steered sharply to starboard, crossing most of the width of the river to let the debris pile float past, and then eased back toward the east bank, where the homeless camp was located. My first impression was that we were in the wrong place. All familiar landmarks were gone, and what we faced was as foreign as—as what? The moon? No, the moon is rugged, but it's dry.

Here, a massive swath of hillside had moved down and slumped into the river, forming a new peninsula that extended thirty feet beyond the old shoreline. The surface was moving as if alive because of the rapid erosion of the newly formed landmass. The water around us was so thick with mud that it made it a struggle for Alan to even steer *Misty Rose* toward shore.

May

THursday 1

Pre-Dawn

Chapter 23

As soon as we were tied up, Alan shut down the engine.

"I don't see any sign of the train wreck," I said—unnecessarily, since we could all see the same thing.

"How do you want to go at this?" Big Dan asked.

"I'm open to suggestions, but my first thought is to work our way uphill along the edge of the slide until we find the train. It can't be too far up there. Let me give Bud a call so that he'll know we're here."

The voice on the phone sounded labored. "It's getting really cold under here. Hurry it up."

"We're coming up from the river now," I told him. "Call back when you can hear us."

We took off our life jackets and hopped ashore with flashlights. Alan and I each carried a shovel, and Big Dan carried the chainsaw. There was a small gap in the vertical rock face that rose from the riverbank, and we were able to work our way twenty feet up to a level bench. Below us, *Misty Rose* thumped softly against the trunk of a fallen fir tree. Looking uphill, to our right was an impenetrable mass of branches, splintered wood, and earth, the surface of which moved slowly downhill in streams of mud.

"The main part of the homeless camp was about fifty feet from the edge of the river—right about there." I pointed in the direction of the slide to a place about ten yards from where we stood.

"That can't be good," Alan observed.

"No. But we know that Bud survived it, so he must have set up his tent somewhere uphill."

Shining my flashlight up the hill, I saw that our path along the edge of the slide was blocked by the trunk of a fallen cottonwood tree.

"Maybe we'll be able to crawl under it," Alan suggested.

We started fighting our way through the tangled mess of brush and branches.

"Step aside," Dan ordered as he pulled the starter cord on the chainsaw.

Leading the way, Dan cut a swath through the branches until we reached the cottonwood. It was huge, perhaps eight feet thick, and it was pressed flat against the ground. There was no way under it. The instant Dan switched off the chainsaw, I heard my phone ringing.

"You're real close," Bud gasped. "Real close."

I could see no sign of a boxcar or any other evidence of the train wreck. But where we stood next to the fallen cottonwood, our view uphill was completely blocked.

"Okay. We have to get around a big log, so hang tight." As if he could do anything else.

Dan again fired up the chainsaw and started cutting a path along the side of the huge tree trunk, away from the slide. It was slow going because some of the branches were close to a foot thick and had to be cut into short pieces that Alan and I could wrestle aside. Fifteen minutes of hard work brought us to a place where we found a small gap under the log.

Alan knelt down and pointed his flashlight into the hole.

"It'll be a tight squeeze, but I think we can get through," he reported.

Lying on his back, he reached both arms into the tunnel, groping around for something to take hold of.

His voice muffled in the hole, Alan called back, "Give me something to brace my feet against so I can push my way through."

Dan sawed off a section of a thick branch and wedged it against the ground next to Alan's boots. He held it fast while Alan pushed off. A couple of inches at a time, he squirmed into the tunnel. This would be a good time to mention that I have an intense dislike for tight places. I wouldn't necessarily call it claustrophobia, but—or maybe I would. In any case, I did not look forward to my turn in the tunnel.

Once Alan was through, I took my position. As an afterthought, I tied one end of a rope around my waist so that Dan could pull me back out if I got stuck. Then I wriggled into the darkness. It seemed like the tunnel got narrower and tighter as I went in deeper. I could almost feel the ground on both sides pressing in, and I had to pause and draw a deep breath just to prove to myself that I could.

I pushed hard against the foot brace and slid farther in, fighting back a growing sense of panic. When my knees were straight, I suddenly was completely unable to move with both arms straight out above my head and nothing to hold onto. I felt Dan reposition the foot brace, and I pushed myself a few more inches. Alan's hands grabbed mine, and he pulled.

Seconds later, I was sitting next to him gasping for breath. We used the rope to pull through first the chainsaw and shovels and then Big Dan. Caked in mud, we looked around. We followed a narrow gap in the cottonwood branches, moving uphill away from the big log.

My phone rang.

"I don't hear the chainsaw anymore," Bud said.

"We just got past the big log. We ought to be able to see something in a couple of minutes."

After fighting our way clear of the branches, we found ourselves on relatively open terrain about fifty feet away from the edge of the slide. Shining our flashlights around, we still found no sign of a train wreck.

"Damn it! He must be on the other side of the slide," I whispered to Dan.

To Bud I said, "Okay, you still with me?"

"Yeah. I'm here. Make some noise. All I can hear is the rain."

I wished I'd thought to bring a whistle.

Big Dan shouted, "Tiernan! Can you hear me?"

"Yes. Yes," Bud wheezed. "Just barely."

We worked our way across the slope, toward the slide. Dan called out again.

"You're getting closer," Bud said. "Keep coming."

Reaching the edge of the slide, we pointed our flashlights across the expanse of debris, wondering if it would be possible to get across it. Alan tried climbing up onto the slide, but the loose mud just slipped down under his feet, rechanneling a stream of water.

"Jesus! Damn it, are you trying to drown me?" Bud shouted.

This time, I heard his voice, not just from the phone, but also from someplace very nearby. I turned my light toward the sound, in the direction of the fallen cottonwood. There was no boxcar anywhere in sight.

"Whatever you just did, undo it!" Bud demanded.

I pointed to the stream flowing around Alan's boots.

"Dam it up! Divert it back the way it was going before," I shouted.

Alan and Dan went to work with the shovels, throwing mud into the rapidly eroding trench that Alan had accidentally created while I followed the course of the new stream down the slide. It vanished into the loose ground right next to the cottonwood log. As I studied the hole where the water was pouring, I got a glimpse of burgundy-colored fabric. Bud's tent was that color.

"There is no boxcar," I shouted to Alan and Dan. "He's under the log, right here!"

"I'm here. I'm here," Bud repeated.

I dug with my hands in the hole the stream had created, pulling at rocks and sticks.

"Okay, we have it diverted back to where it was," Dan said when he joined me next to the log.

"The water is ice cold," Bud complained. "I'm freezing my ass off!"

"He's in a puddle," I said. "We need to find a way to drain it."

"We'll have to do that from the downhill side," Dan said.

"Back through that tunnel," I groaned.

"Gimme that chainsaw," Alan demanded.

He looked around at the jumbled branches of the fallen tree. Finding something he liked, he quickly cut a three-pronged piece of a branch. This he tied to the end of the rope. Holding the coiled rope in one hand, he lobbed the makeshift grappling hook over the top of the huge log. On the second try, it snagged on something.

Meanwhile, Dan took the chainsaw and cut away more of the branches around the pit where Bud lay, leaving stubs that would serve as footholds. With the help of the rope, Dan climbed to the top of the log. He lowered the chainsaw to the ground on the other side, and then climbed down himself. While I climbed over, Dan went to work with the chainsaw, clearing a space to work in.

"We need some light here," I said. "Alan, want to help me bring up the generator?"

"It'll be a pain in the ass to haul that thing up here," he complained.

While we slipped and skidded our way back down to *Misty Rose* to get the generator, Dan started digging a hole next to the log in the area where we estimated Bud to be. Alan was right. It was a bitch of a job to carry the heavy generator up the hill. We stopped when we had it about halfway there.

"This is far enough. Let's just string out the drop cords from here," I said when I caught my breath.

Ten minutes later, we had two quartz-halogen work lights illuminating the area where Dan had been digging. Alan took up the chainsaw and widened the workspace while I attempted to explain to a 911 dispatcher where we were. When I disconnected in order to answer a call from Bud, I had little confidence that the search teams would find us.

"I can hear you digging," he said.

"Good. We're trying to find a way to drain the water out of where you are."

"How're you planning to get this damned boxcar off my back?" Bud asked.

I looked at Dan and Alan.

"There's no boxcar. It's a log!" I shouted

"Okay then, how big is this log?"

"It's huge. Eight feet through, at least."

"You gotta jack the thing up," Bud pleaded.

"That's not possible. The only way we'll get him out is by digging," Dan said.

Alan nodded in agreement.

Digging became increasingly difficult after we'd dug through the loose material of the slide and reached the solid ground below. I cursed my lack of foresight in not having thought to bring a pick. At some point, the hole became large enough for two of us to dig simultaneously. From that point on we rotated, two furiously digging and one resting.

I don't know how long we dug before Alan shouted, "Here it is!"

He pointed at the burgundy fabric of the tent. After clearing the area along the edge of the flattened tent, Alan pulled out a knife and sliced the fabric. A stream of muddy water poured out.

"It's about damn time someone pulled the plug on this bathtub," Bud complained.

While Dan and I worked at burrowing underneath the tent, Alan went back down to *Misty Rose* in search of any kind of tool that would help with the excavation. When he returned, he was carrying an old-fashioned tire iron, heavy and shaped like a spoon on one end. With that, we could pry rocks loose and lever them out of the way.

"I'm suffocating. I need some air," Bud demanded.

I tried to rip the floor of the tent open, but they don't call it ripstop fabric for nothing. Alan handed me his knife, and I carefully cut the fabric, finding myself looking up at Bud's face. His phone dropped into the mud where I knelt.

It took us another hour to move enough dirt to create a cavity for Bud to slither out of his trap. He rolled onto his back and took a deep breath.

"Sweet Jesus, that feels good! I woke up when I heard the train coming, and then I realized that it was a lot louder than normal. It sounded like it was coming right at me, but before I could even get out of my sleeping bag, the boxcar came down on top of me."

"It was a tree, not a boxcar," I reminded him. I could hardly blame him for being confused.

"Oh yeah. The train must've knocked the tree down. It pressed me right into the ground. It's a damn good thing the ground was soft under my tent, or I'd have been squashed. At first, I thought I had been and was just waiting to die. After a while, I figured out that I was still alive, so I wiggled around until I got an arm free and found that phone."

"Good thing you did. Who knows how long it might have taken for anyone to figure out that you were here," I said.

"Naw. You'd a figured it out."

Despite Bud's emphatic reassurances that he wasn't injured, we took the time to lash together some branches to make a crude litter—more of a sled, actually—that we used to transport him down to the tugboat. We helped him down below deck, where we made him lie on Alan's cot, now lacking its mattress.

"Just be careful not to get too close to the exhaust manifold," Alan advised him.

Then turning to Dan and me, he said, "Now we'll see if we can get out of here."

The faint predawn light revealed that during all the time we'd spent exhuming Bud, the streams of mud flowing down the slide had filled the area around the front of the tugboat. There was a good possibility that we might be locked in place.

Dan untied the mooring lines, hoping *Misty Rose* would float free, but she didn't move.

"I don't dare start the engine because if the water intake is in the mud, we'll plug the cooling system," Alan explained.

"How're we going to get loose?" I asked.

He shrugged. "Let's try putting all our weight on the stern and see what happens."

Dan, Alan, and I moved to the very back of the boat, but we could discern no effect. We tried jumping up and down in unison, hoping to pump some water under the bow.

"Let's get a stick and poke around in that mud," Dan suggested. "We can at least figure out how solid it is."

Lacking a better idea, I went ashore and hunted around until I found a twenty-foot fir tree. I cut it down with the chainsaw and quickly trimmed off the branches, ending up with a stout twelve-foot pole. With this, we probed the mud and found it to be still fairly soft.

"We're gonna have to risk starting the engine," Alan finally concluded. "We might be able to wheel wash the mud out from under her."

Without waiting for a discussion, Alan switched on the ignition and pressed the starter button. The big Hemi let out a roar. I looked over the side, where the coolant water outlet pipe was discharging grotesquely muddy water. I felt a clatter when Alan jammed the gearbox into reverse.

The countertorque from the rotation of the huge prop lifted the portside of the boat as Alan pushed the throttle level forward. The stern was sucked downward until it looked like water was about to wash over the deck. A great swirl of thick muddy water spewed out from under the boat on both sides. But we didn't move.

111

Alan worked the throttle lever back and forth, causing the stern to rise and fall. After a few attempts, he figured out the cadence that amplified the effect. We came loose so abruptly that I lost my footing and went skidding across the deck on my butt. Dan dragged me to my feet, and we both looked over the side at the engine coolant outlet, where we saw a smooth flow of steaming water.

Our trip back downriver was fast and exciting. When we came to the swift chutes, Alan opened the throttle and accelerated downstream in order to maintain the ability to steer. We crashed through the standing waves, with water rolling across the deck, swirling into the pilothouse, around our feet, and pouring down into the engine room.

Barely fifteen minutes after breaking out of the mud, we arrived back at my dock, where we found an ambulance standing by on Water Street, having responded to my 911 call during our downriver run. Despite Bud's protests, the paramedics strapped him into a Stokes basket for the short carry up to the ambulance.

May 1

Morning Thursday

Chapter 24

I went inside and started a pot of coffee while the ambulance attendants strapped Bud in for his trip to the hospital. The coffee was done when the ambulance drove away. I carried a thermal carafe and three cups down to the dock, where Dan and Alan were just finishing securing the boat.

The sky was bright and mostly free of clouds. We shook the rainwater off some folding chairs and sat down to unwind from the night's festivities.

"Do you think there ever was a train wreck?" Alan wondered.

"I don't think so. I've heard people describe landslides and tornados as sounding 'like a freight train,' and if they're right, that's probably what Bud heard."

"That was *some* landslide," Dan commented.

"Bud said that there were four other people staying in the camp," I said.

"Not much hope for them."

"I'm going to have to go back up there and try to talk my way past the roadblock. I doubt that anyone there has any idea where the camp was or that there are people down there."

Alan said, "I'm gonna go up to Mike's place and sleep until tomorrow."

We all walked together up to Water Street. Alan handed me his empty cup and headed toward his brother's house. Before Dan left, I offered him two hundred dollars for the fuel he'd given us, but he refused to take my money.

"If you'd used it for water skiing, that'd be one thing. But I can't take your money for this."

Standing under the shower, I tried to remember what day it was: Friday or Saturday? No, that wasn't right. It was Thursday. Barely twelve hours had passed since I'd suspended my computer search for commercial crab fishermen and Harvey Walters's brother, but it seemed like days.

"Did you know there was a big landslide that blocked the highway?" Martha asked when she came in.

"Yeah. I heard about that," I said.

I then told her the whole story before driving back up the highway to the slide site. In the morning sunlight, things looked much different than they had in the middle of the night. The officer at the roadblock listened to my story and let me drive to the staging area where all the emergency vehicles were parked.

"Our guys are down there looking for someone pinned under a boxcar," one of the sheriff's deputies told me.

"There's no boxcar," I said. "That was a mistake. The guy was pinned under a cottonwood tree. He thought it was a boxcar."

"That doesn't make any sense. How would anyone mistake a tree for a boxcar?"

"It was dark. He was inside a tent, and he thought it sounded like a train wreck."

"How do you know all of this?"

At that point, I repeated the whole story and explained where the homeless camp had been—right in the path of the slide—and that four people were probably still there. I drew a sketch, using the huge cottonwood as a reference point, showing where the camp had been.

"We've already called for rescue dogs. Doesn't sound like there's much hope though."

"No, I guess not."

After leaving the slide site, I stopped at Giles Svensen's place. We shared our stories about the previous night's adventures, and Giles told me his theory about the slide.

"About five years ago, some genius decided to improve visibility at the curve in the highway. So they cut down a bunch of trees on the slope above the roadway. Basically stripped it bare. It made for a nice, wide shoulder, but it destabilized the slope."

"Isn't that where the kudzu was growing?"

"Yeah. Someone apparently planted it after the trees were taken down. Then the highway department had to take it out before it took over the whole county. They got rid of the kudzu, all right, but didn't do anything about the hillside.

114

"Even at that, everything would've been okay, but last year the guy with the house up above built a big covered arena for his wife's horses. That was okay, but it had about a half-acre of roof, and guess where the runoff went whenever it rained."

Without waiting for a response, he continued, "All he cared about was keeping the ground dry in the arena, so he piped the rain drains over to the top of the slope and daylighted it there. And guess where the arena is now. It's scattered all the way down to the river. The hillside has been getting saturated all winter, and last night it simply let go."

I whistled.

Giles said, "I hope he has good insurance. The repair bill ain't gonna be pretty."

"The cost of the repairs is the least of his problems. Four people are missing down below."

"Ouch!"

"Yeah. We'll see how that comes out. But listen, I left a portable generator, a chainsaw, and a bunch of other things down there. I'll probably come back tomorrow with some help and try to carry my stuff up to the trail that leads to your place. That is if you don't mind letting me park down there at the end of the trail."

"Sure. No problem with that."

When I got back to the office, Martha said, "You look like crap. Why don't you go get some sleep?"

"I'm gonna go up to the hospital and check on Bud first," I said.

"He's fine. I just talked to the doctor. He's bruised up, but X-rays show nothing broken. They're going to keep him until tomorrow because of hypothermia."

"I feel like I ought to do something—"

"I told the hospital that the billing will go to our workers' comp insurance. They had a hard time understanding how a resident of a homeless camp would be covered by workers' comp, but I think I convinced them to go along with it."

I flopped into my chair and rubbed my eyes. "I need to get back on the Walters investigation."

The ODFW would have records on everyone who had a commercial license for crabbing on the Oregon coast, but the history files were not open to the general public. Law enforcement could request the information, but with Kim gone, I had nobody to make the request.

So I continued checking the business directory websites for the towns surrounding each of the estuaries where a commercial crabber was likely to operate. Martha and I divided the list in half, and with each business name found, we'd search the ODFW website for current licensing information, looking for someone named Walters.

Six hours and two pots of coffee later, we still had nothing. Eventually I reached a point where not even caffeine could keep me awake.

May 2 Friday

Chapter 25

With my mind clear, I was able to take an objective look at the progress of our investigation. Realistically, the chances were pretty slim that we'd find the brother of Harvey Walters the way we were going. While we couldn't abandon the search, it didn't make sense to concentrate all our efforts in one direction where there was a very limited chance of success.

But first things first. When Martha came in, I said, "I'm going to leave you with the search for Walters. I'm going to go get the things I left behind at the slide."

She nodded. "Last night I had another idea. Do you still have that boat registration list from the Marine Board?"

During our investigation of "the Girl in the Carpet" case, we'd acquired a list of every boat registered in Oregon between 1996 and 2004. We'd spent many hours thumbing through the eleven-inch stack of green bar computer paper in search of one boat. It had taken weeks, but we finally did find the boat.

I pointed to the old-fashioned printer stand next to my desk. On the lower shelf, which was intended to hold a pin-feed paper supply, sat the complete Marine Board printout. For the past year, it had served as a platform to elevate my laser printer to a more convenient height.

"The time frame isn't exactly right, but it might be worth a try," I said.

"The witness who told me about Harvey's brother said that the boat looked well used when he saw it. That would have been in 2005 or 2006. I think there's a good chance that the boat is listed somewhere in that printout."

"Good point. Let's give it a shot."

I dug the heavy stack of paper out from under the printer and dropped it on Martha's desk.

"Bet you never hoped to see *that* back on your desk," I said.

"This time, I'll start at the other end."

The entries on the printout were arranged according to the date of each registration or renewal. We'd started our search with the earliest dates and worked forward, so what Martha was proposing was to start with the most recent registrations and work backward. It made sense.

While Martha set about doing that, I made a call to a day labor center in Clackamas. After admonishing me that I should make arrangements at least a day in advance, the lady admitted that despite the high demand for their services, there actually *might be* some workers available on short notice.

"How many workers do you need?" she asked.

"Two ought to be able to get it done."

"What kind of work will this be?"

"Outdoors. I need help carrying tools and equipment about half a mile over rough terrain."

"How heavy is this equipment?"

"There's a generator that weighs 130 pounds. That's why I need two men to carry it. The other things—a chainsaw and some odds and ends—will be easier to carry."

"We have a four-hour minimum, you know."

"That's fine. Two laborers for four hours. When can they get here—I'm in Oregon City."

"How about eleven?"

I gave her my address and debit card number.

"That gives me just enough time to go up and get Bud," I told Martha.

"Now, you're not going to take Bud with you," she scolded.

"I wasn't planning to put him to work, but it wouldn't surprise me if he wants to go along."

Martha sighed. Her message was clear enough.

As it turned out, Bud didn't have any interest in going along. He was so bruised up that he could barely walk.

"Didn't they give you something for the pain?"

He showed me a bottle of pills. "These are pretty good. But I want to save 'em for when I'm feeling better so I can *enjoy* 'em."

I offered to let Bud hang out on my sofa, but he just wanted to take a shower and go to bed. I helped him out of my Yukon and urged him to call Martha or me if he needed anything.

A few minutes before eleven, an old Ford pickup pulled up in front of my place. I watched the workers climb out and shook my head.

"You the one who needs help?" the taller of the two women asked.

I swallowed. "Did they tell you what I need?"

"They said we gotta carry some shit."

"It's pretty heavy—"

The shorter woman struck a defiant pose while the other asked, "You think we can't do it?"

"I just want you to know what you're getting into," I said quickly.

"We didn't come here for no tea party."

I led them—Lexi and Kasandra—around to the garage, where we got into my Yukon for the drive up to the slide. Once again, I had to talk my way past the roadblock. I couldn't help noticing that my two passengers turned away and avoided making eye contact with the state police officer. I drove down into Svensen's place and parked on the slab where the mill had been.

We walked up the trail, past Sunny's gravesite, and started down the path toward the homeless camp. A hundred feet down the path, we came to the slide. From there we had to beat our way downhill through thick undergrowth. When we got to the cottonwood that had trapped Bud, we stopped to talk about the situation.

"We can either lift the things up and over this log or see if we can find a way around it."

"How far is it to go around?" Lexi asked.

"I don't know. We never got that far."

"Okay. It's over the top then," Kasandra said.

The rope was still in place from two nights before, so I demonstrated how to scale the log using the branch stubs for footholds. Lexi climbed to the top and waited there while I climbed down next to the muddy pit we'd dug. I handed the shovels, chainsaw, and lights to Lexi, and she passed them down to Kasandra on the other side.

Once finished with the lightweight stuff, Kasandra and Lexi came with me down to the generator.

"How'd you get this son of a bitch down here?"

"We brought it by boat and carried it up. But it's too dangerous to bring the boat back now."

I started coiling the drop cords while the girls started uphill with the generator. At the log, I cut two pieces of rope and tied them to the handles. I tossed the lines to the girls up on the log, and they hoisted it over.

When I got on top of the log, I spotted a search team out on the slide with a dog, searching for the missing campers. I took the lead going up the hill with the chainsaw, cutting the worst of the obstacles out of the way until we got to the established path. After lugging the generator back to Svensen's place, the girls welcomed my invitation to have a beer.

"They looking for bodies up there or what?" Kasandra asked, pointing back toward the slide.

"Yeah. There were people camped down near the cottonwood tree."

"I camped there once, a few years back," she said.

"No kidding," I said. "Did you meet a guy named Harvey Walters there?"

"Shit. Who remembers names?"

We hiked back and retrieved the rest my things, which were considerably easier to carry than the generator had been. Giles was there and invited us to go up to his warehouse to hose the mud off our boots. He offered the girls a tour of his museum, but they weren't interested.

Back at my place, I thanked the girls and sent them on their way but not before they got me to promise that I'd ask for them next time I needed help. Once they were gone, I drove back up to the slide.

"How's the search going?" I asked the deputy who seemed to be in charge.

She looked at me. "You're Corrigan, aren't you?"

"That's right. I helped pull a survivor out the night of the slide."

"I heard about that. He must be the luckiest guy on earth."

"No, the luckiest guy on earth was someplace far away from here, cozy in bed, when the slide happened."

I gestured down toward the river. "They find anyone yet?"

"They've found three so far. Haven't started the recovery yet though. We have some extra help coming for that. The guy you pulled out—you think he'll be any help identifying the victims?"

"Maybe. He was only there a couple of days before the slide."

"How'd you know he was trapped?"

"Cell phone."

"So homeless guys have cell phones now?" she asked sarcastically.

"He wasn't homeless. He was just camping out—kind of a social call."

The deputy looked at me, her eyes penetratingly intense. "You're investigating something down there."

I hesitated. "Your people found some remains down there a few weeks ago."

"What's your interest in that?"

"Families of missing girls. They want to know who she was."

"You think you know something that we don't?"

"Not yet."

"Sheriff Jamieson know you're on this?"

"I've been in contact with Michael Wheeler." By that, I meant I'd asked him once about the identity of the girl.

She stared at me long enough to make me uncomfortable.

"The dog found something else down there—skeletal remains. The forensics team is down there right now."

It was my turn to stare.

May 3 Saturday

Chapter 26

I studied the unfinished cabinetry in the forward stateroom, trying to remember exactly what I was doing when I stopped work. It had been weeks since I'd been aboard *Annabel Lee*. I'd always found working on the Project to be a good way to relax and take my mind off—well, things. But it couldn't take my mind off Kim's absence. That was a storm cloud that hung above me and wouldn't blow over.

Without enthusiasm, I looked at a scrap of wood on the table saw, where I'd written notes and dimensions for a piece of cabinetry. I picked up another scrap of wood and puzzled over what was written on it. A number. A phone number? Vera Lyons's phone number! I'd written it there on the day she came to visit Kim.

Why hadn't I remembered that? I pulled out my phone and punched in the number. It rang twice, and I recognized Vera's voice when she answered.

"Vera, this is Corrigan. I'd like to—"

"I'm sorry. You have a wrong number," she interrupted.

Then she disconnected. I stood staring at my phone.

Five minutes later, my phone rang. The number on the screen was the one I'd just called.

"Sorry I hung up on you," Vera said. "I couldn't talk right then."

"Well, thanks for calling back. I wanted to talk—"

"She's here. That's why I couldn't talk."

"Kim is with you?" I repeated stupidly.

"Listen, Corrigan, you think you know Kim, but there are things that she's never told you. Things she may *never* tell you."

"If I could just talk to her—"

"No. That's not a good idea right now. Whatever happened up there sent her back twenty years, to a very bad time."

I didn't know any details about Kim's marriage. She never talked about it. Ever. But I knew it had ended badly. It had always been the unspoken barrier that stood between us.

"But what—"

"Corrigan, you seem like a decent guy. I hope that you and Kim can get back together. I really do. But right now, you just have to leave her alone. There's nothing you can say or do that will change what happened."

Before I could answer, the phone went dead.

"Damn!"

Helplessness is a feeling I am not accustomed to. I had no idea what had happened to Kim. What I *did* know was that the discovery of the skeleton at the homeless camp had reopened the old wound. I needed to figure out the connection—I needed to find Harvey Walters and find out what had happened to Brittany Harlan and Sunny. That was the only way I could find out why Kim was gone. And then I could get her back.

I abandoned any thoughts of working on *Annabel Lee*, locked up, and went back home.

Honestly, I'd been procrastinating on the Brittany Harlan investigation because my next move was the thing I most dreaded: I had to talk with Brittany's family. There is nothing in my line of work that I like less than making a cold call to someone who had lost a loved one to crime. No matter what therapists might say, there is no such thing as closure. The surface might heal over, but the wound would be there forever.

But the discovery of another skeleton at the homeless camp and the possibility that it might be Brittany meant that I had to make the call. Saturday was always the best time to find people at home. I knew that before I even started thinking of working on the ship—or of any other excuse to do something other than make the call. So I made a fresh pot of coffee and sat down in front of my computer.

I retrieved the notes I'd compiled from my searches for missing girls and pulled out the file for Brittany Harlan. During my initial online searches, I had printed a thick stack of news articles, most of which had been posted for anniversaries of the abduction.

I carefully read all of them, marking anything that might help me find Brittany's family. Her parents were Teresa and Roger Harlan, and they'd lived in the Cedar Hills area of Beaverton at the time their daughter was abducted.

One of the news reports, dated December 22, 1990, told of the tragic death of Brittany's mother, Teresa Harlan. She had been driving south on Interstate 5 when her car veered into a concrete bridge pylon—the only one in a fifty-mile stretch of highway that was not protected by a guardrail.

It was ruled an accident but only because there was no way to prove otherwise. To everyone involved, though, it was clear that Teresa had taken her own life rather than face another Christmas morning without Brittany.

That made it all the more difficult to make the call to Roger Harlan. When searching for contact information, I found nobody by that name in Oregon but several in other states. One of the old newspaper articles mentioned that Roger was an employee of Freightliner, and I knew that many Freightliner employees had been transferred to other locations when the Portland assembly line was shut down in 2007.

On the chance that he was one of them, I looked for his name in Charlotte and Cleveland. I called the one in Cleveland and introduced myself as a private investigator in Oregon. I asked if he was the same Roger Harlan who had lived in Beaverton in the 1980s.

"Yes, I used to live in Beaverton," he answered warily.

"I wonder if you'd be willing to talk with me about Brittany."

The long sigh told me as much as his words. "I have no patience for anybody's morbid curiosity, Mr. Corrigan. Do you want to know what happens to a family when this kind of thing happens? Marriages break up. People die—killed by the stress. Some turn to alcohol or drugs. Nobody comes out unscathed."

"Believe me, I understand that. But something was brought to my attention that may turn the whole investigation in a new direction."

"And what is that?"

"A man found Brittany's name carved in a wooden beam from an old building that was recently torn down."

"So?" His impatience was obvious.

"The name was scratched into the wood with a broken piece of glass, and it was dated in 2001. I've analyzed the inscription, and it shows every sign of being authentic."

"Wait. Are you saying that you believe Brittany was alive in 2001?"

"I think it is possible."

"On the basis of something scratched in an old board? Anybody could have done that. In case you hadn't noticed, there are sick people out there who do things like that."

"Of course, there are. But like I said, I've studied the inscription and even attempted to replicate it. By my estimation, it took at least twenty hours to put Brittany's name on that beam. I find it very unlikely that any prankster or sicko would spend that much time on a hoax."

"If what you say is true, then why am I hearing this from a private investigator and not from a law enforcement official?"

"What I'm saying is true. Local police were shown the inscription, but without making any kind of forensic analysis, they declared it to be a prank."

"And you know better than they do—"

"I tested some stains on the beam in the area of the inscription. They are blood. I think the person who scratched the name in the wood cut a finger on the broken glass."

"Apparently the police didn't agree."

"They didn't test it. I did. What's more, I think there's a good chance that a DNA profile can be developed from the blood."

"If that's the case, why aren't the police doing it?"

"I don't know. I think the officer they sent out to look at the inscription was a rookie who simply didn't take the time to see what is there."

"Okay, so what's next?" He sounded tired.

"I want to hire a forensic lab to take samples and submit them for DNA analysis. If they succeed in developing a profile, I'd like to compare it with yours. It's the only way to determine if the inscription is authentic."

"And who's going to pay for all that? Do you have a client, or are you expecting me to write the check?"

"I don't have a client. I'll pay for the analysis myself."

"Why would you do that?"

"A couple of months ago, human remains were found buried a quarter mile from where the beam was found."

I hastily added, "Not Brittany's. That's been established. But they belonged to a young woman about twenty years old, and she was killed about five years ago."

"That doesn't sound anything like Brittany's case," he challenged.

"Not unless you consider the possibility that this victim, like Brittany, was abducted as a child. If the inscription is real, then Brittany was held captive for at least twelve years after she was kidnapped. I think there's a chance that they both were."

"What do you want from me?"

"At this point, nothing. But would you be willing to provide a DNA sample for comparison if we are successful in getting a profile from the blood on the beam?"

"What would happen then?"

"If DNA proved that the blood is Brittany's, the authorities would have a whole new case—one that has a good chance of being solved."

"You sound pretty confident."

"I may sound more confident than I am. I would describe my position as cautiously optimistic. I have no intention of stirring up any false hopes.

There are a lot of if's that all need to be pinned down before I can be confident in the case. But I will tell you this—if that is Brittany's blood, I have a pretty solid suspect for her abduction."

"You never did tell me why you are investigating this," he reminded me.

"I have no choice. How could I walk away from it, knowing what I know?"

"Okay, here's what I'll do. If you get the DNA profile, I'll give you a sample to compare it with."

"As to what happens after that, I make no promises."

"Fair enough."

May

Sunday 4

Chapter 27

My effort to identify Sunny among the names on my list of unsolved child abductions in the region had to start with arithmetic. If she died five years ago at age twenty, she would have been born in about 1990—plus or minus two years.

My profile of the hypothetical perpetrator implied that Sunny might have been five to seven years old when kidnapped, so that would have been between 1993 and 1998. On my list, there were five girls of the right age who were abducted in that time frame: Alyssa Marquam, Lacey McCredie, Makayla Imbler, Megan Moro, and Lisa Jewell.

Taking them in order, I looked first at Alyssa Marquam. Tyler and Francine Marquam were on vacation from Alpena, Michigan, when their five-year-old daughter Alyssa was snatched from Beacon Rock State Park in August 1993. News articles at the time mentioned that there were two witnesses but did not reveal their identities. But when I searched for Tyler Marquam in Alpena, Michigan, I got an address.

With that, I called 411 and got a phone number. This call was more difficult than the call to Roger Harlan. For him I had at least the hope that his daughter might still be alive. But with Tyler, I was trying to identify a murder victim. Instead of offering hope, I was potentially destroying it. My call was answered by a woman.

"Is this Francine Marquam?" I asked.

"No, I'm sorry, she is not available at this time. May I take a message?"

"How about Tyler Marquam?"

"I'm sorry. Neither is available."

"My name is Corrigan. I'm an investigator calling from Oregon regarding their daughter, Alyssa."

I thought I heard a gasp on the other end of the line.

"My god! Has something been found?"

"I really need to talk with the Marquams about that."

"I'm Fran's mother, Susan Mosier. Fran and Tyler are traveling in China right now."

"When will they return?" I asked.

"It's an extended trip. They'll be gone for the rest of the month. Can you tell me why you're calling after all these years?"

I took a deep breath. This was the hard part. "We've found some evidence that Alyssa *might have* been held captive for some time after her abduction."

"You mean she might still be alive?"

The hope in her voice was heartbreaking because I could offer no hope in return.

"Mrs. Mosier, I'm very sorry that I cannot offer you that hope. At this point, I'm just gathering information in an effort to connect Alyssa's case with another, where some hard evidence has recently been found. I really need to talk with Tyler or Francine."

"Oh," she said simply.

"I don't think it's a good idea to disrupt their travel with this. It can wait until they return. But I'd appreciate it if you would leave them a message to contact me when they get back."

She agreed with that and took my phone number, and I moved on to the next name on my list.

I approached the Lacey McCredie case with low expectations. Lacey's mother, Andrea, had been the prime suspect in the disappearance of the five-year-old. According to Andrea, Lacey had been taken from the fenced yard of the family home when she went to use the bathroom. There were no witnesses.

Investigators quickly zeroed in on Andrea. One news report quoted an anonymous spokesman as saying, "Lacey's mother reeks of guilt." But despite many hours of interrogation, Andrea's story never changed. Then, three months later, when Andrea put a .38 revolver in her mouth and pulled the trigger, the case was dropped—not officially closed, just dropped.

That left me with only Lacey's father, who had stood by his wife until her death. The family had been living in Gresham, Oregon, in 1995, so that was the first place I searched for Thomas McCredie. When that produced no result, I expanded the search to all of Oregon, and again I came up dry.

But when I added California and Washington to the search, I came up with several hits. Only one came with a phone number, so that was the one I tried first.

"McCredie here," came the answer to my call.

"My name is Corrigan, private investigator. Is this Thomas McCredie?"

"It is. What can I do for you, Mr. Corrigan?"

"Just Corrigan, please. Are you the father of Lacey McCredie?"

"Will you people ever leave this alone? I've said all that—"

I interrupted. "I'm investigating a case where abducted girls may have been held captive, some of them for over ten years."

I heard an audible gasp.

"Are you saying that Lacey is alive?"

"I wish I could. But no, that's not what I'm saying. I have evidence that another girl was still alive at least twelve years after her kidnapping, and I think her abductor may have taken other girls."

"Lacey?"

"I have no evidence of that. What I have are the remains of a girl or young woman who died about five years ago. She was found a couple of months ago very close to where I believe the other girl was held captive. Her age at the time of death was estimated to be around twenty. That would mean she was born about the same time as Lacey."

"You know that they always blamed my wife," he said. "They never had any evidence, but they said that she acted guilty. But the thing is she *did* feel guilty—for leaving Lacey alone."

"Lacey is on a list of ten missing girls whose abductions seem to fit the profile of the one known case. If the recently discovered remains can be matched to one of the missing girls, then we'll have a solid connection with the other case."

"I can see where this is going."

"Would you be willing to provide a fluid sample for DNA profiling to see if—"

"Yes. Of course."

"Okay, I'll have a forensics lab send you a kit for collecting the sample. It's pretty easy."

"How long will it take to get the results?"

"That's hard to say. It won't take long to process yours, but it can take months to get a good profile from human remains."

What I didn't mention was that before that second part of the process could take place, I'd have to convince Michael Wheeler that there was a good reason to spend the taxpayers' money.

I knew from the outset that it would be difficult to track down witnesses involved with the 1996 abduction of Makayla Imbler because the initial news reports indicated that the girl's mother, Olivia Imbler, had never been married. The father's name was nowhere to be found.

My initial searches for Olivia Imbler came up dry. No matter which search engine I used, I found nobody by that name. On the genealogy websites, I found many entries for the surname Imbler but none—at least in this generation—for an Olivia. This led me to suspect that Olivia might be a middle name. Knowing that people are often named after parents or grandparents, I searched among the descendants of the two Olivia Imblers I'd found. No luck.

In 1996 news reports I was able to find the names of two witnesses to Makayla's abduction. I tracked down one of them, a man named Jerry who had seen the kidnapper come out of the Walmart store in Woodburn, Oregon, with the girl.

After introducing myself, I said, "A person with your name is listed among the witnesses to the abduction of Makayla Imbler in 1996."

"Yeah, that's right."

"I know you've told the story before, but can you tell me what you saw?"

"The whole thing took maybe five seconds. I was walking across the parking lot at Walmart when I saw this guy coming out of the store with a little girl. He was holding her hand, but she was acting like she didn't want to go with him. He scooped her up and carried her to an old motor home. He pushed her in the driver's door, climbed in after her, and drove away. Then a lady came running out from the store, shouting for someone to stop the man."

"Can you tell me anything about him?"

"Just what I told the cops. He was a white man, maybe five ten, 170. Brown hair, kind of long. Like I said, he was gone in a few seconds."

"What about his motor home?"

"It was about a twenty-two-footer, and I think it was a Dodge or maybe a Ford. It was white and blue with Oregon plates."

"Anything else you can tell me?"

"Not really. There was a spare tire mounted on the back. It had a white cover with a picture of an eagle on it."

"Do you know anything about the girl's mother?"

Jerry paused. "I was the nearest person when she came out of the store. After the motor home sped away, she grabbed my arm and tried to get me to follow it. But my car was too far away. She was hysterical. Neither of us had a cell phone, but someone else did and called the cops. The lady wouldn't let go of me, begging me to do something."

"I haven't been able to track her down. Do you know anything that might help?"

"Well, I know where she lived. Not the address, but I know the place. See, the Woodburn cops took us to the police station to give our statements. We were there for a couple of hours. Then they drove us back to Walmart 'cause our cars were there. But after the cops left, she kind of fell apart, so I gave her a ride home."

"Would you be able to retrace your way to her place?"

"I think so."

"It would be a big help if you could do that if it isn't too much trouble. And then call me back?" I asked.

"Sure, why not. I can do that."

I spent the next hour attempting to track down the other witness, a woman who had seen the kidnapper lead Makayla away while her mother was trying on a pair of shoes. I searched her name in every way I could think of but without success.

When Jerry called back, he gave me an address in the 900 block on Marion Street in Woodburn. Google Street View showed it to be a modest one-level single-family home. With the help of Kaylin Beatty and her real estate software, I was able to determine that the current owners bought the house in 2004. The prior owner was not identified on the old listing. Kaylin did not have access to any records older than that.

Further investigation in that direction would require a trip to the Marion County assessor's office in Salem, so I put that file aside.

I shifted my attention to the abduction of Megan Moro, just three months after Makayla was taken. Megan was kidnapped from a Burger King restaurant in Salem where the family had stopped for lunch on their way to Seattle.

I found a phone listing in Grants Pass for Megan's father, Jeffrey Moro, but when I called, nobody answered. Instead, I found myself listening to the greeting message on what sounded like an old-fashioned Code-A-Phone answering machine. After the tone, I left my name and number, saying that I was a private investigator looking into cases involving missing children.

A newspaper article a week after the abduction included the name of a witness who saw the kidnapper leading Megan across the parking lot to a gray van. I was able to get a phone number for her using a subscription cell phone directory service.

"This is Carolyn," came the voice on the phone.

"My name is Corrigan. I'm an investigator in Oregon City, and I'm looking into some cases involving missing children. I understand that you witnessed an abduction back in 1996, and I'm hoping you can give some details.

"Oh dear," she said. "Hardly a day goes by that I don't think about that poor little girl. I can't help feeling that I might have stopped it if I'd just done something."

"Can you tell me what happened?"

"Well, it was at Burger King. I'd just gotten out of my car and was approaching the door when a lady came out with a little girl. The lady started across the parking lot, holding the girl's hand, but the girl started to resist. I heard her ask, 'Where's my mommy?' Something about it just didn't seem quite right to me, ya know what I mean?"

"How far away were you?"

"Maybe ten feet, but they were walking away from me. Anyway, when the girl started to resist, the lady picked her up and carried her to a van that was parked at the curb—not actually in the Burger King parking lot. The lady pushed her into the passenger door and climbed in right behind her, and the van sped away."

"Who drove the van?"

"There was a man already at the wheel. They were rolling before the lady even got the door shut, and I knew right then that it was a kidnapping. It all happened so fast. I went inside, thinking I should do something, but I didn't know what. And then some people started calling, 'Megan, Megan,' and I knew right then that they were the little girl's parents.

"I told them what I saw, and then we got someone at the counter to call the police. It seemed to take them forever to get there, and those poor people were in complete panic, not knowing what to do. And I just can't help thinking I should have done something—right when they walked past me."

"You couldn't have known—"

"But that's the thing. I *did* know. I could just *feel* it!"

Feeling the need to redirect the conversation, I asked, "Can you give me a description of the woman?"

"Oh, I gave all that to the police."

"I know, but I'd like to hear it myself if you don't mind."

"Well, she was very plain. Like no makeup, straight hair, drab clothes. Her dress looked almost like an old sack—just gray cloth with buttons down the front and a fake buckle at the waist. And she wore funny shoes, like boys' high-top sneakers."

I thought, if only *all* witnesses had Carolyn's observation skills.

"She was about average height, maybe five five, but she was as skinny as a rail. She might not have weighed as much as a hundred pounds. She looked like she was in her twenties, except for one thing. See, she had a tattoo. It was an omega symbol on her left forearm. But the thing is it looked faded and old, you know? When a tattoo is new, it's dark and sharp edged. So maybe she was older than she looked."

"How about the driver?"

"I only got a glimpse of him while the door was open and the lady was pushing Megan in. I told the cops he looked like a homeless man. Hair all shaggy and uncombed and a scruffy beard. He was wearing a red plaid shirt. He wore glasses. The frames looked like the cheapest kind you can buy, that beige-colored plastic."

"You said you didn't get a license number off the van. Were you able to see what state it was from?"

"It was an Oregon plate—the kind with the pine tree in the middle, but it was all faded."

"Can you describe the van?"

"It was a Ford. When I was telling the police about it, they showed me pictures, and we figured out that it was about a 1990 model. It was all gray except for something painted on the side door. It was like that omega symbol with lettering underneath. It said something like Frenchman and then had two more words below that."

When the conversation was over, I looked over the notes I'd taken. The involvement of a woman in the kidnapping set this case apart from the others. When women participate in a child abduction, it is usually for something other than sex, and that didn't fit with what I believed about Brittany Harlan's case. If someone kept her captive for twelve years, it was almost certainly for sex based on the case histories I'd found so far for long-term captivity of kidnapped girls.

So while I would forever marvel at Carolyn's eye for detail, I doubted it was going to be much use in finding out what happened to Brittany Harlan or identifying Sunny.

The last name on my list was Lisa Jewell, abducted on June 26, 1998, from the ice arena at Lloyd Center in Portland. A pair of witnesses saw a middle-aged woman talking with Lisa, and a few minutes later she was gone. Other witnesses saw a woman carrying a girl wearing ice skates in the mall's underground parking lot. Like the case of Megan Moro, the involvement of a woman made me question the connection with Brittany and the others.

I used every resource available but was unable to find contact information for Lisa Jewell's parents or any of the witnesses. In the end, I put the file in the drawer next to Megan Moro's—under the heading "Probably Not Related."

May 5 Monday

Chapter 28

ud insisted, "Oh hell, I'm okay. I just feel bad for those that didn't get out."

"Last I heard, they had found three," I said.

"Yeah, I heard that too."

Martha said, "There was also something about a skeleton."

"When I talked with the deputy up by the highway on Friday, she told me about that," I said. "I think the CSI people were down there trying to figure out if it was a crime victim or maybe an old Indian grave. But I think it's unlikely that you'd find two people in shallow graves within a hundred yards of one another unless they're somehow connected."

"You think it might be related to Sunny?" Martha asked.

"I'd say the odds favor that conclusion."

"Well, they almost had *my* bones to add to the collection," Bud reminded us.

"So what can you tell us about the people living out there?"

"They were what used to be called hobos. Or maybe bums. That's different from just being homeless. Homeless is temporary. These people were permanent."

"Any chance that one of them was Harvey Walters?"

"None. A couple of them knew Walters—they'd been there that long. They told me all about how he'd sometimes poach a deer and give it to 'em. They wouldn't have talked about him if one of them *was* him."

"Did you find out anything about the pot farm?"

"Not much. It'd been there awhile. Then—maybe three or four years ago—the crop got harvested by the county sheriff, and the growers got busted. But there's still some plants growing wild, and the folks in the camp help themselves. Well, they *did* before they was killed."

Something there didn't quite add up. Sunny was supposedly killed five years ago—that would be a year or two before the raid, which meant that all the people going to and from the pot farm had walked right past the body. How had they done that without smelling something?

"Well, now that you've had a taste of what can happen in an investigation, are you still interested in getting involved in the Tacoma thing?" I asked.

"They're not going have a landslide, are they?"

"I doubt it."

"Then I guess I'm still in. This deal was going along just fine until that damned hillside came down on top of me."

"Dakota Mutual wants us to move forward with it," Martha said. "We'll probably have everything ready in another week."

"Sounds good to me," Bud said.

After Bud left, I turned my attention back to the Brittany Harlan case. I'd promised Roger Harlan I'd follow through on the DNA profiling, so I put in a call to Intermountain Forensic Labs in Portland and asked for Catherine Williams. I'd worked with her on the "Girl in the Carpet" case and trusted her work.

"I have some blood smears that probably date back to 2001," I explained. "They're on a piece of wood that has been out in the weather for about seven years. Is there any chance of getting a DNA profile?"

"If it's been rained on for seven years, there can't be much left," she said.

"Well, there are several smears and one place where there seems to be a drop of blood that ran down the wood. It looks fairly thick."

"Then either the deposit isn't as old as you think, or it wasn't exposed to the weather."

While she was talking, I e-mailed the photos I took of the blood.

"I just e-mailed photos. Suppose the wood was turned so that the side with the blood was facing down? Would that have been enough to shelter it from the weather?"

"Okay, I'm looking at the photos. I'd have to say that these don't look like they've been washed by rain or weathered in the sun."

"So making the assumption that the samples were sheltered—by whatever means—is it worth your time trying to get a profile?"

"As long as you pay me, it's worth *my* time," she kidded. "But yeah, there's a reasonable chance we can do something with it."

We made arrangements to meet at Svensen's place the next day to collect the samples. Then I gave her the mailing addresses for Roger Harlan and Thomas McCredie and asked her to send them the sample kits.

"Got it. I'll see you tomorrow."

When I put down my phone, Martha said, "So you decided to do it."

"Yeah. But like I told you, this is on my dime."

"Right. And like I told you, that's not how partnership works—not *this* partnership, anyway. Either we're partners, or we're not. I'm in this as much as you are."

"Let's just see—"

"No. It's done. We'll both pay our share, and that's it."

"Okay, okay," I said.

And I immediately started thinking of ways to weasel out of the deal. There really was no reason Martha should help foot the bill for my investigation.

Martha turned back to her desk, where she was working through the boat registration printout. Sliding a ruler down each page, she scanned the columns that listed the boat owners by last and first names, looking for a boat registered to someone named Walters. In this way, she was able to scan the names almost as fast as she could turn the pages.

Leaving her to do that, I drove to Salem to follow up on the house on Marion Street in Woodburn where Olivia Imbler lived at the time her daughter was abducted. I sat down at the public computer in the assessor's office and figured out how to do a property history search.

It took about half an hour to determine that the house was owned by Gregory Dilley from the time it was built in 1966 until the current owners bought it in 2004. Nothing in the records mentioned Olivia Imbler.

I pulled out my iPhone and logged onto the public Wi-Fi. My search for a current address or phone number for Gregory Dilley came up empty. Next I did a Google search for his name. That returned about 350,000 hits, so I refined the search by adding Oregon, cutting the list down to about fifty.

Gregory Dilley had bought a new house in 1966. I figured that he had to have been thirty years old or more to be buying a new house, and that meant he would be about eighty now. This led me to look first at the obituaries that came up in my Google search. And that's where I found him.

Gregory R. Dilley passed away at the age of sixty-eight in November 2003. He was survived by a son, Howard Dilley, in Atlanta and a daughter, Olivia. So I knew I was on the right track. Olivia was living with her father at the time Makayla was abducted. But there was no clue as to where the Imbler name came from.

A Google search for Olivia Dilley led me, surprisingly, to half a dozen women in Oregon with that name. Some were conspicuously the wrong age, either too young or too old to have had a five-year-old child in 1996. But one stood out. She was a hairdresser—in Woodburn.

By then, the battery in my phone was getting low, so I went out to the parking lot and plugged into the USB port in my Yukon. I tried calling Shear Fashion Salon and got a message saying that all stylists were currently unable to answer the phone. I left my name and number in voice mail, asking for Olivia to call back.

Confident that I'd found the person I was looking for, I drove to a nearby McDonald's and ordered lunch at the drive-through. I was down to the last few French fries when my phone rang.

"This is Olivia. You asked me to call?"

"Is this Olivia Imbler?"

The extended pause answered the question before she did.

"I don't use that name anymore."

"I'm an investigator in Oregon City. I'd like to talk with you about Makayla."

"I'm sorry. I can't talk about that now. I'm working."

"Is there a convenient time?"

"Uh, Mr. Corrigan, I don't know who you are—"

"I'm investigating a local case where at least one girl was held captive for many years after being abducted as a child."

"And you think—"

"At this point, I know of no connection between this case and Makayla's abduction. I'm just exploring the possibility. Is there a time and place where we can meet?"

I waited for an uncomfortable length of time before she answered.

"I have an open appointment at three thirty this afternoon. We could talk then. There's a café next door to the shop."

I looked at my watch. I could get to Woodburn by then if I didn't get hung up in traffic.

"That sounds fine. I'll see you then."

I got to the café first, so I grabbed a booth with a view of the door. Five minutes later, Olivia Dilley came in and looked around. She was dark haired and pretty despite being a bit overweight. I stood and walked toward her.

"Mr. Corrigan?"

She took a seat in the booth and sat with her hands folded in her lap. I ordered a cup of coffee, and Olivia ordered a Diet Pepsi.

"So what is this about someone holding girls captive? And why haven't I heard anything about it in the news?"

"It's been kept it out of the news to avoid compromising the investigation."

"Well, what leads you to think it might have something to do with Makayla?"

"I want to be really clear on this. We have no evidence that Makayla is any part of this. I'm merely exploring the possibility. Right now, all I have is time frames. Makayla's age and the time of her abduction are consistent with a profile we are developing."

That's when the tears started running down Olivia's cheeks. "I was hoping—"

"Let me explain. We have solid evidence that a seven-year-old girl abducted in 1989 was still alive twelve years later. She may *still* be alive for that matter." Even as I said that, I thought about the skeletal remains found at the landslide site, and I gritted my teeth for what I had to say next. "But please, I don't want to give you any false hopes. In the same area where we believe *that* girl was held, remains have recently been found. They haven't been identified, but the proximity makes us suspect a connection."

I could see the crushing effect that had on her, and she dropped her head and sobbed.

"I'm really sorry to bring this to you. The unidentified girl we're talking about died about five years ago at about age twenty."

"Okay, I get it now. Makayla would be twenty-four now."

"We could compare your DNA with—"

"Yes. Of course! I have to know."

"I'll have a lab send you a kit. It'll come with instructions. All they need is a saliva sample. And please understand that this will take time— maybe several months."

———

May
Tuesday 6

Chapter 29

My first call of the day went to Michael Wheeler.
"I thought I ought to bring you up to date on what I'm doing on your Jane Doe case," I told him.

Wheeler laughed. "As if we had only one Jane Doe case."

"The one from the homeless camp down here. I'm still working on the theory that the girl was abducted as a child in the midnineties and held captive for about fifteen years before being killed."

"So you still believe that your Brittany Harlan carvings are real?" Wheeler asked.

"That's right. And if Brittany Harlan was held captive out there, then it's possible that this girl was too."

"That's a pretty big stretch."

"We'll know soon enough. That's why I called."

"What's happening?"

"I'm having a lab try to develop a DNA profile from blood on the beam with Brittany's name on it, and Brittany's father is sending a sample for comparison."

"That's a pretty big gamble, isn't it? I hope you aren't expecting *us* to pay the bill."

"If we get a match, that's exactly what I expect."

"That's a pretty big *if*. Who's doing the work?"

"Intermountain—same lab I used for the 'Girl in the Carpet' case."

"Who's your client?"

"I don't have one. This is all on me."

"*Okay*," he said, drawing out the word. "*I'd* have to be pretty desperate before I'd gamble *my* money on a long shot like that—or the taxpayers' money, for that matter."

"I don't think it's such a long shot. But regardless, I've identified a couple of possible candidates for your Jane Doe. The lab is sending sample kits to the parents. All we ask from you is to compare their profiles with the victim's."

"You're assuming that we *have* a profile."

It was my turn to laugh. "Of course you have."

Wheeler said, "I can't make any promises."

"What can you tell me about the remains they found after the landslide?"

"Three slide victims and one John Doe."

"So the skeleton is male?"

"That's right. The preliminary report is male, aged about thirty, buried at least twenty years ago. And there's a bullet hole in the back of the skull. How're you going to fit *that* into your theory?"

"Well, you got me there," I admitted.

It certainly wasn't what I'd expected. And it didn't do any good for my belief that Sunny's death was connected with Brittany Harlan's. Now I had to consider the possibility that it was connected instead to this new case. Wheeler had already reached the same conclusion.

"Like I told you before, we believe that the Jane Doe was a resident in the homeless camp. So we know that something bad was going on out there, and whatever it was, it just might be what put the bullet hole in John Doe's skull."

I drove out to Giles Svensen's place at eleven thirty to meet Catherine Williams. I met Giles in the parking lot, and he unlocked his warehouse, where the beam with its inscription was stored.

"I heard they found another skeleton when they were looking for slide victims," Giles commented.

"I was talking with the sheriff's office about that before I came out here. They're calling him a homicide victim, and they say that he died about twenty years ago. Does that ring any bells with you?"

"That'd be just about the time I moved in. I didn't know anyone in the neighborhood at the time, so I wouldn't have noticed if anyone disappeared."

"I didn't really expect that you would, but if you hear any talk around the neighborhood, I'd appreciate a call."

A white minivan turned off the highway and came over to where I had parked. The emblem on the side read "Intermountain Forensics."

After introductions, Catherine Williams suggested, "Let's go take a look at the blood smear."

"Are you certain that this is blood?" she asked when I showed her the beam.

"I did a Kastle-Meyer test on one of the smears. It's definitely blood."

I pointed out the smear that I tested as well as half a dozen others, all barely visible against the dark brown color of the wood. Then I showed her the one short streak that appeared to be where a drop of blood ran down from the letter *R* in the inscription. To my eye, it appeared to be undisturbed and thus would be the most likely place to get a good sample.

After studying the drip and the smears under a magnifying glass, Catherine pinned a small, numbered yellow tag next to each. She then shot close-up photos of each area marked by a tag as well as photos showing the position of the blood relative to the scratched inscription.

Over the next few minutes, she collected samples from the blood she had identified with the numbered tags. Throughout the process, she dictated everything she did into a tiny digital audio recorder. Each of the samples was placed in a glass vial and labeled with numbers matching the tags on the old beam.

"What do you think? Will these produce a profile?" I asked when she was finished.

"I can't say. But I think chances are good. When you told me that the beam was outdoors for five years, I didn't have much hope. But the stains are in pretty good shape. I really doubt that they were exposed to the weather."

Giles said, "When I first saw the inscription, I'd just pushed a couple of sheets of plywood off the pile of timbers. The plywood might have sheltered the beam."

"It had to be something like that," Catherine said. "Anyway, I'll get these sent off to Seattle, and we'll see what we get."

When I returned to my office, Martha triumphantly announced, "I think I've found Harvey Walters's brother!"

She showed me the boat registration printout where she had highlighted the line showing that in 2002, Delbert Walters registered an eighteen-foot Smoker Craft Sportsman. The address given was in Tillamook on the Oregon Coast—an ideal place for a commercial crabbing operation.

The information was twelve years old, but it was the best lead we'd come up with in the week since we first learned that Harvey Walters had a brother. I copied the address into my little spiral notebook and then walked over to Kaylin Beatty's house. Her real estate software was a lot more reliable than most of my subscription search engines.

Kaylin's first search was statewide property-tax rolls, where she found no records for Delbert Walters. She searched again for anyone named Walters with a first initial D and came up with about thirty hits, but none of them fit the man I was looking for.

Next, Kaylin did a tax-roll search for the address that Martha found on the boat registration printout. This turned up a single-family residence with a current assessed value of $184,000, making it a pretty modest property. The present owners purchased the property in 2010. A search of old MLS records turned up the 2010 listing, which showed the seller's name to be Delbert Walters.

I tried the phone number given on the 2010 listing, but not surprisingly, the number was not active. Rapidly approaching another dead end, I searched for the phone number of the people who bought Walters's Tillamook house in the feeble hope that they might know where the former owner went.

"Alcatraz," came the answer to my question.

"He went to Alcatraz?" I repeated.

"Yeah, he got some kind of a job there with the park service. It was like a joke with him—telling people that he was going to Alcatraz."

"Any idea what kind of a job he got?"

"No. If he ever told me that, I've forgotten."

Posing as a property manager, I phoned the human resources office for the Golden Gate National Parks Conservancy and asked for verification of employment for Delbert Walters.

"Yes, Mr. Walters is an employee in good standing."

"And could you tell me his job title, please?"

"Sales associate. He works in the gift shop on the island."

I then said, "And I have his address as—let's see—1410 Balboa Street."

It was a made-up address. I was hoping that the HR lady would correct me.

Instead, she said, "I cannot comment on employees' addresses."

Still, it wasn't a total strikeout. At least I knew where Delbert Walters worked. But no matter how many ways I tried, I could not come up with a phone number or address for Walters anyplace in the San Francisco area. Nor was I able to phone him at his workplace. It appeared that the only way I was going to talk with Delbert Walters was to go there and find him at work.

On the news that evening, it was reported that a body had been recovered from the Willamette River in the area of the Oregon City Marina.

It was reported to be that of an adult male approximately sixty years old, who matched the description of the last missing resident of the homeless camp. Apparently, the landslide had carried him all the way down into the river.

Chapter 30

I complained to Martha, "Until the DNA results come back, there's not much more we can do toward identifying Sunny."

"What about the new skeleton?" Martha asked.

"It appears to be unrelated."

"Just a coincidence that he was found thirty yards from where Sunny was found," she said.

I could see what she was getting at. I'd always told her that there was no such thing as coincidence in criminal investigation.

"We may come back to it later," I said in order to avoid having to explain my deviation from what I had given as an inflexible rule.

Then I changed the subject. "Is everything set for Bud's trip to Tacoma?"

"He has an appointment to see Dr. Gaston next week. I set him up as an electrician working for Tacoma Power and Light. They have workers' comp insurance through Dakota Mutual and agreed to help with our sting."

"That ganglion cyst is supposed to be a repetitive motion injury," I reminded her. "How does an electrician get that?"

"Turning a screwdriver. Anyway, that's going to be his explanation. It probably doesn't matter what we tell him. The doctor is looking for any case where he can overbill the insurance company. Besides, I thought it was important that his job be something he knows."

"Good point. All we need is a car for him to drive."

"I have one reserved from Enterprise in Vancouver. That way it'll have Washington plates. I'll drive Bud over there on Tuesday, and he'll go straight from there to Tacoma, where he'll spend the night in a motel. Then he'll go see the doctor on Wednesday."

"How's he feeling?"

"Still sore, but he's okay. We'll be practicing his lines for the next few days, so he'll know exactly how to answer the doctor's questions."

Unable to think of anything Martha hadn't already thought of, I simply said, "Good."

"What about you?" she asked. "Are you going to go talk with Delbert Walters?"

I'd been playing mental ping-pong with that question ever since my phone call the day before. It seemed like a lot of effort and expense just to ask him where I could find his brother, but I couldn't think of any other way to get the information.

"You know, those boat rides out to Alcatraz sell out—sometimes weeks in advance," Martha said.

I leaned back in my chair and rubbed my eyes. Martha had a point. I Googled "Alcatraz tours" and found that she was right. All the tours were booked up for the next two weeks. Then I had another idea.

Not wishing to spend a lot of money on a hotel room where I'd do nothing but sleep, I looked up the more reasonably priced Holiday Inn at Fisherman's Wharf. After checking the availability of room for the next few days, I phoned the desk.

"I'm going to be there for a couple of days, and I was wondering if you knew how I might get tickets for the Alcatraz tour—their website says they're all booked up."

"I know a guy. He has a connection with the concierge at the Sheraton. They routinely buy blocks of Alcatraz tickets, but most days they have a few extras. My guy has access to those. It's almost a sure thing."

"Can you get tickets for me?" I asked.

"No, I can't do it. Here's how he works. He has a tiny storefront next to the cable car stop on Taylor Street, with a sign on the sidewalk advertising Alcatraz tours. He'll call the Sheraton while you wait and let you know what tickets are available. Strictly last minute. If you want the ticket, you have to buy it along with a bus tour of San Francisco—it's the only way he'll sell it."

"Any other way to get a ticket?"

"Stay at the Sheraton, I suppose."

The difference in price between a room at the Sheraton and one at the Holiday Inn would pay for a bus tour and Alcatraz ticket several times over.

"Do you have a nonsmoking queen room for tonight?"

"Just one left. You want to reserve it?"

"For tonight and tomorrow night," I confirmed.

Next I logged on to Kayak and found a $380 round-trip ticket on an Alaska Airlines flight that would put me in San Francisco at 8:10 p.m. With my hotel room at Fisherman's Wharf, I wouldn't need a car, so I looked at the shuttle bus schedules and found the one that could get me to the Holiday Inn in less than two hours.

I took Bud along when I drove to the airport and had him drive my Yukon back home. It was cheaper and safer than putting it in the long-term parking lot.

"I can see why you don't want to park there," Bud said. "I saw on the news that somebody's been stashing bodies of murder victims in randomly selected cars in airport parking lots."

"That'd be an unpleasant surprise," I agreed.

"It'd be the end of that new-car smell, that's for sure."

"If all goes according to plan, I'll be back here Friday at 4:00 p.m. I'll call Martha if there's any change in my schedule."

Everything I took along was crammed into a small carry-on bag so I wouldn't have to wait at baggage claim only to be told that my luggage was in Denver, Minneapolis, or some other damned place. So upon landing at San Francisco International, I walked straight to the shuttle bus stop. At that, it was still nine before the bus pulled away from the curb.

As we approached the 101, I caught a glimpse of a solid parade of taillights four lanes wide for as far as I could see. The ninety-minute ride took nearly three hours, and I checked in just before midnight. I could've made the trip faster on a bicycle.

May

Thursday 8

Chapter 31

Down the block from the Holiday Inn, I found Joanie's Happy Days Diner open for breakfast. In fact, breakfast was all they served. I recommend the crab benedict. I lingered over my coffee because the clerk at the Holiday Inn told me that his friend with the Alcatraz tickets didn't open until nine.

It was, by San Francisco standards, a beautiful warm spring day. And by that, I mean it was cloudy, but there was no fog, the temperature was over fifty, and there wasn't much wind. I walked two blocks up Beach Street to Taylor and paused on the corner. Looking to my right, I spotted the "Alcatraz Tours" sign on the sidewalk, exactly as I had been told. The guy placed a phone call and confirmed a reservation on the ten-thirty ferry to Alcatraz. Then he tacked on $39 for the Yellow Bus Tour and told me that a shuttle would pick me up in front of the Hyatt at ten.

For the next forty-five minutes, I walked the neighborhood and looked at all the tourist crap I wasn't going to buy. The shuttle bus took us to Pier 33, where everyone lined up in a Disneyland-style queue to wait for the ferry. The ride to the island took about fifteen minutes, and we docked at the same pier where Al Capone and Clint Eastwood first set foot on Alcatraz.

The building nearest the pier contained the bookstore and gift shop, so I departed from the rest of the group getting off the ferry and went straight there. I looked around the store, getting a feel for the layout and looking for anyone who might be Del Walters. Along one wall, there were racks containing replicas of the inmate uniforms, and that's where I spotted a rugged-looking man who appeared to be in his sixties, dressed in the prison blues.

"Del Walters?" I asked even though he was wearing an employee badge with his name on it.

"That's right. What can I do for you?"

"My name's Corrigan. I'm from Oregon City, and I'm trying to track down your brother, Harvey."

"First, I'd like to hear why you want to find him."

I fell back on the script Martha had used when she canvassed Harvey Walters's old neighborhood.

"I'm working for an insurance company. Harvey may be owed some money."

"That's a load of shit," Del said quietly. "You wouldn't come all the way out here for that."

He had me, and I regretted having used the ill-chosen line. "You're right. It is more complicated than that. Is there someplace we can sit down and talk?"

"If you want to tell me what it is you *really* want, you can buy me dinner. Then we can have a proper conversation over a beer."

"I'd go along with that," I said.

"There's a place on Leavenworth Street—Jack's Cannery—decent bar, and we won't have to pay for our drinks. Bartender's a friend of mine."

"I know the place."

Actually, I didn't, but I remembered having seen the sign while walking around a couple of hours earlier.

"Get a table next to the gorilla so we don't have to wade through the place looking for each other. I'll be there at about six. Now you have to let me get back to work."

I browsed the book counter and bought a book about the 1962 escape that was the subject of Clint Eastwood's movie. Leaving the gift shop, I wandered up the road to the old penitentiary building, where I was given an iPod-style headset for a self-paced audio tour.

At one point, I'd toyed with the notion that Del might have participated in the things that his brother had done in the old cedar mill. But the things that I believed had happened there were not part-time aberrations. They were not the kind of things a person would dabble in. On the contrary, doing those things demanded a level of psychosis that could not be picked up and set aside at will. It was a full-time obsession. But whether or not Del would rat out his brother was an open question.

I approached the entrance to Jack's Cannery Bar with mixed expectations. Del Walters had seemed willing to talk, but I also got the feeling that what he really wanted was a free dinner. On my left, just inside the door, there stood a huge, stuffed gorilla. I selected a table about ten feet away.

"Sorry I'm late," Del said. "I couldn't get a ride up here, so I walked. Been here long?"

"Just long enough to read the beer list," I lied.

A waiter appeared and took our orders, and for the next few minutes, we talked of inconsequential things—the weather, baseball, and Alcatraz.

"So why are you trying to find Harvey?" Del asked after our beers were served.

My carefully planned answer was close to the truth but skirted the probability that Harvey had committed at least two murders.

"A friend of mine recently bought the property where your brother's boat repair shop used to be. He discovered evidence of a large marijuana farm and the remains of two people. I'm trying to find out who was growing the pot, and I'm running out of ideas. I'm hoping that Harvey might have seen something that'll help."

"That whole place was overrun by druggers after Harvey moved out. There's no telling what went on out there."

"Their meth lab got raided. But the time period I'm looking at was way before that."

"I was thinking that the druggers were there all along—and just moved into the old mill after Harvey moved out," Del explained.

"You could be right. Do you know anything about them?"

"Only what I heard from Harvey—which wasn't much."

"If they were there before Harvey moved out, where did they live?"

"Hell if I know. I remember there were some little houseboats tied up down below. Maybe they lived there."

"Harvey would know that, wouldn't he?" I asked.

"Yeah, probably. But he never said anything to me about it."

"Well, that's why I'm trying to find him. What did he do after he shut down the boat works?"

"That was real hard on him. It was always his dream to have his own business. Then he got some insurance money when his wife died, and that's what he used to open the boat shop. I think in his mind, the shop wasn't just financed by his wife's death. It *was* his wife. He put everything he had into that business—not just money—everything. It gutted him when he had to shut down."

I repeated my question. "What then?"

"He had nothing left. The bank was taking his house, and a dozen different people were trying to collect debts from him. But by then, he just didn't give a shit. He showed up on my doorstep like a lost dog. Everything he owned was crammed into his old Jeep Cherokee. I let him stay a while, but he didn't contribute anything, so I basically tossed him out."

"Where'd he go from there?"

"Last I saw him, he was heading south on 101. He talked some about looking for gold in the Rogue River or someplace down there."

"Did he have any connections in the area?"

"He talked about a guy who was working a claim on some creek in the Rogue River canyon—said he was gonna go to work for him."

"Do you remember this guy's name or the name of his mine?"

"You know of a place called Merlin? I think that's where the guy lived. After Harvey left, I found a bunch of calls to a number in Merlin charged to my phone."

"Still have that phone bill?"

"Oh hell no. That was six—seven years ago. All I remember is that the phone number belonged to a storage facility of some kind."

We continued talking through dinner, but Del was unable to tell me anything else that might help me track down Harvey Walters. When the bill came, I noted that there was no charge for the beer. I added the price of the drinks to the tip and paid in cash. Del gave me his phone number, and I promised to let him know if I were to find Harvey.

The next day I flew home, wondering if the whole exercise had been a waste of time and money.

May

Saturday 10

Chapter 32

H arvey Walters might be prospecting for gold, and he had known someone who worked at a storage yard in Merlin, Oregon. That was the extent of what I'd gotten out of my trip to San Francisco. I didn't need an accountant to do a cost-benefit analysis on that. The information that Del gave me was pretty thin, and it was seven years old.

The idea that Harvey might have gone out hunting for gold made logical sense. It was one of the few things a man on the run could do and leave no tracks. If a man could find a little bit of gold, he could live a cash-only existence without ever having to show a Social Security card or driver's license. It could make him almost impossible to find.

It was also logical that he would choose the Rogue River canyon as the place to go look for gold. For a century and a half, prospectors have worked the Rogue and its tributaries, and there are hundreds of active claims and innumerable unregistered wildcat operations. It would be impossible to canvas all the mining operations in search of a man who *might* have been there six or seven years ago.

So the only remaining lead was the phone bill showing calls to a storage facility in Merlin. Searching online, I found only five listings for storage in Merlin. But even if I knew which one Harvey had called, it would be difficult or impossible to determine who had spoken with him.

Watching the gate and answering the phone was often a minimum-wage job with high turnover, so there was a high probability that the person Harvey called was long gone and forgotten. Still, it was the only lead I had, so I had to follow up on it. But how?

This person had to have been Harvey's friend. What could I possibly say that would motivate Harvey's friend to tell me how to find him? My "insurance settlement" line had totally bombed with Del Walters. I needed something more convincing. And I needed to say it in person. This couldn't be done over the phone.

I phoned Jerry Midland at his Vancouver pawnshop and explained what I needed. Jerry said he knew someone who could do the job on short notice. I told him I'd be over in a couple of hours. I searched the back of my dresser drawers and found a little travel kit containing stage makeup. Fifteen minutes later, my hair was gray, and I looked at least ten years older than I was.

Next, I pulled the bright-blue blanket off my bed and tacked it to the wall beneath the vanity lights in the bathroom. I set up my camera on a tripod and shot a series of photos of myself in front of the blue backdrop. I picked the best one and e-mailed it to Jerry Midland. With that done, I searched the Web for lodging. The nearest motel to Merlin was the Travelodge in Grants Pass, so I reserved a room there.

DC, who was already miffed about my trip to San Francisco, glowered at me as I packed a bag and prepared to leave again. The leftover chicken in my refrigerator wouldn't last until my return, so I gave it to DC, and while it didn't completely atone for my impending departure, it did at least briefly distract him from his grudge.

The drive to Grants Pass, by way of Vancouver, took nearly seven hours. I checked into the motel at six thirty. This would let me get an early start in canvassing the storage yards on Sunday. I figured I'd probably have to make the rounds twice because typically a different staff would be working on Monday.

After touching up my gray hair, I put on a baggy, oil-stained pair of jeans, a sweatshirt with the sleeves cut short, and a tattered baseball hat from NAPA auto parts. I passed up the free self-service waffles in the hotel lobby and got a more substantial breakfast at the restaurant next door.

As I finished my breakfast, I looked at the map showing the locations of the storage facilities. Three of them were clustered together off Monument Drive, so I decided to start there. I spotted the sign for North Valley U-Store as I drove up Monument Drive and parked next to the office.

"Name's Del Walters," I said, showing my freshly made driver's license.

The lady behind the counter asked, "What can I do for you, Mr. Walters?"

I scratched my forehead and said, "Uh, well, I'm trying to find my brother—Harvey Walters—but I don't know his address."

Looking perplexed, the lady asked, "So do you want to see the phone book?"

"No, I already tried that. Thing is last time I talked to him, he told me he was coming here to see a friend."

"What's the friend's name?"

"If he ever told me that, I've forgotten it now. But his friend worked here, and I think he might have been working a gold claim too. Any idea who that might be?"

She let out a derisive laugh. "*Everyone* around here prospects for gold, one time or another."

"Yeah, I get that. But I think this guy had a pretty big operation. See, Harvey was gonna go to work on his claim. I guess that was about five years ago," I added.

"I can't think of anyone like that."

"Is anybody else working here today?"

"Yeah, there's an assistant manager and a maintenance man."

"Could I talk to the assistant manager?"

"If you want to hang around, he'll be back here as soon as he finishes with his customer. It shouldn't be long—he's just inspecting a unit that's being vacated."

I went outside and waited until a man carrying a clipboard approached the office. I intercepted him and went through essentially the same script that I'd used with the lady inside.

"Well, I don't know who that could be," the assistant manager said. "Nobody here owns a gold claim as far as I know."

"How many other people work here? Maybe one of them knows who my brother's friend is."

"There's two others, but they don't work weekends."

Half a mile away, I found Affordable Mini Storage on Flaming Road where I went through my same routine with the same result. In all, that day I talked with eleven people at the five storage yards. The only possible lead came from a teenager at Merlin Self Storage, who told me that the man who owned the place had a gold claim on Galice Creek about twenty miles away.

"How can I get in touch with him?" I asked. "What's his name?"

"Name's Curt Hubbard. I ain't supposed to give out his phone number."

"When will he be here?"

"Who knows? He doesn't have any schedule."

After leaving there, I found a phone book and looked up Curtis Hubbard. The address given was a rural route box number, and the phone number rang through at the ministorage. I coughed and growled, "Wrong number," rather than talk to the teenager again.

I drove past Merlin Self Storage again and noted that there was a residence on the hill behind the fenced storage yard. A gate in the fence indicated that the residence and the ministorage were connected, and I concluded that it probably was where Curt Hubbard lived. But when I knocked on the door, nobody answered.

Exhausted, I returned to the motel to rest up in preparation for doing it all over again in the morning.

May

Monday 12

Chapter 33

Back at North Valley U-Store, I found the manager at the front desk and introduced myself as Del Walters. I told the same tale I'd used all day on Sunday.

"You sure it was here?" the manager asked.

"Well, I *think* it was," I answered.

"I can't think who that might be. But there's a guy up in town who has a gold mine—Curt Hubbard. He owns Merlin Self Storage. He's the only one I can think of."

The temptation was to skip canvassing the rest of the storage yards and go straight to Hubbard's, but I'd learned long ago that it doesn't pay to deviate from the plan. It's all too easy to get distracted by a false lead and never get back to the original task.

My discipline produced another potential lead when I talked to the attendant at MAC Mini-Storage.

"There's a guy named James Oakland. Goes by the nickname Raider, and he always wears a Raider shirt or hat. He don't work here anymore, but he does a lot of gold mining. He has a suction dredge, and he goes wherever there's a crick on public land, like under bridges and things. Some folks say he's a claim jumper, but he seems to get away with it."

"You know where I can find him?"

"I don't know where he lives, but I see his truck around town sometimes. It's easy to spot—a blue Ford three-quarter ton with a pickup bed from a red Dodge. He calls it a Forge. Pretty strange-looking rig."

"Any particular place I should look for him?"

He shrugged. "Grocery store. Sometimes at the Mexican restaurant down the road."

Returning to Merlin Self Storage, I asked if Curt was around.

"He's probably up at his gold mine."

"I'm trying to find my brother—Harvey Walters—I heard he worked for Curt a few years back."

"There was an old guy—Curt let him live in his garage for a while. Maybe looked a bit like you."

"Any idea where he is now?"

He shook his head. "I didn't know him. Never even talked to him."

"How can I find Curt?"

"Best bet would be to go up to his claim. He has a trailer up there, and sometimes he goes for weeks without coming down here."

"Up Galice Creek?"

"Yeah. There's a sign by the road—Golden Goose Mine. About five miles up the road."

After a quick lunch at the Riffle Restaurant, I headed up the road toward the dot on the map named Galice. After about fifteen miles, I spotted a wooden sign pointing up a gravel road to the left: Galice Creek Road.

Seven miles up the road, I was looking for a place to turn around, thinking I'd passed the Golden Goose Mine without seeing it, when I spotted the crude hand-painted sign planted next to a single-track access road. I bumped a hundred yards down the deeply rutted driveway to an open area filled with broken-down machinery and rusting old cars and trucks. An old travel trailer sat half concealed in a manzanita grove.

Nobody answered my knock on the trailer door, so I followed the sound of an engine running. From the high bank, I looked down at Galice Creek, which was heavily excavated, with piles of rock on both banks. The machine I'd heard was a floating sluice box fed by a Venturi pump.

A man wearing a wetsuit, mask, and snorkel held the suction hose in the riverbed, picking up sand and gravel from the creek bed. There was no way I could get his attention without getting into the water, so I found a place to sit and watch. When the man finally looked up, he waved to acknowledge my presence and then resumed working.

After a few more minutes, he stood up and pulled his mask off. He waded over and shut off the machine and then approached me.

"If you're here to complain about the mud in the water, you might as well leave now 'cause everything here's been approved by DEQ and EPA."

"Don't worry about me. I'm not here to cause trouble. You Curt Hubbard?"

"That's right. Who are you?"

"Del Walters. I'm just here looking for my brother—Harvey Walters."

He squinted at me. "You don't look nothing like Harvey."

My pulse quickened. I extracted a pint of Jim Beam from my jacket and took a swig before offering the bottle to Curt. He accepted the bottle and took a long pull.

"So they tell me," I said, suppressing the compulsion to show him my fake driver's license. "When's the last time you saw Harvey?"

"Been a few months."

"Can you tell me where I can find him?"

"Shit, I don't know where he is. He's somewhere up in the hills. Only time I see him is when he has some color to sell."

Pretending to know more than I did, I said, "So he's still living the life of a hermit."

"I don't know nothing about that."

We talked for another ten minutes, but I was unable to pry any additional information out of him. Finally, after passing him the Jim Beam a couple more times, I pocketed the bottle, thanked him for his time, and turned to go.

"Walters!" Curt called after me. "You find your brother, tell him he owes me twenty bucks on the Super Bowl. Fool went and bet on Denver!"

I tried to figure out a way for Curt to contact me next time he saw Harvey. The problem with that was that he thought I was Del Walters, so if he saw Harvey, the first thing he'd do would be to tell him that his brother had been here looking for him. If Harvey was able to contact Del, the whole thing would be blown.

Low on fuel, I stopped at a gas station in Merlin. While waiting for the attendant to bring me the remains of my hundred-dollar bill, something caught my eye in the parking lot of a grocery store up the street. Blue cab, red pickup box—it was James Oakland's "Forge." As I watched, a tall man wearing an Oakland Raiders baseball hat came out of the store, heading toward the mutant pickup.

Leaving behind the biggest tip I ever gave an undeserving gas station attendant, I raced up the street and into the parking lot of Ray's Groceries. I pulled up behind the Forge just as the tall man reached for the door handle.

"James Oakland?" I shouted out the window.

"Nobody calls me James—at least nobody I know."

"They say folks call you Raider," I answered quickly.

He took a hard look at me. "Who're you?"

"Name's Co—Del Walters. I just drove down from Tillamook."

"Who?"

"Del Walters—Harvey Walters's brother."

"So?"

It was a good sign. He didn't ask who Harvey Walters was. That might mean he knew Harvey, so I signaled him to wait and took the parking space next to his.

"Curt Hubbard told me that you might know where I can find Harvey."

"How the hell would Hubbard know that?" he demanded.

"Damned if I know. It was just something he said."

"Hubbard don't know nothing."

Having clearly gotten off on the wrong foot, I started over. "I really need to find Harvey and warn him."

"Warn him of what?"

I hesitated. "It's personal." And then, as though I had reconsidered, I added, "It's about the law."

Raider looked interested. "What about the law?"

"I really need to talk to Harvey."

"How do I know *you* aren't the law?"

"I'm not. I'm—" I paused, patted my pockets, and said, "Here. Look at my ID."

He studied my phony driver's license.

"Listen. I know Harvey wants to be left alone. But this is really important."

"He said something about a brother once. Said you tossed his ass out."

Trying to look embarrassed, I said, "Yeah. It was a bad time for both of us."

"Looks like you're doing all right now," he said, pointing at my new Yukon.

I laughed. "I *wish* this rig was mine! Insurance company rented that for me. Lady rear-ended me up on Stage Road Pass. They towed me in on Saturday. My old Suburban's probably totaled. Adjuster's going to look at it today."

For effect, I pulled out the remains of my Jim Beam and took a gulp. As if an afterthought, I offered the bottle to Oakland.

"Go ahead and finish it," I said when he reached for the bottle.

"I haven't seen Harvey in a while."

I waited while he drained the last of the whiskey.

"He was working up on Bunker Crick last time I talked to him."

"Bunker Crick?" I asked, mimicking his pronunciation.

"Up off the Rogue—in the wilderness area. Probably not legal."

"Yeah, that won't help if the law tracks him down. How do I get to Bunker Crick?"

"Same way he does. Ya walk."

"I don't know where Bunker Crick is," I said.

"Well, ya know where Graves Crick is," he said. "Bunker Crick is about ten miles down the trail from there. Then, I figure, you just follow the crick 'til you find him."

Many years before, I'd taken a raft trip down the Rogue River, so I knew where Grave Creek was located. It was the final access point to the river before it entered the wilderness area. A hiking trail ran above the north bank of the Rogue for forty miles, all the way to Illahe at the other end of the wilderness area.

"Guess I should've brought my hiking boots."

"You want to find him, that's how you'll have to do it."

As the conversation wound down, I asked Oakland, "What did folks call you when the Raiders were in Los Angeles?"

The question seemed to puzzle him.

"Raider, of course. What else would they call me?"

I had plenty of time to consider my options back at the motel. I was looking for a man who had most likely committed multiple murders and who was in hiding and didn't want to be found. If I found him, there would almost certainly be a confrontation. I would need to control the situation from start to finish, and the only sure way to take control was with my Colt .45 automatic.

But then what? Maybe he'd break down and confess and then willingly accompany me back to Clackamas County Jail to face charges. Right. And rabbits lay colored eggs on Easter. Oregon is a death-penalty state. The chances of Harvey Walters voluntarily facing multiple murder charges were somewhere between miniscule and nonexistent.

If he refused to walk, even under the threat of being shot, I would have no options. I wouldn't shoot him, and I couldn't carry him. He would know that. What's more, if I forced him to accompany me and was then unable to prove his guilt, I could be charged with kidnapping.

That left me in an impossible situation. If I did nothing, Harvey would eventually come into town and talk with Curt Hubbard or Raider Oakland, and as soon as he determined that it hadn't been Del who was looking for him, he'd take off, and I'd probably never find him again. And since I didn't have the authority to arrest him, just mentioning the murdered girls would most likely send him on the run.

So I hadn't been as clever as I had thought. I tried thinking up some kind of ruse that would make him willingly come out of the wilderness. It's something I'm good at. But this was a unique situation, and for the life of me, I couldn't think up any plausible story that would do the trick. One way or another, I had to accept the fact that whatever I did—or if I did nothing—Harvey was probably going to find a new place to hide.

Chapter 34

In the morning, I phoned Jerry Midland's pawnshop and explained my problem.

"I need to track a person—for weeks, maybe even months."

"Can you attach something to his vehicle?"

"He's on foot. He lives in the woods—kind of a hermit."

"And I take it you don't want him to know you're tracking him?"

"That's right. I believe that he is a serial killer, but there isn't yet enough evidence to make any charges stick. So I need to track him in case he takes off."

"Okay. First off, in GPS trackers, the batteries are the issue. They're bulky, and the longer you want them to last, the bulkier they are. That'll make it damn difficult or outright impossible to conceal. But there might be an option."

"What's that?"

"New product—just came out in January. It's solar powered and very small—about the size of three nickels stacked up. It's called Retrievor, and it works with Android or iPhone. I've never actually used one, but it's getting good product reviews."

"What's it cost?" I asked warily.

"It's priced at $299, and then there's a monthly fee for monitoring—but it's only a few bucks."

"What about concealment?"

"Now, there's the problem. If it's concealed, it won't get sunlight, and it'll go dead."

"What's it look like? Can it be camouflaged or made to look like something else?"

"The solar collector itself looks kind of like a button. But the device is too thick to actually be *used* as a button. You might be able to work it

---

159

into the crown of a baseball cap, where the button goes, but I think it'd be pretty easy to spot."

"Isn't there any other option?"

"Like what? You're talking about concealing a long-life tracking device *on his person*, for Christ's sake!"

"Well, maybe if you could hide it in something that he'd *want* to carry around and which he'd leave in the sun for four or five hours a day, I could give it to him," I suggested half sarcastically.

"You know, that's actually not such a bad idea. I could conceal it in a solar-powered radio."

"If I were in his position, I'd be suspicious of a radio—especially presented as a gift from a stranger."

"Could you leave it someplace where he'd just find it—like it was dropped accidentally?"

"That's a possibility. But not a radio. How about a flashlight?"

"That might work. There're lots of solar flashlights. I ought to be able to find one that has room inside for the tracker."

"But it still has to get sunlight—"

"No. I'm thinking I'd take the tracker apart and discard the case and solar collector. That'll make it a lot easier to hide. I'll just wire it to the flashlight's power pack."

"Okay. Let's go for it. If you can get that for me, I can make it work."

"Give me a couple of hours to see what I can do. I'll call you back."

"Just one more thing," I said. "I need it yesterday."

"I assumed that. I'll get back to you."

"I don't know much about it, but there's a guidebook for hiking the Rogue River Trail," the desk clerk at the Travelodge told me. "It'll tell you everything you need to know."

"Any idea where I can get a copy?"

"I'm sure you can find it online at, like, Amazon or something."

"Can I get it locally?"

"Maybe at a backpacking store. The only place I know *for sure* that has it is the Galice Store. You know where that is, up out of Merlin?"

"Yeah, I've been there."

The drive to Galice took me back through Merlin and past the road up Galice Creek. Along the way, I tried to think through the actual mechanics of finding Harvey Walters.

First, I'd need to completely outfit myself with backpacking gear, from hat to boots, because there was no way I could hike to Bunker Creek *and back* in one day. It would be easy to spend a thousand dollars on equipment I'd probably never use again. But then again, I probably could get half my money back selling everything on Craigslist when I was finished with it.

At the Galice Store, I pulled up a chair at the lunch counter and ordered a hamburger.

I checked the waitress's name badge and asked, "Debbie, do you know of a guidebook for hiking the Rogue River Trail?"

"Sure. Want one?" she asked, pointing to a rack behind the cash register.

"Yep. Believe it or not, I drove all the way from Grants Pass just to get it."

Debbie gave me a curious look. "What could possibly make that little book so important?"

"I've never hiked the trail before. I want to know what I'm up against."

"Depends on the weather. It can be pretty muddy in places when it rains, and it gets hotter than hell in the summertime. But it's a very pleasant hike when the weather's right."

While eating lunch, I skimmed through the little guidebook, finding Bunker Creek 9.1 miles from the trailhead at Grave Creek. But even while reading about the hiking trail, I started considering an alternative. I could get to Bunker Creek by raft a lot easier than on foot.

When Debbie came back around, I asked, "Do you know how I can get in touch with the lodges—Black Bar and Paradise?"

"They don't have direct phone service. Just message lines."

"Can they deal with walk-in customers?"

Debbie laughed. "For most of the season, they're booked full months in advance."

"What about right now?"

"You mean on your hiking trip? I can't speak for the lodges, but I'd say your chances of getting in would be pretty good. Their prime season starts at Memorial Day, and after that, there's no way you'd get in. But right now, you'd probably be okay."

Driving back to Grants Pass, I found myself leaning more and more toward the idea of taking a raft down the river. Debbie had quoted me a pretty attractive price for the rent of a fully equipped raft and the shuttle back from the takeout at Foster Bar. I could float to Black Bar Lodge in one day and then make the short hike to Bunker Creek and back the next day. From there, with or without Harvey Walters, it would be a two-day float to Foster Bar with an overnight stay at either Paradise Lodge or the lodge at Half Moon Bar.

My phone started chirping as soon as I got back in the Verizon service area. I pulled over and listened to a voice message from Jerry Midland. He had located the components needed and figured out exactly how to put together the flashlight-tracking device we talked about.

"Just calling to give you the green light on that little project," I told him.

"I'm way ahead of you, Corrigan. I have all the stuff on my bench right now, and I'll start putting it together as soon as I get off the phone. I can get it to the Greyhound terminal in time for the morning bus to Grants Pass. You can pick it up at the bus station on Fifth Street around 1:00 p.m."

"One last thing. Can you weather it—make it so it doesn't look brand-new?"

"No problem."

After I got back to my room, I phoned Debbie.

"My name's Corrigan. We talked earlier today about a raft rental. Can you have one at Grave Creek, ready to go at nine, Thursday morning?"

"Sure. Do you have a permit?"

"I hadn't thought of that. What do I have to do?"

"Phone the Forest Service office at Rand. This time of year, they're sure to have open permits."

We pinned down the remaining details, and then I gave Debbie my credit card number.

"I'll see you for breakfast on Thursday," I said to end the call.

I spent all day Wednesday getting ready for the raft trip. When I phoned the river permit office, it was just as Debbie had predicted. Once the ranger finished lecturing me on the hazards of running the river by myself, she reserved the permit for me.

Next, I went shopping for appropriate clothing for the raft trip, including rain gear, polypro long johns, and fleece, plus shoes that I could wear in the water and on my hike up Bunker Creek. I also found a detailed guidebook for floating the Rogue River, which seemed like a good thing to have along, since my one trip down the river had been more than twenty years before. In the middle of the afternoon, I picked up my parcel from the Greyhound station.

Back at my room, I checked in with Martha, who reported that Bud had gone to Tacoma and was probably with Dr. Gaston at that very moment.

"That's good. Sounds like you have that under control. In the morning, I'm going to set my phone to forward all calls to your number. There won't be any cell service where I'll be for the next few days."

"And where is that?"

"I'm going into the Rogue River Canyon to see if I can find Harvey Walters. I probably won't be back until Monday. I'll cancel the call forwarding when I get back to civilization, probably Sunday afternoon or evening."

"What're you going to do if you find him?"

"Just have a nice, friendly talk and leave him with a little gift."

"What kind of gift?"

"The kind of gift that keeps on giving—a GPS locator."

After finishing the call, I opened the package from Jerry and found the device to be perfect. It was a pocket-sized LED flashlight with a solar collector built into the body. A handwritten note told me how to download the software and activate the tracking. I packed the flashlight into the bag with everything I was taking on the raft, and when I couldn't think of anything else to do, I sat down to study the guidebook.

Chapter 35

ebbie looked at me curiously when she came to take my breakfast order, and it dawned on me that she was focused on my hair, which had been predominantly gray two days before. I offered her a quick explanation.

"I washed out the gray—it was just theater makeup. I was trying to get the senior-citizen discount at Denny's, but it didn't work."

I don't think she believed me, but she laughed—no doubt thinking that I'd done a fresh treatment with Just For Men.

"Your raft is on the trailer, all set to go. Someone will drive you to Grave Creek and get you launched whenever you're ready."

"Can we stop and pick up my permit on the way?" I asked.

"Sure. No problem."

At the Forest Service office, the ranger issued my permit and gave me the compulsory lecture about safety and conservation and then inspected the raft.

"The river is up some," she said. "It shouldn't be a problem—but you need to be extra careful at Blossom Bar."

It was a beautiful morning and promised to be a warm day. While the driver launched the raft, I changed into my river clothes. Debbie had fixed me up with a boxed lunch, which I put in the cooler along with a rack of bottled water and a six-pack of beer. Everything else went into a dry bag that I strapped to the vacant front seat on the raft.

I can't say that I didn't feel apprehensive as I rowed away from the boat ramp at Grave Creek. The first big rapid was just fifty yards away. I'd learned to row when I was a kid on Lake Coeur d'Alene in North Idaho. I had plenty of experience rowing, and on still water, I could make a boat do whatever I wanted it to do. Moving water didn't change the basic rowing technique, but it demanded a whole new skill—timing.

I'd been telling everybody that I'd been down the river before, letting them assume that I'd rowed. But I hadn't. It was a fishing trip organized by some of my friends at Pacific Northern Insurance, and I was a passenger on someone else's raft. And it was twenty years ago. This was a really poor time to have misgivings about what I was doing.

There's no telling what the Galice Resort driver thought as he watched me blunder my way through the first rapid. For my part, I was happy that I'd spent the extra money for a self-bailing raft because I plowed into some pretty big waves that would have left a conventional raft swamped and unmanageable. A hundred yards after the first rapid, I came to the second, an abrupt drop called Grave Creek Falls.

I'd memorized the instructions from the guidebook, so I knew to approach the drop close to the left bank, but I found it unnerving that the rapid was not visible until I was already in it—that's how steeply it dropped. After a moment of extreme intimidation, I was swept cleanly down the chute without taking so much as a splash.

The next falls, two miles ahead, was the real thing. Rainie Falls, I'm told, is sometimes run by thrill seekers and fools. I am neither. There is a narrow chute to the right of the falls that allows boaters the option of going around the big drop, and that was where I elected to go. I went down the chute like a pinball, bouncing off rocks left and right, getting turned around backward, and somehow coming out the bottom intact.

Ahead, the water was fairly smooth. I gulped down a bottle of water and looked ahead in my guidebook to see what I had to do in the next couple of big rapids a mile or two downstream. At Tyee Rapid, I edged my way through along the right bank, earning no style points but staying dry.

The guidebook instructions for Wildcat Rapid were detailed and complex with half a dozen different maneuvers required to dodge various obstacles throughout the quarter-mile rapid. I entered on a row of waves down the center of the right channel and rode the wave train through the entire rapid without spotting any of the rocks, holes, or ledges described in the book.

That was the benefit of the high water. Many of the features that make the Rogue a technically challenging river trip were submerged and not a factor. I found myself in the next series of rapids before I had a chance to consult the book, so I winged it.

As I went downstream, I got disoriented and lost track of where I was relative to the guidebook. There were plenty of photos, but none of them resembled what I was looking at—no doubt the result of the high water. Because I was concerned about possibly of floating past Black Bar Lodge without knowing it, I pulled ashore to figure out where I was.

Eating lunch while studying the map, I finally determined that I was just above the rapid called Slim Pickens, two miles from Black Bar. Going into Slim Pickens down the left side, I failed to see a large submerged boulder that created a small but abrupt waterfall. I went straight over it, and I very nearly flipped when one side of the raft was pushed underwater. Losing my grip on one of the oars, I attempted to control the raft with the other while getting swirled violently in the angry water beneath the pour-over.

When you manage to fill a self-bailing raft with water, you can be sure that you've done something monumentally wrong. I held on for dear life until, for no apparent reason, the raft broke free of the hole and wallowed downstream. I frantically unstrapped the spare oar and got it into the oarlock just as the raft floated into calm water at the foot of the rapid, where I retrieved the oar I'd lost. Without an ounce of cockiness left, I resumed rowing downstream—but with renewed caution.

Several more rapids, concluding with a narrow chute into a flat pool, led me to Big Windy Creek, which I recognized from my earlier trip. Across from Big Windy, Bunker Creek tumbled into the river. I found a landing spot on the right bank and tied up the raft in order to take a look at Bunker Creek.

I scrambled up over the rocks to the Rogue River Trail and walked upstream to the bridge over Bunker Creek. I found backpacker campsites on both sides of the creek and a trail leading up one bank. I wasn't ready to confront Harvey Walters, but it was good to be familiar with the location before returning the next day.

Two big rapids almost back-to-back led into flat water, where I spotted the tie-up for Black Bar Lodge. Iron rings were cemented into the bedrock for tying up boats along the left bank, and a well-beaten path led up from the river. When I got to the lodge, I found that my voice mail hadn't gotten through, but it didn't matter. They were holding space for a good-sized party coming in later but still had a few vacant cabins.

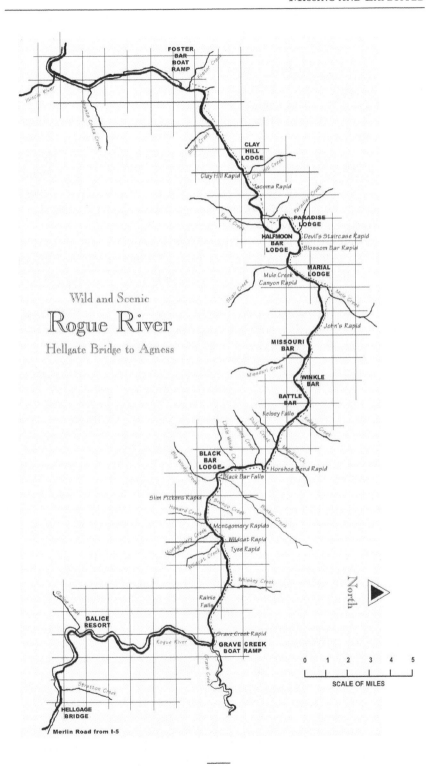

FOSTER
BAR
BOAT
RAMP

Foster Creek

Illinois River

Blanca Godas Creek

Grave Creek

CLAY
HILL
LODGE

Clay Hill Creek

Clay Hill Rapid

Tacoma Rapid

East Creek

Paradise Creek

PARADISE
LODGE

HALFMOON
BAR
LODGE

Devil's Staircase Rapid

Blossom Bar Rapid

MARIAL
LODGE

Mule Creek
Canyon Rapid

Mule Creek

Stair Creek

John's Rapid

Wild and Scenic

Rogue River

Hellgate Bridge to Agness

MISSOURI
BAR

Missouri Creek

WINKLE
BAR

BATTLE
BAR

Kelsey Falls

Kelsey Creek

Dulog Creek

Ditch Creek

Meadow Ck.

Little Windy Ck.

Big Windy Creek

BLACK
BAR
LODGE

Horshoe Bend Rapid

Black Bar Falls

Slim Pickens Rapid

Howard Creek

Bronco Creek

Booten Creek

Montgomery Rapids

Montgomery Creek

Wildcat Rapid

Tyee Rapid

Wildcat Creek

Whiskey Creek

North

Galice Creek

Rainie
Falls

GALICE
RESORT

Rogue River

Grave Creek Rapid

GRAVE CREEK
BOAT RAMP

Grave Creek

Stratton Creek

HELLGAGE
BRIDGE

Merlin Road from I-5

0 1 2 3 4 5

SCALE OF MILES

Black Bar Lodge was built in the 1930s, and it is the oldest and most rustic of the lodges along the Rogue. The lodge building itself is a picturesque log structure with a massive stone fireplace. Guest cabins are set in a row along a gravel path that leads to a bunkhouse for the river guides. After dropping my bag in the cabin assigned to me, I got a beer and settled in front of the fireplace to relax and think about how to approach Walters.

Late in the afternoon, members of the big group started arriving. It was a guided fishing trip using aluminum dories. John, the lodge operator, drove an old Suzuki Samurai down to the boat landing to haul everybody's bags up to the cabins. The lodge became busy with excited people sharing their day's experiences with one another.

Dinner was served family style at big wooden tables, and the food was superb. I was able to glean some information about rapids downstream from one of the guides. In his opinion, the only place I had to watch out for was Blossom Bar.

"It ain't hard to make the pull into the first eddy, but your timing has to be perfect. Miss that eddy, and then you're probably gonna lose your boat."

That's a confidence builder.

Chapter 36

B reakfast was on the table at seven. It had been a chilly night, and the fire in the big fireplace invited me to linger in the lodge, but I had a few things to do in preparation for my day. Back at my cabin, I took my cheap little nylon rucksack outside and rolled it in the dirt. I didn't want it to look brand-new.

I packed three bottles of water and a pint of Jack Daniel's in the pack and put the flashlight/tracker into an outside pocket. When I went back to the kitchen to pick up my sack lunch, the last stragglers in the fishing party were heading down to their boats.

"Where're you hiking today?" John asked.

"I'm going up Bunker Creek to see if I can find someone who's supposedly living up there."

"You mean Harvey?"

Surprised, I said, "Oh. You know him?"

"I don't exactly know him, but every two weeks, we carry supplies across the river to him."

That answered a question that had been bothering me. I figured Walters could probably shoot game, but he'd surely need more than an occasional poached deer to survive.

"Harvey hikes down and rings the bell on the other side of the river. I take his supplies down and row them across. He pays in cash and gives me a list for next time."

"Do you know exactly where I can find him?"

"All I know is that he's somewhere up Bunker Creek."

I packed the lunch into my pack and carried it down to the river. I rowed my raft across and tied up where I could see a trail going up the hillside. On a post at the end of the trail, there was a message board and the bronze bell for signaling the lodge.

It was a strenuous quarter mile up to the main trail, but the walk from there to Bunker Creek was easy. The trail up the creek started out easy but became increasingly steep as I went farther from the river. About a mile up, I came to a fork in the creek and had to decide which branch to follow.

By then, the trail had degenerated into a braided network of wildlife paths, and I could see nothing to indicate which fork of the creek might lead to Harvey Walters. The east fork was bigger, so that was the one I followed. The farther I went, the more difficult the climb became, and I had to stop and rest several times.

I had just finished my lunch and drained my second bottle of water. I was stuffing the food wrappers and empty bottle back into my pack when I heard a faint sound. Straining my ears, I held my breath, hoping to hear it again.

"Chunk. Chunk."

It was barely audible and could easily have been an elk walking in the rocky creek bed.

"Chunk. Chunk. Chunk."

But there was a metallic sound to it—like a shovel digging in gravel. Exactly like a shovel digging in gravel.

Slowly and cautiously, I moved in the direction of the sound, edging up the hillside away from the creek. I'd gone maybe two hundred yards, and the sound was quite clear, when I spotted movement. A shirtless, gray-haired man stood knee-deep in the creek and was shoveling sand and rock into a beat-up old bucket.

Trying to make myself invisible, I ducked down behind some brush. Too bad I hadn't thought to bring a pair of binoculars. The old man, who I assumed to be Harvey Walters, worked slowly, digging in the shallow water of a pool beneath a small waterfall. When the bucket was full, he lugged it to a wooden chute that I hadn't noticed before—a sluice box.

The sluice box was nestled along the edge of the waterfall so that some of the water was diverted into the wooden chute. Walters slowly emptied the contents of the bucket into the top of the sluice box. He then knelt down and started carefully plucking rocks out of the chute. I watched him fill and dump another bucket before I started working my way down the hillside toward him.

"Mr. Walters. Harvey Walters," I called out when I was within fifty yards.

Startled, Walters jerked around and looked in my direction. "You scared the livin' shit out of me! Who the hell are you, and what do you want?"

"I'm looking for Harvey Walters."

"You found him. Now who are you, and why're you here?"

He stood in the creek and watched me scramble the rest of the way down the steep hill. It wasn't until I was ten feet from him that I spotted the lever-action Winchester carbine propped against a boulder at the side of the creek. I felt like I'd just stepped into the nineteenth century.

"My name's Corrigan. I'm from Oregon City."

That didn't bring any particular reaction, and Walters didn't reach for the Winchester, but I still kept my right hand ready to pull my .45 from its SOB holster.

"I'm a private investigator."

His expression hardened. "Investigating what?"

"Is there a place we can sit down and talk?" I asked.

"Yeah, sure."

When he waded out of the stream, I saw that he was wearing black rubber boots—the kind I wore when mucking out the stalls in the cow barn when I was a kid. He sat on a rock and raised his feet, one at a time, to let the water run out. Then he picked up a ragged blue plaid shirt and pulled it on.

"Up there," he said, gesturing upstream.

As he turned and started walking in that direction, he reached for the Winchester. In a fraction of a second, I had my .45 out of its holster and my thumb on the hammer. But Walters didn't even look back. He carried the carbine loosely with his finger outside the trigger guard as he led the way up from the creek bed.

I cautiously followed him to a flat area, where a small shack stood surrounded by piles of rock and assorted relics from a much earlier and larger mining operation. Walters stood the Winchester against an old piece of machinery that I couldn't identify and then turned to sit on a stump by the side of his shack. I eased my .45 back into its holster without letting him see it.

He motioned toward another makeshift chair, so I took off my pack and sat down while he pulled off his boots. Leaning back against the side of the cabin, he propped his bare feet up on an overturned bucket.

"Now, what's so important that you'd come all the way up here?"

Walters was playing it pretty cool, acting unconcerned about my unexpected appearance at his hideout. Even before starting up here, I'd reached the conclusion that my best approach would be to work around the edges of the real issue and try to get him to say something incriminating. I used the same line I'd used on Del.

"A friend of mine recently bought the property where your boat repair shop used to be. He discovered evidence of a large marijuana farm—and the remains of two people."

I watched carefully for a twitch or some sign of discomfort, but there was nothing.

"Remains? You mean dead bodies?"

"That's right—skeletal. Been in the ground for years. So I'm trying to find out who was growing the pot, and I'm running out of ideas. I'm hoping that you might have seen something that'll help."

"Well, there was always dopers out there. You could smell 'em smoking that shit all day long."

"Any idea who they were?"

"Hell, I never had anything to do with 'em. Always on drugs and crazy as loons."

"Did they camp out up there or what?"

"Some of 'em camped out. They were totally paranoid about somebody stealing their pot. I think they had someone on guard, day and night."

"Were they armed?"

"To the teeth. Every kind of weapon you could imagine. Doesn't surprise me a bit that they killed someone."

Professional interrogators call this tactic transference. He was attempting to deflect suspicion from himself to these unnamed "dopers" while portraying himself as a victim.

"Did they have access to the building you leased?"

"Hell, they got inside and set fire to the *big* building! I could never use it again after that."

"I was thinking of the smaller building—the old cedar mill."

"Bastards used to break into my shop and steal anything they could carry. I had to keep my tools in my truck and take 'em home every night."

"There is some evidence that one of the crimes may have taken place inside that building."

"Must've been after I moved out. That's when the whole place was took over by the dopers."

"Could anything have happened in there while you were still in business?'

"No. Well, not while I was around. But I wasn't there around the clock, you know."

"What was inside the part of the building that was added on—the part that faced the river?"

"Hell if I know. The kid told me that it was polluted and I shouldn't go in there."

"The kid?"

"Yeah. The snot-nosed grandson of the old fart who owned the place."

"Do you think someone could have been held prisoner in there?"

172

Walters looked startled. "Well, I don't see how. The place was contaminated."

"Contaminated by what?"

"Some preservative shit that they used to treat the shingles. Anyway, there was big padlocks on the doors, and nobody ever went in there."

I pressed. "Did you ever hear noise from in there?"

"No! I told you, nobody ever went in there," he insisted.

"Well, here's the deal. We found the name of a missing person carved in a beam from that room."

"I don't know nothing about that."

It didn't sound like a denial of guilt. It sounded like a statement of fact. I remembered Michael Wheeler once having said that sociopaths are convincing liars because they have no conscience. I reached into my pack and pulled out the Jack Daniel's and, in the process, dropped the magic flashlight to the ground next to the stump I sat on. I pretended to take a much bigger gulp than the little sip I actually swallowed, and then I offered the bottle to Walters.

"How the hell did you know where to find me?" he finally asked.

I laughed. "It wasn't easy."

"But how?"

"I impersonated your brother. If your friend down in Merlin tells you he talked with your brother, he didn't. It was me. Sorry. I didn't figure he'd say anything to just anybody."

We again traded drinks from the bottle.

"You know my brother?" he asked.

"Del? Yeah. I met him."

"How's he doing? Still fishing for crabs?"

"Not anymore. He's in San Francisco. Works at Alcatraz."

"Alcatraz! What the hell's he do there?"

"Salesman. In the gift shop. Says it beats the hell out of being a greeter at Walmart."

Walters shook his head. We talked until the whiskey was gone. It was midafternoon, and I had to get back down to Black Bar. I'd accomplished what I'd wanted to do. I'd planted the tracking device where he was sure to find it, and I'd put him on notice. If he tried to run, it would be as good as a confession—not in court but in my mind, anyway.

On my way back down Bunker Creek, I pondered what I'd learned—most notably that Harvey Walters was cleverer than I'd anticipated. All his answers were plausible while shifting the blame to the pot farmers. Nothing he told me was inconsistent with the known facts.

Something came back to me—a thought I'd had while I was waiting for Del to show up at Jack's Bar. Kidnapping, imprisonment, sex abuse, and murder were signs of deep psychosis. Genuine psychotics do not cure themselves. How was Harvey able to put all that aside and become a hermit?

Or would I discover that he had adapted? Lacking a place to hold women captive, was he practicing a more conventional form of serial murder? Were there unsolved sex murders in the Grants Pass area? These were question I would have to answer.

May 17 Saturday

Chapter 37

After breakfast, I carried my things down to the raft. I had about fifteen miles to float that day, and despite what the guide had told me—that the only rapid of concern would be Blossom Bar—my guidebook showed dozens of rapids I'd have to run before even getting to Blossom Bar.

But by keeping the guidebook handy and reading ahead about the next two or three rapids, I was able to be prepared for what I was approaching and avoid the major hazards. The rapids in the Kelsey Canyon area were particularly rough, but I was fortunate to have a fisherman in a dory out in front of me, so I simply followed his line.

There was a five-mile stretch of easy water after Kelsey Canyon before I ran into another cluster of tricky rapids. Most of them, because of the high water, bore little resemblance to what was described in the book. Still, I tried to position my raft as the book recommended and in so doing managed to avoid obstacles I couldn't see.

Even after twenty years, Mule Creek was easy to recognize. I stopped and ate lunch on the beach next to the mouth of the creek while reading ahead about Mule Creek Canyon. The memory of that stretch of river was increasingly intimidating as I got closer to the relentless series of rapids that lead into the canyon.

Shortly after leaving my lunch stop, I entered a stretch of fast water that quickly increased in speed and gradient. Once again, I was grateful that I was rowing a self-bailing raft because there was no time to bail. Two boulders in the river ahead marked the entry to the canyon, which in places is too narrow to even put out the oars.

The tension as I entered the first chute was almost paralyzing, but I focused on what I could see. Where the river piled into the left wall, I turned the raft and pulled to the right. Then, looking ahead and seeing the river piling into the right wall, I pivoted again and pulled the other way.

That continued as the river ricocheted back and forth between the canyon walls. After the first couple of turns, I realized I was having fun.

My experience in Mule Creek Canyon built up my confidence, so when I recognized Blossom Bar Rapid ahead, I knew what I had to do. Still, I wanted to see it for myself, so I pulled over to the right bank and climbed up over the boulders until I reached a place where I could see the entire rapid. A full-page series of photos in the guidebook showed exactly what I had to do, and that helped me see the critical places.

Feeling very uneasy, I rowed to the extreme left side of the river. Where the current started accelerating and dropping into the rapid, I turned the raft to face the left bank and pulled hard into the tight eddy that would carry me past the main hazard, an area called the Picket Fence. I brushed against the rock as I turned the raft around to face the center chute.

The guide and the guidebook had both said that once in the center chute, I would be in the clear. There was still a lot of rough water ahead, but the critical part was behind me. Maybe I relaxed too much. As I approached a Volkswagen-sized boulder, I experienced a moment of indecision. The book said I should go left, but there didn't seem to be time. I started right, only to see that a boulder blocked my path.

Going broadside against the Volkswagen rock, I had to drop the oars and shift my weight to keep from flipping. Momentarily pinned against the rock, I watched both oars pop out of the oarlocks and disappear downstream. I clawed at the rock and managed to pull myself and the raft around the left side, back into the current. I unstrapped the spare oar—there was only one—and attempted to control the raft using a nine-foot oar as a paddle.

I bounced off one rock and then another but made it into the eddy at the bottom of the rapid. I spotted one of my oars floating in the middle of the eddy and paddled frantically to get to it. But before I could catch up with it, I was pulled into the next rapid, something called Devil's Staircase.

Out of control, spinning around and around, I bounced down the first part of the rapid. I was washed up against a wall on the right bank and again was nearly flipped. But as I slipped downstream, one of my lost oars surfaced right next to the raft. I leaned over and pulled it aboard. By the time I got both oars into the oarlocks and regained control of the raft, I was out of the rapid.

I'd cut my hand somewhere in the process, so I pulled a Band-Aid out of the first aid kit that came with the raft. It wouldn't stick on my wet skin, and I had to toss it aside and open another. I drifted past Paradise Creek Falls, blowing on my hand in a futile attempt to get it dry enough for the Band-Aid.

Just as I got the Band-Aid to stick, I started into another riffle. It wasn't much of a rapid, but I'd entered it in the wrong place and had some hard rowing to do to get on track to land at Paradise Lodge just ahead. That's when I spotted my other lost oar. I went chasing the oar and lost my chance to land at Paradise Lodge.

Fortunately, the route I'd taken to recover the lost oar led me to the landing for Half Moon Bar Lodge on the opposite side of the river from Paradise. Out of breath and bleeding again where I'd already lost the Band-Aid, I hopped ashore and tied up the raft. I sat on the beach and gulped down a bottle of water.

The ten miles from Half Moon Bar to my takeout at Foster Bar featured only two significant rapids. I rowed downstream through a couple of long flat stretches and got to Foster Bar at twelve thirty. I ate my lunch and waited for the van from Galice Resort, which arrived at two. It took three hours to get back to Galice on a road that led right past Curt Hubbard's Golden Goose Mine.

"Well, you survived!" Debbie said cheerfully. "That's a promising sign. How was the trip?"

"It went well. I couldn't have done it without your help, though."

"No problems with the river?"

"A few but nothing big. You think one of your burgers will hold me until I get back home?"

"Sure. And it's on me. You're the best customer I've had all week."

The drive home took five hours, and I pulled in an hour before midnight. DC was so happy to see me that he went into a purring, drooling episode that monopolized my time for about half an hour. I postponed the dreaded task of going through my messages and went to bed.

May
Monday 19

Chapter 38

My first order of business was to make sure that Harvey Walters's GPS tracker was doing its job. I logged on and was at first discouraged to see that the planted flashlight/tracker hadn't moved. But when I zoomed in, I was able to see that it had moved several times—first to a place about twelve feet from where I'd dropped it. That meant that Walters had picked it up and moved it, probably to a windowsill in his cabin.

There were two additional movements, one at 2:30 a.m. on Saturday and the other at 3:45 a.m. on Sunday. Both went about ten yards southwest from the cabin and back. Now I knew where Walters's outhouse was located. But mainly I knew that he was using his gift.

I set the software to immediately notify me if Walters carried the tracker more than half a mile, and then I leaned back in my chair and contemplated all the what-ifs. Chances were, if Walters was abandoning his hideout and going on the run, he'd take key possessions along. I had to trust that he'd consider the handy little flashlight worth carrying, and if he did, I'd be notified.

The question was what would happen next. As far as I knew, Walters did not have any kind of vehicle in Merlin or Galice. His first act in making a getaway would have to be acquiring some means of transportation. That probably meant selling some gold and buying a car—stealing one would put the law on his tail, and he'd know better than to do that. This would give me time to either notify local law enforcement or drive to Merlin and intercept him.

On the other hand, if he were making one of his occasional trips to Merlin, he probably would leave the flashlight behind. The only indication I'd have would be that the tracker would remain stationary for a few days.

I knew from my conversations with James Oakland and Curt Hubbard that it had been a few months since Walters had made a trip to town, so one might guess that he was due. Knowing that he got his supplies from Black Bar Lodge, I concluded that his purpose in going to town was to sell gold for cash to pay for supplies.

A trip to town and back would take at least two days and probably three, since he'd have to hitch rides wherever he needed to go. But if the tracker ever went beyond three or four days without moving, I'd have to assume that something was wrong, and for that I had no good plan. All I could do would be to drive back to Merlin and hope to track him down through Hubbard.

I went next to the task I'd been putting off. When I opened my e-mail, I found that my inbox was overflowing, but once I finished deleting all the spam, the number of messages was manageable. Not unexpectedly, there was nothing back yet from the forensics lab and nothing new from the sheriff's office.

For the next hour, I plowed through the messages, some of which were two weeks old. When Martha came in, I took a break and let her bring me up to date on what had taken place while I was gone.

"Well, we know how Dr. Gaston's insurance scam works. Bud went in last week and showed the doctor his ganglion cyst without making any suggestion that it might be job related. But the patient information form that he had Bud fill out asked his occupation. The doctor spotted that and started asking a bunch of questions about tasks involving repetitive motion.

"Bud played it just right, at first saying there were none and then coming back with an offhand comment about turning a screwdriver. That's all it took to launch Dr. Gaston. For half an hour, he had Bud demonstrating things he did on the job, and in the end, he declared that not only was the ganglion cyst caused by repetitive motion but also that Bud had the early symptoms of carpal tunnel syndrome."

I said, "I can see where this is going. He'll treat the cyst but bill for that *and* carpal tunnel treatment."

"It's even better than that. He suggested that Bud might want to take a couple of weeks off work to recover. Bud said he didn't have enough sick leave for that, and the doctor said, 'No problem, I can get workers' comp to pay for that.' As soon as Bud agreed to that, the doctor gave him a form to sign, saying that it was painful to work."

"How's the doctor make money on that?"

"Return visits. He's going to have Bud phone in a 'progress check' every couple of days while he's off work. Based on past cases, Dakota Mutual thinks that every time Bud phones in, the doctor will bill for an office call. They're expecting him to keep Bud off work for six or eight weeks."

"And Bud got the whole visit on video?"

"Sure did. He took off his watch so that the doctor could diagnose his carpal tunnel syndrome, so the video is stable and clear. He'll wear the watch and try to get video when he goes back this week for the treatment."

Martha then handed me a page of notes from the messages left on my voice mail while I was in the Rogue River canyon. Near the bottom of the page, there was a message to call Tyler Marquam in Alpena, Michigan. It took a second to register.

He was the father of Alyssa Marquam, the girl kidnapped from Beacon Rock State Park in the Columbia Gorge in 1993. When I'd attempted to call them early in the month, the Marquams had been with a church group smuggling Bibles into China.

I checked my watch. It would be about noon in Michigan.

"Mr. Marquam, my name is Corrigan. I'm a private investigator in Oregon City, Oregon."

"Hold on."

There was a pause, and I could tell the Marquam was moving to a different room.

"Okay," he said after a few moments. "I didn't want my wife to hear this. It's been very hard on her. I'm sure you understand. My mother-in-law said you have something you want to tell me about our daughter, Alyssa."

"The first thing I want to say is that whether good or bad, this is a long shot. The odds are very slim that your daughter is actually any part of this."

"Go ahead."

"Some evidence has been recently uncovered that another girl, abducted six years before Alyssa, may have been held captive and was still alive twelve years later. A short distance from where we think that happened, remains of a twenty-year-old girl were discovered. I'm trying to identify the girl."

"Damn! You don't pull your punches."

"You sound like you can take a punch."

"This isn't easy, you know."

"Yes. I know. But—"

"That's okay. We need to know, one way or the other. If it's Alyssa, at least we'll know. I'm guessing you want a DNA sample."

"That's right. I can have a forensics lab sent you a kit. It's pretty easy—all we need is a saliva sample."

Tyler gave me the address of his office because he didn't want his wife to know about it until or unless there was a positive match.

May
Thursday 22

Chapter 39

I heard tires crunching on the gravel out front. I put my notes aside and went to the door, where I found Giles Svensen coming up the steps.

He took note of my well-cluttered desk, "Am I interrupting anything important?"

"What's up?" I asked.

"I found something you might like. I was tearing some old cabinetry out of the office in my warehouse building, and I found this in an envelope. It looked like it'd slipped down behind the cabinet."

He handed me what was obviously a very old photograph."

"What am I looking at?"

"Turn it over," Giles suggested.

Written in ink that had turned brown with age was the inscription, "Railroad Construction Camp 1877."

"Where is this?" I asked.

"It's my place. There in the upper right, where those shacks are—that's where my warehouse building is. See where the railroad tracks curve to the right?"

"Interesting but—"

"Now look at the building in the lower right. I'm pretty sure that's the original building—the one that they added onto when they built the mill."

I took a closer look at the photo.

"That can't be it. The proportions aren't right. I've seen the old foundation. It's long and narrow. This building is too wide."

"Maybe. It's hard to tell for sure, but look at that railroad siding next to the building. It stops right there. It doesn't go past the building."

Feeling dense for not seeing his point, I said, "So?"

"There's a loading dock there. You can kind of see it at the corner. The roof covered the loading dock, but the building itself was only half the width of the roof."

Then I could see it. If the loading dock were removed, the remainder of the structure would indeed have the long, narrow proportions of the old foundation next to the mill slab.

"It was probably where they stored the tools and supplies for building the railroad," Giles explained. "They'd roll a flatcar up next to the dock, load up, and then head down the line to the construction site."

I said, "You know, if they stored rail plates and spikes in there, it might explain why the building was so overbuilt with those big timbers. All that steel is heavy."

"One thing I can't figure out is the clothesline. Why would you hang your laundry from the equipment shed?" Giles asked.

I studied the photo for a minute before speculating, "Didn't Captain Alan tell us that Chinese laborers lived there? It'd be *their* laundry."

"They wouldn't be living in the equipment shed. I still don't understand why the clothesline is there."

I speculated, "The little shack on the other end of the clothesline— maybe it's not an outhouse. It could be a pump house. That'd be where they got the water for doing the laundry. The only reason the clothesline is attached to the storage building is that it was convenient."

"I guess I can buy that."

But then another idea came into my head. The tunnels. They led to the end of the building where the clothesline was attached. And suddenly it made sense.

"Well, I'll be damned! *I'll be damned!* Giles, have you tried digging inside the old foundation walls?"

"No. Why would I do that?"

"Because there might have been a *basement* under the storage building. There had to be! *That's* where the Chinese laborers were hidden."

"How do you figure?"

"They had to keep the men hidden. That was the reason for the tunnels, so it stands to reason that there would be a dormitory concealed beneath the equipment shed."

"I suppose that makes sense. But what does—"

"Could old man Walters have found a better place to hide Brittany Harlan for twelve years?"

"Oh, sweet Jesus!"

"I need to do some digging. And I mean today," I told him.

"Fine with me," Giles said. "I'm on my way to Spokane. I won't be back 'til next week. But go ahead and dig it out if that's what you need to do.

It wasn't yet noon, so I loaded a pick and shovel into the back of my Yukon. As an afterthought, I grabbed an eight-foot ladder, thinking that I might want to get out of whatever hole I might dig. At Svensen's place, I parked on the slab where the mill building had been.

In the distance, I could hear the heavy equipment still working to repair the slide damaged highway while I carried my pick and shovel over to the corner of the old foundation. I chose to start digging next to the west wall of the foundation. Once I broke through the sod on the surface, I found the digging to be pretty easy.

After two hours, I'd dug a trench about six feet long and six feet deep, and that was enough to confirm what I had guessed in looking at the old photo. What's more, at the north end of my trench, I found the top of a brick-arched doorway through the north wall. I was sure it would prove to be the entrance to one of the tunnels that Alan had described.

This conclusively proved that there had been a cellar of some kind under the equipment shed. I phoned Kaylin Beatty and asked her if she could contact Lucky about doing some more backhoe work. Five minutes later my phone rang.

"Are you up for doing some digging this weekend?" I asked.

"Sure, what do you need?"

"Remember that foundation you uncovered when you cleared the slab up at Svensen's place? Well, it's actually a basement, and I need it dug out—as soon as possible."

"How deep is it?"

"I don't know yet, but based on what I can see, I'd guess ten or twelve feet. When are you available?"

"I could do it anytime Saturday, providing you can get me a backhoe."

"Let's plan on nine. I'll call you back if I can't get the equipment, otherwise I'll see you then."

My next call went to the equipment rental company and arranged to have a backhoe delivered first thing Saturday morning. Then I called the day labor center and asked if Lexi and Kasandra were interested in working on Saturday.

Once all the arrangements were made, I resumed digging—continuing the trench until I reached the northeast corner of the foundation wall, where Alan had described stairs leading down to the tunnels entrances. It was early evening when hunger finally overwhelmed me. By then I'd dug deep enough to reveal paint on the north wall that showed clearly where the stairway had been.

I went back on Friday to continue the excavation. I found the top of another brick arch, probably the entry to the other tunnel, and also found evidence along the west wall of there having once been partitions within the cellar space, forming five rooms in addition to the stairwell.

Chapter 40

Kevin arrived at eight thirty, and I led him over to where I'd been digging and explained what I needed. Lexi and Kasandra showed up right behind the equipment trailer with the backhoe. I set the girls to work in the stairwell area while Kevin unloaded the backhoe. With my blistered hands and aching back, I assigned myself to a supervisory role.

Kevin set up next to the southwest corner of the old foundation wall. Once he had the stabilizers set, he started scraping the sod off the surface. As I had found the day before, once the surface was broken, the fill underneath was loose and easy to dig. When the hole was about eight feet deep, Kevin started finding chunks of concrete.

I climbed down into the hole to get a closer look. There were two distinctly different kinds of concrete. Some were the heavily weathered old concrete broken from the top of the original foundation; but others were fragments of concrete block with mortar and plastic foam sticking to them. Uncertain what that might mean, I poked around with a shovel to see what else might be in the bottom of the hole.

Something caught my eye, and when I took a closer look, it turned out to be a broken piece of white porcelain china, identifiable as part of a toilet tank. That was not something that could have been part of the nineteenth-century construction. Taken together with the modern concrete, it suggested that the old cellar dormitory had been remodeled, and I had a very bad feeling about the purpose of the update.

"We're going to have to dig this out by hand from here down," I told Kevin. "Can you move over and excavate the whole thing down to this depth?"

"Sure, no problem."

While Kevin moved the backhoe to his right, I dug down through the debris in the bottom of the pit, finding more pieces of the toilet and a lot more pieces of concrete. About eighteen inches down, I reached the floor slab. I paused to consider whether or not I should call the sheriff's office. I believed that this was a crime scene, and in that regard, it should be excavated by the authorities.

On the other hand, there was no real evidence that a crime had been committed here. All I had so far was Brittany Harlan's name scratched into a piece of wood, and the Canby police had already declared that to be the work of a prankster. But the simple truth of the matter was that I didn't *want* to call the authorities. I didn't believe they could find anything I couldn't, and I could get this done a lot sooner than they could.

I figured I could defend my decision to do the excavation myself, so I kept digging. I was too deep in the pit to throw my diggings out of the hole, so I merely heaped them in one corner. When I was about eight feet from the end wall, my shovel struck something solid. A few minutes of careful digging revealed the broken remains of a partition wall extending about a foot above the floor slab.

At that point, I called Lexi and Kasandra over to help while Kevin continued excavating the rest of the cellar down to the debris layer.

"What we seem to have here is a small room built within the original cellar walls," I explained to the girls. "I'd like to clear it out—all the way down to the slab."

"We have to put all this stuff someplace," Kasandra complained.

"For now, let's just pile it over on the part that Kevin has already dug out. We can figure out what to do with it later."

By the time we had the floor completely uncovered, Kevin had finished digging the full length of the cellar down to the two-foot level. What we found confirmed my worst fears. The remains of the partition walls showed that there had been a room—or cell—that was eight feet square. The doorway to the cell led to a narrow hallway that ran along the east side of the cellar.

In the northwest corner of the cell, there were two drain pipes—one for a toilet and one for a sink. The pipes were ABS plastic, clearly proving that they were of modern construction. I asked myself if there was any possible innocent explanation for the existence of the cell. Could it have been something as innocuous as a restroom for the mill workers?

Again I paused to consider calling the sheriff. It would be humiliating to raise the alarm only to find that there was an innocent purpose for the little room. The only way to be sure was to keep digging. I climbed out of the pit and waved to Kevin.

"If a crime took place here, it is possible that there is evidence in what we're digging out of the bottom layer," I explained. "I don't want to mix it with what you've already excavated."

Kevin pointed to the opposite side of the pit and suggested, "I could pile it over there on the slab."

"That's what I had in mind. The other thing I was thinking was that we should handle the debris kind of gently so that we don't break it up any more than it already is."

"Digging with the backhoe, I can't guarantee that things won't get broken."

"Yeah, what we'll have to do is shovel it by hand into your bucket, and then you can take it up and pile it off to the side."

"Not the fastest way to do the job," he pointed out.

"No, but it's the way it has to be done."

Over the next six hours, we exposed three more identical cells. By four thirty, when the equipment rental company arrived to pick up the backhoe, we'd excavated the entire cellar down to the slab. Kasandra took a tape measure down and called the dimensions up to me while I drew a floor plan.

Everything about the cellar reeked of evil. At the north end of the cellar, we found what looked like a utility room next to the stairwell. In one corner, I could make out a circular rust stain where a water heater had been. Next to the west tunnel entrance, there was a black pipe for natural gas next to a rectangular pattern where there may have been a furnace.

Next to the furnace, it appeared that there had been something like a kitchen counter. Plumbing in the floor at one end suggested that there had been a sink there. Most of the floor appeared to be the original nineteenth-century slab, but there was a strip of newer concrete covering a utility trench that carried the newer plumbing.

From the utility room, a hallway ran the length of the cellar, providing access to the four cells, the walls of which had been eight inches thick. And the builder had not been content with simple concrete block construction. He had filled the blocks with polyurethane foam, presumably to prevent sound from penetrating the walls. The tiny, dungeonlike rooms reminded me of the isolation cells in D Block at Alcatraz.

The next day, I created a scale drawing of the dungeon, all the while wondering how Harvey Walters had found the money to undertake such a project. It had to have come from the proceeds of his wife's life insurance. In the afternoon, I went back out to take a closer look at the material dug from the bottom of the cellar.

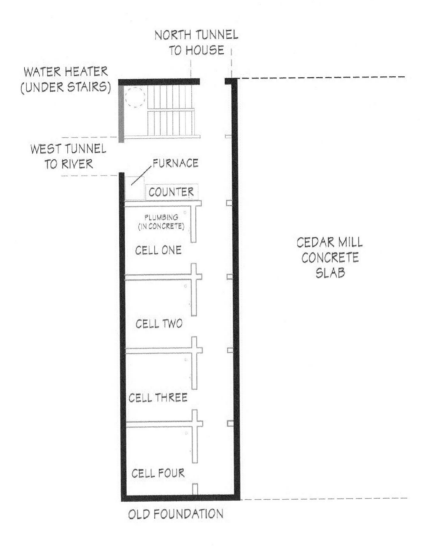

I worked my way through the piles of debris that Kevin had stacked on the slab, looking for anything that would tell a story. Obviously, with his boat business faltering, Walters had removed Sunny and any other women still alive and then attempted to destroy the evidence.

It appeared that he'd removed any furnishings, along with the doors and fixtures, before breaking down the concrete walls. I could only imagine what the building's owner thought when he found all of that rubble in the old cellar after Walters moved out.

When Douglas Roy finally demolished the building, he'd bulldozed the top of the foundation wall into the pit on top of the wreckage that Walters left behind. Some of the chunks of old concrete were fairly large, and a few still showed where the heavy beams had been. It occurred to me that it might be possible to match the wood grain cast into the concrete with the ends of Brittany's beam. That would prove conclusively where the beam had come from, not that I had any doubt.

May
26
Monday

Chapter 41

The morning news revealed the identity of the John Doe found at the homeless camp after the landslide. Twenty-six-year-old Keith Heppner lived alone but was reported missing in August 1984 after failing to show up at work for several days. There was no record that there had been any kind of investigation. There had been indications that he had skipped town to dodge creditors.

Those basic facts might support Michael Wheeler's theory that the dead man had been a resident at the homeless camp—assuming the camp had been there at the time. The fact was I didn't know how long the camp had been there.

But there was one man who was sure to know—Captain Alan. Unfortunately, I didn't know where Alan was. He'd been tied up at my dock when I left for San Francisco, but he was gone by the time I returned. He could be anyplace on the river.

My boat was still in the garage. I blamed that on the crappy weather and high water, but the truth was that in Kim's absence, I just hadn't been motivated to launch the boat. Besides, whatever time I might have had for boating was consumed by my desperate search for the key to bringing Kim back.

Maybe I was just looking for an excuse to do something that might make things seem normal. It really wasn't important when the homeless camp was built. But I was weary. I couldn't remember the last time I'd given myself a day off. I called Martha.

"Do you know how to tow a trailer?" I asked.

"I can do it as long as I don't have to back up," she said.

"That's good enough. I need to get my boat launched. Can you tow the trailer back here? I can get back by boat before you get back with the trailer. You'll never have to back it up."

I uncovered the boat and checked all the equipment before hitching up. We stopped at the gas station and filled the fuel tank on the way to the West Linn boat ramp. The engine fired on the first try, and I easily beat Martha back to Canemah.

Once I had the trailer parked, I threw some snacks and a couple of beers into a cooler and went back down to my boat. There was something about sitting in the driver's seat of my little Tigershark that just made me feel good. At least, that's the way things *should* have been. But without Kim, it was just a hollow parody of how it should have been.

I took off upriver, keeping my eyes open for *Misty Rose*. I figured Alan would be needing some income to pay for the repairs on his boat, so there was a good chance I'd find him salvaging logs, building a dock, or cutting trees somewhere along the riverbank. These were typical of the things he did when he needed money.

In the four weeks since our mad dash upriver to the landslide, the water level had dropped back to normal, and the river looked nothing like it had when I'd last been on it. As I approached the site of the landslide, I pulled back the throttle and looked up to where the homeless camp had been. A broad swath of bare earth extended all the way down the hillside, intersected only by the repaired highway and railroad.

The big cottonwood that had pinned Bud to the ground was prominent just to the left of the slide as I looked up at it. Most of the debris that had flowed into the river had been washed away, and the riverbank at that point consisted of a mud cliff.

I pushed the throttle forward and accelerated up toward Wattles Corner. It was a holiday, but there was surprisingly little traffic on the river. I ran at full speed up past Hebb Park and beyond. I had to slow down and wait for the Canby Ferry to cross the river. After the ferry passed, I resumed cruising speed, and that's when I spotted a peculiar sight in the distance upriver.

There was a small boat towing an old-fashioned black rubber raft downriver toward the washed-out boat ramp at Molalla River State Park. But what caught my eye was that the raft carried two outhouses. As I approached, I was surprised to see Captain Alan and Slalom Jim in the towboat and Kaylin's friend Kurt Riley on the raft with the outhouses. I looped around and pulled up beside the little green towboat.

"This your idea of a houseboat?" I asked.

Jim said, "Yeah. It's an *out*house boat."

"Salvage project," Kurt explained.

When they pulled up at the broken remains of the boat ramp, which was destroyed in one of the big floods, I beached my boat off to the side.

Together, we unloaded the outhouses from the raft onto the old boat ramp. They were fiberglass chemical toilets that appeared to be in good shape but were thickly caked with mud.

"We salvaged these up along the Pudding River. They probably were washed down from a farm somewhere upstream in the floodwater last year," Alan explained. "We brought the raft so that we could float them down to here."

Waiting for an opportunity to ask Alan about the homeless camp, I sat back and watched as he and Jim set up the water pump we'd used to raise *Misty Rose*. With that, they started hosing the mud off the outhouses.

"I see what you're doing!" came a voice from above us. "That's disgusting!"

I looked up to see man wearing Spandex bicycle shorts waving his cell phone and shouting at us over the roar of the water pump motor. Jim shut down the pump to find out what the ruckus was all about.

"I swim in that river!" screamed the indignant bicyclist.

Raising his hands in a "What the hell?" gesture, Jim said, "I piss in this river. So what?"

I didn't calculate that to be the most diplomatic response he could have given. It was clear to me that Mr. Spandex thought they were emptying the outhouses into the river.

Kurt said, "We're just washing off mud. It's the stuff riverbeds are made of."

But that explanation was too late. Spandex Man was in a lather and had become deaf to any rational conversation.

"I'm calling the sheriff! You guys are in big trouble!"

About then, he must have realized he was badly outnumbered, and he disappeared somewhere up beyond the parking lot. Jim backed a trailer down next to the boat ramp, and I helped load the two outhouses onto it. Jim and Alan were tying them down, and Kurt was deflating his raft when the Clackamas County Sheriff's cruiser pulled into the parking lot.

"We had a report that someone was emptying chemical toilets into the river," one of the deputies said as he approached.

"That's not what we were doing. We just salvaged them out of the Pudding River," Jim said.

Alan added, "They probably were carried into the river by the flood last year."

"We were just hosing off the mud," Jim said.

One of the deputies walked around the trailer studying the old outhouses.

"My keen powers of observation tell me that these outhouses haven't been used in some considerable period of time," he said with mock gravity.

After the deputies left, Jim and Kurt got busy loading the green boat onto its trailer, and I took the opportunity to ask Alan if he knew when the homeless camp was built.

"Oh hell. It's hard to say. I mean, there's been homeless camps on and off for I don't know how long—only they used to be called Hoovervilles or hobo towns. I'll bet even the Indians had homeless camps there."

I don't know where he'd have gone from there if I hadn't interrupted. "I'm just talking about the latest camp."

"Well, I guess I first noticed it in the midnineties. Maybe '96 or '97."

"So you don't think it was there in '84?" I asked.

"I can't say for sure. I guess it *could've* been, but I think I'd have noticed it. I go by there a lot."

As I motored back downriver, I contemplated what Alan's observation might have meant. If there had been no homeless camp there when Keith Heppner vanished from Canby, what was he doing there? The first thought I had was that he might have been involved in illegal agriculture. Had the pot farm been there thirty years ago?

Heppner had been killed by a bullet in the back of the head. That was typical of executions for reasons associated with the drug trade. None of these things suggested that his death could be connected in any way with Sunny, who had died over twenty years later. It had to be just a coincidence that they were buried ninety feet from each other.

June 3 Tuesday

Chapter 42

A month to the day after collecting the blood samples from Brittany's beam, I received a FedEx envelope from the DNA lab in Seattle. Hoping to find a match between Roger Harlan's DNA and the blood samples, I tore open the envelope and pulled out two sheets of paper, each containing a profile. They were from Roger Harlan and Olivia Dilley—but not from the blood.

I was disappointed but not surprised. It takes more time to develop a profile from a tiny blood sample than from fresh saliva samples. A match between the blood and Roger Harlan would have proved my theory and made the case for comparing the other profiles with Sunny's. Without that, I had to consider what it would take to get the sheriff's office to order the comparison.

I had Michael Wheeler's cell phone number, and I knew he was in line to become the head of the Homicide and Violent Crimes Unit—HVCU— now that Larry Jamieson's position as Clackamas County Sheriff had been made official in the May election. Calling Wheeler directly was a lot more efficient than trying to go through the normal channels.

"Make it quick, Corrigan. I have a meeting in two minutes," Wheeler said.

"I got the profiles back on the samples from a couple of the people I think might be the parents of the Jane Doe. I'd like your folks to make the comparison."

"Can we talk about this later? I really have—"

"You remember when I told you about the beam with Brittany Harlan's name on it?" I asked him.

"Sure, what about it?"

"We've been excavating the old cellar where I think the beam came from. I believe we've uncovered a major crime scene."

"Tell me what you have."

"There used to be an old building there—originally built during the railroad construction era in the nineteenth century. We excavated the foundation and found a basement, and in it we found what appears to be a row of prison cells in a concealed bunker."

"And you're thinking—"

"What I'm thinking is pretty perverted. The cells were built in modern times—plastic plumbing and concrete blocks. I think they were built to house kidnapped girls—and one of those cells was Brittany Harlan's. Another might have held your Jane Doe."

Wheeler let out a long, low whistle. "Okay, you have my attention. Let me call you back after this meeting."

For the next hour, I sat nervously waiting for that call. I couldn't find the focus necessary to do any constructive work, so I went back and reviewed all my notes on the Brittany Harlan–Harvey Walters investigation. When the call finally came, we agreed to meet at Svensen's place in half an hour.

I phoned Svensen while I drove up Highway 99 and told him that he was about to have visitors.

"You know, I looked into that hole you dug. I've been wondering when you'd get someone out here to take a look."

Svensen met me in the parking area next to his Studebaker museum. After removing the lock and chain, he rolled the big door open. He switched on the lights to give the mercury-vapor bulbs time to warm up and come to full brightness before Wheeler arrived.

While we waited, Giles showed me the Studebaker he brought back from his trip to Spokane last month. It was a 1963 Gran Turismo in nice unrestored condition, showing only eighty-five thousand miles on the odometer.

"The original owner died last year, and his daughter put the car up for sale. She turned down a couple of offers because the buyers said they wanted to make it into a hot-rod. She liked the idea of putting it in a museum, so she gave me a good price."

Michael Wheeler drove down off the highway, and I recognized Carrie Silverton in the passenger seat. Silverton was part of the CSI team who had recovered the evidence from the El Camino that Kim pulled out of the Willamette River two years before.

"First, let me show you what got this whole thing started," I suggested.

I led Wheeler and Silverton over to the corner of the old warehouse where the beam was stored. Silverton knelt down and studied the Brittany Harlan inscription with a magnifying glass, making no comment.

"What are the yellow tags?" Wheeler asked.

"That's where the blood samples were taken for DNA profiling," I said.

"What do you think, Carrie?"

"There definitely are chips of glass in the inscription. I'm sure that we'll be able to recover enough for analysis."

"Let's see what else we have before we call the forensics team," Wheeler said.

I pulled out a tape measure and put it alongside the beam, showing Wheeler and Silverton that it was thirteen and a half feet long. We then went outside and walked over to the long trench next to the old mill slab. The first thing I did was show him that the cellar was twelve and a half feet wide. Allowing six inches for a socket to support each end, the beams would be thirteen and a half feet in length. That was no coincidence.

"What do you know about the history of this place?" Wheeler asked.

"The original foundation dates back to the early 1870s. There was a railroad storage building on top of it. We think that the cellar here was built to hide Chinese laborers. Then sometime in the early twentieth century, the mill building was put up next to the old shed. We think that the plumbing and partition walls were added in the late 1980s."

"By whom?"

"The building was leased in 1986 by a man named Harvey Walters, who ran a boat repair business there until going bankrupt in 2007. Brittany Harlan was kidnapped in 1989. My theory is that Walters built the cells sometime between 1986 and 1989," I explained.

Silverton climbed down the ladder into the pit and looked closely at the broken remains of the partition walls and plumbing. She walked up what used to be the hallway to the north end of the underground bunker.

"What are these brick arches?" she asked.

"We believe that they go into tunnels that were used to smuggle the Chinese laborers in and out of the cellar."

"What makes you think they were tunnels?"

"Do you know Captain Alan—the old tugboat operator?"

"I know who you're talking about," Wheeler said.

"Alan told me about the tunnels. He used to hang around here with the owner's son back in the 1960s. He says that they used to play in the tunnels. One went from here to the old house, and the other went down to the edge of the river."

"How do you figure they played into your idea about the 'cells' down there?"

"They probably didn't. We think tunnels were probably collapsed by then."

"Okay, well, there's plenty here to investigate," Wheeler concluded.

He turned to Silverton and said, "Let's get the team out here and work the scene. I want that beam taken to the State Police lab, and I want everything that came out of that hole run through a strainer."

"I guess that means you're starting to like my theory," I said to him.

"Let's just say I can see why you've stuck with it. Do you have any idea where the boat repair guy is?"

"I tracked him down. He's working a little gold claim in the Rogue River canyon."

"Does he know you're investigating him?"

"I talked with him but told him that I was investigating the drug dealers who used to be down here."

Wheeler scratched his head. His expression showed skepticism. "If he suspects that you were looking at him, he's probably already on the run."

"I don't think he is. See, he's carrying a GPS tracker."

I went on to explain how I'd planted the flashlight-tracker for Walters to find.

"So would you like to compare the DNA profiles I have with Jane Doe's?" I asked.

"E-mail them to me," he said.

"Already done. I did that before I came out here."

With the investigation now in Wheeler's hands, I had to take a fresh look at what I could do without interfering. I considered phoning Vera to let Kim know what we'd found, but since we hadn't yet established a positive connection between Sunny and the dungeon, I reluctantly decided that it would be premature. That call would have to wait for Wheeler to confirm a DNA match.

When I talked with him about the pending analysis of the blood from the beam, Wheeler said that he needed to see a match on Sunny's DNA before he'd ask the county to pay for the profiling of the blood samples that Catherine Williams had collected. But if Sunny was one of the abducted girls, then there would be ample justification for spending taxpayer money to authenticate Brittany's etchings through DNA analysis.

Wheeler had also made it clear that he did not want the media to hear anything about what we'd found at Svensen's place, which was an unnecessary admonition. I didn't want this to blow up in public any more than he did.

"Maybe this was a bomb shelter from the 1950s," Martha speculated when I showed her the drawing of the cellar.

"It isn't that old," I explained. "ABS plumbing did not come into common usage until the late sixties, and by then the bomb shelter construction craze was long past."

"But doomsday preppers still build bomb shelters."

"No self-respecting doomsday prepper would build a shelter under a wooden ceiling. This cellar shows none of the characteristics of a survivalist enclave. For example, there is no apparent facility for storage of a long-term food or water supply, and these things are basic requirements of a survival shelter."

"I guess I just didn't want to believe that anybody would actually be so twisted as to build a dungeon—especially one for little children."

"I know what you're saying. This whole thing pushes the boundaries of sanity. In any case, the state crime lab will be analyzing the composition of the concrete and plastics used, and they'll be able to determine its age with a fairly high degree of accuracy."

Switching topics, Martha said, "Bud came back from Tacoma last night. I guess the treatment for his ganglion cyst was uneventful. He has a bandage on his wrist. He managed to get away with wearing the video watch on his other wrist throughout the whole thing, so if the doctor tries to bill for anything he didn't do, we'll have the proof."

"Sounds like that investigation is about wrapped up."

"Yeah. Bud's already bugging me about what he can do next."

"I never promised him that this would be a full-time job," I reminded her.

"Oh, he knows that. It's just that he likes doing it."

June
Friday 6

Chapter 43

In the middle of the afternoon, I got a call from Michael Wheeler telling me that the forensics lab had completed the comparisons between Sunny's DNA and the first two profiles we had provided.

"We compared it with both—Roger Harlan and Olivia Dilley—and there was no match. Jane Doe is not related to either of them."

That was a disappointment for me. Even though I never believed that Sunny was actually Brittany Harlan, I really thought there was a good chance that she might have been Makayla Imbler. That left Lacey McCredie and Alyssa Marquam on my list of possible victims. The DNA profiles from their fathers had not yet come back from the lab.

"What's happening with your tracker? Is the suspect doing anything?" Wheeler asked, changing the subject.

"We check it twice a day. So far, the only the only thing he's done is make a nightly trip to the outhouse and back."

"You'll let me know the minute he deviates from that pattern."

"Sure. If Walters carries the tracker more than half a mile, we'll know it immediately and give you a call. On the other hand, if the tracker sits still for more than twenty-four hours, that warrants a look as well. It might just mean that he's constipated, but it might also mean that he's left his camp."

"In other words, he could be long gone before we would know it."

"Afraid so. The best we can hope for is that the little flashlight is worth enough to him that he'll take it along if he decides to run."

"Oh boy, I don't know. That seems like a lot to hope for."

"I know, but the fact that he's still there and carrying the flashlight to the outhouse every night is encouraging. It proves that he doesn't easily get spooked. And he's regular. Besides, what's the alternative—put a stakeout up on his gold claim?"

"Well, we certainly can't do that. What was *your* plan for dealing with him?"

"I figured if he missed a trip to the outhouse, I'd have to make a quick drive to Merlin. By then, he'll have been gone for as much as a full day. But without a car, he'll have to hitch a ride from Grave Creek. He'll probably go to Curt Hubbard's place to sell some gold, so that's where I'd figure to pick up his trail. But now that you're involved, you can simply call the Josephine County sheriff and ask them intercept him."

"I'd hate to send 'em out there just because Walters didn't eat his prunes."

"That's not such an unusual thing, is it? I don't mean Walters getting constipated—I mean nobody expects every stakeout to be successful, do they?

"They'll go along with it a couple of times, but if they both turn out to be false alarms, we'll have a hard time getting them to do it again. Then what do we do?"

"Let's not let it come to that. What can I do to help you get an arrest warrant? Then this won't be an issue."

"We're a long way from that, Corrigan. Right now, we can't even prove that a crime was committed, let alone that Walters is responsible for it."

"Can you put a rush on processing the DNA from the blood? Then you'll have both."

"That's still *your* baby, remember?"

"I think that if you expressed your official interest in the outcome, it might give it a higher priority," I suggested.

While I wrapped up my conversation with Wheeler, I was distracted by what I was overhearing from Martha, who was talking on her phone. She was talking to someone about Harvey Walters, but until I hung up my phone, I could only pick up bits and pieces.

The last thing I overheard was, "Okay, I'll see you in twenty minutes."

"What was that about?" I asked.

"When I was doing interviews up where Walters used to live, a couple of people told me they thought Harvey was good friends with his next-door neighbor. The problem was the neighbor was never there. I tried about five times, and finally all I could do was leave a note on his door. Well, that was him."

"Was he out of town or what?"

"No, he says he's been around the whole time. I guess we just missed each other every time I was there."

"But that was over a month ago. Why'd it take him so long to get back to you?"

"He says he never uses his front door. He didn't find the note until a UPS delivery man rang his doorbell this morning."

"Well, if he really was Harvey's good friend, you might find something worthwhile."

A FedEx truck interrupted the conversation, and I anxiously tore open the overnight envelope to find the DNA profiles from Tom McCredie and Tyler Marquam. I e-mailed them to Michael Wheeler and urged him to follow up with the comparisons to Sunny's profile.

When Martha returned two hours later, she wore a big smile.

"Well, I volunteered you to clean out George Spray's basement. I hope you don't mind."

"Whoa there! You did what?"

"You'll love it. I decided that my best approach was to tell George the simple truth. At the time I left the note, we were looking for Harvey Walters, but since then you'd tracked him down and visited him. I never even had to explain why we're looking for him.

"So anyway, George started talking, and I just let him go. He said that Harvey used to come over and watch sports on television—he has one of those huge old big-screen sets that take up half the room. Sometimes they'd go watch the high school football games together because it was cheap and within walking distance."

"That's heartwarming but—"

"Okay, the thing is George knew that Harvey was going downhill. Financially speaking. When the foreclosure finally came down, Harvey loaded everything that would fit into his car, and then he prevailed on George to let him put the rest in his basement. And then Harvey hit him up for fifty dollars before leaving."

"Hold it. Are you saying that we're going over there to get—"

"I saw the pile of stuff Harvey left behind. There's a few pieces of furniture and things and maybe a dozen cardboard boxes."

I recalled, "Del Walters told me that Harvey showed up in Tillamook with only what he could pack into his car. So this is what happened to the stuff that didn't fit."

"Well, there you have it. I asked George if he knew what was in the boxes, and he said he'd gone through them, looking for something that would tell him where Harvey went. He said there were photos, some books, and some old papers."

"Okay. When's the party?"

"Right now! He's expecting us."

On the way up to Van Buren Street, I stopped at an ATM and got fifty dollars. I took my proof of insurance out of its dirty envelope and put the cash in. After Martha introduced us, I gave the envelope to George Spray.

"Harvey asked me to give this to you. But he forgot to tell me where you lived."

"Well, I'll be damned. I figured I'd never see that money again."

I told a simplified version of how I'd found Walters working his gold claim without giving any hint where. I never had to explain why we'd been looking for Harvey. George never asked. He was just happy to have his money.

After folding down the seats in the back of my Yukon, Martha and I carried Harvey's furniture—an antique bentwood chair, an old wooden icebox, and a round table with a marble top—and fourteen cardboard boxes up from the basement and loaded them in.

Back home, I moved my boat trailer out of the garage to make room for Harvey's things. We put the furniture in the corner and lined up the boxes along the wall. One by one, we opened them to see what we had. While I was looking in a box full of what I thought were family photos and memorabilia, Martha poked through a box of old mail.

"Aha! Look at this," Martha exclaimed.

She held an open envelope addressed to Harvey Walters. It bore the return address of Stevens Marine. She waved the contents and handed me the top sheet. It was a rejection to Harvey's application for employment as a mechanic in their boat repair shop.

"But here's the good stuff. They returned the résumé he'd sent them. Take a look."

Walters listed his work experience in the traditional way, newest to oldest. So it started with his ownership of Walters Marine Repair and worked backward. I'd never wondered what he did before opening his shop. I just took it for granted that he'd worked in boat repair. He had, but that was fifteen years before he opened his own shop.

In the intervening years, he'd worked for Diamond Heating and Plumbing in Milwaukie. He claimed to be experienced in rough plumbing and installation of heating and air-conditioning systems. That told me he was capable of planning the mechanical systems in the cells.

I scanned the résumé and e-mailed it to Wheeler. One more strike against Walters.

"Okay! This makes the whole thing worthwhile. Let's call it a day and finish this tomorrow."

As it turned out, we didn't get back to the project in the garage. Martha had to make an unexpected trip to Seattle to help her mom, who had fallen and was hospitalized. I got up on Saturday morning planning to go back to work in the garage, but it was such a beautiful morning that I couldn't resist taking my boat out for some high-speed cruising before the crowds got out on the river.

Skimming over the perfectly flat water, I pushed the throttle to its limit, enjoying the wind in my face as I raced upriver. I decided to keep going until something forced me to slow down. About two miles past Wilsonville, I spotted *Misty Rose* tied up at an old boathouse along the right bank, so I pulled back on the throttle and circled over to say hello.

The boathouse was big enough to keep a forty-foot boat, but its steel roofing was rusty, and some of the wall panels were missing completely. As I idled in toward *Misty Rose*, Captain Alan appeared from inside the boathouse.

"Good timing," he said. "I was wondering how I was going to do this by myself."

"What's up?"

"I need to get this thing up to Slalom Jim's place in Newberg. I could tow it, but that's kind of hard to do. The best way is to push it, but then I can't see where I'm going. If you want to come along, you can stand out front and tell me where to steer it."

"Sounds like fun," I said.

I was ready to do something meaningless that required no particular brain work, and this would fill the bill. I tied up my boat along one side while Alan maneuvered *Misty Rose* into the boat well. When we were both ready, I untied the boathouse and signaled Alan to give her the gas.

Slowly, we pulled away from shore and out to the middle of the river. With *Misty Rose* completely hidden from view inside the boathouse, we gradually picked up speed. I stood next to an open window on the upstream end and made hand signs to tell Alan which way to steer. Making about five knots, it took an hour and a half to get to Slalom Jim's place.

We were still in the middle of the river, reducing speed in preparation for landing, when a Yamhill County river patrol boat raced toward us with blue lights flashing. The boat made a wide circle around us, and Alan cut the throttle.

"We had a citizen report of a runaway boathouse," the deputy called.

"They thought it was drifting *upstream*?" Alan asked.

"I guess they didn't notice which way it was going. Looks like you guys have it all under control."

The sheriff's boat took off back upstream, and we eased the boathouse over against the bank down below Slalom Jim's new house. He came down and offered us beers from the cooler on his beach. Alan took him up on the offer, but I waved it off.

"Why don't you stick around," Jim said. "I'm going to barbecue a prime rib roast, and some of the neighbors are coming over."

I ended up staying for the picnic and cruising back home in the twilight.

June
Tuesday 10

Chapter 44

M ichael Wheeler said, "Okay, Corrigan. Now you have my undivided attention on this thing. The girl from the homeless camp is Lacey McCredie—the girl from Gresham."

Even though it was what I'd believed to be true, the confirmation left me numb. Lacey was five years old when kidnapped. That meant she spent twelve years in Harvey Walters's bunker before he killed her. I would later learn that it was even worse than I had imagined.

Wheeler continued, "We've contacted our grief counselors, and they're going to break the news to the family."

"I don't envy them. Are you aware that Lacey's mother took her own life because she was suspected of being responsible for her daughter's disappearance?"

"No, I didn't know that. Thanks. I'll pass it along to the counselors. Anyway, now I'm ready to believe that there really is something to that Brittany Harlan inscription."

"Well, let me tell you what I found out. Harvey Walters worked for a plumbing and heating company before he went into the boat repair business. He *knew how* to build those cells."

"That's a start. Send me what you have. I need to build a case pretty quick now because it's only a matter of time until the media pick up the story, and when they do, we need to be ready to make an arrest."

The possibility that Kim might hear about this on the news instead of from me was something I hadn't considered before. Given the circumstances leading up to her departure, I believed that she would feel betrayed if I weren't the one to tell her. I pocketed my phone and walked down to the river. Sitting in my boat, I called Vera Lyons.

"This is Corrigan. Can you talk?"

"Hi, Corrigan. Yes, I can talk. What's happening?"

"I really need to talk with Kim."

"Of course, you do. And when she's ready, she'll call you. But you can't force it."

"Vera, Kim left here because she was upset about a case involving the unidentified remains of a young woman and a possible connection to a child abducted twenty-some years ago. We've identified the remains, and we've identified a suspect. It'll be in the news any day now, and I'd prefer that she hear about from me instead of—"

"Corrigan, listen to me. You think you know what this is about, but you don't. You just don't."

"I know what happened out there—out where she found the girl. I need to tell her—"

"Believe me, it would be a big mistake for you to do that. She'll come around. You just have to let her do it her way. You have to give her time."

"That's just it. There is no time. This could be on the evening news any day now."

"Right now, she is unaware that you know where she is. So she won't blame you for not telling her what you know. But if you go and blow it, she won't trust either of us, and there's no telling what she'll do. You're going to have to trust me."

"But—"

"Like I said before, there's a lot you don't know. Just leave her alone for now. It has to be that way. She'll call you when she's ready."

So there it was. Vera could be infuriating with her whole fanciful approach to life—things will take care of themselves because that's what they're supposed to do. I couldn't do a thing, and the feeling of helplessness was overwhelming. There was, however, another call I needed to make, and I couldn't put it off.

"Is this Tyler Marquam?" I asked.

"Yes. What can I do for you?"

"This is Corrigan. We talked a couple of weeks ago."

"Of course, yes. Have you found out something?"

"We have. Your DNA does not match the remains we found out here."

"I don't know if that's good news or bad. I mean, it would be a relief if we just knew—"

"Mr. Marquam, there's more. We have a list of girls who went missing under circumstances similar to what happened to Alyssa. We made other DNA comparisons. And we found a match. Now let me tell you what that means. That girl was kidnapped at age five, but she died probably twelve years later."

"So she was held captive—"

"That's right. And we're pretty sure another girl was too. Now we have to consider the possibility—I would say *probability*—that there were others. And Alyssa is still on the list of potential victims."

"I can't tell that to my wife," he said quietly.

"It's going to be in the news. I don't know when the story will break, but it'll probably be within the next couple of days. And when it does, the news media will start looking at other child abductions. It won't take them long to find Alyssa's name. I don't know if there's any way to prepare your wife for that, but it's something you should consider."

"This nightmare just never ends."

"For what it's worth, we've identified a pretty solid suspect."

"Has he been arrested?" Marquam asked quickly.

"Not yet," I explained. "We know where he is, but right now we're quietly collecting evidence."

"Do you think we might find out—"

"I can't make that promise. But I don't plan to let go of this until we know everything there is to know."

"I appreciate that. I really do. Keep me up to date, will you?"

After disconnecting, I told Martha, "I'm going to go out to the garage and finish going through the boxes."

I'd intended to have it done by then, but somehow I got sidetracked onto a bunch of inconsequential tasks. But after talking with Tyler Marquam, I felt a renewed sense of purpose. I started where I'd left off, going through the box nearest the door, removing each item and asking myself if it could have any connection with the bunker or the abducted girls.

It is strange what people find important enough to save: hand-labeled audio cassettes featuring old country music, a tube-type clock radio with a broken dial, a box of watercolor painting supplies, a stack of crocheted doilies, a flattened Portland Beavers baseball cap, a Sony Walkman, a full set of engineering drawing tools, a collection of cigarette lighters, the circuit board from an unknown electronic device, a set of tiny silver-plated wine goblets, and five tiny glass figurines.

And that was just the first box. I put everything back into the box, padding the fragile items with wadded-up sheets of newspaper. Then I moved on to the second box and the third. In the corner of the box, I found a very old tin box. The words U-ALL-NO AFTER DINNER MINTS were embossed on the lid of the box, and when I picked it up, something rattled inside. I poured the contents out onto the floor. There were several necklaces and chains, all of low quality, some earrings, an old fashioned brooch, and a tarnished silver bracelet.

I picked up the bracelet and looked closely at it. It seemed to be a fairly cheap piece of jewelry, and it was very small. As I turned it over in my hand, I read the engraving on it. Lacey. I stared, not ready to believe what I was holding. It was a child's bracelet—Lacey McCredie's bracelet.

Tears came into my eyes as I looked at this artifact from a stolen childhood. In it, I could see the innocence of a five-year-old girl, helpless in the grasp of a man with nothing but evil on his mind. I pulled a small evidence bag from my shirt pocket and dropped the bracelet into it. It was a pathetic remnant of a once-happy life. But for Harvey Walters, it was a trophy.

I couldn't continue what I'd been doing, and I couldn't go into the office. Instead, I walked down to my dock where I sat and stared at the slow-moving river. I should have felt a sense of triumph. I'd found the thing that would put Harvey Walters on the execution table. But all I felt was sadness.

That evening, I resumed my search of Harvey Walters's belongings. Now that I knew that Walters was one of those psychopaths who keeps souvenirs of his crimes, I paid special attention to the small and seemingly trivial items in the boxes. I kept working into the night.

I picked up an old-fashioned jewelry box and carefully opened it. Inside I found a disorganized mess of costume jewelry and trinkets. There was nothing there that I could immediately identify as having belonged to any of the missing girls, but it seemed conceivable that this was a trophy collection. I set it aside for Michael Wheeler.

In a box filled with old clothing, most of which had apparently belonged to Harvey's deceased wife, I found a small knitted blue sweater with Snoopy on the back. Which of the missing girls had worn that, I wondered.

The last box was the one where Martha had found the rejection letter from Stevens Marine. She hadn't finished going through it, so I picked up where she'd left off. There were old greeting cards, letters from family members—mostly on his wife's side of the family—and there were even a few love letters from his wife. Deeper in the box, there were newspaper clippings but none related to the missing girls.

June
Wednesday 11

Chapter 45

First thing in the morning, I drove to Michael Wheeler's office and gave him Harvey Walters's résumé, the bracelet, the sweater, and the jewelry box.

"Last week, I got a call from Harvey's former neighbor. When he learned that I'd been in contact with Walters, he said that he had a pile of his stuff and asked me if I could take it to him."

"Don't you think you should have called *us* to pick it up?" Wheeler asked.

"This was before you got the DNA match. Remember, you weren't interested."

"You're on pretty thin ice here, Corrigan," he cautioned.

"I didn't know what was there until last night," I said defensively.

Wheeler turned the little plastic bag holding the bracelet over and studied it. "We'll have to ask Tom McCredie if he recognizes this."

"Will that be enough to get an arrest warrant?"

Instead of answering my question, Wheeler said, "There's more. Out at the Studebaker guy's place, the CSI team has been digging in an old fire pit. Under a mess of burned fiberglass, they're finding teeth and fragments of bone."

I let out a long, low whistle, thinking of the other missing girls on my list.

"I'll send someone down to pick up the things from your garage. And you need to get off the playing field. This isn't your game anymore."

He was wrong about that. It was my game until Kim came back. I returned to my office and told Martha about the bracelet and the other things I'd found.

"Is Walters still eating his prunes?" I asked.

"Seems so. He took his nightly walk at three thirty this morning."

"That's good. I think he's going to have some visitors pretty soon."

With nothing better to do, I started straightening up my desk and organizing all my files related to the case. I looked again at my list of missing girls, wondering how many more would be connected to Harvey Walters. Undoubtedly, one of those ten names belonged to the remains in the fire pit.

Except for Brittany Harlan, I hadn't made files for the first five girls on the list because they hadn't been in the age range that would fit with Sunny. All were still possible victims of Walters, and I was tempted to start digging into their cases, but I couldn't ignore Michael Wheeler's admonition to stay out of it.

At the bottom of a stack of miscellaneous case notes, I came across the file I'd made regarding the cases where girls or women had been held captive by their kidnappers—Ariel Castro, Cameron Hooker, Thomas Hose, Phillip Garrido, and Brian Mitchell. Now we could add the name of Harvey Walters to that list. As I put the collection of notes into a file folder, my attention was drawn to something in one of the news clippings.

It was the hand-drawn sketch of the cell where a kidnap victim in Salt Lake City was held for at least fifteen years before being left drugged and naked in a city park. She didn't even know her name. I dug through the papers on my desk until I found the drawing I'd made after we uncovered the bunker. I laid it next to the old news clipping. That girl's cell was identical to the ones in Harvey Walters's dungeon.

"Holy shit!" I whispered.

I quickly reread the clipping. A couple of details jumped out at me. The girl had said that her cell was close to a busy railroad, where twenty trains a day went past. And her description of her captor matched Harvey Walters. Papers spilled to the floor as I flipped through files in search of the DNA profiles from Olivia Dilley and Tyler Marquam.

"Martha, get Salt Lake City Police on the phone and find out who's handling this case."

I handed her the clipping about the mystery girl.

"And get an e-mail address," I added. "We may know who that girl is."

The confirmation came back in the middle of the afternoon. "Sassy" was Alyssa Marquam. I suggested to the detective in charge that I be allowed to contact Tyler Marquam, since I'd already spoken with him about his daughter.

211

"What do you have?" Marquam asked.

"We have a positive DNA match," I told him. "Pack your bags. You're going to Salt Lake City."

"What are you talking about?"

"That's where your daughter is—alive and well."

I heard him gasp, and then I waited through a long moment of silence.

"Alyssa is alive? How? What happened?"

"Tyler, I need to tell you that it isn't all good news. Yes, Alyssa is alive and well, but she endured seventeen years of captivity during which she never saw daylight, and she was abused in ways that neither of us can imagine."

"Dear god!"

"She was found in a park in Salt Lake City four years ago. Since then, she's been recovering and learning how to live. By all accounts, she's a very strong young lady and has made remarkable progress."

"When can we see her?"

I gave him the contact number in Salt Lake City and said that the police department there would make all the necessary arrangements. When I got off the phone, I went to my computer and booked a flight to Salt Lake City. Next I called Wheeler and told him about this new development.

"How in hell did you make *that* connection?" he asked.

"When I was looking at cases of long-term captivity, I ran across a newspaper clipping about a young woman in Salt Lake City who had been held since she was a child. She had no idea who she was or where she had lived, but she drew a sketch of the cell where she was kept. It looked exactly like what we found in the bunker. I sent the DNA profiles, and bingo."

"Give me the contact information," he demanded.

"Check your e-mail. I just sent it along with the news clip."

"What about the girl's parents?"

"They're in Michigan. SLPD let me make the call. I just got off the phone. I'll be on a flight to Salt Lake City in three hours. The family has asked that the media be kept out of it until after the reunion. That'll happen in the morning. But it'll be all over the news by tomorrow night—Friday at the latest."

"What kind of shape is the girl in?"

"She seems to be okay, but who knows what this kind of thing does to her—emotionally speaking."

I was led to a small meeting room at the Salt Lake City Police Department headquarters. As I glanced around, I noticed video cameras in each corner, up near the ceiling. About a dozen chairs were arranged in a semicircle opposite the entry door. The patrolman who had escorted me in introduced me to the detective in charge.

"Donald Loraine," he said, extending his hand.

"Corrigan. Nice to meet you."

"The girl's parents will be here in a few minutes. They're with a psychologist right now getting a quick briefing."

"How's Alyssa doing?"

"She's fine. She doesn't know why she's here."

The door opened and a middle-aged couple entered, accompanied by a woman and two men, all in their twenties or thirties.

"This is Tyler and Francine Marquam, Alyssa's parents. And these are her sister, Danielle, and brothers, Jason and Ryan."

"I'm Corrigan," I said, stepping forward.

Francine rushed ahead of her husband and hugged me. "Thank you, thank you," she whispered.

I shook Tyler's hand.

"We can't express—"

"You don't need to. Just being asked to be here is all the thanks I need," I said.

Detective Loraine gestured for us all to take seats. I stepped back and leaned against the wall, attempting to look insignificant.

"Alyssa knows that she's here to meet some people, but she hasn't been told who you are. Her counselor will introduce her under the name she has adopted for herself."

Nodding toward Tyler and Francine, he said, "They say that she probably won't recognize you, so don't expect too much at first."

Nervous conversation continued until there was a quiet knock on the door. When the detective opened it, a lady in conservative business attire led a young blond woman into the room.

"Let me introduce Addison Snow," the counselor said.

"Addie," the younger woman corrected shyly.

As she looked around the people in the room, she froze when she made eye contact with Francine.

"Alyssa?" Francine asked.

"Mommy? *Mommy?*" Alyssa whispered.

They rushed into each other's arms, both in tears. The rest of the family gathered around, and for ten minutes, they all shared hugs and tears. I stayed in the background and wiped the tears from my own eyes.

"I'm not Addison Snow anymore. I'm Alyssa—" She burst into tears again. "I don't know my last name."

"It's Marquam," Tyler told her.

"Alyssa Marquam," she said, testing the sound of it.

"*M-A-R-Q-U-A-M*," one of her brothers said.

"Alyssa Marquam," she repeated. "We had a black-and-white dog."

"Toby," Francine said.

"I guess he's not alive anymore," Alyssa said. She shook her head as if to free herself from the sad thought. "What happens now?" she asked.

"That's up to you," the counselor said. "What do you want to do?"

"I want to go home."

Off to the side, I asked Detective Loraine what the plans were regarding the questions he wanted to ask Alyssa.

"I can't do that now," he said. "She just needs to go home. Maybe in a few days, we can set something up. But this is a very special time. Let's just leave it for them."

I nodded in agreement.

On the flight back to Portland, I had time to consider what was coming in the next few days. There would be press conferences in Salt Lake City, Alpena, and Clackamas. I realized I had to talk with Roger Harlan and Olivia Dilley and let them know what was coming.

That evening, I made the more difficult call first.

"Olivia, this is Corrigan. We talked a few weeks ago."

"Yes. What did you find out?" she asked.

The hope in her voice was heartbreaking because I could offer her no hope in return.

"First, there was no match with your DNA. That means that we still don't know what happened to Makayla."

"Oh," she said simply.

"But now I have to tell you what the investigation has uncovered. We found a place where at least three young girls were kept captive for fifteen years or more. We know that two are dead. One of them is still unidentified. One girl is known to have survived."

"Is it—"

"No," I interrupted. "It isn't Makayla. It is a girl from Michigan. You'll hear all about it on the news in a day or two. I just thought you should know what's coming."

"I see."

"I'm sorry. I really wish I could have brought you better news."

Next I called Roger Harlan.

"Does this mean you got the DNA results back?" he asked when I introduced myself.

"Some of it. We know that the girl they found in March is not Brittany—but then, we never considered that a serious possibility. She was just too young to be."

"What about the other thing—the blood you found?"

"Nothing's come back on that yet. I'm sure we'll know pretty soon. But other things have developed that you'll be hearing on the news, probably within the next two days."

"Can you give me a preview?"

"That's why I called. First, in the area where we found the beam with Brittany's name on it, we uncovered an underground bunker that contained a row of cells. We believe that the beam came from the ceiling in one of the cells."

"Cells. What does that mean?"

"Roger, it's a goddamned dungeon. I don't know how else to describe it. At least two girls are known to have been killed, and one of them was held for twelve years first. The other—well, we may never know. There are just bone fragments."

I heard him groan.

"One girl is known to have survived. She was reunited with her family this morning."

"So maybe Brittany—"

"I have to be honest, Roger. I don't think there's much chance that she survived. I've seen the dungeon."

"But what about the girl who survived? How did that happen?"

"Four years ago, she was found in a Salt Lake City park, drugged, unconscious, and naked. She didn't remember anything of her life before the kidnapping. It's a heartbreaking story. We don't know why or how she was taken to Utah. But like I said, all of this will be in the news tomorrow."

Chapter 46

Sometime in the middle of the night, it occurred to me that there was a problem. Why I hadn't realized it sooner, I can attribute only to my euphoria over reuniting Alyssa with her family. The problem was that Alyssa was released in 2010. Harvey Walters went bankrupt and abandoned the old cedar mill in 2007. Who held Alyssa after Walters left town?

I could understand why Detective Loraine had chosen not to initiate a fresh interrogation of Alyssa right after the reunion, but there were some questions that had to be answered. Or maybe they already had been. I reminded myself that all the information I had about "Sassy" was what I'd read in the old news clipping. It was entirely possible—even probable—that the police had withheld some of what they knew.

The news clipping made no mention of there having been *two* perpetrators or that "Sassy" had been moved to a *second* cell. But in any case, the conclusion was almost inescapable. Walters had to have had an accomplice. The only alternatives were that either Walters was completely innocent and *someone else* was responsible, or Alyssa had blocked from her memory whatever had taken place between 2007 and 2010.

Traumatic amnesia could do that. But *had* it? Or had Alyssa been kept drugged for that entire period of time? The week that she remained unconscious after having been found in the park may well have been a detoxification period, even though that was not stated in the article.

But the one thing I knew for sure was that Harvey Walters had not taken Alyssa or anyone else along when he went to Tillamook to stay with his brother. If he wasn't completely innocent, what had he done with her? And if he *was* completely innocent, how could he have Lacey's bracelet?

These questions swirled in my brain for hours before physical weariness overtook mental activity and put me into a troubled sleep.

My first thought of the morning was to figure out what had taken place between 2007 and 2010. I decided that the best place to start would be with a visit to Giles Svensen, but I never got there.

"Walters didn't go out last night!" Martha nearly shouted.

"When's the last time he moved?" I asked.

"Not since three in the morning yesterday."

"Dammit! Call Wheeler and let him know."

I was already on the move, grabbing my keys and wallet. During my four-hour drive down I-5, I calculated all the possible scenarios. Dismissing the optimistic possibility that he'd simply skipped his prunes, I figured a man hiking out from Bunker Creek would make an early start.

He could probably do the ten-mile hike in four or five hours, so he'd have been at Grave Creek before noon yesterday. From there, he'd have needed to hitch a ride to Galice. That could take anywhere from thirty minutes to a couple of hours—it would just depend on how busy the boat landing was.

Once at Galice, he could use the phone—but who could he call? If he needed cash, he'd need to sell some gold. For that, he'd probably go to Curt Hubbard. It was possible, then, that he might have called the mini-storage yard owned by Hubbard. That had to be my first stop.

When I walked into the storage yard office, I pulled my baseball hat down to conceal the fact that my hair was no longer gray.

"Remember me? Del Walters. I was here a couple of weeks ago looking for my brother—Harvey Walters."

"Oh yeah. A guy by that name was here yesterday afternoon. Got his car and drove away."

"Car? *What* car?" I asked stupidly.

"*His* car. The old Jeep Cherokee."

I wanted to ask him why in hell he hadn't told me the first time I was here that Harvey had a car. But then I remembered that I had never asked him to look in his customer records for someone named Harvey Walters. I'd only asked about a man who worked a gold claim.

"Do you know where he went?"

Instead of answering, he simply pointed toward the road to Galice. That probably meant he'd headed off to sell his gold to Hubbard. I drove up the winding road to the Golden Goose Mine and found Hubbard sitting on the steps next to his trailer.

"You ain't Harvey's brother," he said before I opened my mouth.

"I guess you must've talked to him," I said.

"That's right. And he said you ain't his brother."

"Yeah, I told him that I'd tricked you with that."

"Why the hell'd you do that?"

"I figured you might not talk to me if I didn't."

"Damn right."

"So do you know where he is now?"

"Shit! *You* know damn well where he is. He's on his way to see his brother just like you told him. He sold me a little bit of gold, took the cash, and headed down the road."

He had a full day's head start on me. If he really went to see his brother, he'd be there already. Or had he simply told a tale to Hubbard in case someone like me came looking for him? I had to figure that it all depended on whether or not he knew we were closing in on him.

The press conferences had concluded about three hours earlier. He might know now that his secret had been uncovered, but he couldn't have known the day before. His departure from Bunker Creek couldn't have had anything to do with the news. Maybe it was exactly what he'd told Curt Hubbard—that he wanted to go visit Del.

"Hey, that's great," I said to Hubbard. "I suppose he told you that his brother works at Alcatraz."

"Yeah. He mentioned that. It kind of amused him."

"Good. I'm glad to hear he's going. Just wish I could've talked to him first."

"Well, it might not be too late, you know. He was gonna get his brakes fixed before driving to California. Sounded like he also needed a tune-up."

"Any idea where he'd go to get that work done?"

"Grants Pass, I'd assume," Curt said.

"Any Idea what shop he'd go to?"

"I told you. Grants Pass—Grants Pass Auto Repair—in Merlin. Right on the main road."

Damn! I'd driven right past the place just an hour before.

"What's Harvey's Jeep look like?"

"Looks like a piece of shit. It used to be blue, but the paint is all chalky and looks almost white now. You might be able to catch up with him—you know, if they had to order parts or something."

I hurried back down to Merlin and found Grants Pass Towing and Repair just up the road from the storage yard. The overhead doors were open on all three service bays, and there was no sign of an old Jeep Cherokee.

A man in oil-stained coveralls wiped his hands on a shop towel as I approached. He had a Wyatt Earp–style mustache and the leathery skin of a man who spent a lot of time outdoors.

"I'm looking for Harvey Walters," I said.

"Don't know anybody by that name," Wyatt Earp said.

"He'd have been a customer. Drove a blue Jeep Cherokee and needed brake work."

"He needed a hell of a lot more than just brake work."

"So you know who I'm talking about then?"

"He a friend of yours?"

"Yeah, kind of."

"Well. What he really needs to do is open the hood, take off the radiator cap, and drive a new car under it. And then go get a new radiator cap."

"Sounds right," I agreed. "I guess he's already gone."

"Left an hour ago. Maybe two. He wouldn't let us do but half the work that needed to be done on those brakes. I made him sign off that there's no guarantee on an incomplete job. I told him the wheel cylinders needed new seals and the drums needed to be turned, but all he wanted was the brake linings—the cheapest ones we could get."

I got onto I-5, heading south and hoping that Harvey Walters would stay under the speed limit. Figuring I could get away with driving ten over the limit, it would take at least six hours to catch up with him. By then, he'd be most of the way to San Francisco. The only *good* thing was that I knew where he was going.

I doubted that Harvey knew any more than what I'd told him about Del—that is, that he worked at Alcatraz. By the time he got to San Francisco, it would be too late to go out to the island, so all I had to do was stake out the ticket line at the Alcatraz ferry landing in the morning.

Fifty minutes after getting on the freeway, I was approaching Siskiyou Summit, just north of the California state line, when I spotted the old Cherokee in a wide turnout. The hood was up, and steam was billowing out. Standing with his hands in his pockets, staring into the engine compartment, was Harvey Walters.

I slowed as I went past and then pulled into the uphill end of the turnout. I grabbed my phone and punched the callback button for Michael Wheeler.

"What's happening, Corrigan? Your partner said that Walters might be on the run. I asked Josephine County to watch the trailhead."

"You can call that off," I said. "Has a warrant been issued?"

"Yes. Judge signed off about an hour ago."

"Okay, Walters is on I-5, southbound between mile posts 2 and 1. He's stopped in the breakdown lane with an overheated engine. Pale-blue Jeep Cherokee."

"Have you made contact?"

"Not yet."

"Do what you need to do to keep him there. I'll get OSP on the way!"

After Wheeler disconnected, I looked in my rearview mirror. Walters was still standing next to his open hood, looking in my direction. As quickly as I could, I clipped my holstered .45 to the waistband of my jeans at the small of my back and pulled out my shirttail to conceal it.

I slowly backed down the hill toward Walters, stopping when I was twenty feet away. He looked at me with a curious expression as I cautiously approached him. My right hand was behind my back, and my fingers were wrapped around the grip of my Colt.

"You're the guy who came up to my claim," he said.

"That's right."

"Are you *following* me or what?"

"Not exactly," I said.

"Then what're you doing here?"

"I wasn't following you, but I *was* looking for you. Curt said you came this way."

"Why would you be looking for me?"

I ignored the question and asked, "Overheating?"

"Boiling like a teakettle. You carrying any water?"

"Not enough to do any good with that. I can call a tow truck," I offered.

"Well, shit. I guess it was a dumb idea to take this old heap out on the highway. It ain't hardly been run for three or four years. Probably should've checked it out better."

The first Oregon State Police cruiser sped past in the northbound lane with lights flashing. Another was close behind. Figuring that they'd loop back as soon as they got to the nearest crossover, I kept Walters talking.

"Where are you heading?" I asked.

"Well, I *was* going to go see my brother, but it looks like that's not going to happen."

"Like I said, I can call a tow truck."

"Tow truck would probably cost more than this old thing is worth."

Looking down the road over Harvey's shoulder, I spotted a procession of blue lights rapidly approaching. The first car came to a stop with brakes locked and tires screeching. Harvey spun around and stared at the OSP cruiser as the driver jumped out with gun drawn.

"On the ground, right now!" the officer ordered. "Hands behind your head! Both of you, on the ground!"

I complied as did Walters.

Two more cruisers arrived, and while the first officer held his position and kept us covered, the new arrivals approached.

I said, "Officers, I want to let you know that I am legally carrying a concealed weapon. It is holstered behind my back."

While one officer held his weapon at the ready, another pulled up my shirt and removed the Colt from its holster.

"I am a licensed private investigator. My ID is in my billfold."

"Please stay where you are," the officer said while he pulled my billfold from my hip pocket.

He found my driver's license and investigator's license, looking back and forth between the photographs and my face.

"You the one who made the call?" he asked.

"That's right. My name's Corrigan."

"Okay. You can get up"

He then turned to Walters. "Are you Harvey Walters?"

"Yes. What's this all about?"

"There is a warrant for your arrest in Clackamas County. We are going to take you into custody."

"My arrest? What the hell for?"

Instead of answering, the officer made the compulsory Miranda rights declaration.

"Do you understand your rights?" the officer demanded.

"Yes," Walters answered, "but what's this about?"

One of the officers knelt down and handcuffed Walters and then helped him to his feet.

"You are wanted on charges of kidnapping and murder," the officer told him.

"That's ridiculous! Who was kidnapped? Who was murdered?"

"I'm sorry, sir, I do not have that information. Everything will be explained when you get to Clackamas County."

Walters looked at me and said, "You—Corrigan—tell me what this is all about!"

"Here's the deal, Harvey. They want to talk to you about those people buried out by your old boat repair shop."

221

"I told you. That was those dope heads. I don't know nothing about it."

"You'll have to tell that to the sheriff's investigators in Clackamas County."

"We really have to go all the way up there?" he asked.

"That's where they are—that's where the crimes took place."

"Hell of a long way to go just to tell them that I don't know anything."

At that point, Walters was led to one of the patrol cars and eased into the backseat. He looked at me as the door closed as if pleading for me to help.

"His vehicle will be taken to our impound lot. What happens to it from there I can't say."

"If his engine hadn't overheated, he'd be a hundred miles into California by now," I commented.

"Yeah. Lucky break for us. Not so lucky for him."

I followed the police cruisers to the crossover at Siskiyou Summit to get over to the northbound lanes and then started down the long grade. As I approached Medford, I saw a sign advertising a steak house and realized how hungry I was. I hadn't eaten all day. While I waited for my steak, I phoned Wheeler and brought him up to date on the arrest.

"The takedown was pretty uneventful. Walters didn't put up any kind of resistance. And naturally, he claimed to know nothing about the kidnappings or murders."

"I have to tell you, Corrigan, I was *not happy* when your partner told me that you'd taken off to find Walters. That was way outside your authority," Wheeler told me.

"It would have taken all day for the Josephine County officers to catch up with what I already knew. By then, Walters's engine would have cooled down, and he'd be in California."

"You could have worked with Josephine County—told them what you knew—instead of running off half-cocked. They might have grabbed him before he even got on the freeway."

"And they might have missed him altogether. Look, what's done is done. Let's just make sure that this guy doesn't get away from us now."

"As long as you understand that I won't tolerate this kind of thing in the future."

After that crappy phone call, I punched Martha's number.

"I just heard on the news that state police captured Harvey Walters," Martha told me.

"There's more to the story than that, but it can wait. Anything new going on there?"

"News media people have been calling all day. The press conference in Salt Lake City mentioned your name and gave you a lot of the credit for solving the case. The video of the reunion was—well, it brought tears to my eyes. When Alyssa recognized her mother, it was really something! Your name is all over the news here, and everybody wants to do an interview."

"Honestly, I can't even think about that right now. All I can think about is what happened between 2007 and 2010."

"What do you mean?"

"Alyssa was released in 2010. Walters shut down his boat works in 2007. So what happened in between?"

"Oh. Oh! I hadn't thought of that."

Chapter 47

I was bone tired when I got home late Friday night. I really should have spent the night in Medford, but I wanted to get back to the office and try to find an answer for the three-year problem. The one thing that kept me awake on the long drive home was the nagging worry that I'd overlooked something.

Whatever hope I had of sleeping in was swept away by the ringing of my phone at seven thirty. It was the first of about two dozen calls from reporters. After talking with Martha the night before, I had decided that the only way I could deal with the onslaught would be to have my own press conference. I told this reporter—and all the others who called—that I'd answer all their questions at three on the steps of the Carnegie Library on John Adams Street.

DC showed up while my coffee was brewing, demanding that I maul his head and rub his cheeks. It had been three days since I'd paid any attention to him, but you'd think it had been three months from the way he acted. I was able to distract him with a bowl of fresh food, long enough to bring in the morning newspaper and pour a cup of coffee.

The front page and two more pages in the middle of section A were filled with the news of Alyssa's reunion with her family. I read every word, hoping that Alyssa had said something that would explain the three-year riddle, but nothing she said hinted that anything ever changed during the course of her captivity except for the day the TV in her cell was connected to CNN—September 11, 2001. I could not miss the fact that that was the same day that Brittany Harlan had scratched her name in the old beam.

In between phone calls from more reporters, I went through the rest of the newspaper. When I reached the obituaries on the last couple of pages, I closed the paper, but just as I was tossing it aside, something registered in what I'd seen. A name: Keith Heppner.

I took another look, and sure enough, someone had written an obituary for the man whose bones were found after the landslide. Born in 1959, Keith Heppner was twenty-five years old when he died. He had been a member of the Canby Union High School class of 1977, and he lived and worked in Canby. He had never married. But that wasn't what caught my attention. Keith Heppner had worked in his family's business—Premium Concrete and Masonry.

That changed everything.

Someone had put a bullet in the back of Keith Heppner's head in 1984 and buried him four hundred yards from the cedar mill and the bunker, which had been constructed by someone proficient in concrete and masonry. That couldn't possibly be a coincidence.

But it was more than just a coincidence. It was also a major problem—at least in regards to the theory of Harvey Walters's role in the construction of the bunker. He didn't open his boat works until 1986, after his wife's life insurance provided him with the capital to go into business. Before that, Walters had never had the money to spend on a project like the bunker.

Still, Walters *had* to have been involved. How else could you explain him having Lacey McCredie's bracelet? And what about those other items—the child's sweater and the other things he'd stored in George Spray's basement?

I leaned back and stared at the ceiling, walking myself through the thought process that had led me to Harvey Walters. I asked myself what it was that had first led me to suspect Walters. At least in part, it was my knowledge of Oregon landlord-tenant laws. When you lease a property, nobody—not even the owner—could enter the property without your permission. That's the law. Between 1989, when Brittany Harlan was abducted, and 2001, when she carved her name on the beam, Harvey Walters was the only person with unlimited access to the old cedar mill.

It had always seemed impossible that anybody else could have kept Brittany in the old mill without Walters's knowledge. But when I first zeroed in on Walters, I didn't know about the cellar and the tunnel that connected it to Charles Roy's house.

What I now knew was that it actually *was* possible that other people had access to the mill building—and not just the building but the specific *part* of the building where the girls had been imprisoned. That opened the door to the possibility that someone *other* than Harvey Walters had kidnapped and held the girls.

And Harvey had insisted that he never had access to the old part of the building—the part with the basement where the cells were constructed. If he was telling the truth about that, then the only person who had access to the bunker was the owner of the property, Charles Roy. Was there a connection between Keith Heppner and Charles Roy?

Heppner could not have been simply an innocent victim. It was inconceivable that he could have participated in the construction of the cells without knowing what they were for. I needed to find out how he had become involved in a plot so elaborate as to involve the construction of the bunker. I searched for his name in the criminal databases online, but I came up empty.

A Google search of Heppner's name produced nothing I didn't already know, so I did a search for Canby Union High School, class of 1977. Among other things, I found a newspaper article about a class reunion in 2002 and a complete 1977 yearbook. Strangely, when I scrolled through the senior class pictures, I did not find Keith Heppner.

I scrolled to the staff pages and looked at the photos of the teachers. I copied down the names of four English teachers. Everybody takes English. My first phone call went to Doreen Adel.

"My name is Corrigan. I'm a private—"

"Oh, I know who you are, Mr. Corrigan! You're the one who reunited that girl with her family. I can't believe I'm talking to you." She paused a second and then asked, "But why on earth *did* you call me?"

"I'm interested in one of your former students," I said. "You may have seen him in the news lately too. Keith Heppner."

"Keith Heppner," she repeated. "I know it's a terrible thing to say, but it didn't surprise me one bit to read that he'd been shot in the head. That one had trouble written all over him."

"I'm exploring the possibility that he had a connection with some illegal activity in the area where his remains were found."

"He was always getting into trouble in school. Way back when he was in sixth grade, he and another boy got caught drilling holes through the wall from a janitor's closet into the girl's locker room. They should've sent them both to MacLaren right then, but for some reason, they left them for us to deal with.

"As he got older, he just got worse. Always getting in fights. Stealing things. Vandalism. Seems like hardly a month would go by without him getting in trouble over something. Oh, and he was nasty! And I don't just mean his filthy language."

"Can you elaborate on that?"

"Well, that was what finally got him expelled from school. He threatened a girl and tried to make her take off her clothes. There's no telling what those two would have done if a witness hadn't broken it up."

"It seems like the police should have been involved," I commented.

"Well, they were. But then the judge told Keith that he'd drop the charges if he joined the army."

"I didn't know they still did that in 1977."

"I guess they didn't, but the judge didn't know it. Anyway, the army wouldn't take him. But he never did get called back into court. The other kid got off scot-free too."

"Who was the other kid?"

"Douglas Roy. He was a year younger than Keith, but those two did everything together. Peas in a pod. I don't know what makes kids like that."

Doreen kept talking, but I wasn't listening. My mind went off on its own track the instant she spoke Douglas Roy's name. That was the connection I was looking for. They weren't just school friends. They were both involved in sex-based crimes as far back as grade school.

What had Giles Svensen said about Douglas Roy? "By all accounts, the grandson wasn't much good. He's the one who rang up all the debt and got foreclosed on."

Had he rung up all those debts paying Keith Heppner to build the cells in his bunker? Now, there was a theory I could sink my teeth into. Douglas Roy's dad was killed in Vietnam. Growing up without a father, his moral compass pointed every direction but north. By the time he went to live with his grandfather at age seventeen in 1978, Douglas was beyond reclamation.

Douglas Roy had walked away from the property in 2010 after falling into arrears on payments to the hard-money lender he had borrowed from. It was from that foreclosure that Giles Svensen had bought the property. 2010. That was when Alyssa was left in Salt Lake City. Coincidence?

My own words came back. "There is no such thing as coincidence in criminal investigation."

Damn! I tried to call Michael Wheeler but got only his voice mail. I told him I had something important to tell him but didn't attempt to go into any detail.

I made good on my promise to be on the front steps of the library at three, and for the next ninety minutes, I got to play Hero for a Day. Word had leaked out that the sheriff's office had a "person of interest" in custody, but I denied any knowledge of that.

One reporter asked if it was true that I was the one who had found the cell where Alyssa Marquam had been held, and I said it had been brought to my attention by the new owner of the property. When he then asked the location of the property, I said I was not at liberty to disclose that while the official investigation was still underway.

Another reporter seemed determined to make the sheriff's office look incompetent, asking pointedly why it took a private investigator to uncover the truth.

"This was never a Clackamas County case," I told him. "Alyssa wasn't kidnapped in Clackamas County or even in the state of Oregon. She was kidnapped in Washington. There was no reason whatsoever for the Clackamas County Sheriff's Office to be involved in this until I reported what I'd found after a call from the property owner."

"Is it true that other girls were held prisoner in the same place?"

"That is a possibility, but at this time, there is no proof to support that theory."

"What other girls might have been kept there?"

"The sheriff's office is investigating whether or not others were involved. I am not part of that investigation. You'll have to get that information from them."

This reporter was one of those who love to make law enforcement officials look like incompetent fools, and I was not about to assist him. Sure, I wished Michael Wheeler had come around to my point of view sooner, but I never questioned his judgment in the course he took.

June
15
Sunday

Chapter 48

I'd silenced my phone before going to bed, so I managed to catch up on some of my lost sleep. When I became aware of DC scratching on the door, my clock read nine twenty. I couldn't remember the last time I'd slept that late. I checked my voice mail, but Wheeler hadn't returned my call.

Nor had I received the call I really wanted—the call from Kim. I really expected her to call after the Salt Lake City press conference. I guess it was possible that she hadn't seen it. She was, after all, with Vera, and for all I knew, they might have gone off to the mountains of Tibet in search of a higher truth. I didn't waste my time trying to call Vera.

After reading all about myself in the Sunday newspaper, I showered and fried some eggs. As much as I felt the need to jump into an investigation of Douglas Roy, I made the decision to do nothing until after talking with Michael Wheeler. He was already ticked off about my run to intercept Harvey Walters. There was no need to risk getting myself on his wrong side.

Leisure time on the beach was when I most missed Kim. We should have been out skiing on the early morning smooth water, or we should have been sharing barbecued chicken with the neighbors on the beach on the Sunday after my press conference.

But nobody comes around to see what the single guy is doing by himself. Nobody, that is, except DC, who was impatiently waiting for me to toss him scraps of chicken from the hamburger I was grilling, or Bud, who was just happy to hang around and share my beer.

After even Bud and DC left to pursue other avenues of entertainment, I sat gazing at the river contemplating all that had taken place in the past two weeks. But I'm really not very good at sitting still, so I gathered a few tools and went to work on my perpetual punch list of loose-end projects on my beach and dock.

I was tinkering with the wiring on my boat when I looked up to see a couple pedaling Kaylin Beatty's yellow paddleboat toward me.

"Kaylin sent us up here to invite you over to her place. It's nothing fancy—just a gathering of friends. We'd give you a ride, but I think the rear seats are just for little kids."

Well, I was running out of little things to do, and I wasn't about to take on the next major project, which was building a new shed to replace the one taken away by last year's flood. So I went up to the house and put on a shirt with a collar and clean shorts.

I walked up the street and crossed the railroad tracks in front of Kaylin's house. Looking down on the patio slab that sat on a level area about eight feet above the river level, I saw perhaps a dozen people sitting and standing around a propane fire pit.

As I approached the group, I recognized many of the people, but there were some I'd never met before. Kaylin made the introductions: Sandy and Dave from her real estate office, Susan and Dennis from somewhere up the hill, Mark and Linda from Wilsonville, and Connie, who was conspicuously solo. I immediately sensed a setup.

"Connie works in our West Linn office," Kaylin said.

Connie held out her hand and said, "I've heard of you. Now, is Corrigan your first name, or is it your last name?"

"It's my *only* name," I answered a bit more impatiently than I'd intended.

The truth is, I should have known it was only a matter of time before my friends would start setting me up with their single friends. Kim had been gone for nearly three months. There was no reason I should feel irritated that Kaylin or anybody else would fail to understand that it wasn't over between Kim and me despite all indications to the contrary.

And to be completely fair to both Kaylin and Connie, she really was an attractive woman. Tall and slim with short blond hair and a pretty smile. There had been times in my life when I would have welcomed a setup with Connie or someone like her. But this wasn't the time.

Once everybody went back to their seats, the only place left for me was on a two-seat iron-and-oak replica of an old-fashioned park bench. Connie was already sitting on one end of the bench. I took the other and accepted the beer that Kaylin offered me.

"We were just talking about that poor girl in Salt Lake City," Linda said.

"How did you ever make the connection with the Beacon Rock kidnapping?" Connie asked.

Mark said, "I heard on the news that there is a suspect in custody."

To her credit, Martha refrained from revealing what she knew about the case. But it was pretty clear that I had to say something. So I shifted into storytelling mode and delivered a sanitized version of how the case had developed from the discovery of Sunny's remains to the theory that she may have been abducted as a child and kept in captivity for years before being killed.

I avoided saying anything about Brittany Harlan, since the DNA connection was still unproven. Instead, I focused on my list of missing children and how I tracked down parents to get DNA samples for comparison with Sunny's. Glossing over the discovery of the bunker and its connection to the drawing in the Salt Lake City newspaper article, I merely said that I'd sent the DNA "on a hunch."

Connie leaned against my shoulder and gushed, "That's really quite remarkable,"

"I think that before this is all done, we'll solve several more missing-child cases," I said.

"Oh, so will there be more reunions?"

"I wouldn't want anybody to be optimistic about that. We've already identified one girl who didn't survive captivity, and there are indications that at least one other died."

"That's *so* sad," Connie said, placing her hand on my arm.

Kaylin said, "Corrigan's the one who solved the Mendelson-Devonshire case too."

As I looked around the group, I counted at least four Realtors. I didn't want to remain the center of attention, so to change the subject, I said, "I've heard that real estate can be pretty entertaining at times."

"I told Corrigan about the time I was out on broker tour," Kaylin said. "I had my tour sheet, so I didn't notice that there were no open-house signs set out. The door was unlocked, so I walked in with my clients—a couple from Boston. We'd just walked up the stairs when a door opened just a few feet in front of me. Out stepped a woman wearing nothing but the towel on her head.

"We all stood there for a second, and then I tried to explain that the house was listed on the broker tour sheet. To emphasize the point, I waved the tour sheet. She said that she'd canceled the open house and didn't understand why it could still be on the tour sheet. As diplomatically as I could, I ushered my clients back outside."

"You'd think she would have had the door locked," Susan commented.

"I think she did it on purpose," Kaylin answered. "I mean, it wasn't just that the door was unlocked. When she walked out of the bathroom, she never tried to cover up. She just stood there holding the towel on her head."

Connie spoke up, "I had a different kind of thing happen just a couple of months ago. I work with another agent—Mona—in a kind of informal partnership. We had some clients who found the house they wanted to buy, so we wrote the offer for them.

"We phoned the listing agent and made an appointment to present our offer. When we got to the listing agent's office, she introduced her clients—Mr. and Mrs. Jones. That's not their real name, of course. Throughout the whole presentation, I just let Mona do all the talking. 'Mr. Jones' avoided making any eye contact with me. When we were finished presenting our offer, we left to let the listing agent talk with the sellers.

"A couple of hours later, we were back in our office, and Mona answered the phone. It was the listing agent calling to say that the sellers wanted to accept the offer. After hanging up, Mona—obviously embarrassed—said, 'I don't know how to say this, but the seller doesn't want you involved in the transaction. He wants to deal only with me.'

"I broke out laughing, which was the last thing Mona expected. So then I explained, 'Well, when we first walked in, I recognized 'Mr. Jones' right away. Last weekend I spent an entire evening dancing with him in a singles bar.' Mona cracked up in uncontrolled laughter. We went forward and got the transaction closed without me ever having to see 'Mr. Jones' again."

Throughout the telling of the story, Connie had somehow managed to slide closer to me, and by the time she wrapped it up, her bare leg was pressed against mine, and she had one hand on my shoulder and the other on my thigh.

Now, for any man—and I don't exempt myself here—this kind of thing is a huge ego booster. I was obviously irresistible to this very attractive woman. By all appearances, in fact, she was ready to accompany me back to my place.

So confronted with the challenge of extracting myself from this without hurting feelings, I got up and helped myself to another beer and suggested that Kurt tell the story of the outhouse salvage. Avoiding the park bench, I hung around Kaylin's little three-sided beach shack, showing others the little metal tags that marked the high-water lines from major floods over the past century and a half.

In the end, I strolled around the block with Connie and explained the reality of my situation. She made sure I understood that she didn't feel rejected but that if I ever changed my mind, I shouldn't hesitate to call her. I told her I'd keep that in mind.

June **16** Monday

Chapter 49

The caller ID said that it was Michael Wheeler.

He started out by saying, "I got your message. I assume you were calling about the DNA."

"No, it was—wait. What about the DNA?" I asked.

"From the blood. I got the package Saturday. It's Brittany Harlan's blood. You were right about that all along."

"Jesus! Has anybody talked with Roger Harlan?"

"We called Cleveland, and they sent out a chaplain yesterday to tell him about it. I spent most of the weekend interrogating Harvey Walters. He's a tough nut to crack."

"What's he saying?" I asked.

"I think he's spent a lot of time preparing for this interrogation. He insists that he never went into the part of the building where the cells were, and he has an answer for just about everything."

"What about Lacey's bracelet? How does he explain away that?"

"He says he found it in the gravel outside the mill and kept it because he has a granddaughter named Lacey. Says he always intended to give it to her."

"Does he *really* have a granddaughter named Lacey?" I asked, amazed.

"It turns out that he actually does," Wheeler said glumly.

So I dropped the bomb. "Did you know that Keith Heppner was a concrete mason?"

"Heppner? What's that got to do with anything?"

"Who built the cells in the bunker? You saw it yourself. It was professionally done. Walters was no brick mason. He couldn't have done it."

"What are you telling me?" he asked.

"Heppner was killed two years before Walters leased the cedar mill."

"Uh-oh."

"Yeah. And there's more. I talked with Heppner's English teacher at Canby High. She had a lot to say about Heppner."

"Yeah? Such as?"

"Heppner was expelled from school for assaulting a girl and tearing off her clothes—him and another kid. And that pair had been in trouble before, going back to when they were in seventh or eighth grade and got caught drilling holes to look into the girls' shower room."

"Who's the other kid? Don't tell me it was Harvey Walters!"

"No way. It was Douglas Roy—grandson of the owner of the old cedar mill."

"Spell it out. What are you saying, Corrigan?"

"Douglas Roy and Keith Heppner planned and built the bunker together. When it was all finished, Roy executed Heppner. Maybe he didn't trust him to keep the secret. Or maybe he decided that he wanted the girls all for himself."

"Shit. This has trouble all over it. You know, some reporter has found out that we have someone in custody. We've scheduled a press conference for this afternoon. Now we have to tell them we have the wrong guy? Not to mention that we could end up with a wrongful arrest suit from Walters."

"You don't need me to tell you how to play it," I said while contemplating the way *I'd* play it.

"You're right. What's the name of that teacher you talked to?"

"Doreen Adel." I added the phone number.

"I need to get back with Walters and see what he knows about this Douglas Roy guy."

"Well then, I'll get off the phone and let you go to work."

"Did I understand that right?' Martha asked. "Did you just tell Wheeler that Harvey Walters didn't do it?"

"It looks that way. I never even looked at Douglas Roy. He was just a kid—in his early twenties when all this started. His grandfather Charles was still the owner of the mill. There just wasn't a reason to look at Douglas."

"What ever happened to his grandfather?"

"Well, that's something we'll have to take a good look at. He was found dead in his burning house. And he'd been dead for a while before the fire—like a couple of weeks."

"Didn't anybody suspect the grandson? I mean, that's pretty strange."

I agreed. "There was no apparent evidence of arson in the fire, and the old man's cause of death couldn't be determined. People may have had their suspicions, but there was no evidence to act on."

"So what happens now?"

234

"I'm going to go have a talk with Giles Svensen—see if I can get a lead on where Douglas Roy went when he abandoned the mill property."

I found Giles in his Studebaker museum polishing his 1963 Gran Turismo.

"I wish I could afford to make all the cars look this good. I can't really ask people to pay to look at those," he said with a gesture toward the rest of the warehouse.

"Wouldn't it be great to be rich?" I commented.

"Any idea when the sheriff will be done with their investigation?"

I looked out the open door toward the old cedar mill site. Two CSI vans were parked down by the railroad tracks. Yellow crime-scene tape was strung across the driveway where it crossed the railroad, and there was a large portable shelter set up over the pile of material we had dug out of the bunker. There were three smaller shelters set up along the slope where the old path led down to the riverbank.

I could only shrug. "I guess they'll keep working the scene until they're satisfied that there's nothing more to find."

"I saw 'em digging up the old trash pile. I remember the night that it caught fire. I guess there was a bunch of fiberglass scraps on the pile, because once it got started, it made a vicious fire—flames thirty feet high. It was the middle of the night, and nobody was around. My wife woke me up because the light from the fire was flickering on the wall next to the bed. At first, we both thought that our house was on fire.

"I called the fire department, but by the time they got here, the fire had mostly burned itself out. Nobody ever figured out how it got started. The best guess was that some oily rags started the fire—spontaneous combustion. But old Harvey Walters claimed he'd never tossed anything like that on the trash pile. Now, one of the cadets who've been guarding the scene at night told me that they've found bones in the ashes."

"I heard the same thing. Do you remember when that fire happened?"

He scratched his head. "The wife died in oh-three, so it was sometime before that—probably two years—and it was in the fall. Some of the leaves on the ground caught fire."

I pointed to the other small shelters. "Any idea what's going on there?"

"Not really. They had search dogs all over the property for two days. If I had to guess, I'd say the dogs found something at those spots. But nobody's told me anything."

"Figures. When you first leased the warehouse, did you deal with Charles Roy or his grandson?"

"Old Charlie was a long time dead when I rented this place. I never even met him. I approached Douglas Roy about taking over the warehouse lease from Harvey Walters after the building was damaged by fire. Douglas agreed as long as I repaired the fire damage, which wasn't that much—but it was more than Walters could afford."

"What can you tell me about Douglas Roy?"

Giles made a derisive sound. "He wasn't likeable—wouldn't look you in the eye. Always smelled like pot."

"If I remember right, you said that he was living in a houseboat down on the river."

"That's right. As I understand it, he picked it up in an auction from the outfit that rents 'em over on Lake Billy Chinook. From what I could see, it was pretty well used."

"And he abandoned the property in 2010?"

"That's right. He'd stopped making payments a couple of years before that but hung around until the power was shut off."

"Any idea where he went?"

"No clue. After he tore down the mill building, he just up and left. Someone must've bought the houseboat, because it was moved away."

"Where to?"

"Who knows? Just one day it was gone."

"Did Douglas have visitors? I mean, did you see people come and go around the place?"

"I couldn't say. There were cars, but I always assumed they had to do with the boatyard. Douglas had an old Chevy Nova from the seventies and his grandpa's little RV. He kept 'em parked in a broken-down garage over where Charlie's house burnt down."

"You think that lender—Birkenfield—would know where he went?"

"Not a chance. Birkenfield had to jump through all kinds of hoops to foreclose on the property because he couldn't find Douglas."

"Hard to believe he could simply vanish."

"Why all the interest in Douglas Roy?" Giles finally asked.

I dodged the question. "Just trying to get all the details straight."

June 17 Tuesday

Chapter 50

L ooking concerned, Martha asked, "Should we even be doing this? I mean, it's the sheriff's case now."

"We're not interfering with their investigation. We're just searching public databases. We'll give Wheeler anything we find."

"Okay," she said cautiously. "So where should I start?"

"Do general searches for anything with Douglas Roy's name on it—especially anything more recent than 2010. I'm going to go ask Kaylin if she can find anything in the property tax or real estate records."

I carried a respectable bottle of Cabernet over to Kaylin's place and knocked on the door.

"Kind of early for that, isn't it?" she asked.

"Just wanted to thank you for inviting me to your gathering the other day," I said. And then I added, "And ask for a few minutes of your time—on the computer."

First, she searched the current tax rolls for Douglas Roy. That produced no hits. So she expanded the search for anyone with the last name of Roy. That produced dozens of hits, including one for a prominent former member of the Portland Trail Blazers basketball team.

I scanned the list in search of anyone whose name contained Douglas or any variant of Douglas. I didn't see anything right off, but I asked Kaylin for a printed copy that I could go over more carefully later. Next, she searched the transaction history in search of any sale that involved Douglas Roy, and again she came up empty.

"Try looking for Charles Roy. He was Douglas Roy's grandfather, and my understanding is that Douglas had power of attorney in Charles's later years."

That search turned up the property that Giles Svensen now owned. When the lender had foreclosed on the property, it was still in Charles

Roy's name. Four other properties formerly owned by Charles Roy had been sold off between 1993 and 2006—all long after Charles had died.

I asked Kaylin to print the transaction notes in case I found some reason to contact the current owners.

```
11-3-1993   Residence on Elm St. in Canby sold to Richard
            K. Farmington
5-20-1999   9 acres on New Era Rd. sold to Christian
            Evangelical Ministry
7-25-2003   Duplex on High Street in Oregon City sold to
            Nathan S. Riddle
9-15-2006   Residence on Hwy 99E outside Oregon City sold
            to D. E. Langlois
```

When Kaylin ran out of things to search for, I drove up to the Clackamas County records office. I searched for births, deaths, marriages, and court records, finding only the recorded copy of Douglas Edward Roy's durable power of attorney for Charles Roy, dated 1982. That was the document that enabled Douglas to spend his grandfather's money building the cells in the bunker.

I could find nothing regarding any trouble with the law. But, of course, his juvenile records, whatever they may contain, would be sealed—if not outright expunged.

In the tax assessor's office, I searched the history for all the properties Charles Roy had once owned, confirming the transactions Kaylin had found. All in all, it was a lot of tedious work with very little to show for it.

Back in the office, I asked Martha if she'd had any luck.

"Not much," she admitted. "Douglas Edward Roy's driver's license expired in 2009, and he never renewed it. He owned a 1972 Chevy Nova that was abandoned near Salem in 2010. It looks like he either left the state or changed his identity."

"There's one other place to look," I said.

"Where's that?"

"He lived in a houseboat—the kind with a motor. That should have been registered as a boat."

"Oh no! You don't mean—"

I nodded and pointed at the old Marine Board printout. "He bought the houseboat from a marina on Lake Billy Chinook. It was a thirty-three-footer with a seized-up outboard motor. It was twelve years old when Roy bought it in the eighties, and he still had it in 2010. It must've been built around 1970. Unless he somehow avoided licensing it, you'll find it in there."

"But it would just have the address of the cedar mill, wouldn't it? What good is that?"

"If we can get a registration number, we might be able to find out where it is now. It's a long shot, but maybe the current owner can give us a lead on Roy."

"Now you're just grasping at straws," she said.

I reminded her, "It's what led us to Harvey Walters."

"I'm going to wear out that old stack of paper," she complained. "And this time, I'm going to burn it when I'm done."

Leaving Martha to her project, I went outside and sat down on my porch steps, gazing out at the river. Nearly every conscious thought these days began with the same pair of questions. "Why hadn't Kim called, and what can I do to change that?" Surely the arrest of the person responsible for Lacey McCredie's death and the captivity of Alyssa Marquam and Brittany Harlan would serve as the painkiller for whatever was bothering Kim. And that's why I had to find Douglas Roy.

What I knew so far was that Douglas Roy apparently had lived his life off the grid. It was almost inconceivable that a person could go through life without leaving a paper trail, but with the exception of his driver's license and the power of attorney, Roy had done exactly that. The POA had enabled him to conduct business in the name of his grandfather long after the old man had died.

But when he abandoned the mill property in 2010, he had to have gone somewhere, and he couldn't have continued hiding behind his grandfather's name. That left only three possibilities: either he had assumed a new identity, he had left the state, or he was dead.

All of the information I had showed that Roy was desperately short on money from the time Harvey Walters shut down his boat works and stopped paying rent. He had been borrowing against the mill property for years until he was no longer able to make the mortgage payments. Under these circumstances, where could he have come up with the money to establish a new identity? I knew what I'd had to pay just to get a fake driver's license, and that was only a fraction of what it would cost to create a whole new identity.

So if Roy couldn't afford to buy a new identity, that meant he probably was either gone from Oregon or dead. On the first possibility, I would have to search public records in forty-nine other states, starting with those closest to Oregon. On the latter possibility, I'd have to compile a list of all unidentified male bodies found since 2010 and screen them against what I knew about Douglas Roy—which wasn't much.

His approximate age in 2010 was fifty. I had a physical description given to me by Giles. He had not finished high school—at least in Canby. He associated with pot growers and meth cooks. And most of all, he was a sexual predator. The first two items might help in connecting him with an unidentified corpse. The last three might help find him if he still was alive.

When my phone rang, the caller ID said Michael Wheeler.

"We're going to have to cut Harvey Walters loose. We simply don't have anything to justify holding him any longer."

"I have to say, I'm feeling pretty guilty about having pinned this on him," I admitted.

Wheeler waved it off. "It happens all the time. That's why we call them persons of interest now instead of suspects. Walters was a witness. Nothing less, nothing more."

"What's next, then? For Walters, I mean."

"We'll buy him a bus ticket back to Medford where he can pick up his vehicle, and we'll give him a couple of days per diem for food and lodging. He's already signed a waiver for any future claim of wrongful arrest."

"Would you ask him to give me a call before he leaves town? I still have some things of his in my garage."

After I disconnected that call, I looked up the number for Grants Pass Towing and Repair—the people who had worked on Harvey Walters's brakes.

"I'd like you to pick up the Jeep Cherokee from the OSP impound garage in Medford. Take it into your shop and finish the brake job, clean the cooling system, and give the engine a tune-up."

"Who's paying for all of this?"

"I am. What do you need to get started?'

After I gave him my debit card number, he said, "You know, this is going to be somewhere between a thousand and fifteen hundred dollars."

"That's what I would have guessed. I'll let you know when OSP has been authorized to release the vehicle to you."

About an hour later, Harvey Walters called.

"I'm really sorry that I caused all this trouble for you," I told him.

"In a way, you kind of did me a favor," he said. "This whole affair has proven to me that I made the right choice when I decided to make my own way. If I ever get to thinking about moving back into town, all I'll have to do is remember what city life really is like."

"Nevertheless, I feel like I owe you something for the trouble I caused you, so I've arranged to have some work done on your Jeep. Maybe you'll be able to make that trip to see Del."

"You don't have to do that," he said. "It hasn't been so bad."

"It's a done deal," I said. "All you need to do is get the impound garage to release the Jeep to the towing company. They'll take it to Merlin, and you can pick it up there."

"Detective Wheeler said you have some things of mine in your garage."

"Yeah, some furniture. An old ice box, a chair, and a table."

"Oh, those. I'd forgotten all about them. They belonged to Daisy— my wife. I held onto them because . . . Well, you know. Just sentimental reasons. But I don't have any need for them. Maybe you want 'em or know someone else who does."

"I'll take care of them for you. There is one favor I'd like to ask, though."

"What's that?"

"Did you find a little flashlight after I visited you up on Bunker Creek?"

"Sure did. I figured it was yours."

"Well, it's more than it appears to be. There's a GPS tracker built into it. I was hoping it would let me track you if you went on the run," I confessed.

"I'll be damned. Never would have guessed that was possible."

"Anyway, I'd appreciate it if you'd take it down to John at Black Bar Lodge and ask him to mail it to me. It's kind of expensive."

"Sure. I'll do that," he said.

"And you'll find a replacement for it in your Jeep. Only it won't have the tracker. Just one more thing. Give me a call when you pick up the Jeep—let me know if everything's okay. And again, I'm really sorry for putting you on the spot."

"No problem."

My conscience thus appeased, I went out to the garage and took a good look at Harvey's furniture. There was no place in my house, office, or ship for the items, but I had an idea. While visiting Kaylin, I'd noticed that she had a magnificent antique buffet in her dining room. So I asked her to take a look at what I had. She was thrilled to give Daisy Walters's furniture a good home.

Chapter 51

I spent the rest of the week trying to find Douglas Roy with my computer. I subscribe to about a dozen different online search engines that give me a wide variety of options for finding information about people. But I always start with the obvious.

A Google search produced nearly sixty-three thousand hits—including a physician, a civil engineer, a sculptor, and an Elvis impersonator—but nobody who could possibly be the man I was looking for. I found seventy-nine profiles on Linked-In, including most of those found by Google—the Elvis impersonator being the exception—but again, nobody with credentials anything like my Douglas Roy.

Many of the specialized database search engines can search only one state at a time since their search results come mainly from state records. That made searching them a slow and repetitious process even when I limited my searches to the six Western states. Hour after tedious hour, I plodded through hundreds of dead-end leads.

I was nearing the point of going back to take another look at that Elvis impersonator when I took an accidental shot in the dark. I was doing a search for Douglas Roy in the state of Montana when I mistakenly entered his first and last names in the wrong fields and wound up searching for Roy Douglas. But the mistake brought an interesting hit.

There was a two-year-old article in a weekly newspaper in Hamilton, Montana, regarding a man named Roy Douglas, who was picked up on suspicion of vagrancy and public intoxication. He was subsequently released when he was able to show that he owned a recreational vehicle that was parked nearby. He stated that he was on his way to Yellowstone Park with his teenage niece.

Three things jumped out at me: the man's name, the RV, and the fact that he was traveling with a young girl. Douglas Roy's grandfather had owned an RV that had still been in the garage long after he had died. And

I recalled that a witness I'd interviewed about the local abductions had said something about an RV. Had Douglas Roy switched his names around and built a new identity? While I was still skeptical that he had the wherewithal to do that, the coincidence was too big to ignore.

I did a few searches, looking for unsolved abductions in the Bitterroot Valley region of Montana in the time frame of 2010 to 2014, and I found three—all involving girls under the age of ten. That was troubling. It suddenly appeared that Douglas Roy might have somehow set aside enough money to move to Montana and set up a new base of operation.

Peyton Ismay was at her father's rural home outside Pinesdale when she vanished on December 12, 2010. She had been playing with her dog in freshly fallen snow while her father was working on machinery in a nearby shed. The dog started barking insistently, something that he rarely did. Seven-year-old Peyton was gone. Tracks in the snow indicated that she had walked out to the road, possibly to get the mail. There was some speculation that the girl's estranged mother had picked her up, but to date, neither the mother nor the child had been found.

Six-year-old Emma Roberts was last seen on September 9, 2011, walking home from school in Conner, Montana. She never made it. Extensive searches proved fruitless. There had been reports of a particularly aggressive grizzly bear in the area, leading to speculation that it may have carried the girl into the forest, but there was no evidence that a bear attack had taken place.

A year later, on September 23, 2012, eight-year-old Taylor Austin was hiking in a wildlife refuge outside the town of Stevensville with a group of Brownies. When the group leader noticed that Taylor was missing, none of the other girls could say for sure when they had last seen her. It had been about fifteen minutes since the last head count. In that time, the group had walked less than a mile. The best guess was that she had fallen into one of the many ponds, but despite days of searching, no trace of Taylor was ever found.

Three missing girls and no witnesses. In each of the three cases, there was a plausible explanation—a parental abduction, a grizzly bear attack, and a simple drowning. But it was equally plausible that someone had stalked and seized the girls. And then there was Roy Douglas driving around with a teenage girl in his RV in July of 2012, within twenty miles of all three disappearances.

I phoned the Ravalli County Sheriff's Office, which had been mentioned in the newspaper article, and spent ten minutes explaining why I wanted to talk to the deputy who had picked up Roy Douglas. Fortunately, the department was small enough that the dispatcher was able to identify and put me in touch with the deputy, who was off duty that day.

"I'm trying to track down a man who may be in your area—Roy Douglas. A newspaper article says that you picked him up a couple of years ago in Hamilton on suspicion of vagrancy and intoxication. He was travelling in a motor home with a teenage girl."

"Yeah. As I recall, the girl was his niece."

"Were you able to verify that?"

"The girl had a school ID card that said her last name was Douglas—same as the guy she was with. They said they were on their way to Yellowstone Park and had stopped in Hamilton to do their laundry and shopping after a week in Glacier Park. The man had been drinking, but he was on foot, so once we checked out his story, we let him go."

"Have you ever seen him or the girl again?"

"I don't think so. But then, I wasn't on the lookout for them. It's possible that I've seen them, but I didn't have any reason to pay attention."

"What about his vehicle?"

"The RV? I've seen one that looks like it a few times, up around Victor. That's about ten miles north of Hamilton. But I can't say for sure that it's the same one."

"What's it look like?"

"Well, it's not one of those big ones. It's a C class, built on a van chassis—a Dodge. White with blue trim. It's pretty old—probably from the seventies—and it's showing its age."

"Did you notice if it had out-of-state plates?"

"It has Montana plates with current tags. I always look at that as a matter of habit."

We talked for five or ten more minutes, but I didn't learn anything new. However, the deputy's description of the RV sounded very familiar. I leafed through the notes I'd made while interviewing witnesses to the local abductions. It was Jerry, the witness to the kidnapping of Makayla Imbler, who had described the vehicle her kidnapper drove. It was a white-and-blue Dodge motor home.

I did an exhaustive name search for Roy Douglas in Montana and, other than that little news report, came up dry. He did not own any real estate, and there was no motorhome registered in his name. That could mean a variety of things. Maybe he was living with a friend or relative. Or maybe he was Douglas Roy.

To Martha I said, "Giles Svensen told me that Charles Roy had some kind of recreational vehicle that Douglas apparently inherited. Can you see if you can find any records on it?"

"Any idea when it was first registered?"

"Could be clear back in the seventies. But Charles still owned it when he died, and it was still on the property until Douglas Roy took off."

While Martha went to work on that, I went to work on MapQuest. It was six hundred miles to Victor, Montana—basically an all-day drive. The last thing I wanted to do was take another long road trip. But I couldn't think of any other way to search for the RV the deputy saw in Victor. Next, I booked a room for Saturday night in the Super 8 Motel on the north end of Hamilton.

"If you find anything on the RV, leave a note on my desk. I'm going to go get an oil change. I'll be driving to Montana tomorrow."

When I got back to the office an hour and a half later, there was a note on my desk. Charles Roy had registered a 1973 Dodge motor home in 1978. Color was shown as white and blue. The licenses were renewed every two years up through 2010. There was no record of a sale, and the vehicle had not been licensed in Oregon since.

But maybe in Montana . . .

Out the door at five thirty, I drove straight through with stops only for gas and fast food. I drove into Victor exactly eleven hours later. The town was four blocks long and seven blocks wide, with US-93 along its eastern edge. I cruised slowly up Main Street hoping—but not expecting—to see the old motor home. It took less than twenty minutes to cover the entire twenty-eight-block grid. No luck.

Sunday morning, I bought a map of Ravalli County. While waiting for breakfast, I folded the map to show Victor and the rural roads surrounding the town. With that, I systematically drove slowly along the roads, marking them off with a blue highlighter. By lunchtime, I'd covered over a hundred miles of roads, mostly gravel, and had seen no sign of the RV.

After lunch at an old-fashioned restaurant on Main Street, I resumed my search, fighting back the growing feeling that the whole exercise was a waste of time. In the middle of the afternoon, about two miles west of town on Sweethouse Creek Road, I spotted a white-and-blue RV parked under a low-cost tarp shelter next to a rundown farmhouse, about a hundred yards from the road.

I parked in the shade of an enormous fir tree and got out my binoculars. The front of the RV was clearly that of an early-seventies Dodge. I watched the house for five or ten minutes without seeing any sign of occupation. I got out and walked over to a small cluster of mismatched mailboxes and looked for names. Crudely panted on the third box was what I was looking for: Douglas.

Before driving up the dirt driveway, I clipped my holstered .45 to my waistband under the back of my windbreaker. There was no answer when I knocked on the door, so I walked around the house to see if someone might be in the backyard. There was nobody in the yard, but the door stood open on a single-car garage.

"You looking for something?" asked someone from inside the garage.

"Looking for Roy Douglas," I said.

As I approached the open door, a man stood up from behind an old Ford tractor. He was about five eight or five nine, maybe 175. Sandy hair, and he hadn't shaved for a few days. I guessed his age to be about fifty. All of that fit with what I knew about Douglas Roy.

"That's me. What can I do for you, then?"

"Is that your motor home out there?" I asked, pointing toward the tarp shelter.

"What about it? And who the hell are you?"

"I'm sorry. My name's Corrigan. I'm a private investigator."

When Douglas stepped out from behind the tractor, I saw that he was holding a twelve-inch Crescent wrench in his right hand. As I spoke, his eyes showed a sudden intensity, and his grip on the wrench seemed to tighten. I kept my right hand on my hip, ready to pull the .45 if he made a move toward me.

"Why's a PI want to know about my RV?"

"How long have you owned it?"

"I ain't telling you nothing until you tell me what this is all about!"

His words were confrontational, but he did not make a move. I couldn't think of anything to say that would lower the tension.

"An RV matching the description of that one was involved in a kidnapping."

He looked hard at me. "What kidnapping? Where?"

"Can you tell me how long you've owned the RV?"

"About ten years. So what?"

"Two years ago, were you picked up by a sheriff's deputy in Hamilton?"

He slammed the wrench down on a workbench, and I grabbed my Colt.

"That was bullshit! I wasn't even drunk. I just tripped over a bad spot on the sidewalk."

"They said you were traveling with a teenage girl."

"Yeah, my brother's kid, from Missoula."

"What were you doing in Hamilton?"

"Washing clothes at the laundromat. I don't have a washing machine here. Rachael just came down here from a week in Glacier Park. We were getting ready to go catch up with her family in West Yellowstone."

"Have you ever driven the RV to Oregon?"

"Oregon? Hell no. I was pushing my luck to take it to Yellowstone!"

"Do you know a man named Keith Heppner?"

"Never heard of him. Who the hell is he?"

"Are you related to Charles Roy?"

"Charles who?"

"Charles Roy. Roy is his last name."

"Oh. I don't know anybody by that name."

"Have you ever used the name Douglas Roy?"

"Is *that* what this is all about? A mix-up on the name?"

"You tell me. Douglas Roy owned an RV just like yours," I told him.

"Well, it wasn't *this* one," he insisted. "This one belonged to my old man for twenty years. That guy you're talking about never owned it."

This wasn't going the way I wanted. The coincidence of someone named Roy Douglas owning an RV matching the description of the one owned by Douglas Roy was more than I could accept.

"There's one way to find out," I said. "Let's go look at the VIN."

"Shit," Douglas complained. "I don't have time for this."

But he put the wrench on the tractor seat and started walking toward the RV. I followed a few feet behind him. He ducked under the canopy and dragged an apple box over next to the left front wheel. Standing on the box, he wiped the dirt from the lower corner of the windshield with his thumb. The number he read from the VIN tag did not match what Martha had written down.

"Can you read that again?"

"It don't match, does it? You want to check it out for yourself?"

After he stepped down from the box, I cautiously stepped up onto it. He'd read the VIN right. This was not Charles Roy's RV. Only then did I take my hand off the Colt.

"What are the odds? Douglas Roy and Roy Douglas have matching RVs, six hundred miles apart."

"Maybe you should go buy a Power Ball ticket."

"Would you like a beer? I've got some in my rig."

"No thanks. I don't drink much anymore."

"Well, I'm sorry to have wasted your time. Good luck with that tractor."

All the way home the next day, I cursed the coincidence that had cost me three days behind the wheel and left me exhausted. There's no such

---

247

thing as coincidence in criminal investigation, I reminded myself. This must have been something else. It couldn't have been a coincidence.

As for the missing girls in Montana, I had no answers. Their disappearances would have to remain mysteries.

June 24 Tuesday

Chapter 52

"I finished going through the boat registrations," Martha told me. "I found a few houseboats that match the description, but none of them was ever registered to Douglas Roy."

"Well, I didn't have any more luck than you did. The guy in Montana is not Douglas Roy."

"So where do we go from here?"

I said, "I've been thinking about my list of missing girls. When I made the list, I was looking only for girls who were the right age to have possibly been Sunny. But now we know that Roy could have been abducting girls two years before and fifteen years after the time frame I was looking at."

"Dear god, no. You mean there might be others?"

"I think we need to find out. You want to take that on?"

"I'll give it a try."

Pointing at the tall stack of green bar paper that made up the boat registration list, Martha then asked, "What do you want me to do with this?"

"Just put it back underneath my printer. Who knows—we may need it again sometime."

"God forbid!"

"But before you put it away, jot down the info on the houseboat registrations you found. Maybe we'll find that one of them belongs to a friend of Roy's."

"Already done," she said, handing me a sheet of paper.

I slipped the list into the file and said, "I'm going to see if I can track down the druggers who took over the mill after Walters left. They had to have known Douglas. He let them camp there and let them set up the meth lab in the old mill. Maybe they took him in when he abandoned the property."

"How do you go about finding a bunch of meth cooks?"

"Nobody can find a drugger faster than another drugger. I'm going to start with Red Harper."

Red Harper was a neighbor who had a pot-growing operation in his garage. He was in business long before legalization, so I thought he might know something of the pot plantation out by the old mill. On some level, networking is a part of every business—even illegal ones.

I banged hard on the door of Red's garage because I knew the blowers running inside would obscure the sound of a gentle knock. Red cracked the door open and suspiciously peered at me.

"Oh. It's you," he said.

He slithered outside and pulled the door shut behind himself.

"I was hoping you could tell me something about one of your competitors," I said.

He spit on the ground, saying nothing.

"They were growing marijuana on a couple of acres up next to where the big landslide came down."

"Those guys pulled out three or four years ago," Red told me. "They were just a bunch of amateurs. The stuff they produced was about the same as what the hippies grew back in the sixties. There's a reason they called it weed. It was all crap."

"Are any of those guys still around?"

"If you're looking to score some cheap shit, this ain't the way to go about it!"

I thought perhaps he was making a joke. Anyway, I treated it that way and laughed politely.

"No, I wanted to ask them about the old cedar mill."

"Well, why don't you just talk to the people who own the place, then?"

"I've already done that. But he's only owned the property for a few months and doesn't know much of the history."

He gave me a penetrating stare. "What is it you're trying to find out?"

"You heard that some people camping up there got buried in the landslide? Well, I'm trying to find out who they were. Since their camp was right next to the farm, I thought I'd ask the growers if they knew who the people were."

"What makes you think they'll talk to you even if you do find 'em?"

"I'm not trying to pin anything on them. *They* didn't start the landslide. I just want to know who the victims were. Their families deserve to know."

Silence. I held my ground and waited him out.

At last, he said, "They're meth cooks too, you know. They might not be too friendly."

I noticed his use of the present tense. "Are they still around?"

"They got warned that there was gonna be a raid at the mill, so they packed up and moved out in the middle of the night. But they're still around."

"Do you know where they are?"

"Not specifically. Word around is that they're squatting on a vacant farm somewhere east of Canby."

"Do you know any of their names?"

Red stared at me. "I ain't no rat."

I hadn't expected to get much from Red. Talking with him was more a matter of procedure than of expectation, but his tip that the meth cooks might be on a farm east of Canby gave me something to do. The area between Highway 99E in Canby and Highway 213 was not heavily populated, and there weren't many roads out there. If the druggers were still growing marijuana, it might be possible to spot them from the air.

But even if they didn't have an outdoor pot plantation, they might still be identifiable from the air. According to Giles, they lived in a collection of old RVs and travel trailers during the time when they were at the old cedar mill. If they still did, that should be fairly easy to spot.

Barry Walker's red-and-white floatplane was moored fifty yards downstream from my dock. I called Barry and asked if he had some time available to do some aerial reconnaissance. An hour later, I walked out the ramp onto Barry's dock, where he was already warming the engine in preparation for our flight. The Piper Cub is a three-seat aircraft of high-wing design, and visibility from the right-hand passenger seat is exceptionally good with the door removed.

Carrying my digital Nikon with a telephoto zoom lens, I climbed into the plane and strapped myself in. Barry pushed us away from the dock as he stepped aboard, and once he had his belts fastened, we idled out to the middle of the river. Accelerating into the wind, we lifted off the water and climbed to 2,500 feet.

I had printed a map that showed the area I wanted to cover, and I pointed to our starting point about seven miles southwest of where we took off. From Canby, we flew east above Bremer Road. I kept my eyes on the ground, looking for an isolated farm with a collection of trailers and RVs. The first thing I learned was that people with acreage tend to keep a lot of vehicles on their property.

Trying to distinguish between RVs that were occupied and those that were merely stored, I looked for the obvious signs—well-used driveways and footpaths, sheds and shelters adjacent to the RVs, tended gardens, and cars that were not sitting on blocks. Where Bremer Road ended, we continued flying east along Carus Road, until we reached Highway 213. Barry turned the plane and followed the same path going the other direction.

We repeated our east-west flights along two more roads leading out of Canby, and then we started tracking the north-south roads that crossed or branched off from the roads we'd already covered. In the course of our two-hour reconnaissance, I shot photos of about a dozen places that looked like possibilities—clusters of RVs on isolated parcels of land where a meth lab might go unnoticed by neighbors and passersby.

Back in my office, I downloaded the photos to my computer and studied them carefully. I was able to zoom in and identify such detail as boots left on porches and tools on the fender of a pickup truck. I made notes of what I could see at each of the locations, and by the time I finished going through the photos, I had eliminated all but three places.

The most promising one sat at the end of a quarter-mile driveway that branched off to the south from Union Hall Road. The house on the property had a partially collapsed roof and was heavily overgrown by blackberry vines. But the metal-roofed barn had well-worn footpaths leading to a cluster of seven travel trailers and RVs. And most revealing was a heap of trash behind the barn, containing many gallon jugs and a number of twenty-pound propane tanks. These are the hallmarks of a meth lab.

What to do with that information was a whole different question. The lyrics from one of my mother's favorite old songs came to mind.

Paranoia strikes deep
Into your life it will creep
It starts when you're always afraid
Step out of line, the man come and take you away

Red had it right when he said that the meth cooks wouldn't talk to an outsider. Paranoia is a way of life for people deep in the drug culture, and they have an inherent distrust for outsiders. What's more, they have a sixth sense for knowing when someone isn't one of their kind. There was absolutely no way I could walk onto that property and start asking questions.

The alternative to that would be to find someone who could do it for me—someone who would not be summarily deemed a threat to the druggers. That meant it had to be another drugger. A couple of ideas came to me. One was a teenage meth head who had briefly been a suspect in my "Girl in the Carpet" investigation—Shane Keasey. The problem with Keasey was that he was as squirrely as a chipmunk. He wouldn't trust me any more than the meth cooks would.

My other idea was Mickey Odell, who had been a witness in the Mendelson-Devonshire case. He was a retired Clackamas County sheriff's deputy, and like most law enforcement people, he had, over the years, developed working relationships with many people, some of whom operated on the wrong side of the law. In other words, Mickey would know someone who could talk to a meth head.

"I never had a chance to thank you for your testimony in the Devonshire trial," I told Odell.

"Don't get the idea I was doing you any special favors. I just said what happened," he said.

"There were plenty of people who wouldn't do that. But that's not the reason for my call. I'm looking for someone who can talk freely with some people who are probably running a meth lab."

"People like that don't talk to *anybody*."

"I'm not looking for any information about them. I'm just trying to track down the owner of a building they used to lease."

"So you know who these people are?"

"I don't know any names, but I think I know *where* they are. The thing is I can't exactly walk up and knock on their door."

"You're crazy, Corrigan. *Nobody* can walk up and knock on their door."

"I was thinking someone could approach one of them when he's on neutral ground—like in a tavern or maybe a grocery store."

"Why not the library?"

"Look, Odell, I know what the difficulties are. I'm just hoping that you can connect me with someone they might not distrust on sight. I'm not asking for any guarantees on what happens after that."

"Okay, there is a guy. He got clean while he was in the joint. He works with ex-cons who want to go straight. But the point is he can talk the talk and walk the walk."

"Can you ask him to call me?"

"He won't do that. You'll have to approach him in person. Best place to find him is at one of his AA meetings."

"Where and when?"

June
Wednesday 25

Chapter 53

I was at the VFW hall before the AA meeting opened. Alonzo Diamond had the look of a career felon, with jailhouse tattoos that were barely visible against his dark skin and a deeply lined face with features hardened by hard time.

"Odell told me you might be here," he said after I introduced myself.

"Did he tell you what I need?"

"He said you want me to pump some information out of some megatweakers."

"Do you think it's possible to do that?"

He shrugged. "If he's sellin' something and I'm buyin' it, he might spill."

"They're meth cooks, and I think their operation is pretty big. There's at least seven or eight men in the gang. And they've been in business for at least seven years."

"Gang like that doesn't stay around by talking out of school. What is it you want to know?"

"I'm trying to get a line on a guy who owned a place they used to rent—about four years ago."

"Why do you want this guy?"

"I'm investigating the kidnapping and murder of little girls."

He snapped his fingers. "You're the guy on the news—the guy who found that girl's parents."

"That's right. I think the guy I'm looking for might know something about it."

"I can't make any promises. But I'm willing to give it a try. What's your plan?"

"I'm fairly sure I know where they are operating now. They're on rural property south of here. It's all fenced, and there's no way to see for sure what's going on. But their trash pile tells a story. My idea is to find a concealed location to watch their driveway until someone leaves. We follow to a place where you can approach him."

"What the hell do we do while we wait for someone to leave?"

"Do you play cribbage?" I asked.

In the end, I did the stakeout alone. Alonzo didn't want to play cribbage for hours on end, and he suggested that I just phone him when the subject was on the move. Out on Union Hall Road, I talked with the man who lived across the street from the meth lab. He was happy to let me use his barn for the stakeout if it would help get rid of his unwelcome neighbors. From the hayloft in the old-fashioned wood barn, I would have a clear view of the property.

The next problem was my car. My Yukon was bright red. When I bought it, I rationalized that in any color, a large SUV was not the ideal surveillance vehicle anyway, so color didn't matter. But now that I was faced with a real-life situation, I felt the need for a lower-profile vehicle, so I borrowed Martha's Subaru wagon.

It was Thursday afternoon when I parked behind the barn and climbed to the loft with my camera, binoculars, a folding chair, and an ice chest filled with bottled water and sandwiches from the Fred Meyer deli. With the long lens, I shot pictures of the trailers in hopes that Giles Svensen might be able to confirm that they were the same ones that had been parked at the cedar mill. Through the binoculars, I watched people move between the trailers and the pole building. There was no question that something significant was going on there.

I stayed until long after dark, and nobody ever left the property. There was nothing to be gained by spending any more time there, so I went home to get a good night's sleep. In the morning, Martha informed me that she needed her car to go visit her mother in Seattle. I offered to let her take my Yukon, but she refused on the grounds that she was afraid to drive anything that big.

That left me with two bad alternatives. Either I drive my high-profile Yukon, or I borrow something else—and the only thing immediately available was Bud's old Pontiac Phoenix, which had lost its muffler during the Clinton presidency and sounded like the old washing machine on my grandmother's back porch. But if I could tolerate its clatter and if it didn't break down while tailing my subject, it would most certainly provide a low profile.

Bud readily agreed to let me borrow the Pontiac.

"I'll clean it out some first," he offered.

"You don't need to go to any trouble," I answered.

When I actually looked inside it, I wished I'd kept my mouth shut. There was a kind of hollowed-out space around what was left of the driver's seat, and the rest of the car was filled with fast food wrappers, soft drink cups, newspapers, and stuff I couldn't quite identify.

"When you step on the brake, you want to be ready to steer to the left. It'll pull kind of hard the other way," Bud warned.

"Anything else?"

"Don't pay attention to the low oil light. It always stays on. Oh yeah—you'll want to keep your window open a bit too because of the exhaust fumes."

It wasn't too late to change my mind, but it seemed somehow impolite to tell him no thanks at this point. So I made the ten-mile drive to Union Hall Road in Bud's rattling, smoking, and barely controllable Pontiac. There were only a few defects in the car that Bud had neglected to mention—the loose steering that required constant back-and-forth correction as the car wandered all over the road and the totally nonfunctional shock absorbers that let the car continually bounce up and down even on pavement that I knew to be smooth.

As I was finishing a sandwich three hours into my surveillance, an old brown Chevy C-10 pickup came up the driveway toward the gate. I grabbed my phone and called Alonzo as I hurried down to the Pontiac, which protested energetically when I tried to start the engine. With some groaning and sputtering, the engine finally fired, and I was able to get out to the road before the C-10 was out of sight.

"We're heading toward Oregon City on Highway 213," I told Alonzo after we passed the little convenience store that constitutes downtown Mulino.

North of Mulino, the highway goes up a long, sustained grade, and Bud's car slowed from 55 mph to 40 mph before dropping into second gear. I kept the gas pedal on the floor as the C-10 pulled away. By the time I got to the top of the hill, it was nowhere in sight. Throwing all caution aside, I took the old Pontiac up to 70, which was as fast as it would go. In the mirror, I watched a blue plume of oil smoke following me.

Fortunately, a traffic signal stopped the C-10 long enough for me to catch up before we got into Oregon City. At Molalla Avenue, we turned left, and I relayed that information to Alonzo. The right turn signal came on, and I thought he was going to turn into the post office, but he kept going for another long block, finally turning into the parking lot at Wichita Pub.

"That's it," I told Alonzo. "He's going into Wichita Pub. Look for a guy wearing a badly faded orange T-shirt and a ragged OSU Beavers baseball hat."

While I was saying that, Alonzo pulled into the parking lot. We nodded at each other as he strode toward the door. Before he got there, his gait changed to an ambling shuffle, and he dropped his shoulders into a sullen slouch.

Just before going inside, he said, "Com check."

His transmitter was working. I gave him a thumbs-up signal, and then he turned and went inside.

It was still early, so there wasn't much background noise. In the earpiece, I could hear Alonzo's footsteps as he walked around, presumably looking for our guy.

"Oh, hey! How're you doing?" he said, sounding surprised. And then he quickly added, "I remember you from before."

"Before what?" came the suspicious answer.

"Well, before—you were with the guys down there by the river, where the guy used to fix boats."

"Yeah, so what? I don't know you."

"Diamond. Alonzo Diamond. We never actually met. I just remember seeing you out there. I used to work for the guy with all the old cars—Svensen. Hey, let me buy you a beer."

Without waiting for a response, Alonzo said loudly, "Can we get a couple of beers over here?"

"Thanks," the other guy mumbled.

"I came up on the train from Salem yesterday, and when we went past the boatyard, I couldn't believe it! The building you guys were in was completely gone."

"It's been gone a long time. Where the hell've you been?"

"I been in the joint—a five-year stretch for GTA."

"The main yard or the farm?"

"Main yard. They said I was incorrigible."

"You know a dude named Fletcher? David Fletcher?"

I held my breath. It was probably a name he'd just made up. It's the oldest trick in the book to catch someone in a lie.

"Don't remember the name," Alonzo said. "I'm shitty with names."

The conversation was briefly interrupted by the delivery of the beers.

"Here's to life on the outside."

257

For about ten minutes, the Alonzo talked about his life in prison—something that I knew he didn't have to make up. The younger man admitted to having spent some time in the county lockup but never in the state pen.

"So what happened to the boat repair building? Did it burn down or what?"

"I think it was just tore down. We was out of there before that."

"You guys moved out? I thought it was a pretty sweet setup for you."

"Someone tipped us off that there was going to be a raid. We didn't wait around."

"Good move. Hey, want another beer? I don't suppose you know where I can find the guy who owned the place out there—Roy?"

"Who knows?"

"He was keeping some stuff for me. Now I need it, and I don't know where he is."

"What kind of stuff?"

"Stuff you don't want to know about."

"Guns?"

"You know where he is?"

"He's around. I saw him a while back—down at Fisherman's Marine. Didn't talk to him though. Just saw him, that's all."

"Damn! I really need to find that dude."

"I'd look for him somewhere by the river."

"Why do you say that, man?"

"He was buying crawdad traps. You wouldn't need crawdad traps if you didn't live by the river, would you?"

I couldn't find fault with that logic. If Douglas Roy was buying crawdad traps, he probably *did* live by the river or perhaps in his old houseboat. Alonzo kept the conversation going for another ten or fifteen minutes without producing any other hints. But just knowing that Roy was still in the area was worth the effort. The fact that he might be living along the river was intriguing because it greatly reduced the search area.

"Were you able to hear everything okay?" Alonzo asked.

"Yeah. I got it all. You did well. How can I pay you for your help?"

"You know that I'm officially off the wagon now. I was over a thousand days clean, and now I'm back to zero."

"I'm sorry. I never anticipated that."

"It was what I had to do to get him talking. If I didn't drink with him, he never would've trusted me. So don't worry about it."

"Still, I'd like to pay you—"

"Just make a donation to Salvation Army. That's all. They're good folks."

June 28 Saturday

Chapter 54

A pile of paper waited for me on my desk. This included everything from the mail to a list of phone calls I'd missed. I quickly determined that neither Kim nor Vera had called. Then I spent the next hour attempting to return all the phone calls I'd missed.

After setting aside my bills, I started going through the notes from Martha. Following up on our conversation about missing girls, Martha had scoured the Internet in search of other possible victims of Douglas Roy. Her initial list had included nine names, but she had crossed off five as she dug deeper into the case histories.

Martha had arranged her notes on the four remaining names in the order of their abductions. The first name was Shannon Coburg, who was kidnapped in 1986. The nine-year-old was playing soccer in a large city park in the Hillendale neighborhood of Oregon City. Her mother was watching the game but didn't notice when the girl disappeared from the sideline.

A witness had seen a man in his twenties showing the girl a puppy. Another witness saw the girl get into a green compact car. Using the puppy to lure the girl to his car was a tactic we hadn't noted before, but everything else fit Douglas Roy's style, nearly three years before the abduction of Brittany Harlan.

Danielle Flora was only four years old when she was taken from an unlicensed day-care facility in Gladstone. It had been a warm spring day in 1997, and the five preschool children were playing in a fenced yard. Nobody saw the actual abduction, but a white-and-blue bus was seen driving away at the time someone noticed the girl missing. My immediate thought was that the back of a motor home could easily be mistaken for a bus.

Courtney Talent was five when she disappeared on October 17, 2000. She was last seen taking a nap in her bedroom in the family home on Imperial Drive in West Linn, almost directly across the river from my place in Canemah. This turned into another case where a family member was suspected, but no evidence was ever produced. It sounded disturbingly similar to Lacey McCredie's case.

The final name on Martha's list was Emily Marcola, abducted from a popular snow park on Mt. Hood on January 16, 2010. The girl was not yet four years old and had been riding a plastic toboggan with an older brother and sister while the parents watched from their car a hundred yards away. The boy was pulling the toboggan back to the top of the hill with his sisters following close behind. A man in a brown parka was walking briskly down the hill, and as he passed the Marcola children, he snatched Emily and carried her down the hill.

Even as Emily's father gave chase, the abductor vanished in the busy parking lot. Nobody saw them get into a vehicle or leave the parking lot. One of the posts included a photo of the three children in their snowsuits sitting on their toboggan next to the family car. I was just about to put the print aside when something caught my eye. In the parking lot behind the kids, a couple of rows back, sat a white motor home with blue trim.

Inexplicably, Emily was found unharmed three weeks after her abduction wandering alone in Washington Square Mall near Beaverton. The child was unable to say where she'd been, and all she could say about her abductor was that he was "a daddy."

All four of these cases fit into what we knew about Douglas Roy and his methods. Knowing that there were unidentified remains from the search at the mill property, I forwarded Martha's notes to Michael Wheeler so that he could get someone busy finding people to give DNA for comparison.

With all the backlogged paperwork taken care of, I allowed myself the luxury of a few minutes to consider my next move. The idea that Douglas Roy might be living somewhere on the river was tantalizing because there were few realistic possibilities.

The *un*realistic possibility was that he was living on riverfront property that he owned. He abandoned the mill property because he couldn't make his mortgage payments. It seemed very unlikely that he could have had the money to buy another property, and in any case, his name was nowhere to be found on the county property tax rolls—although it now seemed likely that he was living under an assumed name.

Thus, it boiled down to just two possibilities. Either he was living in property he didn't own—renting, squatting, or imposing on a friend— or he was living in the apparently unregistered houseboat that he'd had up at the cedar mill. I pulled out the list of houseboat registrations that Martha had compiled and looked it over without seeing anything of immediate interest.

There wasn't much I could do to find Roy if he was living on somebody else's property, but it would be pretty easy to spot a houseboat, registered or not. I carried ten gallons of fuel down to my boat, grabbed some snacks and my camera, and took off upriver.

Half a mile past the West Linn boat landing, I paused to shoot a picture of the houseboat at Pete's Place, where Alan's tugboat had sunk. It occurred to me that I never heard Pete's last name. As I thought about it, Douglas Roy would be in his early fifties—and that's about how old Pete was.

I'd never seen a photo of Douglas Roy, so maybe he was going by the name of Pete these days. Almost as quickly as the idea came to me, I had to reject it. Captain Alan knew both Pete and Douglas Roy. If they were one and the same, he'd have said so.

Another mile upstream, I passed a houseboat tied up to one of the private docks in the area known as Coalca. I had seen it many times, and had never seen any sign that it was occupied. Still, I shot a picture of it before continuing upriver, past the old mill property and the landslide. I didn't see another houseboat until I got to Wilsonville.

There were two houseboats in the moorage at the public marina. The larger of them was a rental. It was available for such things as wedding receptions, company picnic cruises, and similar functions. It was not occupied. The smaller houseboat sat with all its window shades closed, making it impossible to determine if it was occupied, so I shot pictures of it.

Continuing upstream, I found two more houseboats moored along Dog Ridge Road in Newberg. One belonged to a part-time member of the Yamhill County sheriff's marine unit, but I took pictures of both, just so my documentation would be complete.

I went on upriver, past the mouth of the Yamhill River, slowing my boat to idle speed because of the presence in this area of shifting sandbars that are notorious for grabbing careless boaters. I went as far as I dared without finding any houseboats. I even explored up the Yamhill River, where I found *Misty Rose* tied up to Captain Alan's old barge. Alan, however, was no place to be seen, and his pickup was not in its usual parking spot at the head of the boarding plank for the barge.

On my high-speed run back downstream, I evaluated what I'd accomplished. Of the five houseboats I'd photographed, I considered only one to be a viable possibility for Roy's hideout. That was the one at Wilsonville. As I idled through the no-wake zone opposite the moorage, I took another long look at that houseboat, but still saw no sign of life.

Back at my desk I compared the registration numbers on the houseboats I'd photographed with those on Martha's list. All five were there. As I checked them off, something caught my eye. I recognized the name of the Yamhill County deputy, but it was another name that seemed oddly familiar. It was an unusual name: D. E. Langlois.

I'd seen that name before, but where? It was the registration for the houseboat at Pete's Place. Could Langlois be Pete's name? I was fairly sure that nobody had ever mentioned Pete's last name—and even if someone had, that wouldn't explain why the name *looked* familiar. I'd never heard the name spoken. I wasn't even sure how it was pronounced.

Setting that aside, I made a Google search of the name on the houseboat at Wilsonville, finding that it belonged to a well-known home builder who lived in West Linn. When I called him, he said that the houseboat was his family's weekend getaway place. Douglas Roy wasn't living there.

That put me back to considering the likelihood that he was living on someone else's property, and that could be screened only by a door-to-door search. There was no such thing as a comprehensive directory of rental properties.

I was interrupted by the ringing of my phone. And after that, nothing would ever be the same.

"Are you the one who's been on the news about that Michigan girl?"

As much as I enjoyed being told what a wonderful thing I'd done, I was becoming tired of the phone calls, many of which were from people wanting to talk to me about movie rights, ghost-written memoirs, or guest appearances at their local service clubs. And all too often, it was another reporter wanting an exclusive interview.

I forced myself to sound cordial. "Yes, this is Corrigan. What can I do for you?"

Fully prepared to say no thank you and goodbye, I had my finger on the disconnect button.

"My name is Jeffrey Moro. I believe you phoned me a couple of months ago."

It took a second for me to recognize the name. He was the father of Megan Moro. I flipped through my files until I found Megan's. She was the girl taken from Burger King in Salem. I'd largely ruled out her case as being connected to Douglas Roy because witnesses said she was taken by a woman.

"Yes," I confirmed. "I did call you."

"I'm sorry I didn't call back. There've been so many calls over the years—most of them from people satisfying their idle curiosity and a few from sick people who claim they know something when all they want to do is pretend to be heroes."

"I understand. And I have to tell you out front that the success we've had with the investigation that led to Alyssa Marquam probably doesn't extend to Megan's case."

"Oh. Why do you say that?"

"Megan was abducted by a woman. Everything we know about the person who kidnapped Alyssa and a number of others is that it is a man who acts alone."

But I didn't want to leave him completely without hope, so I added, "Even though no arrest has yet been made, a suspect has been identified. When he is found, we will find out whether or not he really did act alone as we believe."

"I heard that there are some unidentified remains," Jeffrey said.

"That's true. If you wish, I could ask to have a kit sent to you for taking a DNA sample for comparison."

"I'd be willing to do that. You can't imagine how devastating this has been to our family. Not knowing is the worst. Even bad news would be better than not knowing."

To whatever degree I could force my brain to multitask, I read through my notes on Megan Moro's case while her father talked. The witness had provided an extraordinary amount of information with a level of detail rarely found.

"Can you tell me how the abduction happened?"

"We were on our way to Seattle from Grants Pass. The girls—Megan and her older sister—needed to take a restroom break, so we stopped at Burger King to get something to eat. I escorted the girls to the restroom while my wife ordered lunch. I let the girls go into the ladies' room. I figured I could go to the men's room and be back out before the girls finished.

"I finished and waited by the door until Tiffany—Megan's sister—came out. But Megan didn't. Tiffany said that a lady had told the girls that their mother wanted them outside, but Tiffany was on the toilet. Megan had already finished, so the lady took her, saying she'd come back for Tiffany.

"I looked all around and saw no sign of Megan, so I went to where my wife was still standing in line. But Megan wasn't there either. Then we knew that she'd been kidnapped. We started out toward the parking lot and ran headlong into a witness who had just seen a woman carry a little girl to a van, which sped away as soon as they were inside."

I said, "I've talked with that witness. She is very observant."

"It took forever—or at least it *seemed* like forever—for the police to arrive. By then it was too late. Megan was gone. We were desperate to get her back. We stayed in Salem hoping that the police would bring her back, but after a couple of weeks, I knew it wasn't going to happen. I had to get back to my job, and Tiffany had to get home to start school.

"Kimberly—my wife—stayed in Salem. She was adamant that she had to be there in case they found Megan. I didn't know it, but that was the end of our family. She never said so, but she couldn't help feeling that it was my fault. If I had stayed outside the door until the girls came out, it never would've happened.

"Anyway, Kimberly never came home. Even after all hope of getting Megan back was gone, she stayed in Salem. I sent her money. She got an apartment, a car, and a job in a store downtown. At Christmas, she refused to leave Salem, so I took Tiffany there to spend the holiday with her mother. By the middle of the next year, we'd just kind of given up on each other. Kimberly thought it was my fault Megan was taken, and she felt that I'd given up on her too easily. It was like she believed that if I hadn't left Salem, Megan would have been found.

"For some reason I didn't see it at the time, but Kimberly had lost her sanity. She really should have been under professional care. Instead, she went to the police station every day until someone told her that she was impeding the investigation. So she tried doing her own investigation, driving all over Salem in search of the van the witness had described. In a year, she put a hundred thousand miles on her car without ever going twenty miles outside of town.

"A year and a half after Megan was taken, I filed for divorce. It had gotten to a point where I couldn't even talk to Kimberly. She was completely irrational. She immediately switched back to her maiden name. Tiffany stayed with me because her mom by then had enrolled in the Oregon State Police Academy—she was going to become a cop so that she could find Megan."

I was feeling very uneasy about hearing the personal impact of the abduction. I sensed that Jeffrey was suffering the lingering effects of the trauma almost as much as his wife had. I wished I could think of something to say that would give him some comfort.

"Tiffany and I didn't hear from Kimberly for a long time—maybe seven or eight years. She just scrubbed us from her life. From time to time, we'd hear from Tiffany's grandmother, and she'd tell us what was happening with her. She graduated from the police academy—top of her class, I guess. Anyway, she got a job with the sheriff's office in Clackamas County."

At that moment I knew. My eyes filled with tears, and I was barely able to choke out the question. "What is your ex-wife's name?"

"Stayton. Kimberly Ann Stayton," he said.

I don't know what else was said or how the conversation finally ended. And I don't remember how long I sat at my desk gazing out at the Willamette River.

———

June
29
Sunday

Chapter 55

Things that had never made sense before suddenly had become clear. Now I knew why Kim had become so emotional over the discovery of Lacey McCredie's remains and why the subject of Brittany Harlan's inscription was so upsetting. I had always known that Kim's marriage had ended in some great trauma—how can a marriage end *without* trauma? But this was far beyond anything I could have imagined.

I tried calling Vera and Kim, but both had seemingly blocked calls from me. I knew of no other way to get in touch with her to tell her that I knew about Megan and would help her find out what had happened to her.

As I brought my own emotions under control, an action plan gradually took shape. Step one was still to find Douglas Roy. Even though I didn't really believe that he was connected with Megan's case, the only way to definitively eliminate that possibility was to find him and interrogate him. That led me back to my desk, where my file on Megan Moro still say open on top of the houseboat registration file.

I went online and searched for Megan. I found pictures of the girl, and her mother's features were all over her face. It was heartbreaking to stare into the innocent eyes of the child. I had to close my browser and force myself to set Megan's file aside.

Once again staring at Martha's houseboat registration list, my eyes landed on the name D. E. Langlois. I *knew* that name. It was—I pulled open the drawer where Martha had organized all the files related to child abductions, and I pulled out Kaylin Beatty's list of transactions involving the property of Charles Roy. The name D. E. Langlois jumped off the page.

I mapped the address of the property that Charles Roy, ten years after his death, had sold to D. E. Langlois. As I stared at the map and tried to orient the property to some familiar landmark, I switched the display to satellite imagining and confirmed that the Langlois residence was directly across Highway 99E from Pete's Place.

The connection was too much to ignore. I jumped up from my desk and tripped over DC, who was hanging around mirroring my moods, acting like he'd lost his best friend. The momentary distraction was just enough to stop me from running straight out the door. Instead, I paused long enough to grab my binoculars, camera, and .45 automatic.

I drove straight up to Pete's Place and pulled onto the shoulder. To my left was a century-old bungalow set back about fifty yards from the highway, surrounded by tall fir trees. I aimed my camera at the old house and zoomed in, and that's when I saw the RV parked under a sagging carport. It was a white Dodge with blue trim. I pressed the shutter button.

Even while I was mentally processing the information, I became aware of movement. Someone had come out of the house—a man. He got into a green Toyota sedan. I put down my camera and stepped on the gas, accelerating out of the turnout into the southbound traffic lane while watching the Toyota in my rearview mirror.

It turned the other direction, back toward Oregon City. I braked hard and spun the big Yukon into a controlled skid, whipping around into the northbound lane. I stomped on the gas. Who says you can't spin the tires on an SUV? I closed to about two hundred yards and tailed the Toyota toward town. At Canemah, the speed limit drops to 40 mph, so I eased off the gas to keep from overrunning the Toyota.

I followed him through Canemah and up the hill, past the falls viewpoint, and then down through the tunnel under the railroad tracks. He turned right onto Main Street and, within a block, pulled to the curb. I went past and took a parking space in a lot that had signs with ominous warnings to anyone who wasn't a customer of the adjacent store.

"I have him!" I shouted when Michael Wheeler answered his phone.

"Is that you, Corrigan?"

"It's Douglas Roy. He's right here on Main Street. It looks like he's going into The Wheel."

The Wheel was a tiny restaurant and bar on the corner of Highway 99 and Main.

"Are you sure it's him?"

"As sure as I can be. Can you get someone down here?"

"Don't do anything, Corrigan. Just sit tight."

At that moment, Roy looked straight at me. From fifty feet away, I could see the recognition register on his face. He'd seen me on television. He looked quickly both ways. A city police car turned from 99 onto Main and momentarily blocked my view of Roy. When the car continued past, Roy was gone.

"He's running," I said to Wheeler. "Hold on. I've lost him."

I ran up the sidewalk toward Roy's parked car. He wasn't there, so I continued past it to the intersection of Highway 99 and Main Street. I looked first right and then left, just in time to get a glimpse of Roy scrambling up the embankment next to the railroad overpass.

"He's going up to the railroad tracks!" I shouted to Wheeler.

"I've called for support."

Not waiting for the pedestrian signal to change, I danced my way across the busy highway dodging cars and waving my .45 to encourage their drivers to give me some space. I scrambled up the embankment where Roy had disappeared. Sirens screamed somewhere in the distance.

A broken-down fence ran parallel to the railroad tracks. To the left, there was nowhere to go, so I ran to my right. I went only a few steps and saw fresh skid marks in a steep path leading down into the abandoned Blue Heron Paper Mill. I caught a glimpse of Roy as he disappeared behind one of the old buildings.

"He's on the Blue Heron property, heading south between the buildings," I reported to Wheeler.

I slid down the embankment to the asphalt between the tall building on my right, where semitrailer loads of wood chips used to be unloaded, and the metal-sided building on my left, which had housed the de-inking machinery for recycling used paper. I ran to the corner of that building, where I could see up and down what used to be Main Street, and saw Roy enter the number 2 paper machine building.

Switching my phone to speaker, I caught the tail end of what Wheeler was saying.

"—are on the way. Do not follow him! You hear that, Corrigan? Stay back and wait for our people!"

"He just went into the number 2 paper machine building," I said, pretending I hadn't heard him.

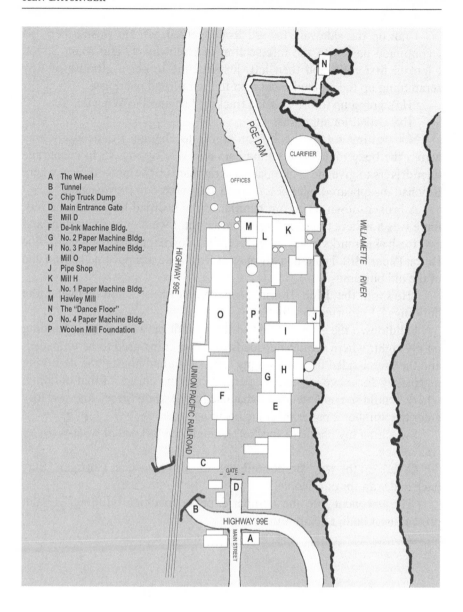

The Blue Heron paper mill occupied a twenty-two-acre parcel of land lying between downtown Oregon City and Willamette Falls. The mill went bankrupt in 2011, and all the machinery was removed as part of the court-ordered liquidation. What remained of the mill was an ugly collection of decaying industrial buildings constructed throughout the twentieth century without an overall plan and with a conspicuous disregard for esthetics. Most of the buildings, including the one where Roy had just disappeared, featured rusting corrugated sheet-metal siding over steel or concrete frames.

As I entered the building, the sound of running footsteps echoed through the cavernous empty space, telling me that Roy was still on the move. I couldn't see him, so I had to follow the sounds. That was becoming increasingly difficult as the scream of sirens got louder.

"I lost him!" I shouted to my phone.

"Stay back, Corrigan! You hear me?"

I holstered my .45 and backtracked outside the building. From beneath the oversized lettering on the side of the building spelling out "Working Together for Safety," I watched the arrival of a swarm of police and sheriff's vehicles at the gate to the mill site. While two officers struggled to cut the lock from the gate, another backed his SUV up against it and rigged a tow chain from the gate to his trailer hitch.

With a shouted warning, the SUV driver advised everyone to stand clear. He gunned the engine and tore the gate from its hinges, allowing a swarm of officers to run onto the mill property. I motioned toward the last place I'd seen Roy, careful to keep my hands visible.

"He was heading toward number 3!" I shouted.

Over the next few minutes, chaos reigned as an ever-increasing number of emergency vehicles arrived. I recognized Sheriff Larry Jamieson and made my way toward him. I gave him a quick summary of how events had developed.

"Are you sure it's Douglas Roy in there?"

"I don't know what Roy looks like. But this guy owns a house and a houseboat that both used to belong to Roy, and he has an RV that matches one seen by witnesses to some of the kidnappings," I explained.

"I sure hope you're right!"

To everyone within earshot, Jamieson shouted, "We're setting up a command post right here! Get a communication rig over here and make room for SWAT."

In the interest of self-preservation, I stayed close to the command center. There had to have been at least three dozen armed officers swarming over the area, with more arriving by the minute, and the last thing I wanted was to be mistaken for the target.

Jamieson was on his VHF saying, "I want officers up on the railroad grade—all the way up to the falls. Don't let anyone climb up there, and report immediately if you think you see our guy."

I saw Michael Wheeler arrive, followed by Oregon City's massive armored SWAT vehicle. Only when he was out of his car and approaching the command center did I disconnect and put my phone away.

He asked the same question Jamieson had. "Are you sure it's him?"

"As sure as I can be. But if this guy isn't Roy, he damned sure is guilty of *something*."

"You stay here," he ordered. "I'm going to set up a forward post."

"You don't know what he looks like," I told him. "I'm going with you."

"Fine. Just stay out of the way!"

Officers were fanning out and entering the old buildings on both sides of Main Street. I followed Wheeler up Main toward the distinctive concrete Hawley Pulp and Paper building at the south edge of the mill property.

"He's in Mill O," someone shouted on the radio. "Mill O. He's heading west—toward the river."

"In pursuit!"

"Ten-four. Heading south into the pipe-shop building."

"Not in sight! Repeat, he's not in sight."

A number of officers rushed out of the huge number 4 paper machine building on our left, swarming across Main Street to the foundation of the old Oregon City Woolen Mill and into Mill O. Others moved south, ahead of Wheeler and me, into the number 1 paper machine building. Wheeler stayed on the asphalt, following the paper mill's rail spur between the two rows of buildings.

The tall structure that housed the Blue Heron offices stood before us, and off to our right, a causeway went between the Hawley building and the stagnant water of the basin created by the dam around the brink of Willamette Falls. Wheeler paused there, with an unobstructed view west, toward the river. Thirty yards ahead of us, a man suddenly burst from Mill H, frantically looking left and right.

"That's him," I told Wheeler. "That's Roy!"

Seeing us and half a dozen uniformed officers behind us, Roy ran the other direction. But that led to a dead end. With officers swarming through all the buildings behind him, the only way he could go was onto the walkway atop the dam. I followed Wheeler and the other officers in pursuit onto the dam, past the huge circular concrete basin that used to be the clarifier pool.

Roy continued out on the dam, above the rusting penstocks of one of the old Willamette Falls power plants. At the end of the walkway, he reached the platform called the Dance Floor, where the last of the powerhouses on the Oregon City side of the falls had stood until just a few years ago.

Cornered on the Dance Floor, Roy had no place to run. His only option would be to scale the chain-link fence and make a suicidal leap toward the river forty feet below. He started clawing at the fence in a desperate attempt to climb it, but perhaps recognizing the futility of trying to escape, Roy dropped back down onto the steel-grate deck and raised his hands.

Two deputies ran forward and forced Roy down to the deck, quickly pulling his arms behind his back and cuffing him. The chase was over.

The suspect was pulled to his feet to face Wheeler, who recited the Miranda statement.

"Are you Douglas Roy?" Wheeler asked when the subject acknowledged that he understood his rights.

"I am Douglas Langlois," he said. "I want an attorney."

With that, there could be no further questioning. Wheeler ordered the arresting officers to escort Langlois back across the dam to a patrol car waiting next to the Hawley building.

"Langlois is Roy," I told Wheeler. "Langlois is the name he's been using since he abandoned the old cedar mill."

"How do you know that?" Wheeler asked.

"We found it in the real estate transactions involving his grandfather's property, together with registration records on the houseboat that used to be moored up at the mill."

"I want to know how this whole stampede started," he said.

I ignored that. "You need to search his house."

"We'll get to that. First, though, we need to get him booked and get search warrants."

"No," I insisted. "You can't wait for warrants. He could have captives in there!"

Wheeler stared at me for several seconds. "Let's go talk to Jamieson," he finally said.

We hurried back down Main Street to the command center, where Jamieson was busy on the radio, disbanding the huge army of officers from the Oregon City, West Linn, Gladstone, and Canby police departments, the sheriff's office, and the Oregon State Police.

"What makes you think there could be captives in his house?" Jamieson asked me after Wheeler explained the situation.

"Alyssa Marquam, Brittany Harlan, Lacey McCredie," I said. "Do you need more than that?"

"No. Let's go."

Leaving an OSP officer in charge of the command center, Jamieson quickly commandeered two sheriff's office SUVs. I piled into the backseat of one alongside Wheeler. With sirens and lights, we led the way out to Highway 99, screaming south through Canemah. As we passed an old mobile home park, I pointed to the faded blue bungalow where the old RV was parked.

We skidded to a stop on the gravel driveway with the other SUV and two patrol cars right behind. Officers with weapons drawn fanned out around the old house.

Someone yelled, "Clear!" after checking the RV.

The weighted steel battering ram took down the backdoor, and four officers rushed inside. I had to wait outside while they went from room to room, calling out when each was clear. When I finally got inside, two deputies were standing at the bottom of a stairway to the basement, looking at a steel door that appeared to be secured by a deadbolt.

An officer screwed a slide hammer into the deadbolt lock, and with two sharp pulls, he extracted the cylinder. He then used a screwdriver to retract the deadbolt. Cautiously, he pulled the door open, with two officers behind him holding their weapons at the ready.

"Clear! Clear! Clear!" the officer shouted, waving for those behind him to lower their weapons.

That's when I heard a faint voice say, "Thank you."

I was the fourth one into the tiny room, where a small brown-haired woman stood wide-eyed with her back to the corner furthest from the door.

"It's okay," Wheeler said quietly. "You're safe now."

Remembering the photo from 1987, showing a smiling child with her kitten, and I saw something familiar in her eyes.

"Brittany?" I asked.

She turned her face toward me and stared for a second. "Yes," she said quietly. "I'm Brittany. He wanted me to forget. But I remembered."

"We found where you scratched your name in the wood," I said.

At that point, Brittany started to cry and said, "Where are Mommy and Daddy?"

"We'll call them as soon as we get back to our office," Wheeler told her.

I didn't know if Wheeler was aware that Brittany's mother took her own life a few years after the kidnapping. I surely didn't want to be the one who'd have to tell her. I scrolled through the recent calls list on my phone until I found Roger Harlan's number, which was easy to spot because of its Cleveland area code.

"There's someone here who wants to talk to you," I said when he answered.

Brittany looked confused when I handed her my phone.

"It's a telephone," I said, realizing that she'd never seen a cell phone. "It's your dad."

"Hello?" she said tentatively.

"Brittany?" I heard Roger ask. "Is it really you, Brittany?"

"Daddy?"

The next few minutes were filled with tears and smiles as Brittany was led up the stairs and into a world she hadn't seen in twenty-five years. Overwhelmed, Brittany crumbled to the ground and cried. Officers had to help her to the car.

Later that afternoon, a massive press conference was staged in the gymnasium at Clackamas High School. As the news spread, the major networks went wall-to-wall with their coverage. Sheriff Jamieson and his PIO, Cal Westfall, took center stage with Wheeler close behind. All the reporters demanded to know the identity of the suspect, but the officers deferred, explaining that it would take some time to determine his actual name.

"Is this case connected with the Michigan girl—Alyssa Marquam?" shouted an ABC reporter.

"We currently believe that is the case," Westfall said.

"Are there others?"

"We do not know of any other survivors at this time."

I was on the main floor, off to the side of the stage, having been dragged along from the sheriff's office to the high school by Jamieson. I declined to go up on stage because it wasn't my show, and I wasn't looking for a gold star from anybody. Inevitably, though, one of the reporters from Channel 12 recognized me and dragged his cameraman over to where I'd been keeping a low profile.

Hours later, I got home, exhausted and numb. I got a can of beer out of the refrigerator and flopped into a chair on my porch. DC appeared from somewhere, landing heavily in my lap. Bud showed up about ten seconds after I snapped my beer open.

"Hey, Corrigan, you're big news," he said.

"Go get yourself a beer. I can't get up." I gestured with my beer can toward the huge cat.

The rest of the evening passed quietly, though one after another, most of my neighbors stopped by to congratulate me.

Deputies met Roger Harlan at the American Airlines gate when he arrived in Portland a little after ten thirty. They drove him to the sheriff's office for a private reunion with the daughter he had not seen in twenty-five years. At Roger's request, no cameras were permitted.

Chapter 56

When Martha came in on Monday morning, she said that her mother was very impressed that her daughter worked for the famous detective Corrigan.

"We're partners, remember?" I said.

"Ten-four, boss."

"You know what finally did it?" I asked her.

"No."

"It was the houseboat registration. You get all the points for that."

"Please say you'll never ask me to go through that printout again!"

"Not on this case," I promised.

"Now that it's all wrapped up, do you think Kim will come back?" Martha asked.

I let that hang in the air for perhaps half a minute before answering. "I learned something last Saturday," I finally said. "Something I never knew."

Martha waited for me to elaborate.

"Do you remember the name Megan Moro on the list of missing girls?"

"Was she the one grabbed by the woman in Salem?"

"That's right."

I paused to collect my emotions. "Megan Moro is Kim's daughter."

Martha stared at me. "Dear god," she whispered.

Neither of us said anything for several minutes.

At last, Martha said, "So we aren't finished yet."

"No. We aren't."

"What can I do? *Anything!* I'll even go through those damned boat registrations again, if it'll help."

"Back about the time of the landslide, I talked with a witness to Megan's abduction. She gave me a lot of detail. She's either an extraordinary witness, or else she's really good at making things up. I plan to talk with her again and find out which. And, of course, if Kim comes back—"

"When," Martha correct. "Not *if.* She'll be back."

"What you can do," I said, "is dig up every scrap of information you can find about Megan Moro. I've already scoured the Internet, but I suspect that a lot of the news coverage hasn't been digitized yet."

"So I guess I'll have to start in the newspaper archives."

"Right—in Salem, since that's where the kidnapping took place, and it appears that the entire investigation was done by Salem PD. See what you can find in the *Statesman Journal* archives."

After Martha left, I made the call I'd been dreading. Kevin Fox had a history with Kim. I didn't know any of the details about it, and I didn't want to. But Fox was a detective for the Salem Police Department, and if anybody could get me a copy of the investigation files on the abduction of Megan Moro, it was Fox.

"Am I *really* talking with the famous PI Corrigan? Please, give me a minute to catch my breath," Fox said with his customary sarcasm.

"How you doing, Fox?" I asked.

"Kidding aside, Corrigan, you did good—getting those girls back."

"Thanks. But I'm not finished. That's the reason for the call."

"What's up?"

"Megan Moro—abducted from Salem in 1996. I need the file on your investigation."

The long silence told me what I'd suspected. "I assume you know—"

"Yeah. I know. Can you get me the file?"

"What makes you think you can solve it?"

"I *have* to."

"Of course, you do. Sure, Corrigan. I'll copy the file for you."

"When can I pick it up?"

"It's a pretty big file. You'll have to give me a couple of days. I'll call you when it's ready."

"Thanks, Fox. I owe you."

"You've said that before. Just solve this one, okay? Then you won't owe me a thing."

The interrogation of Douglas Roy was scheduled to begin at one, and Wheeler had invited me to be there as an observer. Since Roy had invoked his Miranda rights at the time of his arrest, no interrogation could be conducted without his attorney present. And since he couldn't afford to pay an attorney, the whole process had to wait until one was appointed by the court.

I was given a seat in a room adjacent to the interrogation room, where I could watch on a closed-circuit video monitor. The lead interrogator was Vince Norway, a tough-as-nails deputy with a Marine haircut and a vast amount of training and experience at getting suspects to talk. Roy's attorney was a public defender named Martin Mayger.

When asked to state his legal name, Roy said, "My name is Douglas Edward Langlois."

"Have you ever used the name Douglas E. Roy?"

"Yes. Roy was my father's name. He was killed in Vietnam. My parents never married, but I used his name because it made it easier to get survivor's benefits from the Veterans Administration."

"But your legal name is Langlois. Is that correct?"

"Yes."

That answered the question of how he'd managed to establish a second identity. He'd had two identities all his life.

Martin Mayger then shocked everyone by saying, "Against my legal advice, my client wishes to make a statement."

Norway looked at Langlois and asked, "You understand that this session is being recorded and that anything you say can and will be used against you in court?"

"Yeah, yeah, yeah. But I figure I ain't getting out from under this thing anyway, so it don't matter much."

I wondered if he'd forgotten that Oregon is a death penalty state.

"In that case, say what you want to say."

"Okay, well, I had this friend, see? Keith Heppner. We was in school together until we both got tossed out, and then my mom sent me to live with my grandpa. I wasn't supposed to see Keith after that, but he used to sneak out to Grandpa's place. We'd do stuff—like go fishing or play in the old tunnels."

"Tunnels?" Norway asked.

"Yeah, there was a tunnel that went from Grandpa's house to a cellar under the old cedar mill. And there was another one that went from there down to the edge of the river. Grandpa told me that they were a hundred years old and were built to smuggle Chinamen in and out."

"What did you do in the tunnels?"

"Nothing special—smoke dope or whatever. It was just a place to hang out and not get disturbed. Anyway, Keith had this idea that we could take girls in there and make 'em do things."

"What kind of things?"

"Well, sex, mainly. Different kinds of sex, you know. Keith had a bunch of ideas about that, but when we tried to talk girls into going into the tunnels, they freaked out and wouldn't go in. But Keith said we could just rough 'em up a little bit, and then they'd go in.

"We only tried that once, though. Keith had to beat her up pretty bad before she did it. Afterward, he wanted to kill her and throw the body in the river. But we just let her go. I guess she never told anyone, though, because we never heard nothing about it. But it scared the hell out of me, just thinking what that girl could've done to us."

"How old was that girl? What was her name?"

"I don't know what her name was. She was just a girl we knew from school. I think she was a year younger than me. Anyways, after that, Keith started talking about how we could make a room where we could lock a girl in, and then we wouldn't have to kill her or worry about her talking."

"When was this?"

"Well, I guess he first started talking about it maybe a year after I went to live with Grandpa. That'd be around '78 or '79. At first, it was just hot air. But he went to work for his old man—they had a masonry and concrete business. After a couple of years, Keith knew how to build things, and when he talked about building a room for keeping girls, it kind of turned from bullshit into a plan."

"How were you going to pay for it?"

"Oh, well, when I got to be twenty-one, I got a power of attorney for my grandpa, because he was going blind and stuff, and he needed my help with all the paperwork. I found out that he had a bunch of money."

"Are you saying that you stole money from your grandfather?"

"It wasn't stealing. It was legal. Like I said, I had that power of attorney. So anyways, me and Keith started talking serious about building a place to keep girls, and we decided that the cellar under the mill was the best place for it. Then Keith got the idea of building a whole row of rooms so that we could keep more girls in there.

"The mill was shut down, and the building was empty, so Keith got a whole load of concrete blocks delivered out there and then a bunch of ready mix. We laid everything out on the floor in chalk and then started building. And we filled the insides of the concrete blocks with plastic foam to make them solid so that sound wouldn't go through.

"And Keith knew a guy named Brad who helped a lot too. It would've been real hard to get that job done without him. Brad was older, maybe thirty or thirty-five, but he knew how to do plumbing, electrical, and heating—stuff like that."

"What is Brad's last name?"

"If I ever knew it, I've forgotten what it was. Altogether, it took like almost a year to build the rooms. They had everything—toilets, heat, lights, even TV. We bought good, comfortable beds too. And we built a kitchen—but that wasn't for the girls to use. We set it up so that we'd cook those TV dinners in the oven and then take 'em to the girls. That way we didn't ever have to let them out of their rooms."

I was starting to feel sick, listening to the offhand way Langlois described the imprisonment of girls. The more detail he provided, the more twisted he seemed to be.

"When did you finish building the cells?"

"Oh, that would've been in '84, probably."

"Okay, then what?"

"Well, *then* we had to get some girls. But first we had to get rid of Brad. He was a dumb shit. We told him to meet us at the boat ramp in Wilsonville in the middle of the night—we told him we were going to have a party on a houseboat. Instead, Keith knocked him over the head and sent him and his car down the ramp into the river. Bye-bye, Brad.

"Next night we went to a high school football game in Portland and picked up a girl. We told her we were taking her to a dance with a live band, but she started getting scared, and then she started trying to open the car door to jump out, so we had to tape her up. She fought real hard, and we had to hurt her pretty bad in order to get her tied up.

"She just up and died in the car, so we didn't take her to the mill. Instead, we took her up in the mountains somewhere around Estacada and put her under some branches and stuff, way off the road."

"What was the girl's name?"

"Oh hell, I don't know. Anyways, not too long after that, we picked up a girl out at that college in Gresham—or Troutdale, whatever."

"Mt. Hood Community College?"

"Yeah, probably. Anyways, Keith slipped her some kind of drug, so he wouldn't have to fight her. We carried her down to her room and, you know, took all her clothes. Only thing is, when she woke up, she went wild!

"We didn't even dare to open the door, because she was just going crazy. She wrecked everything in the room. But finally she wore out, maybe from not eating. We knew we'd never be able to do anything with her, so Keith took care of her."

"You mean he killed her."

"Yeah, whatever. Anyways, we took her up in the mountains like we did with the other one. So after that, I got to thinking we needed to get younger girls because they wouldn't be able to fight so hard, and we could raise 'em up to do what we wanted. But Keith didn't like that idea, so I had to get him out of the picture."

"You mean you killed him."

Langlois gave an indifferent shrug. "I told him I had something to show him, and he followed me up an old path away from the mill. I popped him and buried him out near where the hobos live. Then I had to find the kind of girl I could deal with."

"You mean a child—"

"Basically, yeah."

"When was this?"

"It was winter—end of '84 or maybe early '85. I picked her up in a grocery store in Salem. She was just wandering around alone, so I took her hand and led her outside. I figure she must've walked away from her parents. Anyways, she turned out to be too young—she wouldn't pay any attention to the things I told her, and she never stopped crying. I had to shut her up before she made me crazy."

"How did you shut her up?"

"I think I just put a pillow over her face. Yeah. Probably, that's what I did. Then I was going to take her up into the mountains, but I got caught in a traffic jam. All of a sudden, there was a cop shining his light in my window telling me that the road was closed by a wreck, and I'd have to turn back. The body was just laying on the backseat, not even covered up, but the cop didn't notice.

"Anyways, I got the hell out of there and dropped the body in a ditch somewhere around Damascus. It was found the next day, and that made me pretty nervous for a while, but luckily nothing ever came out of it."

"Can you give me the names of these girls?"

"I'm no good with names. I never paid no attention. Those was one, two, and three."

I found this extremely troubling—because of his indifference to these human lives but also because none of these three had previously been recognized as potential victims of Langlois. As he continued talking, I frequently referred to the notes Martha and I had compiled relating to missing girls, and in that way, I was able to attach names to some of his numbers.

1—unidentified, abducted as a teenager in 1984, dumped in mountains

2—unidentified, abducted as a college student in 1985, dumped in mountains

 # 3—unidentified, abducted as a toddler in 1985, was nearly caught with body in car
 # 4—Shannon Coburg, held for 10 years, died in childbirth, buried at the mill, not found
 # 6—Brittany Harlan, held for 25 years
 # 7—Caroline Lowell, held for 16 years, remains found buried at the mill
 # 8—Evelyn Curtin, held for 15 years, died in 2007, remains were burned
 # 9—Alyssa Marquam, held for 17 years, released in Salt Lake City in 2010
 # 10—unidentified, abducted 1986, buried at the mill, not found
 # 11—Lacey McCredie, held for 15 years, killed in 2010, buried near homeless camp
 # 12—Makayla Imbler, held for 11 years, killed in 2007, remains were burned
 # 13—Danielle Flora, held for 5 years, died in 2002, remains were burned.
 # 14—unidentified, abducted 2005, not on lists because body was found near abduction site
 # 15—unidentified, abducted 2007, held for 3 years, remains tossed into the Snake River
 # 16—Emily Marcola, released unharmed

All told, Langlois confessed to sixteen murders, including his grandfather's. Significantly—at least for me—none of the cases he described sounded anything like Megan Moro's abduction. That was a huge relief. It would have been horrifying to know that he'd done to her the things he'd done to the other girls.

The confession was sprinkled with details regarding the way he treated the girls who'd been in his hands for long periods. Langlois talked all afternoon, completely without emotion, describing in horrible detail how he'd captured each girl and what he did to her.

When he spoke about September 11, 2001, he said he was so overcome with emotion about what had happened in New York that he decided to connect the TV sets in the cells to CNN. Prior to that, they were connected to a VCR where he played *Sesame Street* and porn videos. He acted as though he had done something noble by letting the girls watch the world outside on CNN. That was the day Brittany Harlan stood on the table in her cell and scratched her name in the beam.

His story eventually came around to his last few years at his grandfather's mill. Sometime after Harvey Walters shut down his boat repair business in 2007, Langlois fell into serious financial difficulty. Missing the monthly lease checks from Walters, he rented the building to the meth cooks, but they proved to be unreliable and didn't always pay. When it became apparent that he couldn't continue to live on borrowed money, Langlois started making plans.

The fact that he already had two identities was a big help. His ownership of the mill was all done as Douglas Roy, and he had a driver's license and Social Security number under that name. But he also had a driver's license as Douglas Langlois, which was the name he had used to buy the houseboat back in the 1980s in order to get out of his grandfather's house.

Between 2007 and 2010, he transferred as many of his grandfather's assets as possible to Langlois so as to protect them from his creditors. This included the bungalow on Highway 99 where I finally found him.

When he realized he'd have to abandon the mill, he already had a place to go. Early in 2010, when foreclosure was imminent, Langlois knew he had to destroy the bunker. At the time, he was holding four girls—Brittany Harlan, Alyssa Marquam, Lacey McCredie, and an unidentified ten-year-old girl. The basement of his little bungalow couldn't accommodate all four, so he made a plan to release all except Brittany Harlan.

Why Brittany? Langlois had deluded himself into believing that she loved him and really wanted to live as his slave. In reality, Brittany had created for herself an effective survival strategy that kept her alive for twenty-five years.

But what could he do with the others? He said he didn't want to kill them, but the reason had nothing to do with compassion. He simply didn't want to deal with the disposal of three corpses because, as he explained, "that's how people get caught." So he got his hands on some kind of drug—he claimed he didn't know what it was—that would render the girls semiconscious.

He told the girls he was giving them polio shots and injected them with the drug. Then he got them into the back of his grandfather's old motor home, bound them with duct tape, and hit the road, planning to drop girls in Salt Lake City, Phoenix, and San Diego.

But the news coverage of "Sassy's" inexplicable appearance in the park in Salt Lake City took him by surprise, and he panicked. On his hasty drive back home, he dumped his youngest captive into the Snake River in Idaho. When asked if he'd killed her first, he just gave an indifferent shrug. He arrived back in Oregon with Lacey McCredie still in the motor home because he hadn't found a convenient place to dump her.

It was late at night when he approached the old cedar mill. Recalling where he'd buried his long-time friend, Keith Heppner, he decided that would be a good place to dispose of Lacey. He parked his motor home in the turnout along Highway 99 at the head of the trail that led down to the homeless camp. In her drugged condition, Lacey was barely able to walk. Langlois half carried, half dragged her down to the junction with the trail that went to the pot farm.

That's where he suffocated her with a plastic bag. In the dark, he simply tossed the body into a bramble patch, but the next day, he carried some scraps of metal roofing up the trail and laid them over the body, adding some heavy rocks to keep animals from disturbing the grave site. There she had remained until the day Kim was waved ashore by the homeless man.

He took Brittany to his bungalow and locked her in the basement cell. Over a period of weeks, Langlois pulled everything of value out of the mill building. When there was nothing left to sell for salvage, he leveled everything with a bulldozer rented under the name of Douglas Roy. He used that to demolish the cells and fill the bunker with dirt. Finally, he moved his old houseboat down to the moorage across the highway from his bungalow, where it became Pete's Place.

The houseboat provided him with a monthly rent check, and he got a part-time job cleaning cars for a nearby used-car dealer. That gave him enough income to maintain his low-profile life in the bungalow.

When Langlois finally stopped talking, there were still many unanswered questions. Some of them would *never* be answered.

Chapter 57

The call I'd been waiting for finally came in while I was sitting on my porch with a soggy cat in my lap and my first cup of coffee. It was raining lightly, and I was wondering if the weather would improve before the holiday weekend—not that I had any plans.

Caller ID said Vera Lyons.

"Vera," I almost shouted. "Thank god you called! I take it you've seen the news and know what's been happing here. Is Kim still with you?"

"Slow down, Corrigan. Yes, Kim is still here, and yes, we've seen the news."

"I really need to talk to her! I need to tell her—I need to tell her that I know about Megan."

"I always knew you'd figure it out. But listen to me. You still don't know the whole story."

"Can't you just let me talk to Kim?"

"Be quiet, Corrigan, and just listen."

"Vera, I—"

"No! Just listen! I need to tell you about Kim's life. You don't know anything about that."

"We've been pretty close for a long time," I protested. "I probably know more than you think."

"You know less than you think," she corrected.

I sighed. "Have it your way."

"Did Kim ever tell you that she was a neglected child?"

"Neglected child—what are you talking about?"

"It has a lot to do with the way she thinks and the way that this whole thing has affected her. Yes, she was a neglected child. I'm not proud to admit that. I'm afraid her father and I treated her as an inconvenience."

"I think you're wrong. She never said—"

"That's my point! She never told you about it. But it is the heart of the issue. You probably know that she was born in Corvallis. Her dad was a professor of business administration at Oregon State at the time."

"I know that." Then to lighten the mood, I added, "And she was born on October 4, 1970—ten-four. She was destined to be some kind of a cop."

Vera groaned. "That's a pretty old joke. And pretty lame too. Anyway, I assume you know that she had no brothers or sisters. When Kim was two years old, her dad took a position in the business school at the University of the Pacific in Stockton, and that's where she grew up."

"I know that," I said impatiently.

"Yes. Well, I'll admit right now that we weren't the best parents on earth. My husband and I were academics—he the professor and I the perpetual student. We were never much interested in parenting. We simply expected our child to be like a pet—and conform to our lifestyle. And that might have worked if not for the girl who lived next door."

"Would that be Tiffany?" I asked. "Kim has occasionally talked about her childhood friend."

"That's right. But the thing is Tiffany was from a large family—she had four older brothers—and the family had a boat. The boys were—well, they were boys. Tiffany's mom started inviting Kim to go along when they went boating so that Tiffany would have someone to play with."

"And that's how she got into water skiing. I know all that."

"My husband and I were quietly happy to be relieved of the obligation to entertain her. It is very hard for me to admit that. And Kim will never say how much that hurt her. I could see that it did, but I never did anything about it. Anyway, over time, Kim went on so many boat outings that I think she started to feel like a member of Tiffany's family. I think she spent as many nights at their house as she did at ours.

"And at the same time, things were coming apart for me. For a long time, things weren't right between Kim's dad and me. He was absorbed in the school and his job, and I was increasingly restless. Then one day, I got on a bus to San Francisco, leaving my husband to deal with Kim. I guess he did his best, but he really didn't have a clue. And I was so self-absorbed, I didn't care."

"I don't think Kim sees it that way," I said.

"You're wrong. She was hurt to the core when I abandoned her—so much so that she still can't talk about it. And to make things worse, when Kim was in her senior year, her dad accepted a job in New York. He didn't bother talking about it first. He simply told Kim that they were moving.

"Kim, of course, threw a terrible fit. She didn't want to leave all the things she liked to do, and she didn't want to live in the big city. But most of all, she didn't want to leave the only people who loved and cared about her. Tiffany's folks could see that. So they went to my husband and suggested that Kim be allowed to stay with them until she finished high school."

"Did you know all this was happening?"

"I was completely out of the picture. By then, I'd gone back to using my maiden name— Lyons—and I'd become what people in those days called a free spirit. I joined a band of drifters and went on a ten-year nationwide odyssey to 'find myself.' Then when my stepfather died and left me some money, I left the travelling commune, bought a small motor home, and have been on the road by myself ever since.

"So in 1987, Kim graduated from Stagg High School. Her father was too busy to make the trip back to Sacramento, so he sent her a card. I was too spaced-out to even do that. I can't even imagine how that made her feel. Anyway, she started dating a guy—Jeffrey Moro. He was a former Stagg High student who was two years older than Kim and had been attending community college.

"Jeffrey had been involved in high school sports, but I guess he wasn't good enough to get a scholarship. In any case, he still lived with his family—and he had access to the family boat, which was all that Kim needed to know. She had been accepted into University of the Pacific, so she got a job at Dairy Queen through the summer of '87 and spent virtually all her time off with her friends out on the Delta boating and skiing.

"She didn't know it, but by the time she started the fall term at the university, she was pregnant. I imagine that she started to suspect the situation in October and undoubtedly knew for sure by mid-November. Her dad withdrew his financial support for her education and basically disowned her.

"Of course, I didn't know about any of this until years later. Jeffrey and Kim got married in a civil ceremony in January 1988. Their daughter, Tiffany, was born on May 14, 1988. Jeffrey dropped out of school and went to work in construction.

"In 1990, they moved to Oregon—trying to lower their cost of living and find a better job. Jeffrey went to work for the Department of Transportation in Medford. By then Kim was pregnant again, and their second daughter, Megan, was born on November 16, 1990.

"Jeffrey did well at ODOT and earned some good promotions. In 1993, Jeffrey's grandfather left him some money, and he used it to buy a house on the shore of the reservoir behind Savage Rapids Dam in Grants Pass. For Kim, it was like a dream come true, because the lake was just big enough for water skiing. They bought a little ski boat, and their house on Savage

Lake became their own private boating paradise. The girls grew up around and in the water.

"Kim stayed home to raise the girls, planning to get a job after they both were in school. She was interested in law enforcement—maybe it was that whole ten-four thing—anyway, she started taking police sciences courses at Rogue Community College. It was just in the evenings, but she intended to take on a full class-load after Megan started kindergarten. As 1996 rolled around, Tiffany was in second grade, and Megan was going to start kindergarten in the fall."

I knew what came next.

"In August, they decided to take a road trip, intending to visit Seattle and Victoria, BC. They stopped for lunch in Salem. Jeffrey needed to use the restroom, so Kim got in line to place their order. Then the girls decided that they needed to go too, so they went with him. Kim never saw Megan again. I guess you know all about the abduction."

"Jeffrey told me the details," I said, "and I've talked with one of the witnesses."

"But think about this. Kim—who never got over the feeling that she had been abandoned by her parents and who had vowed to be a better parent to her own children—suddenly has lost one. It was crushing to her. She still hasn't recovered from that.

"When Jeffrey came back, Kim could tell just by looking at him that something was wrong—and then she noticed that Megan wasn't with him. He told her that he had walked the girls to the door of the ladies' room and then let them go in alone. Then he went into the men's room, thinking that he'd be back out long before the girls got done.

"But only Tiffany came out. She said that a lady came into the restroom and told them that their mother wanted them to come outside with her. Tiffany was still busy and told that to the lady, who just said okay and then left with Megan. By the time Tiffany told the story to Jeffrey, Megan was gone.

"Jeffrey and Kim frantically looked in all the cars in the parking lot, while an employee called the police. There was a witness who said that she'd seen a woman and little girl get into an old van driven by a male, described as looking like a homeless person, whatever that meant. In the days before the AMBER Alert system was created, the only thing the police could do was put out a bulletin on the van. But by the time that was done, the van and Megan had been gone for nearly an hour.

"For two weeks, Kim and Jeffrey stayed in a Salem motel with Tiffany, hoping that Megan would be found. The police received a bunch of tips from people who thought they had seen a gray van with a little girl in it, but none of the leads panned out. By the end of the week, the van could have been as far away as New York or Alaska. Jeffrey could tell that the police were losing hope, but Kim held on.

"Jeffrey had to go back to work, and it was almost time for Tiffany to go back to school. But Kim insisted that she had to stay in Salem in case Megan was found. And by then, she was starting to blame Jeffrey—he shouldn't have let the girls go into the restroom alone. At the very least, he should have waited outside the door until they came back out. Once that feeling took root, I think, she couldn't get it out of her head. It started to undermine their marriage.

"Kim stayed in the motel for another week or two but eventually got a cheap little apartment. Weeks passed. Jeffrey begged her to come home, but she simply could not go home without Megan. Months passed. She stayed in Salem. At Christmas, Jeffrey took Tiffany to Salem, but the visit was a disaster. The hard feelings would never go away.

"By the middle of '97, it was clear that Jeffrey and Kim were through with each other. She thought that he was the reason Megan was taken, and she felt that he'd given up on her way too soon. She had the notion that if Jeffrey hadn't been in such a hurry to get home, Megan would have been found. Irrational logic, for sure, but she'd gone around the bend, you know?

"Kim had a burning desire to get personally involved in the search. She eventually enrolled in the Oregon State Police Academy, financing her life with a part-time job at Nordstrom's. A year and a half after Megan disappeared, Jeffrey and Kim divorced. She let Jeffrey have custody of Tiffany because she wouldn't have had time to take care of her and remain in school.

"After graduation from the academy in 1999, she landed a job with the Clackamas County Sheriff's Office. Her experience with boating led to her being assigned to the marine unit. She was good at what she did and worked her way up the promotion ladder.

"Gradually, she let go of any hope that Megan would ever be seen again. She forced herself to block the emotion out of her mind in order to remain sane— though most people who knew her believed that she was too late on that score. Years passed. She put away the photos because seeing them just made her cry.

"She met Kevin Fox at a law enforcement conference in 2005. When she learned that he was a detective with Salem Police Department, she started dating him, hoping that it might somehow get her into the investigation. They dated for a couple of years, but eventually Kim called it off because she just didn't have the same intensity of feeling toward Fox that he had for her.

"Then she simply stopped talking about her past. She had to. It just hurt too much. That's why she never told you about Megan."

I finally asked the question I'd been holding back. "So what happens now?"

"Well, like I said, Kim knows about the things you've been working on. We've seen you all over television. I think she's been holding her breath—uncertain whether to hope for a solution to Megan's case or to dread it."

"I haven't given up hope for Megan," I said earnestly.

"See, that's the problem. She did. And then all of this has brought it back, and she can't decide if she wants that. I don't think she could stand another disappointment."

"Tell her I'll figure it out. There has to be a way—"

"You still don't understand what she's been through, Corrigan. This isn't something that just goes away."

"No, but—"

"Listen. I can't explain all this right now. I have to go."

In the middle of the afternoon, Martha returned from her second day in the archives at the *Statesman Journal*. The thick folder she dropped on her desk indicated that she'd found quite a bit of news about Megan Moro.

She said, "I copied everything I found with Megan's name in it, but I haven't actually read very much of it yet." She leafed through the file and handed me the top ten or twenty pages, which had small Post-It notes marking relevant paragraphs. "Last night, I went through those articles and marked the things that looked like they might give us something to work with."

The first sheet in the stack was a front page article from August 4, 1996. Under the headline "5-Year-Old Girl Abducted in Salem" was a photo of Megan. The accompanying article described the abduction and police response, but it didn't provide any details beyond what we already knew.

Martha had put a sticky note where the article said that police were interviewing *several witnesses* who saw the abduction. I was aware of only one—Carolyn Gervais. I had spoken with her back in early May. If there actually were other witnesses, their observations would be found in the investigation file that Kevin Fox was copying for me.

Further down in the article were descriptions of the abductors and their van. This was the information that had gone out in the police APB right after the abductions. Most of it coincided with what Carolyn Gervais had told me on the phone, although the van was described as a "late model" Ford cargo van. Carolyn had said it was about a 1990 model, which would be significantly different in appearance from more recent vans. If Carolyn's description was right, it would help explain why the van was not intercepted after the APB.

There were discrepancies, as well, in the descriptions of the abductors, hinting that some of the details may have come from witnesses other than Carolyn. As good a witness as Carolyn seemed to be on the phone nearly twenty years after the crime, no witness is infallible. In fact, eyewitnesses are notoriously unreliable. I made a note of the discrepancies in the descriptions—that was something else I'd have to investigate.

The newspaper coverage on the second day after the abduction focused more on Megan's family than on the abduction itself, and it included a photo of Kim and Jeffrey Moro looking haggard and distraught. It felt strangely surreal to look at the image of a twenty-five-year-old version of the Kim I knew. There was a sense of vulnerability and even a hint of naïveté that I'd never seen in her face. I stared at the image for a long time before reading the text beneath it.

It seemed clear that most of the article was a copy-and-paste job from a police department press release. It expressed optimism about finding Megan and quoted "an unnamed source," saying that police were following up on a number of unspecified leads. The article concluded with a description of the woman abductor and a police artist's sketch, followed by the compulsory plea for public help.

As I read through the news reports, it gradually dawned on me that I actually had followed the story when it was headline news back in 1996. At the time, I'd looked at it from the perspective of an insurance fraud investigator, whose default mind-set is built around suspicion. The inherent cynicism that grows out of this mind-set is an occupational hazard in my business.

But I remembered having watched Megan's parents in televised interviews and being unable to attach any culpability to them. In fact, I found myself uncharacteristically sympathetic toward their obvious helplessness. How could I have known that fifteen years later, I'd meet Kim and have no idea that she was the same young mother I'd seen in the news?

Page by page I worked my way through the newspaper articles, which gradually tapered off in length and frequency. I watched the images of Kim as she went from distraught to shattered. I tried to relate her situation to my own at the time—when I was, by all accounts, happily married with a son of about the same age as Megan's older sister, Tiffany. How would I have reacted if someone had taken Daniel when he was five years old?

Putting that aside, I tried to focus on the abductors—a woman and a man. As I had concluded way back in May, the involvement of a woman in the abduction put this case into a whole different category from the Douglas Langlois kidnappings. In studying the profiles of child abductors, I found that over 95 percent are males. And of those involving a woman perpetrator, nearly all acted alone. They were women who, for one reason or another, had failed to complete their own pregnancies and were looking for infants to raise as their own.

But multiple witnesses had seen a male driver in the van when Megan was kidnapped. I went to the computer and tried to find a profile for couples who abduct children, and what I learned was troubling. Most abductions involving couples are custodial fights—not stranger abductions. In the handful of cases—I found only four—where a couple participated together in abducting an unrelated child, *all* were centered around sexual abuse, with the female either *facilitating* the abuse or *participating* in it with the male.

I did not look forward to the task of explaining that to Kim, though in all likelihood, she'd done the research herself and already knew the bad news.

The profile for the male in these cases is almost identical to that of males who act alone in sexually motivated abductions. He would be Caucasian, age 20 to 35, and he would have a history of failed relationships with women. He probably was a victim of childhood abuse. He would be socially inept and would *not* be employed in a job that required interaction with other people.

What is different is that in most cases, the male abductor-predator is a loner. He lives alone, he is unable to maintain friendships, and he commits his crimes by himself. But in a few cases, the predator somehow connects with a like-minded partner—usually of the same sex, as with Douglas Langlois and Keith Heppner or the infamous "Hillside Stranglers." The partners in these crimes tend to fit the same profile, though one will invariably be dominant.

The rarest sexual predator partnerships are those involving a male and a female. Both partners are reclusive and insecure. They did not go out looking for one another. On the contrary, their normal inclination when meeting a member of the opposite sex is to retreat and avoid contact. It becomes highly unlikely that two people thus avoiding one another will ever form a bond.

Yet it does occasionally happen. And when it does, the female is invariably the submissive partner. She is likely to be painfully shy and withdrawn. The relationship with her partner is most likely the only relationship she has ever had. She participates in her male partner's sex crimes either because she believes she will lose her partner if she doesn't, or because she believes it is her duty.

The unlikely conjunction of two people trying to avoid one another is then further complicated by the need for the male partner to be a sexual predator. The odds are astronomical against the occurrence of such a conjunction. That's why these partnerships are so rare.

Exactly how that profile would help with Megan's case wasn't clear. I don't know how long I sat staring at the ceiling contemplating where and under what circumstances two people of these profiles might encounter one another—group therapy, perhaps?

If one of the partners had a criminal record, it would almost certainly be the male. I would need to focus on his description and try to match that with sex offenders. When I talked with Carolyn back in May, she'd said that he had a beard and that his hair was shaggy and uncombed. He wore cheap glasses and looked like a homeless man. There wasn't much there to work with.

I went back and reread the news reports looking for additional details. Nobody had seen the man outside the van, so it was impossible to estimate his height. One witness used the expression "Dachau thin" to describe both the man and the woman. The APB on the van indicated that the man's age was about thirty. That would make him close to fifty now.

I knew I was getting ahead of myself. If there were descriptions of the abductors, I'd find them in full detail in the police investigation files. Trying to work with newspaper articles was a pretty risky thing because inevitably, in the telling of the story—either to the reporter or by the reporter—some of the facts would become garbled.

Martha handed me the remainder of the newspaper clippings with her sticky notes marking what she considered to be potentially helpful information. Most of these later articles were reports on the many tips that were received by police in the weeks and months following Megan's abduction. Among the articles that Martha had marked were three that dealt with potential suspects arrested on unrelated charges, who had been investigated for possible involvement in Megan's case.

One was a woman who had taken a toddler from the day-care room in a church in Eugene, about sixty-five miles south of Salem. Despite having no tattoo, the woman's description otherwise seemed to match that of Megan's kidnapper. She'd simply walked into the day-care room, picked up the little girl, and carried her out.

The teenage girl who had been watching the children was inexperienced and was uncertain what to do when the woman said that she was "Sandra's aunt." She later said that the woman's use of the girl's name had convinced her that she was who she'd claimed to be. Later, it was determined that all the children wore name tags, and the abductor had simply read Sandra's.

Twenty minutes later, the girl's parents came to pick her up and found her missing. A few days after the abduction, a neighbor called 911 to report that the lady next door, who matched the description of the kidnapper, suddenly had a child. When police responded, they'd found Sandra unharmed. The abductor and her same-sex partner simply wanted a child.

A more recent arrest took place in Antioch, California, after a witness had seen two young girls in the company of a man later identified as convicted sex offender Phillip Garrido. The witness was so struck by the sullen and submissive behavior of the girls and their pale appearance that she called the police, who quickly discovered Garrido's history.

When Garrido was arrested for multiple parole violations, it was discovered that he had abducted an eleven-year-old girl in 1991 and kept her as a sex slave for eighteen years, fathering the two children whose appearance raised the witness's suspicion. Garrido's wife, Nancy, had been an active accomplice in the captivity and abuse of the victim and her two daughters.

This was one of the four cases I'd found online when I was researching abductions by couples, so I was familiar with the details of the crime. Looking at photos of the couple taken following their arrests, I had a difficult time reconciling it with the descriptions of the near-skeletal couple who abducted Megan. But then again, there were no photos showing how the California couple had looked fourteen years earlier, when Megan was taken.

After months of investigation, no evidence was ever found to connect the Phillip and Nancy Garrido to Megan Moro. Still, I made a note to take a long look at that case. Toward that end, I logged onto Amazon. com and ordered a copy of the best-selling book written by the survivor of that abduction, with the idea that it could give me some insight into the mentality of the kidnappers.

The most intriguing *Statesman Journal* article was a story picked up from a newspaper in Klamath Falls six years after Megan's abduction. In July 2002, a citizen called 911 to report suspicious activity in a rest area along US-97, just south of Chemult. The caller reported that a woman was loitering outside the restrooms and talking to any children not accompanied by an adult.

When a state police officer arrived at the rest area, the caller told him that the subject had already left, heading south. The witnesses, a young couple from Spokane, had stopped for a picnic lunch at the rest area. Their attention was drawn to the strange behavior of a woman about thirty yards away. She was walking briskly up the sidewalk, waving something at cars in the parking lot.

The strange woman then approached the restrooms, where she intercepted at least four different children in a five-minute period before the witnesses decided to report it. Shortly before the officer arrived, the woman got into a Plymouth Voyager minivan and left. The woman was described as mousy and very thin.

In response to a radio call from the responding officer, a patrolman fifteen miles down the highway stopped a minivan matching the description of the one reported by the witnesses. The driver was thirty-six-year-old Christopher Dayton from Klamath Falls, accompanied by his wife, Michelle. The explanation she offered for her strange behavior was that she'd found a child's sweatshirt in the parking lot and was simply attempting to find its owner. She said when she was unable to find its owner that she'd hung the sweatshirt on a handicap parking sign, but the officer at the rest area found nothing there.

Smelling the strong aroma of marijuana smoke from the vehicle, the patrolman conducted a field sobriety test, which Christopher Dayton failed. By then, another patrolman had arrived on the scene. The subjects were read their rights, handcuffed, and placed in the backseats of the patrol cars.

The patrolmen noted that all the windows in the back of the minivan were painted black, and the rear seats had been removed. A dirty sleeping bag was spread over a thick mattress of bare foam rubber on the floor. Two rolls of duct tape sat just inside the backdoor.

Subsequent investigation had failed to produce evidence of anything other than driving stoned, so Christopher and Michelle Dayton were released. The newspaper article pointed out the similarities between this incident and Megan's abduction but said nothing to suggest that any official investigation of that connection had been conducted.

Late in the afternoon, I received an e-mail from Kevin Fox saying that his clerk had finished copying the Megan Moro investigation files, and the copy would be at the front desk for me to pick up first thing in the morning. If Christopher and Michelle Dayton had been investigated for possible involvement in Megan Moro's abduction, I'd find it in the file.

July
Wednesday 2

Chapter 58

I was at the Salem police station when they unlocked the front door at seven. All the way to Salem and back, the only thing I could think about was my conversation with Vera. The things she told me had filled in some gaps but had also left me troubled about Kim's emotional state.

The best thing I could do, I decided, was to immerse myself in the Salem investigation files. The more I knew about the case, the better I'd be able to understand Kim's situation. On my initial look through the files, I was pleased by how well organized they were. The summary document included a rudimentary cross-index of the major phases of the investigation.

Since there was no physical or forensic evidence, the initial investigation focused on elimination of the pro forma suspects—meaning family members— and then on witness comments, and finally on tips. Given the circumstances of the abduction, family members were never seriously considered suspects. So the investigation had moved quickly to the witnesses and the things they saw.

It turns out that there were four witnesses to the abduction. The witness who provided the most information was Carolyn Gervais—the same witness I'd spoken with two months before. I pulled out my notes from that interview and compared them with what she'd told the police at the time of the abduction.

Another witness was a fifteen-year-old girl who was in the Burger King restroom when the "skinny lady" told Tiffany and Megan that their mother wanted them to go outside with her. The description of the woman given by this witness was less detailed but generally consistent with that given by Carolyn Gervais.

The witness said that the lady came in just a few seconds behind Tiffany and Megan. She immediately told the little girls, "Your mother wants you to come outside with me." Tiffany protested that she needed to pee and told Megan to wait for her. But once Tiffany went into the stall, the lady took Megan by the hand and led her out the door. The witness estimated that it took less than thirty seconds.

Not more than two minutes later, Tiffany left the restroom and found her father waiting outside. The witness was right behind Tiffany, and when she heard her tell Jeffrey what had happened, she jumped in to confirm Tiffany's account. She said that Jeffrey and Tiffany rushed to the seating area of the restaurant and looked around for the missing little girl. It was about then that Carolyn Gervais came in and said what she'd seen in the parking lot—the skinny lady carrying Megan to a van, which then sped away.

The other two witnesses were in the parking lot. One was in line for the drive-up window. He heard a woman say sharply, "You come with me right now!" Turning toward the sound, he saw the woman scoop up the struggling child and hurry to a van parked at the curb.

This was the witness who described the abductor as "Dachau thin." Beyond that, he described her straight hair and plain appearance. The van, he said, was very dirty and seemed to have peeling paint on the roof—he couldn't be sure because the van was so dirty.

The final witness was a woman making a left turn out of the Burger King parking lot when a van pulled suddenly away from the curb and nearly broadsided her. She got a good look at the van's driver before he backed off and swerved around her, heading in the direction of the freeway. She noted that the silver or gray paint was peeling from the hood of the van, which she said was a Ford with a straight bumper and rectangular grille.

A sketch artist from the Oregon State Police had interviewed each of the witnesses, initially creating three sketches of the woman abductor based on what each witness had observed. Then she put the three sketches of the woman side by side, and while playing back video of her sessions with the witnesses, she created a fourth sketch that reconciled the differences between the original three. All the witnesses said that the final rendering was "very good."

The artist went through the same exercise to create a good rendering of the van driver. I scanned the two images and printed copies that I stapled to my bulletin board.

One thing that became apparent as I read through the documents was that the simple chronological arrangement of the files would make it difficult to relate evidence or tips to one another based on content. While the Salem investigators had probably been sufficiently familiar with the entire case to be able to recall related bits of information, there was a lot of material in the file for a newcomer to the investigation—me—to digest and mentally index.

There was an answer to that.

"Remember what you were doing on this date two years ago?" I asked Martha.

She thought about it for a second and then said, "Sure. I was creating the database for everything in the Mendelson-Devonshire files. Why?"

"How'd you like to do it again?"

"For the Megan Moro files?"

"That's right. It's not nearly as big as Mendelson-Devonshire, but still, there's a lot here. Being able to search the files by subject will let us find things that are separated by long time periods in the chronological files."

"No problem. How do you want to do it?"

"Same as last time. I'll start scanning all the documents. You set up the database and then go through the documents. Identify keywords and index them in the database. In the process, we'll get at least a superficial understanding of the investigation, and the database will bring us fully up to speed."

"Cool. Let's do it."

It took me the rest of the morning to scan the files, and while I did that, Martha created an Access database and started entering data.

Recalling what I'd read in the news clippings, I thumbed through the Salem files in search of anything relating to the couple arrested in California—Phillip and Nancy Garrido. I found that Salem detectives had gone to Placerville to look for any possible connection to Megan's case. California authorities were already looking at other cases of missing girls in their investigation of the Garridos, but Megan was not on their list.

In searching the Garridos' property, no evidence was found connecting the couple with any other abduction cases, but they remain "persons of interest" in at least one open case. After interviewing the Garridos, the Salem detectives concluded that there was no connection and returned home empty-handed. Nothing further was done.

I compared the Garrido booking photos with the police sketches in Megan's file—as the Salem police had no doubt done—and I couldn't find any striking similarities. Phillip and Nancy Garrido would have been in their midforties when Megan was abducted. The witnesses had said that Megan's abductors appeared to be much younger than that—in their twenties or early thirties. Still, I wasn't quite ready to set it aside. Cases of abductions by couples are so uncommon that I found it difficult to dismiss one without a long look.

In a rare event of perfect timing, the FedEx truck stopped in front of my house and delivered my copy of Jaycee Dugard's memoir, *A Stolen Life*. In the first few pages, it told how Garrido had stalked Jaycee and used a stun gun to disable her in order to get her into his car. That was quite different from the way Megan's abductor had lured the little girl out of the Burger King restaurant.

Jaycee's story is tragic and fascinating in its study of the psychology of both the kidnapper and his victim. I found that it related more to the victims of Douglas Langlois than to Megan Moro, but that was only because I still had no clue what had become of Megan after the van sped away.

But in the end, it provided conclusive proof that Megan had not been taken by the Garrido couple. The shack where Jaycee was held could not have concealed another victim from her. So, as the Salem cops had done five years earlier, I marked Phillip and Nancy Garrido off the list of possible suspects in Megan's case.

When I finished reading it, I put Jaycee's book in the bottom of a desk drawer under a thick stack of closed files. I did not believe it would be a good thing for Kim to read. As a profile for the kind of people who might have abducted Megan, it was positively terrifying.

Chapter 59

WWhile Martha continued working on data entry, I started looking at one of the obvious areas of discrepancy in the investigation files, and that was the description of the van that had taken Megan away. Everyone agreed that it was a full-size Ford Econoline, and that it was silver or gray with patches of paint missing from the roof or hood.

The police had concluded that the van was most likely about a 1990 model. That didn't seem right to me. Why would the paint be peeling off a vehicle that was only six years old? I read through pages of witness interrogation reports, where the detectives had probed for details that would help identify the van, and followed their logic.

First, all three of the witnesses who had seen the van described it as having a "squared-off" shape in the front end—a short, nearly horizontal hood and wide, rectangular grille. That made it a third-generation Econoline, manufactured from 1975 through 1991. The more recent Ford vans had softer, more-rounded corners and a sloping hood. So what made the detectives exclude all but the last two or three years of production for the third-generation Econoline?

The answer was in the observations of the woman who had nearly been T-boned by the van, who was certain that it had an Oregon "pine tree" license plate on the front bumper. It's actually a fir tree, not a pine tree, but the important point was that Oregon did not begin using those plates until the middle of 1988. That fact was apparently what led detectives to conclude that the van was no older than that time. And they already knew that it couldn't be newer than 1991, so that gave them a pretty narrow range of possibilities.

Only problem with that was that it made the assumption that the van was new when it got its fir tree license plate. But a van of any age could have been brought into Oregon and relicensed after the middle of 1988, and it would have received the new plate. It was also possible that the plates on the van were taken from some other vehicle. If the perps had set out with the intention of committing a capital crime, it was not unreasonable to believe that they'd had the foresight to put bogus plates on their van.

So where did that leave me? I had a seventeen-year age range for the van, and unless I could narrow that down, it would be almost useless as evidence. The condition of the paint was what made me question the age attributed to the van by the detectives in the 1996 investigation. What might have caused the paint on the roof and hood to deteriorate?

We've all seen cars with peeling or flaking paint on their roofs. I started searching around online, looking for an explanation for it. What I found was that at one time or another, just about every car manufacturer has experienced problems with their painting processes. Oddly, it seems that the very popular silver or metallic gray colors were the most vulnerable, no matter what manufacturer made the paint or what vehicle it was applied to.

All of the discussions online focused primarily on how to correct the problems rather than on what had actually caused them. I went from forum to forum, blog to blog, and website to website, learning more and more about the difficulties involved in applying paint to cars but not quite finding the reason for a factory paint job to peel.

I finally landed on a website called Lemon Aid, where consumers share advice on how to get compensation from the manufacturers for things that went wrong with their vehicles. There was a lot of whining by people with absurdly unrealistic expectations, but there were also occasional tidbits that indicated that something actually had gone wrong on the vehicle assembly line that affected a relatively large number of vehicles. I learned that in 1979, Ford had changed paint suppliers in an effort to reduce the quantity of hazardous vapors entering the atmosphere during painting. But the new paint chemistry required some different surface preparation on the vehicles, and someone had neglected to share that information with the people on the assembly line.

The result was what critics had derisively called "Ford's biodegradable paint." Many vehicles—mostly metallic gray—were repainted by dealers at company expense for people with affected vehicles. But far more people simply ignored the flaking paint and lived with the result. Most of the problem vehicles came from the assembly plant in Lorain, Ohio, where the Econoline vans were built.

All of this suggested to me than the kidnappers' van was most likely a 1979 or 1980 model. When the Salem detectives had screened DMV records, they'd been looking for something ten years newer than that.

To further narrow the search, I considered what the exact model of the van might be. The witnesses all agreed that it was a panel van with no side windows other than those on the front doors, making it a cargo van as opposed to the Club Wagon passenger van of the same era. The Econoline cargo van was sold in four primary configurations: half ton, three-quarter ton, and one ton—designated E100, E150, E250, and E350.

If I could determine which model the witnesses had seen, it would narrow the search considerably. The Salem detectives seemed to have had the same thought in mind when they interviewed the witnesses. They grilled them regarding the badges or insignia on the van, without luck. They showed them photos of the different models, pointing out that the most visible difference was the wheels. The half-ton vans had passenger car wheels and tires, while the heavy-duty vans had larger truck wheels and tires, but the witnesses were unable to say which might have been on the van they saw.

One detective had asked how tall the van appeared to be. He seemed to be working from the knowledge that the E250 and E350 vans were nearly six inches further off the ground than the lighter-duty models. But none of the witnesses could give a useful answer to the question.

On about my tenth reading of the witness interviews, I spotted something that raised a question in my mind. The lady who had made the left turn in front of the van, just before it pulled out from the curb, was driving a 1990 Mazda Miata. And she had been able to see that the paint on the hood of the van was defective.

If the van had been one of the newer models with a steeply slanted hood, there would be no question how she'd have been able to do that. But on those third-generation vans, the hood was virtually horizontal. That meant that the witness's eye level had to be above the hood level of the van. Was that even possible from the driver's seat of a Miata? She'd been very specific that "all of the paint was gone from the hood."

I knew that the Mazda Miata was a two-seat roadster and that the driver sat very low. I wondered what the driver's eye level would be. After thinking about that for a bit, I went to Craigslist and searched the car ads for a 1990 Mazda Miata. There were several, but one was in Redland, just a few miles away, so I phoned the seller.

"I'd like to take a look at your Miata. Do you still have it?" I asked the lady who answered the phone.

"Sure. When would you like to see it?"

"Well, I could be there in half an hour, if that works for you," I suggested.

"No problem. I'll be here all afternoon."

I grabbed a tape measure and some masking tape and drove to Redland, about five miles east of Oregon City. I found the address and spotted the Miata, freshly washed, sitting on the driveway in front of a modest ranch-style house from the seventies. As I got out of my Yukon, a lady came out of the house and introduced herself as Carla.

"You must be the one who called," she said.

"That's right. I hope you didn't go to the trouble of washing it just for me," I said, handing her my card. "My name's Corrigan."

She glanced at the card and then took a longer second look. "Investigator? Are you really an investigator?"

"That's right, I'm—"

"Hey, are you the one who rescued those girls in the paper mill?" she asked, suddenly excited.

"Uh, they weren't actually in the paper mill," I started to explain.

"Jimmy!" she shouted. "The detective who saved those captive girls is here! He wants to buy the Mazda!"

I tried to say, "No, I just want to measure—"

But she kept talking. "Wow. I never expected to meet a famous detective! Jimmy! Find that newspaper—the one that tells about how they caught that asshole in the mill—and bring the camera!"

The upshot was that I had to autograph my picture on the front page of the newspaper and have pictures taken with Jimmy and Carla before I could explain that I didn't really want to buy the Miata.

"I just want to take a couple of measurements."

"What for? Wait! Are you doing another investigation?" she asked excitedly.

"Uh, well, yes. I am."

"Oh wow! You hear that Jimmy? Mr. Corrigan—I mean Corrigan—is investigating our old car!"

Jimmy looked at me with suspicion. "What's wrong with the car? Did somebody get killed in it?"

"Nothing like that. I just need to measure—"

Carla said, "Honey, he just needs to take some measurements."

Jimmy said, "This ain't gonna get us in trouble, is it?"

"No chance," I assured him.

After mulling it over, he finally said, "Well, I guess that'd be okay."

I climbed behind the wheel of the Miata and closed the door. After adjusting the seat, I turned to my left and stuck a piece of masking tape on the window at my eye level. Then I got back out and asked Carla if she'd get in and move the seat as if she were going to drive. I stuck another piece of tape on the window at her eye level.

301

The two pieces of tape were only a couple of inches apart. Carla looked to be about five two. I am ten inches taller. It was easy to guess that the witness who saw the van was probably closer to Carla's size than mine, but in any case, the eye level would probably be within the range between the two pieces of tape. Measuring from the ground to the tape, mine was at forty inches. Carla's was at thirty-eight.

Jimmy handed me a Sharpie marker. "Could you put an autograph on the window—next to the tape?"

On the way back through Oregon City, one of the cars parked at the curb on Main Street caught my eye. It was a Ford Econoline, and its squarish profile told me that it was one of the third-generation vans. I whipped into the next parking space and hurried back to the van. It turned out to be a one-ton model—an E350. I quickly measured the height of the hood. It was fifty-one inches above the ground.

"You there! What're you doing with my van?"

I turned to see a large man carrying a long baguette in a paper wrapper. He carried it the way Joe Don Baker had wielded his legendary axe handle when playing Sheriff Buford Pusser in the movie *Walking Tall*, and somehow it made his loaf of bread look terribly menacing.

I hastily said, "Nothing. I just needed to know the height of the hood." He stared hard at me.

"It's part of an investigation I'm doing," I said, offering my card.

Buford Baguette took my card and studied it intently. "What the hell are you investigating?"

"I just needed to know how high the hood is on this model van. I saw yours sitting here, so I stopped to take the measurement. I didn't even touch the van."

He slowly lowered his weapon.

"Hey, aren't you the PI who's been all over the news?"

Back in my office, I searched the Internet until I found the dimensions for the third-generation Ford vans. The overall height for the E100 was 79.1 inches, and for the E350 was 84.8 inches. The bodies themselves were identical, so the difference in height was entirely due to differences in the tire sizes and the suspension. What that meant was that the height of the E100's hood would be 5.7 inches lower than that of the E350.

At fifty-one inches high, even I would have been unable to see the surface of the E350's hood from the seat of the Mazda Miata. But at forty-five inches, someone Carla's size might be able to see the hood of the E100.

I already knew that the road in front of the Burger King where Megan was abducted was level and flat, so the witness who described the hood of the van could not have been looking down at it. In order to see that the paint was gone, the leading edge of the hood had to be below her eye level, which I now knew was about forty inches.

At the instant she looked over to see the van, it was skidding to a stop just short of a collision. In a panic-braking situation, the front of the van could have dived five inches, allowing the witness to see the top of the hood. But it couldn't possibly have dived much more than that. There simply wasn't enough spring range in the front suspension.

So now I knew. The kidnappers drove a 1979 or 1980 Ford E100. I'd spent the entire day figuring that out. I hoped it would prove worth my time. I fired off an e-mail to Kevin Fox, asking for a list of all 1979 and 1980 Ford E100 vans that were registered in Oregon in 1996. Someone on that list might be the kidnapper.

Chapter 60

L ooking over the work that Martha had done on the Megan database, I spotted her entry regarding Christopher and Michelle Dayton, the Klamath Falls couple arrested on Highway 97 in 2002. Leafing through the investigation files, I located the page where the names appeared. The state police, after arresting Dayton for DUII, had issued a perfunctory advisory regarding Michelle's multiple approaches to children in the roadside picnic area.

The Salem detective assigned to Megan's cold case had noted the similarity in the descriptions of Michelle Dayton and Megan's abductor. And it was hard to get around the implications of blacked-out windows and the duct tape found in the van. While there had apparently been some initial excitement over the possible connection, the investigation had been cut short by the discovery that the couple had been living in Edgewood, Pennsylvania, in 1996 and had not moved to Oregon until five years later.

But I couldn't let it go quite that easily. The blacked-out windows, the mattress, and the duct tape in the minivan, coupled with the woman's dubious activities in the parking lot, were just too much to ignore— particularly when taken in conjunction with the similarity in her appearance to that of the woman who had snatched Megan. Either the Salem detective knew something that wasn't mentioned in the report, or he was too quick to accept Dayton's alibi.

After all, the fact that the suspects had lived in Pennsylvania at the time didn't mean they couldn't have traveled to Oregon. On the contrary, the fact that they eventually *moved* to Oregon implied that they may have had some interest in—and reason to visit—the state before moving here.

On my computer, I used some of my subscription software to do a full background check on Christopher and Michelle Dayton. This kind of search was not possible in 2002, even for law enforcement, so I couldn't fault the Salem cops for failing to find what I found—that Michelle's parents lived in Oregon. In fact, they lived in Scio, just outside Salem, only twenty miles from the Burger King where Megan was kidnapped.

I was able to find a photo of Michelle Dayton taken at the time of the couple's 2002 arrest. I made a print of it and pinned it to my bulletin board next to the police drawings of Megan's abductor. There were many similarities: their ages, their emaciated appearance, the straight brown hair, the thin lips, and the pencil-thin eyebrows. But the investigation file contained no mention of a tattoo.

Christopher Dayton's booking photo was not much use in a comparison with the police sketch. The driver of the van that took Megan away wore his hair long and shaggy, he had a scruffy beard, and he wore cheap glasses. Dayton was clean-shaven, his hair was buzz cut, and he was not wearing glasses. I tried drawing glasses, long hair, and a beard onto the booking photo, and the end result looked very much like the police sketch. The problem was that if I'd done the same thing to a photo of Mother Theresa, the result would have been the same.

Focusing my attention on Michelle Dayton's parents, I started a background check on them, only to discover that her father had died in 2011. Her mother, however, continued to live at the address in Scio where the family had lived since the early 1970s. That undoubtedly meant that Michelle had grown up in Scio and would have been quite familiar with Salem and the surrounding area.

Michelle's mother, Grace, was sixty-nine years old. She had no record of arrests or even traffic tickets, and she was a choir singer at Our Lady of Lourdes Catholic church in Scio. This did not seem like a person who would be inclined to cover for criminal activity—except possibly for her daughter. I decided to give her a call even though it was a holiday.

When I got Grace on the phone, I said, "My name is Corrigan. I'm a licensed private investigator, and I'm looking at—"

"Oh, I know who you are! I saw you on the news a few days ago! Now, why on earth would you be calling me?"

I wondered how long this new celebrity status would last. But I had already concocted an answer to her question, which I had anticipated. "I'm just following up on some open cases, including one where a child was abducted from a church nursery in Eugene—maybe you remember that?"

"I vaguely remember when that happened," Grace said hesitantly. "But I certainly don't know anything about it."

"No. I didn't expect that you would. Still, we're obligated to check out something that you might be able to help with. See, we're looking at tip that the woman may have been in Scio."

"I don't get it. Didn't that woman turn herself in?"

"That's right. But an informant says that she may have had an accomplice who has never been picked up."

"What's that have to do with me?"

"You sing in the choir, don't you?"

"Yes, I do."

"So you get to see everyone in the congregation," I explained. "I'd like to show you some pictures and see if you recognize anyone."

"Sounds like a waste of time, but if you really want to do it, I'm willing to take a look," she said.

"I wouldn't ask if it wasn't important."

"It must be for you to be calling on the Fourth of July."

"Holidays don't count where kidnapping of children is involved."

"I see your point. When do you want to show me the pictures?"

"At your convenience. I could get down there this afternoon if that works for you."

I crossed my fingers.

"Well, if you really think it's worth your time—"

On Google Maps, I looked up Edgewood, Pennsylvania, and found it to be a borough in Pittsburgh. Zooming out, I found Carnegie Mellon University just a few miles away. With that, I started fabricating a story that might turn a conversation with Grace in a direction that could produce results. Next, I made fresh prints of a few random photos from prior investigations. My plan was to start with the photos and then engage Grace in a social discussion about her family—ultimately about her daughter and son-in-law.

Grace was surprisingly young for her age. Her dark eyes and olive complexion attested to her Italian heritage, though I honestly couldn't see much resemblance to the old police photo of her daughter. She peppered me with questions about the Douglas Langlois case, and that helped pave the way for the rest of our conversation. When we got to it, Grace carefully studied the photos I placed on the table before declaring with apparent confidence that none of the faces looked familiar.

"Have you lived here a long time?" I asked.

"Oh yes. We—my late husband and I—moved here in 1972. We raised our family here."

"How many children do you have?" I asked, making my voice as conversational as I could.

"Two—a boy and a girl," she answered. "How about you?"

"I have a son. Lives in Pittsburgh now—doing postgrad work at Carnegie."

I do have a son, but the rest was pure fabrication. It was merely intended to steer the conversation in a specific direction.

"Oh, my daughter used to live in Pittsburgh, just a couple of miles from Carnegie," Grace said, taking the bait.

"You're kidding! That's quite a coincidence. What took her from Scio all the way to Pittsburgh? Don't tell me she went to Carnegie too."

"No, but you know how kids are. A couple of years after Michelle got married, her husband said that he had a big job offer in Pittsburgh, so off they went. I didn't believe his story about a job offer because he'd never had a decent job in his life, but it wasn't my place to say so, you know what I mean? Later on, I found out that the so-called big job was driving a U-Haul truck full of Oregon marijuana to Pittsburgh. As far as I know, he never did get a legitimate job back there."

"It must've been hard—having your daughter so far away. Did you ever get to visit her?"

"Pah! I wasn't welcome there. Whenever I talked about going there, they'd come up with some excuse why it wasn't a good time. I think they just didn't want me to see how they were living."

"That's too bad. Did they ever come to visit you?"

"Oh sure. Just about every summer, they'd drive their old van across the country—they said it was just to visit, but I knew it was to pick up another load of marijuana. It's a miracle they never got caught, or they'd be living in a penitentiary in someplace like Iowa or Nebraska."

"You said that they *used* to live in Pennsylvania. Where are they now?"

"After six or seven years there, they moved back here. They live in Klamath Falls now. I think Chris finally started getting his life together. He has a half-decent job in a muffler repair shop, and he's managed to stay out of trouble for the last ten years, so maybe it'll be okay."

"Do they have kids?"

"No, that's one of my big disappointments in life. I always wanted grandchildren. And Michelle wanted to be a mother. But—well, I don't know—I think all that stuff he smoked made Chris, you know, unable to father children."

"Would they consider adoption?" I asked, while thinking *or kidnapping?*

"Oh, they might have—fifteen years ago. In fact, I think they even looked into getting one of those foreign babies—like from India or someplace like that. But it's probably too late for that. They're almost fifty now. Michelle has horses. That seems to make her happy. But listen to me—I just go on and on. What about your son? Do you get to see him?"

"Christmas. That's about it. Maybe I'll see him more after he finishes school."

"Kids."

"Yeah. Kids," I agreed.

My instincts had been right. The alibi that the police had accepted when they looked at Christopher and Michelle Dayton in 2002 was no good. Every summer, they returned to Oregon—in their old van. And Michelle wanted a child badly enough to look at foreign adoption.

It was going to be difficult to wait through the weekend. First thing Monday, I'd ask Fox to find out from Pennsylvania DMV what kind of vehicles had been registered to Christopher and Michelle Dayton back in 1996. If they owned a Ford E100—well, even if they didn't—I was going to take a long, hard look at them.

July
5
Saturday

Chapter 61

I was sitting on my front porch with Bud, talking about his future in undercover investigations, when Kaylin Beatty approached.

"I was wondering if you could recommend a security system," she said.

"Don't you already have one?" I'd been in her house, and I'd seen the sensors and keypad.

"I have one in the house. But I need something down on the other side of the railroad tracks."

"Has somebody stolen something from your dock?"

At one time or another, everyone in the neighborhood—with the exception of Big Dan—had had things stolen from our boats or docks.

"Not from my dock," Kaylin said, "from my garden!"

"Your garden?"

"That's right. I planted a dozen tomato plants last month in a little garden plot on my beach. All that silt carried in by the flood last year looked pretty fertile, so I thought I'd give it a try. And then this morning, I went down to water them, and all my plants are gone! Somebody took every one of them just when they were really starting to grow."

"Somebody stole *tomato plants*?" I asked. I was having a very hard time believing that anybody would steal tomato plants.

"Yes! That's what I'm saying. Every one of them."

Bud said, "Maybe they mistook them for pot."

"Can I get an alarm that will tell me when someone goes down there?" she asked.

"Let's go take a look at the layout," I said. "Then I can make a recommendation."

We walked down the steps from the railroad grade. Kaylin's garden plot was off to the right, and as she had said, all the plants had been pulled from the ground and taken away, leaving two rows of holes filled with potting soil. The ground was firm enough that no shoe prints were left to help identify the culprit.

"Motion detectors are kind of difficult down here. The movement of plants when the wind blows, the vibrations from passing trains, reflections off the water—all these things can give you false alarms. Really, video monitoring is about the only thing that works—and it works mainly as a deterrent. But I don't think it would have prevented this crime."

"Why not?"

I pointed down the steep embankment that led to the river's edge. There were animal tracks in the narrow strip of mud where the water lapped at the shore.

"I'd bet that those tracks were made by your culprit."

"Otters? You think otters took my tomatoes?"

"Otters aren't vegetarians. But those aren't otter tracks."

"They aren't? Then what are they?"

"Nutria—and nutria *are* vegetarians. Farmers hate the things."

"Nutria? What the hell are nutria?"

"It's a nice name for an oversized rat," Bud said.

"Yuck!"

"It's not really a rat," I said. "It's a South American critter that was brought here to breed for fur."

"And they look like big rats," Bud insisted. "I never could figure out why anybody would want to wear rat fur."

"Well, I guess nobody did. Anyway, when the fur business didn't work out, they just turned the animals loose, and sixty years later here they are."

"What can I do about them?"

"You could shoot 'em, or maybe trap 'em, but I don't think either would be legal. Probably the best thing to do is avoid letting them find anything to eat. Then they'll go someplace else."

"So I can't have a tomato garden?"

"Not unless you know how to build a nutria-proof fence."

"Well, crap. If I can't have a garden, maybe I'll just pour a concrete slab like Barry did."

As I leafed through the pages in the investigation files, I found many contact reports bearing Kim's name. There was nothing unexpected about that—it was entirely normal for the victim's family members to be in contact with the investigators. But as I read through the contact reports, it became apparent that as time went by, the investigators had increasingly found Kim's involvement to be more hindrance than help.

The contact reports always referred to Kim by her initials—KAM. A week after Megan's abduction, a detective wrote:

```
09-05-96 Three phone calls from KAM today.
Questions about what witnesses said. Told her
witness reports are confidential. More questions
about vehicle. Told her we are searching DMV
records. Are we looking at local sex offenders—
yes, both local and regional.
```

There were similar entries almost daily:

```
09-12-96 KAM brought a list of people she thinks
may have followed the family from Grants Pass to
Salem. List includes a man who complains about
boat wakes when they water ski, a store clerk
who is unfriendly, a neighbor whose dog barks at
night, and a couple who recently lost a child in
a car accident.
```

As days turned to weeks, the contact reports contained less detail:

```
10-15-96 Phone call from KAM wanting update.
```

The increasing reluctance of the investigators to talk with Kim and their increasing belief that she had nothing to contribute became more and more apparent in the tone of their comments.

```
02-20-97 KAM: 20 min. phone call.
```

```
06-01-98 Phone contact: KAM now studying to
join police.
```

```
11-13-98 Telecon: KAM saw news report about
missing child in Portland.
```

What was never said but was inescapably obvious was Kim's deteriorating mental state. She was driven and desperate. Words like *demanding* and *unreasonable* gradually crept into the contact reports. And then in 1999, she stopped calling and visiting the Salem Police Department. There were no further reports.

July
Monday
7

Chapter 62

Kevin Fox answered the phone, "What do you have, Corrigan?"

"You get my e-mail about the van?" I asked.

"Yeah. What makes you think our guys got the age wrong?"

I explained what I'd found out about paint problems and license plates. It was more difficult to tell him how I'd concluded that the van was an E100.

"You're kidding, right?" Fox challenged.

"Not at all. If that witness could see that the paint was gone from the hood, the van had to be an E100. Either that, or she's about six six."

"You haven't convinced me, but I'll go along with you for now. What do you need?"

"DMV records from 1996. I'd like a list of everyone in Oregon who owned a '79 or '80 Ford E100 that year—silver or gray. And if you can get it, I'd like the same thing from Pennsylvania."

"Pennsylvania? What in hell does Pennsylvania have to do with this?"

"You recall a K-Falls arrest where a woman was approaching children in a rest area along US-97? Last name's Dayton. Michelle Dayton. And they arrested her husband for DUII—Christopher Dayton."

"Yeah. That was, like, ten years after Megan was kidnapped."

"It wasn't that long—more like six or seven. But do you remember the details of the vehicle involved? It was a minivan with black paint over the windows and an old mattress and duct tape in the back."

"That's right. I remember it now. We looked at those people, but we didn't find any connection."

"They lived in Pennsylvania in 1996," I said.

"Yeah. So what makes you think they could be any part of this?"

"The woman grew up in Scio. Her family still lives there. She and her husband used to drive out here every summer. What's more, they drove a van on those visits."

"Where are you getting all this?"

"I talked with the woman's mother. She says her son-in-law was involved in transporting big loads of pot from here to Pittsburgh every time they came to visit."

"Well, shit!"

"Yeah. I'd like to know if Dayton has an arrest record back there, and I'd like to know what kind of van he had in 1996. And I'd *really* like to know if there was a child living with him after 1996."

"I see your point. But listen. Our guys gave him a poly when he was in the K-Falls lockup. The box said he had no knowledge of the '96 case and never tried to abduct anybody."

"The polygraph isn't perfect," I reminded him. "People beat it all the time."

I heard the deep sigh that preceded Fox's answer, "It's a dead end, Corrigan. It was a dead end at the time, and it's still a dead end today."

"You're probably right. It probably *is* a dead end. But it's the best thing I have right now, and I need to pin down the details before I close the book on it."

"Yeah, I know. How can I help with that?"

"Get me answers to a couple of questions. Who was farming pot in your area in the years 1994 through 2002? It had to be a fairly good-sized operation to supply Dayton with the stuff, a truckload at a time. And on the other end, who was distributing the stuff?"

"I'll get you the answer to the first question. As to the second, I'll find out who you need to talk to in Pittsburgh, and I'll ask 'em to work with you. That's all I can do—but remember, *none of this* makes Dayton a kidnapper."

"No, but we can't disregard what brought attention to these people in the first place. It was Michelle Dayton approaching kids in the rest area. Michelle's mother told me that the Daytons were unable to conceive a child. And Michelle wanted a child badly enough to look into adopting an orphan from India or Somalia—someplace like that."

"And on that, you think they might have snatched Megan?"

"I think it's a possibility."

"Then where is she? If they wanted her to keep as their own, wouldn't they still have her?"

"Sure. But a million different things could have happened. Maybe she died. Maybe she ran away. The point is they desperately wanted a child, and they didn't have much respect for the law. They knew the area, drove a van, and might well have been there when Megan was taken."

"You're making it sound easy. But you know as well as I do that what you have is pretty thin."

"Of course, it is. But like I said, it's the best we have right now."

"Yeah, I suppose it is. I'll get you connected with somebody in Pittsburgh who can answer your questions."

While waiting for Fox to get me the Pittsburgh contact information, I went to work on sighting reports. I was quickly able to see that there were two distinct types of sightings: people who saw a van and people who saw a girl. There was a total of 284 sighting reports, spread over the eighteen years since Megan was abducted. Of those, 161 occurred in the first year, including 98 in the first week.

I was automatically skeptical of the van-sighting reports since the APB and early news reports had spoken of a "late model" Ford van. The description was later changed to a Ford van from "approximately 1990," but even that was inaccurate and misleading. If witnesses were reporting that they'd seen vans that conformed with the inaccurate descriptions, their reports probably were irrelevant.

There were two other ways to categorize the sighting reports: location and time. The traditional way to deal with sighting reports was to stick colored pins in a map, and toward that end, I stapled an Oregon highway map to my bulletin board and dug around in my desk drawer for a plastic box full of map pins. I started pushing pins into the map at the location of each sighting, and I quickly realized that so many of the sightings were concentrated in the Salem area that it rendered the result meaningless.

I needed a better way to map the sightings. A few minutes online led me to a piece of software called Maptitude, created precisely for the task at hand—and a multitude of other law enforcement applications. It wasn't cheap, but I ignored the price and downloaded it. Within half an hour, I was ready to start mapping all the sighting reports.

First, I color coded the markers for each sighting: red for a sighting of a girl matching Megan's description; orange for a man or woman matching the descriptions of the abductors; and blue for van sightings. For each marker, I entered the date and time of the sighting. It took just over three hours to figure out how to use the software and enter the 284 sightings.

In the process of entering the data, I noted that during the Salem investigation, all the sighting reports had been indexed according to when the report was received rather than when the sighting occurred. The result was a well-organized but inherently misleading collection of data.

Looking at the display on my computer screen, I saw that Maptitude let me view the sightings in such a way that a few patterns showed up in the blue markers. I was specifically looking for sightings on a time line that might show what direction the van had gone after the abduction.

There were three van sightings reported on Interstate 5 south of Salem. The abduction had taken place at 1:30 p.m. on August 4, 1996. The next day, a witness reported having seen a van matching the description given on the news (a late-model Ford van) at the rest area where I-5 crosses the Santiam River at about 2:00 p.m. Another witness reported seeing a "suspicious van" on I-5 near Cottage Grove at 3:15 p.m. And a third witness saw a van driven by "hippies" going through Medford at 5:30 p.m.

The timing of these three sightings implied that all three witnesses may have seen the same vehicle, and their descriptions of the driver were reasonably consistent. But was it worth anything? What it told me was that a hippie drove a late-model Ford van south on I-5 that afternoon. Unfortunately, the abductors were driving a van that was probably at least fifteen years old.

There was a similar trail of sightings reported along Oregon Highway 22 going east from Salem. These reports all came in after the news media posted a photo of a 1990 Ford van, which would have had the same body style as the 1979–80 van that I had identified as the probable model involved in the abduction.

One sighting was at the Minto rest area just east of Gates on Highway 22 at about 2:15 p.m. Time and distance made this a possible hit. The witness said that the van parked far from the restrooms despite many open parking spaces much closer. She had heard an argument between a man and a woman in the van but had not been able to discern the words. She also thought that she had heard a child crying.

Another witness passed an old Ford van that was laboring on the steep grade approaching the Cascade summit. He said there was heavy black smoke coming from the tailpipe, and he passed the van to escape from the fumes. That sighting was a little over an hour after the Minto sighting. The fuel-rich exhaust smoke implied that the van had a poorly tuned carbureted engine. The fuel-injected engines introduced in 1987 were far less likely to produce black exhaust. This bolstered the possibility that it was the right van—or at least one of the right vintage.

There were two sightings in the small town of Sisters on the east side of the Cascade summit. One was from a gas station attendant who had filled up the van, and the other was from another customer in the same gas station. Both described a very dirty old van with a hippie driving. Again, the timing suggested that it was the same van; however, the security camera at the gas station was so poorly focused that it was impossible to make out anything but the fuzzy shape of the van. It was indeed a third-generation Econoline van, but beyond that, nothing could be determined.

I also found a pattern of sightings on Interstate 84, where four witnesses had seen what could have been the same van in the eastbound lanes on the afternoon and evening of August 4. What drew attention to the van was the driver's apparent inability to stay between the white lines. Either the driver was intoxicated, or the van had severe mechanical problems in the steering linkage—depending which witness you believed.

It was fascinating to me the way the Maptitude software made these patterns visible, where simple pins on a map would have meant next to nothing. I could find nothing in the investigation files to indicate that the detectives at the time had been able to relate the witness reports to one another. Each report was recorded and individually investigated, but the possible connections between them had remained invisible.

I dismissed the Interstate 5 sightings simply because it was probably the wrong model of Ford van. However, either of the two eastbound vans could have been driven by the kidnappers—on Highway 22 or on Interstate 84. If Christopher Dayton was hauling 250 kilos of marijuana and a kidnapped child back to Pittsburgh, he might have taken either route out of Salem.

My money would be on the Highway 22 sightings because of the witness who had heard a crying child. Also, the I-84 van, with its apparent steering problems, might have been incapable of making a transcontinental round-trip. But either way, I felt that there was a better than fifty-fifty chance that Megan was taken east from Salem.

Studying the red markers indicating sightings of a child matching Megan's description, I looked mainly for clusters. Finding multiple sightings over time in a relatively small area might imply that Megan was being held nearby. The largest cluster was in and around Salem. That was predictable, since that's where the case received the most publicity.

Salem detectives had been very thorough in their investigation of these leads. In about half the cases, they were able to determine that the child reported was someone who lived there and had a passing resemblance to Megan. Other leads had been discounted because the children seen were not acting in a manner consistent with being captives.

On that score, I had some second thoughts. In reading Jaycee Dugard's memoir, I had seen that the behavior of long-term captives often does not conform to common expectations. It goes beyond Stockholm syndrome, where captives form a kind of bond with their captors. It is a conscious and deliberate survival strategy employed by the captives to placate their captors in an effort to minimize mistreatment.

But even taking that perspective into account, only a couple of the Salem sightings seemed to be worth further investigation. The others, whether genuine possibilities or not, simply contained insufficient information for further investigation. I stuck Post-It notes on the files that would get another look and moved on.

There was another cluster of red and orange markers at Sisters, Oregon. The orange markers were from the two reports of the van driven by hippies that stopped for gas on the afternoon of the abduction. But there were three red markers in the area as well, representing witnesses who thought they might have seen Megan. These sightings occurred three months, eight months, and four years after the abduction. Again, I applied Post-It notes flagging these for further investigation.

A cluster of Megan sightings around Grants Pass had followed publicity on the one-year anniversary of the abduction. None of the witnesses had ever known or seen Megan before the abduction, when the family lived in Grants Pass. If they had, it might have bolstered the credibility of their sighting reports. But as it turned out, the witnesses were simply good-hearted people wanting to do something to help, and the subjects of their sightings had all been identified.

Except for three places where there were pairs of red markers, the rest were scattered all across the map without apparent pattern. The paired markers were in Troutdale, Seaside, and a remote area south of Burns. Salem detectives had relied on the local authorities to check out the leads in most of the distant sightings, and the files did not contain specifics about those investigations—only the final conclusion, which in all cases was that sightings were not relevant to Megan's case.

July
Wednesday 9

Chapter 63

As she returned the last few sheets of paper to the investigation file, Martha proclaimed, "Well, that does it. The database is finished."

"Good. Now let's put it to work."

I showed her my sightings map. "Every red marker on this map represents a place where a witness reported seeing a girl who looked like Megan. All of these reports were investigated and dismissed. Our job is to take a second look and try to see something that wasn't visible to the detectives who did the original follow-up."

"So how do you want me to do this?"

"First, sort all the sighting reports according to location. You can see on the map that there are hot spots where there have been multiple sightings within close proximity to one another. Based strictly on numbers, that's where we have the best chance of finding Megan."

"Okay, I can take all the witness reports in a specific location and identify keywords, and then I can search the database for other places where the word appears."

"You got it. With some luck, we'll be able to bring seemingly unrelated pieces of information together to see things that were invisible in the original investigation."

"There must be about two hundred Megan sightings in here," Martha said, indicating the database file.

"It's actually closer to *three* hundred. Prioritize according to the number of sightings in a geographic area. The idea will be to look for commonalities that might determine if the different witnesses all may have seen the same girl. If that seems to be a realistic possibility, then we'll try to determine if it was Megan."

I handed Martha the list of locations where there had been multiple sightings, some of them separated by ten years or more. There were sixteen locations where three or more witnesses had reported seeing someone they thought might have been Megan. Of those hot spots, five were within a thirty-mile radius of the scene of the abduction.

While Martha went to work on that, I went to work on the reports where people had seen an individual or couple matching the descriptions or police drawings of the suspects. On the Maptitude display, these sightings were represented by orange markers. There were several places where both red and orange markers were clustered in close proximity. I considered these to be high-priority targets.

I picked keywords from each of the abductor sightings, beginning with the witnesses to the abduction itself, and searched our database for other places where the same word was used. The witness who had the most to say about the abductors, of course, was Carolyn Gervais, so hers was the first file I selected to cross-reference, focusing on her descriptions of the abductors.

I broke down her descriptions into individual features—the hair, the eyes, height and weight, posture, clothing, and so on. Thus, keywords associated with the woman's hair included *straight, brown, oily*, and *chopped*—that being Carolyn's description of her haircut. I quickly found the shortcoming in this process. The database program had no way to match keywords with synonyms. If two witnesses used different words to describe the same thing, my search would miss it. I discovered this when I was looking at one description of the woman's hair as looking drab and dirty, where Carolyn had simply called it oily. A computer would be incapable of seeing that the two descriptions meant the same thing. So the human factor could not be taken out of the process.

Oddly, when I got to Carolyn's description of the tattoo on the woman's arm, I found no matches for it anywhere in the database. The only reference to it was in Carolyn's interview transcript, where she called it a faded omega symbol. The tattoo had been completely left out of the broadcast descriptions of the subject. To me, it seemed like a defining feature, and its omission struck me as a serious oversight.

The only reasonable explanation for that was that perhaps it was one of those details deliberately held back from the public for the purpose of screening false witnesses. But to me, it seemed like something that could spark immediate recognition—people would notice a distinctive tattoo. The word *tattoo* was nowhere in the entire investigation file except for Carolyn's interview.

And yet when I entered the word *omega*, I got a cascade of matches. The police apparently had put a considerable effort into figuring out the *meaning* of the omega tattoo. What first came to *my* mind was the well-known

Swiss timepiece company. But you'd have to be pretty enthralled with your wristwatch to have the omega symbol tattooed on your arm.

Really, all I knew about the omega symbol was that it is the last letter in the Greek alphabet, and as such, it was symbolic of "the end." It is most often used in association with the alpha symbol, the first letter in the Greek alphabet, symbolic of "the beginning." Thus, the alpha and omega represented the beginning and the end. There was something vaguely ominous in the use of the omega by itself—the end.

In attempting to find a reason for the tattoo, the Salem detectives had compiled a list of every group or organization that used *omega* in its name. The list identified half a dozen college sororities whose name included the omega—but always in conjunction with one or two other Greek letters. Was it possible that Carolyn had seen only *part* of a tattoo?

As I considered that idea, I couldn't recall having ever seen or heard of a sorority woman getting herself branded with her sorority name. It seemed to me that sorority girls were far too refined for that. They'd wear tastefully small Greek letters on a gold chain, but they'd never submit to something as uncouth as a tattoo.

When I searched online for omega groups, I came up with dozens of hits, and for a few seconds, I let myself believe that I'd found something. But I quickly learned that omega groups have something to do with higher mathematics.

Then I found a *New York Times* article about an anti-Castro group in Florida that called itself Omega 7. During the early 1980s, the group claimed responsibility for at least two murders and numerous bombings. The group seemingly fell apart after the 1983 arrest of its leader. In any case, it seemed highly unlikely that a group of terrorists would brand themselves with a very visible tattoo proclaiming their affiliation.

I also found a Web page for the Omega Group in Charleston—in the United Kingdom. This group *did* use the Omega symbol, but it was a social organization involved with gardening, home decor, and the arts. I found it extremely unlikely that the little old ladies in East Sussex would put omega tattoos on their arms. Had any of the witnesses who saw our suspect at Burger King reported that she spoke with an English accent, I might have given the connection further consideration. However, under the circumstances, any association with that group seemed extremely unlikely; and that put me right back where I started. Why did this woman wear an omega tattoo?

After two hours of fruitless searching on the Internet, I finally had to set the omega question aside. Maybe it was simply a random selection— something she saw and liked the way it looked irrespective of any literal meaning. Still, I put a Post-It tab on the page, marking the topic as an unresolved loose end for later study.

The most prominent characteristic of the woman was her thinness. To be described as "Dachau thin" suggested something beyond anorexia and far, far beyond "fashionably" thin. This was thinness to such an extreme as to be indicative of severe malnutrition. I was forced to consider the likelihood that the expression was merely a tasteless exaggeration by that witness. All the other witnesses had said she was very thin but had not resorted to hyperbole in their descriptions.

Was there something about her thinness—and that of her companion—that might help us figure out who she was? Maybe she was one of those dietary extremists who had put virtually every edible substance on their forbidden foods list. That too might warrant some research. But the probable answer was the easiest. They were thin because they were living in poverty.

I asked myself why a destitute person would decide to kidnap a child, and I cringed at the obvious answer: to sell. A female child is a marketable commodity in some deeply twisted parts of society. I might have to look at that possibility at some point, but I knew I couldn't be unscathed by what I'd find in that nightmare. So I resolved to look at everything else first and get into that only as a last and final resort.

The basic problem was that there is no mainstream answer to the question of why someone would abduct a child. It is an aberration in and of itself, so the people I was looking for lived their lives somewhere far outside the mainstream. And that led my thoughts back to Christopher and Michelle Dayton. They were deeply involved in the drug culture, and their thinness was quite possibly due to chronic use of methamphetamines.

"This is Captain Glendale with narcotics and vice, Pittsburgh Bureau of Police. I've been asked to contact you regarding an old case here."

"Thank you, Captain, for the call," I said. "If you can give me a couple of minutes, I'll tell what this is all about."

"Please do," Glendale answered. "I'm having trouble understanding why a PI in Oregon needs to know about an old drug case in Pittsburgh."

"For the past four months, I've been working on a case involving abducted girls who've been held captive—you've probably seen it in the news."

"Okay, so you *are* the guy who got those two girls home. Nice work."

"Thanks. But there's still an unsolved abduction—I'm working with Salem PD to try to clear it out of their cold-case file. The crime took place in '96. In 2002, a pair of suspects was identified as a result of a traffic arrest. They were cleared because at the time of the abduction, they lived in Pittsburgh. But I've recently learned that they visited relatives in Oregon on a regular basis while they lived in your area."

"And you're talking about Christopher Dayton?"

"Correct. His mother-in-law told me that he hauled a vanload of Oregon marijuana back to Pittsburgh every time he came to visit. I'm looking for any information that might help pinpoint when he made those trips."

"It's long past the statute on any drug crimes," Glendale said.

"Yeah. I understand that. But if I could put him in Oregon on August 4, 1996, he'd go to the top of the list of suspects in our child abduction case."

"That's a tall order."

"I'd also like to know what kind of vehicle he owned in 1996. The child was taken away in a Ford E100 van, 1979 or 1980, silver or gray. If Dayton owned a van like that or if one of his business associates had one, that would be good to know."

"That's a bit easier. DMV ought to be able to get that info."

"There's one other thing—school records. The missing girl was five years old when she was kidnapped. If Dayton had her there, she should have been in school between 1996 and 2002. Dayton's wife is Catholic, so you'll have to check the parochial schools too."

"Okay. I think I get the picture. Here's what I can tell you right now. Dayton skipped bail on a trafficking charge here in June 2002. He was picked up as a known associate of an operator who distributed everything from pot to heroin."

"He was arrested here for driving while stoned in July 2002. He was driving a minivan with the windows painted black, and in the back there was a mattress and two rolls of duct tape. His wife was seen just before the arrest talking to children in a picnic area, possibly trying to lure them into the van."

"I'll assign someone to do the DMV screening. We'll see about that Ford van. And I'll have someone look at Dayton's file for anything that might hint where he was in August 1996. Give us a few days. We're busy here."

I thanked Captain Glendale and ended the call. Then I leaned back in my chair and stared at the ceiling, where a large spider was tormenting my poor cat, whose full attention was focused on the critter he couldn't possibly reach.

July 11 Friday

Chapter 64

While waiting impatiently to hear back from Pittsburgh, I returned to my search for the reason a young woman would choose to have an omega symbol tattooed on her arm. I don't pretend to understand the attraction to things like tattoos, nose piercings, backward hats, or baggy shorts. But my orderly mind demands that there be a reason why people do things.

Omega. Searching for that alone yielded far too many hits to screen. I'd already tried coupling *omega* with *tattoo* and *group*, without finding anything useful. But I kept at it, entering other keywords that might focus the search. When I entered "omega Oregon," I found a newspaper article from 1989 that talked about what had become of former followers of the Bhagwan Shree Rajneesh, who had started a huge commune in Central Oregon in the early 1980s.

The guru came to Oregon from India in 1981, bought the Big Muddy Ranch, and proceeded to build his utopian commune for his followers, who called themselves Sannyasins. They worshiped their guru, whom they called Osho, to such a degree that they bestowed upon him Rolls-Royce automobiles—ninety-three of them—as tokens of their esteem. Clearly, many of his disciples had more money than good sense.

The massive influx of the new age outsiders inevitably led to trouble. The huge development at the ranch, renamed Rajneeshpuram, set the Bhagwan afoul of Oregon land-use laws and federal immigration laws, and their attempts to dominate local politics resulted in severely strained relationships with long-time residents of the area. The finishing touch, and ultimately the undoing of the Rajneeshees, was when they attempted to swing the 1984 Wasco County elections by bussing in thousands of homeless people to vote for their candidates while simultaneously contaminating restaurant salad bars with bacteria to make the residents too sick to go to the polls.

In 1985, the whole thing fell apart. Osho fled the country, several of his lieutenants were indicted and prosecuted for their roles in the biological warfare, and the Sannyasins split into multiple factions. The true believers, of course, followed their leader back to Poona, India, the destitute people brought in to vote migrated to the streets of Portland, and the wealthy spiritualists migrated back to their California new age meditation roots. A stalwart few remained dedicated to the Sannyasin dream in Oregon and occasionally made news with public statements in defense of the Bhagwan.

Toward the end of the article, there was a single sentence that contained the keyword that had triggered the Google hit: *omega*. Even before the implosion of Rajneeshpuram, there were deep rifts within the residents. The wealthy members, not wishing to live the life of peasants in the kingdom, had built their own accommodations on the ranch. Their separation and their higher standard of living led many to resent their aloofness. At the same time, the true believers also became increasingly disenchanted with the commune leaders for their increasingly militant activities.

A small faction within that final group separated from the Rajneesh movement and declared themselves to be the ultimate believers. They were the Omega—the conclusion of the Sannyasin evolution. Unfortunately, the newspaper article gave no details about the Omega organization beyond saying that its leaders were Swami Dhyan Paul and Ma Prem Antar Dee.

My subsequent Web searches produced no results for those names, which were archetypical Rajneeshee aliases. I then went looking for any of the Sannyasin spin-off groups that were still active in Oregon. That led to a complex maze of Google hits that I had to wade through in search of contact information for anyone who might know something about the Omega organization. After hours of digging, I finally found an e-mail address for what seemed to be the business office for one of the more prominent groups.

I then considered what would be the best way to elicit a good response from the group. I doubted I could convincingly pose as someone interested in joining their group. I simply didn't speak their language, and I strongly suspected that they'd see through such a ruse. Ultimately, I decided to fall back on true statements—well, *mostly* true, anyway.

After struggling with the appropriate wording, I enlisted help from Martha, and between us we came up with something that I hoped would work.

I am trying to locate a woman named Sarah Miller who may have resided at Rajneeshpuram back in the 1980s. However, I do not know the name she used there. When Osho returned to India, Sarah joined an organization called Omega, which I understand was a very small, tight-knit group; but I've been unable to find any information on them.

If someone in your organization can tell me about Omega, I will make a donation to your charity fund in compensation for his or her time.

Corrigan

I pressed the Send button quickly, before I had time to change my mind. Late in the afternoon, a ping from my computer signaled the receipt of an e-mail message.

My name is Tyler. I am responding to your inquiry about Sarah Miller. Unfortunately, I know of nobody by that name. I can, however, tell you what I know about Omega, though I'm afraid it isn't much.

I believe that the organization fell apart after only a short time and never had more than thirty members. They lived briefly in Madras in a rented church building but lacked the financial support to stay afloat. The last few members of the group went to live on a farm, where they worked for board and room.

I wish I could tell you more, but that is what I know about Omega. Please let me know if I can help you in any other way.

Tyler

That wasn't a lot of help. Of course, I didn't expect anybody to know Sara Miller, since I'd made up the name while looking at the can of beer on my desk. The little bit of information about Omega probably wouldn't be much help, although it might be possible to track down the place they'd rented in Madras. But there was one question I had to ask, because any possible value to the pursuit of the Omega organization depended on the answer.

Thank you for your quick response. It occurred to me that I neglected in my earlier message to provide an additional detail about Sarah Miller that might help identify her. She had a prominent tattoo of the omega

325

symbol on her arm. If you remember someone like that, please let me know.

Almost immediately, I received the following reply:

The omega tattoo was something that many of the original members of the group had done as a gesture of their allegiance to the new philosophy. I wish I could be more helpful.

So finally I was certain as to the meaning of the omega tattoo. I thanked Tyler and asked for an address where I could send a donation. The information was well worth the $100 check I put in the mail. Unfortunately, it didn't conform very well with my suspicions about Michelle Dayton, whose mother had said nothing to me that even hinted that she'd ever been involved with the Rajneeshees or their spin-offs.

Then again, if your daughter had joined a cult, it might be something you'd be reluctant to talk about, even thirty years later. Michelle would have been at a very impressionable age then—right around twenty years old. It was entirely conceivable that she could have been attracted to the message of peace, love, and harmony offered by the Bhagwan.

This new insight raised questions about the van. Carolyn Gervais had told me she'd seen the omega symbol painted on the door of the van. Had the Omegas once owned a van? And if they had, why were Christopher and Michelle Dayton still driving it in 1996? It occurred to me that they must have been among the principal leaders of the group in order to take possession of the van when the group disbanded.

July 14 Monday

Chapter 65

I could hardly go back to Michelle Dayton's mother and ask if Michelle had been a Rajneeshee or a member of the spin-off cult called Omega—not given the ruse I'd used to talk with her before. So I phoned Klamath Falls Police Department to ask if Michelle's arrest report had mentioned a tattoo, but the chief told me that there was no arrest report for her. She had been brought in on suspicion of intoxication but was released without ever being charged. Only Christopher had been arrested.

I'd really been hoping for confirmation of the tattoo, because that would pin down Michelle as the abductor. It was looking more and more like I'd have to make the trip to Klamath Falls in order to see for myself if she had the tattoo. But because of my new celebrity status, any contact I made with Christopher or Michelle could tip them off that they were under suspicion and send them on the run, so I wanted to be sure that I had a solid case before approaching them.

The morning mail brought me a list from Oregon DMV showing all the Ford vans of the right model, color, and age that had been registered in Oregon in 1996. There were 593 E100 vans on the list. I had hoped for a smaller number. I quickly scanned the list looking for Dayton's name. I was disappointed, but not overly surprised, to find that nobody with that name owned the van I was looking for.

Next, I scanned the list in search of names that looked anything like the Rajneeshee names that I'd seen in the articles that mentioned the origins of the Omega cult. Once again, I came up dry. I did, however, find half a dozen vans registered at addresses in Madras. Any one of those might have been an Omega member who contributed the van to the cause—a serious step down from the ninety-three Rolls-Royces given to Osho.

"Martha, I have some 1996 names and addresses. See if any of those people are still there—and if not, try to track them down."

"What's their connection to this?"

"They all owned the right kind of van in 1996, and they lived in Madras. I'm looking for any connection they might have to the Omega faction or the Rajneeshees."

"You got it, boss."

Then I had to consider what to do with the other 587 owners of E100 Ford vans. I felt strongly that one of the vans on that list was the one that had carried Megan away from Burger King. To prioritize the search, I highlighted the registrations for vans in the areas where there had been Megan sightings. That brought the number of "possibles" down to sixty-one. We could work with that.

I called Kevin Fox to let him know that I'd received the DMV list and ask if he'd had any luck in his search for pot growers who might have been filling orders for Christopher Dayton.

"I've gone round and round with the vice squad. They don't think that anybody in our jurisdiction could have shipped half a ton of product in those days. So I went to Marion County and asked the same question—who could furnish marketable pot in half-ton quantities."

"Any luck there?"

"Not much. But, of course, their records are only for the ones they caught. It's entirely possible that the one who filled your suspect's orders never got caught. Anyway, they gave me the names of two growers big enough to do the job. One was busted in '96 and the other in '98."

"I can work with that," I told him.

"I'm trying to find out where they are. I have an inquiry in with the parole board—they're both out of prison now—rehabilitated, I'm sure."

"Right. All I need to know is whether they sold a load to Christopher Dayton around the first week in August 1996."

"You understand that they won't have documentation. These guys don't keep books like that."

"Yeah, I know it's a long shot. I'm just hoping we can put Dayton's alibi in question. It won't get us a conviction, but it might tell us that we're on the right track."

"I'll let you know what we find."

"There's one more thing," I said.

"Of course, there is," Fox said tiredly.

"I need to know if Michelle Dayton has the omega tattoo that Carolyn Gervais saw. Maybe you can ask someone in K-Falls to check it out—discreetly. I wouldn't want her to know that we're looking at her."

"I'll see what I can do. No promises."

"Thanks, Fox."

"Hey, Corrigan. You're doing good, okay?"

After a frustrating hour spent trying to figure some way to find out about the tattoo, a plan started to take shape. I needed someone to get close enough to Michelle Dayton to see her forearms. I certainly couldn't do it myself, though, because if she was actually the kidnapper, she'd probably recognize me from all the recent publicity and quickly deduce my real purpose in being there.

"Martha, didn't you once say that you used to have horses?" I asked, recalling that Grace had told me that her daughter had found happiness in raising horses.

"When I was a kid—actually, clear up until I got married. We had a few acres outside Ellensburg, and we had horses. My mom says I learned to ride about the same time I learned to walk."

"So you might be able to strike up a conversation with a horse person," I hinted.

"Sure, if we had something to talk about."

"What might that be?"

"Who knows? Feed, exercise, breeds, competition, tack—it could be just about anything as long as the other person was interested. What do you know about this person?"

"Only that she has horses and that they apparently are the focus of her life."

"Yep, that sounds like a horse person," Martha confirmed.

"Let me think this through," I said, leaning back and staring out the window.

You just can't simply strike up a conversation with a stranger and talk about the things Martha had mentioned. Or could you? The one thing that all horse people have is their tack—saddles, bridles, girths, blankets, and so forth. If we knew a few basics about Michelle's riding style, we'd know what kind of tack would interest her. Then we could approach her somehow with an irresistible offer of some kind.

In Klamath Falls, there really was only one kind of horsemanship—Western. But there was a pretty broad range of styles within that category, each calling for a different kind of tack.

"Got another question for you," I said slowly while forming a plan.

"Sure, what's that?"

"Do you think you could call Michelle's mother with some kind of ruse to get her to tell you what kind of tack her daughter might be interested in?"

"I could say I'm an old friend wanting to give Michelle a surprise gift," she suggested.

"Yeah, maybe." It sounded a bit shaky to me.

"Or I could talk directly to Michelle, posing as someone representing an equestrian organization."

"What organization would that be?"

"I don't know. There's no shortage to choose from. I'd just need to find one that she'd have some interest in."

"How about something relating to water rights in the Klamath Basin? That's been in the news a lot."

"Give me a little time. I'll figure out something."

I left Martha alone in the office and went down to my dock to stare at the river and clear my mind. While confident that Martha would be able to determine what kind of tack might be of interest to Michelle, I needed to come up with a way to put that information to use—an irresistible offer. An offer she couldn't refuse. The vision of a horse's severed head lying on silk sheets in a movie producer's bed came to mind.

But that wouldn't do. We had to offer her something for nothing—something she'd want—and we'd have to offer it in a way that wouldn't arouse suspicion. The big question was how to approach Michelle. You can't just walk up to someone and say, "I have something you want, and I'm going to give it to you." There had to be a better way.

When I wandered back up to the office, Martha announced, "I got the information. Michelle has a dozen horses, all Western Quarter Horses. She breeds and trains most of them for trail riding, but her real passion is for training horses for rodeo events. She keeps the horses on her twenty-acre ranch, which has a year-around creek fed by natural springs. She's concerned that increased use of ground water could dry up the springs."

"Okay," I said slowly. "Could we approach her through the water rights issue?"

"I don't think so. I mean, she listened to what I had to say but didn't really start talking until I asked about her horses."

"Hmm."

I was back to the severed horse head idea.

"How about this?" Martha offered. "I have the saddle that Larry Mahan used at the Ellensburg Rodeo in 1966—the first year he won the PCRA All-Around Cowboy award. I've held onto it forever, but I have no need for it anymore. It would be irresistible to just about anybody who knows about rodeo."

"You'd actually give that up just to see if Michelle has a tattoo?" I asked.

"If she has the tattoo, she'll be going to prison, and I'll be able to get the saddle back. If she's innocent, then she'll probably be a better curator for the saddle than I am."

An hour later, I was still trying to figure out what to do with Martha's idea. It could be, as she'd said, irresistible to Michelle. The question was how to put the offer before her. As I noted before, I could hardly just walk up and say, "I have Larry Mahan's saddle, and I want to give it to you if you'll just let me look at your arms." I simply could not think of a way to approach Michelle directly.

But could I approach her *indirectly*? Slowly, I started putting together a plan based on something Grace had told me about her son-in-law, Christopher Dayton. He had a good job in a muffler shop. I did a quick online search for muffler shops in Klamath Falls. About twenty businesses advertised muffler repairs, but most of them were general auto repair shops. Only four shops specialized in exhaust system repair.

I had Martha start phoning the muffler shops, posing as the credit manager for an appliance store. The second shop she called confirmed that Christopher Dayton was an employee in good standing. We now knew that he was an estimator and supervisor at Davis Muffler Shop on East Main. A person desperately in need of some muffler work might be willing to offer Larry's saddle as payment, even though it was undoubtedly worth far more than a new muffler.

I went to the kitchen and got two cans of beer from the refrigerator and carried them out onto the porch. I sat down, put my feet up on the railing, and snapped open a can.

"Hey, Corrigan. What's happening?" Bud asked casually, pretending he was just happening by.

"Not much. How about a beer?" I asked.

The "Bud Call" nearly always works.

"Don't mind if I do," he said, taking the other seat and helping himself to the unopened beer.

After an appropriate amount of time had passed—half a beer, to use Bud's time standard—I broached the subject.

"Do you think your Pontiac would make it to Klamath Falls?"

He seemed mildly offended. "Of course, it would. It ain't the prettiest thing on the road, but it's dependable. You need to borrow it again?"

"No, I was wondering if you'd be interested in doing some more undercover work."

Bud perked up and gulped down the remainder of his beer. "Sure! What do ya have?"

"I need someone who can get close enough to a woman to see if she has tattoos."

"Where are her tattoos?" he asked with a lascivious, hopeful grin.

"Forget it. They're on her forearms. I think someone who needs a muffler on his car might be able to get close enough to her to see what's there."

"Huh? I don't get it. Got another beer?"

"Sure. Help yourself."

When he was back in his chair, I explained the whole thing to him without revealing why I needed to know about the tattoo.

"So you want me to beg the guy in the muffler shop to take an old saddle in exchange for a new muffler for my Pontiac?"

"It needs one," I pointed out. "The thing is this isn't just any old saddle. It was Larry Mahan's saddle."

"I don't know him."

"Larry Mahan is one of the most famous rodeo cowboys in history," I explained. "Martha can tell you the whole story."

"Okay, so what would make me so desperate for a muffler that I'd be willing to trade a valuable saddle for it?"

"How about a ticket for excessive noise. You can say that you've been ordered to get it fixed, or you'll have to pay a big fine—which you can't afford to do any more than you can afford to buy a muffler."

"Okay, I'm starting to get the picture. I can do that."

"There's just one thing. You'll need to get some work done on your car before you go. Brakes, steering, shocks—that car isn't safe on the highway."

"Oh," Bud said sadly. "If you're gonna make me do all that, I won't be able to take the job. I can't afford to have all that work done."

That was no surprise, and I already had an answer.

"In the morning, take your car across the highway to John's Auto Repair and ask Cyndi to call me with an estimate. That won't cost you anything. Then we can talk about what comes next, okay?"

July **15**
Tuesday

Chapter 66

The price Cyndi quoted for the necessary work on Bud's Pontiac exceeded its total value by a substantial margin. That was hardly a surprise, since the pathetic old car was basically worthless.

"But I'll tell you what. I have a special deal today for Vietnam veterans. For Bud, I'll do the job for half price," Cyndi told me.

It wasn't hard to see that she'd be losing money on that deal. I guess she was just being a good neighbor. I told her to do the work and send me the bill.

When Bud stopped by, I told him, "I'm going to pay the bill for your car repairs and then deduct it from your pay for this job."

"Will there be anything leftover for me?" he asked.

"Probably not much. But your car ought to be good to go for another quarter-million miles."

"I guess that'll be okay—as long as you can give me some money for travel expenses."

"We'll give you some cash and a credit card. That'll take care of you."

"When do I leave?"

"Your car won't be ready to go for a couple of days. In the meantime, you'll need to work with Martha to get your story down pat. She'll tell you everything you need to know about Larry Mahan and his saddle, and you'll need a good story for how you came to own it."

"Okay, I'm cool with that. But how do I work the deal? I can't just come out of the clear blue and offer to trade Larry Mahan's saddle for a muffler repair."

"Right. When you first get to K-Falls, find the Davis Muffler Shop. Then stop at the nearest gas station—make sure it's one that doesn't have a service bay—and ask where you can get a muffler. Get the name of the guy you talk to."

"Why do I have to do all that? Can't I just go straight to the muffler shop?"

"The idea is so that you can ask for Christopher Dayton by name and then tell him something like, 'Jake up at the Chevron station told me that I might be able to make a deal with you.' Then Dayton will probably ask what kind of deal."

"So I tell him a sob story about why I can't afford a muffler," Bud said.

"Yeah, but you have to tell him that the gas station guy told you that Dayton's wife raises rodeo horses and might be interested in owning Larry Mahan's saddle. You have to get that idea planted right up front, and you have to make sure that he understands that the saddle is worth way more than the muffler because he's going to have to pay the repair bill out of his own pocket."

"What if he says no?"

"Your job is to make the deal sound so good that he *can't* say no. Martha will help you with your story. You'll say how much you hate to let it go and wouldn't do it if you had any choice."

"What if he doesn't believe it's really Larry Mahan's?"

"That's exactly what we want. Challenge him to ask his wife about the saddle—she'll know what it's worth—and offer to show it to her. That's the key to meeting his wife. Point out that you have signed documents proving what it is and then remind him that even if it weren't Larry's, it'd still be worth more than a muffler. Convince him to call his wife to take a look at it, because she'll know what it's worth."

"Well, okay then, what if he takes the deal right away without calling his wife?"

"Improvise. You really want to meet his wife just to make sure the saddle is going to someone who appreciates it for what it is. One way or another, you need to give the saddle to her directly so that you can see if she has the tattoo."

Martha went with Bud to the sitting area on my beach to start prepping him for the job. As she'd done in coaching him for the insurance scam investigation, she'd play the role of Dayton and throw him every curve she could think of. What we had in our favor was Bud's natural talent for storytelling. Or as Big Dan once said, "Bud could bullshit his way out of the apocalypse."

When my phone rang, the number on the screen showed the area code 412—Pittsburgh.

"This is Captain Glendale, Pittsburgh Bureau of Police. Sorry it took so long, but I have the answers to some of your questions—but not all."

"Thanks, Captain. I appreciate whatever you can tell me."

"Like I told you before, Dayton skipped bail on a trafficking charge back in '02. His associate was convicted and spent four years in the state pen. We sent his parole officer out to talk to him."

"Were you able to confirm that he was transporting pot from Oregon?"

"He did confirm that. But I know you were interested in specific dates, and he said he had no way of knowing that."

"Any luck with the schools?"

"We talked with the public school where Dayton lived. Nothing. Then we contacted three different Catholic schools. There was nothing there either. If Dayton had a kid in school, he was using some other name."

"What about the van? Did Dayton—or his associate—own a van like the one I described?"

"Not so far as we can tell. The thing is the mutts don't always register the vehicles they drive. Get my meaning? They'll put stolen tags on it and call it good. But we're sending you the DMV records for 1996. Maybe you can find something, maybe not."

"That'll give us something to do, anyway. I do have one general question though."

"What's that?"

"The guys who transport large quantities of pot—do they travel the interstate highways, or do they stay on secondary routes?"

"There's more anonymity on the interstates. On the secondary highways, there's a lot more likelihood of personal encounters, and that's always dangerous to the hauler."

I wondered to myself what traces a drug transporter might leave along the way. He probably wouldn't be stupid enough to use a credit card for food, fuel, and lodging. But what if he had some unexpected expense—some kind of breakdown or a medical problem—that exceeded his cash supply?

"What about credit cards?" I asked.

"Even if we knew what card he used, the records are probably long gone by now. But without knowing what card he used, there's no chance at all."

"Just thinking out loud," I said, a bit embarrassed. "Thanks for the info."

"Good luck with your investigation," he concluded.

It was disappointing. But it had been a long shot from the beginning. At least we'd confirmed the story Grace had told me about Dayton hauling Oregon weed to Pittsburgh. But *what about* those cross-country trips?

An idea suddenly popped into my head—another long shot, but every now and then, the desperation half-court shot scores the game-winning basket.

"What do you need now, Corrigan?" Kevin Fox asked.

"I'm wondering if phone records could tell us anything about Christopher Dayton's travels. How long do the phone companies keep records on phone calls?"

"In theory, ever since the phone companies computerized, they store the records indefinitely. There's probably a giant data bank somewhere that has phone records back to the 1980s. But I don't know how you'd go about finding any particular data in a digital warehouse."

"If the data is stored, it ought to be accessible," I argued. "Otherwise, what's the point of keeping it?"

"Okay, suppose you're right. We don't know what kind of phone Dayton may have had back then. And even if he had a phone, it could have been a throwaway. We can't search for phone calls from a particular phone unless we know the phone number."

I could tell that Fox was getting impatient.

"I think we can find that number. Do you think Michelle Dayton ever phoned her mother? If we can get Grace's phone records, we ought to be able to spot phone calls from Pittsburgh," I suggested.

"You make that sound easy," he complained.

"No, not easy. But possible. Maybe."

"You know, of course, that it takes a court order to get phone records."

"I have faith in your persuasive skills," I said.

"Corrigan, you'd better get this thing figured out pretty soon. You're becoming a pain in the ass."

"So you'll do it?"

"I'll try. No promises."

July 18 Friday

Chapter 67

The repairs on Bud's Pontiac were finished by Thursday afternoon. "Corrigan, we really should have replaced the exhaust system," Cyndi told me when I went over to pay the bill. "That car isn't safe to drive with all that exhaust leaking into the passenger compartment."

"He drives with the window open," I said.

"He'd better. But with all you've spent on that old wreck, I don't understand why you'd draw the line on something as cheap as a muffler."

"It's more than just the muffler," I reminded her.

"Yeah, but still—"

"We'll get it done pretty soon," I promised. "Just not today."

"Okay. But if he asphyxiates himself on exhaust fumes, it isn't our fault."

So I made a special point of warning Bud to keep the window open all the time. It was the same warning he'd given me when I borrowed his car to stake out the meth lab weeks before.

"Man, I can't believe it's the same car," Bud exclaimed when he came back from a test drive. "It handles just like new!"

So Friday morning, with Larry Mahan's rodeo saddle in the hatchback and a bag of sandwiches from Martha on the passenger seat, Bud took off toward Klamath Falls. I gave him a prepaid phone but cautioned him to make sure it was out of sight when he was pleading poverty to Christopher Dayton.

"He's really jazzed about doing this," Martha said as we watched him turn onto the highway. "He was worried you wouldn't let him work again after the landslide and all."

I gave her a stern look. "And I wouldn't if I could prove that he'd started the landslide. But I'm giving him the benefit of the doubt on that."

Parts of the case were coming together. And I liked the fact that they were coming from several different directions. The abductor had the omega tattoo. The Omega faction of the Sannyasins was headquartered in Madras, and its members wore the omega tattoo. The old van with the peeling gray paint was seen three times on Highway 22 after the kidnapping. Highway 22 was the most direct route from Salem to Madras.

"It doesn't look good for Megan, does it?" Martha asked.

I'd been deliberately avoiding that thought. But she was right. So far, we'd found no evidence that Christopher and Michelle Dayton had actually had a child in their household at any time. If they were the abductors, it looked like Megan probably was dead. I wondered how hard that conclusion would hit Kim.

Surely, the rescues of Brittany Harlan and Alyssa Marquam had given Kim reason to hope that Megan, too, might be found alive. And I would have to be the one to tell her that the best we could hope for was a conviction of those responsible. But if Michelle Dayton was the skinny woman with the omega tattoo, Megan was almost certainly dead. There was no escaping that.

"No," I said to Martha. "It doesn't look good for Megan."

"Maybe they did it for someone else," she speculated.

"Nobody does that."

She sighed. "I know. I just don't want it to end this way."

"Keep working on those van registrations. If the van was registered to anyone in Oregon *other* than Dayton, it might mean that other people were involved. It would mean that Dayton got to Oregon some other way and then borrowed the van after he got here. And if that's the case, then maybe they *did* do it for someone else."

"We're getting close," Martha said. "I can *feel* it."

"It all hinges on breaking Dayton's alibi. As long as he can claim that he was in Pittsburgh when Megan was abducted, we don't stand a chance of getting him charged."

"But if Michelle has the tattoo—if we connect them to the van—"

"It won't mean a thing unless we can show that they were in Salem on August 4."

"I don't see how we can prove that!"

"Fox is working on getting a court order to look at phone records. We might find something there."

"How long will that take?"

"Your guess is as good as mine. But it all starts with that court order."

"Maybe—"

Martha left the thought unfinished, but I could tell from the look on her face that she had an idea.

"Those phone records you're talking about—would those be computer data?" she finally asked.

"Well, sure. Everything's computerized. But who knows where the data is stored."

"You remember my son's friend?"

"Shahzad? Sure, I remember him."

Shahzad—I never heard his last name, or maybe that was it—was a seemingly skilled computer hacker, who had helped us with a prior investigation. Martha didn't have to tell me what she had in mind.

I said, "It's worth a try. Give him a call."

"I can't actually call him directly, but I'll call Jason. He'll get a message to Shahzad."

I gave Martha the phone number I had for Michelle's mother. It was a landline, so I felt safe with the assumption that she'd have had the same number in 1996. Then I listened while she explained to her son that we'd like to get the record for all incoming and outgoing calls for 1996.

Two hours later, a text message popped up on my phone.

hello so jsn sez u nd ph#s 2 n frm 5035550633 prbly wl gt jst lng dist frm 96 cuz lnd ln ok?

With some effort, I was able to translate the message to "Jason says you need phone numbers to and from 503.555.0633. I probably will be able to get just long-distance calls from 1996, since this is a landline, and records then covered only long-distance calls. Will that be enough?"

I keyed in my return message.

Shahzad,
    I understand you can get only long-distance records from 1996. That will be fine. Can you estimate how long this will take?
                                                Corrigan

I hoped he'd be able to translate my message into whatever language it was he spoke. I waited for an answer back, but when nothing came in, I returned to my analysis of the vehicle registration records from Pennsylvania.

"Holy crap," Martha commented half an hour later. "That was quick."

She tapped a few keys, and the printer started spitting out Grace's monthly phone bills from 1996. As I looked them over, I was struck by how much things had changed in the last eighteen years—starting with the size of the monthly bill. The average was under thirty dollars.

Page by page, I highlighted every call to and from area code 412—Pittsburgh. It didn't take long, because there were not many calls, and yet they spoke volumes about the relationship between Michelle and her mother. Most of the calls were originated by Grace. Every one of the incoming calls from Pittsburgh was billed to Grace.

There was a twenty-minute collect call from Pittsburgh on May 12—Mother's Day. That, I felt, was pretty solid proof of who placed the call. There were no calls to or from Pittsburgh in the two months preceding Mother's Day, but overall it looked like Grace had talked with her daughter about once a month on average.

I flipped to the July and August bills. Any calls to or from Pittsburgh on those bills would indicate that Christopher and Michelle were at home. There was a collect call from Michelle on July 10. That was all until September 16, when Grace had phoned Michelle. The absence of calls in between didn't prove that the couple was in Oregon, but it also didn't prove they were in Pittsburgh.

On my second pass through the phone bills, I paid closer attention to the long-distance calls to and from area codes *other than* 412. There were many calls to a number in Albuquerque, but if there were incoming calls, they had been paid by the caller and didn't show on Grace's bill. I made a note to follow up on the Albuquerque number but considered it a low-priority task.

As I looked at the August bill, I noted two collect calls from a number in area code 801, an hour apart on August 6. When I looked up the area code, I found that the calls had come from Ogden, Utah, right along Interstate 84—the route Christopher and Michelle would take on their way from Oregon to Pittsburgh. My pulse rate quickened.

The reverse directory indicated that the Utah number was no longer in service. I called the phone company in Ogden and asked if anyone could tell me about the 1996 phone number. My call was handed up the food chain twice before anyone asked who I was.

"My name is Corrigan. I'm an investigator in Oregon, working on a case involving child abductions." I never claimed to be a cop or that mine was an official investigation. I simply neglected to use the word *private*.

"Of course, Inspector. What can I help you with?"

I read off the Ogden phone number.

340

"That number is on the phone bill for a person of interest in our case. I'm wondering what you can tell me about it."

"It was a public phone—a pay phone in a restaurant."

"Can you tell me if the restaurant is still in business?"

"Yes, it is. Would you like their phone number?"

I called the restaurant and confirmed that they'd been in business at that location since 1993.

"Are there any employees still around from back then?"

"I'm the owner. I was here. Tell me again what this is about."

"Like I said, I'm investigating a case involving kidnapped children," I repeated.

"Hey, I know who you are! You're the one who saved those girls!" the lady exclaimed.

"I'm trying to track the movements of someone who made a call from a pay phone in your restaurant in 1996," I answered.

"Goodness! We had the pay phone taken out ten years ago. Cell phones, you know. Nobody uses pay phones anymore."

"Is there a motel close to your restaurant?"

"There are some at the freeway interchange. That's a couple of miles away. Most of our customers are local folks."

"Are there other businesses nearby?"

"Well, sure. We're in a little strip mall. There's a Walgreens, a paint store, a couple of clothing stores—and then there's the AAMCO shop right across the street."

"AAMCO? The transmission repair shop?"

"That's right."

"Was that shop there in 1996?"

"Sure. It's been around a lot longer than we have."

It was pretty easy to see what had happened. Christopher and Michelle were cruising down the Interstate when their transmission went up in smoke. They managed to get to the AAMCO shop but didn't have the money to pay for the needed repairs, so they went to the pay phone and called Grace. She probably wired the money, and the second call was to confirm that they'd received it.

When I called the transmission shop, the manager told me that records that old—if they existed at all—would be stored at the owner's residence. The owner confirmed that he'd have an invoice for any work done on August 6 or 7, 1996, but he wouldn't be able to look for it until he got home later in the day.

I told Martha, "We're really close. If there's an invoice with Dayton's name on it, the alibi is shot."

July
Saturday
19

Chapter 68

When he called in, Bud told me, "I was too late getting into town last night to do anything about the muffler."

"Did you have car problems? I thought you'd get there in about five or six hours."

"Yeah, but I had to stop in Sisters."

"What for?"

"I was feeling kinda sick."

"Don't tell me you rolled up the windows!" I said.

"It was cold up there on the pass. It was only for a little while," Bud protested.

There was no point in admonishing him for his carelessness.

"So you're okay now?"

"Yeah. Just having breakfast at Denny's. Then I'll get started on the job. I just wanted to let you know what's happening."

When I opened the door to go out and pick up the morning paper, DC blasted past, nearly bowling me over, and planted his face in his food bowl. After testing the contents, he gave me an accusing glare, obviously unhappy to find yesterday's crunchies instead of fresh ones.

I came back in with the newspaper in time to hear my phone ringing again. It was unusual to get *one* call before eight on a Saturday morning, let alone two. And then I remembered that Ogden is in a different time zone.

"Okay, I have a couple dozen invoices for those days. None has the name Dayton, but there are some cash invoices that don't have names on them."

"I believe they were driving a Ford van—and it could have had license plates from Oregon or Pennsylvania."

"What year was that Ford?"

"I believe it was a '79 or '80," I said.

"Then if it had an automatic, it would've been an FMX in '79 or maybe an AOD in '80," he said, more to himself than to me. After a moment, he said, "Okay, here's an invoice for a remanufactured AOD, installed. Paid in cash. $1,189."

"What information do you have on the van?"

"I don't have anything. I don't even know for sure that it *was* a van. The transmission came off the shelf, so nobody wrote down the vehicle model. It was a Ford. That's all I know."

"Would there be a warranty on file?"

"Only if they sent in the card. Most people forget."

I thanked him and put the phone down. DC hopped into my lap, purring like a locomotive, demanding that I perform his morning ritual head maul. I obliged while contemplating my next move on the Dayton investigation. I was certain that the Ford transmission on the cash invoice had been installed in Dayton's E100 Ford van. But I needed proof. If Grace had wired money to Michelle, I could probably find a record of the transaction through her bank—but only with a court order.

But just the fact that Daytons were only 775 miles from Salem two days after Megan was abducted was enough to seriously erode their alibi. I was confident that with Bud's confirmation of Michelle's omega tattoo, we could get the court order.

Nothing about this case came easy.

The number that showed up on my telephone screen was unfamiliar.

"This is Corrigan," I said as politely as I could, knowing that the call was probably from a telemarketer wanting to sell Canadian pharmaceuticals.

A quiet voice said, "This is Brittany Harlan."

It took me a second to catch my breath. "Brittany! It's great to hear from you. How are you doing?"

After the initial media storm, reporters had respected the family's request for privacy, and for the last two weeks, there had been nothing in the news about Brittany.

"I wanted to call and thank you. They say that if it wasn't for you, I'd still be—" She left the sentence unfinished.

"When I first saw where you carved your name on the beam, I didn't know who you were. Someone had to explain it to me," I managed to say, choking on the emotion.

"I read the newspaper accounts—how you figured the whole thing out. I used to pray, all the time, that someone would do what you did.

"That man tried to make me forget my name. He said my name was Trina, and he punished me if I tried to say that wasn't right. Sometimes I almost forgot my name. Then one day he came in with a bottle of beer, but he knocked it off the table, and it broke all over the floor. Later on, I found a piece of the bottle in the corner under my bed.

"I stood on the table and scratched my name in the wood where I could see it when I looked up. That way I would never forget who I was. Sometime after that, he hooked up my TV so that I could watch the news— that was the day the terrorists crashed the airplanes. I scratched the date next to my name. I didn't remember what year it was when he took me to that place, so I didn't know how old I was."

I listened without comment as Brittany told her story, recalling that Alyssa Marquam had also spoken about the day Langlois connected the TV cable.

"I could tell there were other girls there. Sometimes I could hear them crying. But he punished me if I ever made any noise, and I guess he did the same to them. We never tried to talk to each other. Anyway, one day he injected something into my arm, and the next thing I knew, I was in a different place—a tiny room all made of wood, and it was moving, like in the back of a truck. I was tied up, and it was mostly dark, but I could see three other girls in there with me. I thought they must be asleep, because they never opened their eyes.

"One of the other girls was naked, and I thought how lucky I was to still have my clothes. Then we stopped, and it was all dark. I pretended to be asleep when the man opened the box. He lifted the naked girl out and closed the door. A little while later, we started to move again. The next time we stopped, the man gave me another injection. When I woke up, I was in the room where you found me."

I said, "We found the wooden box built into the back of Langlois' old motor home. It was Alyssa Marquam he took out when you were awake. The other two girls didn't make it."

"I know," she said quietly. "I pretended I liked him. I think that's why he let me live. The new place where he locked me up was more like a house. I could hear him walking around on the floor above. But it didn't have very good heat. Sometimes it got really cold. I had TV, but all I could watch was video cassettes. They were mostly sex movies. I asked him if I could have the news channel again, and he finally hooked it up.

"Everything I knew about the world came from what I saw on TV. I didn't understand what 'outside' was, because I couldn't actually remember *being* outside. I was always *inside*—inside those concrete walls, inside the wooden box, and then inside the little room. On TV I saw images of the outdoors, but I didn't actually understand what it was like.

"Then the policemen broke the door open and took me outdoors, and I got dizzy and sick. I had to close my eyes and get down on the ground, because I guess my brain just couldn't figure out what I was seeing. The space around me was so big! It still takes my breath away when I look at the sky—especially at night."

"You're going to be okay," I told her, putting as much confidence as I could into my voice.

"My mom is dead," she said.

"Yes. I know." I wondered if she knew the circumstances of her mother's death. "Your dad will take care of you. He never gave up—never stopped looking for you."

"It's all so strange. Sometimes I feel like I'm still seven years old."

There was a long pause, and I could hear her crying quietly.

"Can you come and see me sometime?" she finally asked.

"I would love to do that. Maybe you should ask your dad to give me a call."

July

Monday 21

Chapter 69

ud said, "I'll start back as soon as they finish with the muffler. It was harder to make the deal than we thought it'd be. I did just like we talked about and went looking for a gas station close to the muffler shop. But the guy there said Dayton was an asshole, and he wouldn't trust him to touch his car. So I went to another gas station, and that guy didn't have any idea where there was a muffler shop.

"I finally decided to just make up a name. So I went to the muffler shop, but Dayton wasn't there. They said he'd be in sometime after noon. When Dayton showed up, I told him how I needed a muffler, or I'd have to pay a big fine. He said, 'Tough shit.' So I told him that the guy whose name I made up said that his wife might be interested in the saddle.

"He says, 'Never heard of him,' of course, since I made up the name, and then he says, 'My wife don't pay the bills, and she sure as hell don't need another saddle.' So we got off to a really shitty start, and I told him I'd buy him a beer if he'd just listen to my story.

"We met at a tavern after the shop closed for the day, and I told him how I almost passed out from the exhaust fumes in my car, and a cop pulled me over because he thought I was drunk, and then he gave me a ticket but said he'd tear it up if I got the muffler fixed by today. Meanwhile, Dayton gulped down the beer and called for another, and I hadn't even hardly had time to take a drink of mine."

That, I thought, was a pretty extraordinary thing. Rarely had I ever seen anyone down a beer faster than Bud.

"So I pulled out the magazine Martha gave me with the story of the saddle and the picture of Larry Mahan carrying it on his shoulder, and I pointed to all the little things in the photo that proved it really was the same saddle. I showed him the letter from the Washington Rodeo Association asking if they could display the saddle in their museum and the other letter where someone offered Martha two thousand dollars for it. That's when he first started to look interested.

"He asked why didn't I sell it to that guy, and I told him I couldn't, because it belonged to my wife, but now she's dead, and the saddle is the only thing I have with me to trade for the muffler. Then he asked how was he to know if the letters I showed him were real, 'cause I could've just made 'em on a computer. So I said, 'If your wife knows about this stuff, she'll tell you what it's worth. Just let me show it to her,' and he says she ain't in town.

"I start worrying—maybe she's gone to Disneyland or something—but then he says, 'She mostly just stays out at the ranch,' so I said I'd be happy to take the saddle out there and show it to her. He finally said that would be okay, but it was too late to do it that day. I said I could take it out there the next day—yesterday, and he said all right."

I was finding it increasingly difficult to wait for Bud to get to the point, but I held my tongue and let him tell the story his way.

"So anyway, yesterday I drove about ten miles out of town on a gravel road and found their ranch. The house isn't much to look at, but they have a big barn and a covered arena. It's like they care more about the horses than about themselves. The lady—Michelle—came out from the barn and asked if I was the one with the saddle. She looked at it and asked me a bunch of questions about it and looked at the magazine and everything. Then she said that it didn't look like much, but she'd talk it over with her husband.

"I could tell just looking at her face that she wanted that saddle real bad, though, so when she went to talk to Dayton, I knew she was going to convince him to make the deal."

I couldn't take it anymore. "Dammit, Bud, I don't care about the saddle. Did she have the tattoo or not?"

"Oh yeah. Right. Well, she was wearing this sleeveless blouse, so I could see her arms all the way up to her shoulders, and she didn't have no tattoos anywhere."

"Shit. Why couldn't you have just told me that out front?"

"Well, because of the scar," Bud said.

"Scar? What scar?"

"It was right there on the top of her arm, halfway between her wrist and elbow. Her arm was all tan except for that big pink scar, as big as a silver dollar."

"You think she might have had a tattoo removed?"

"I don't know. I've never seen a tattoo scar. Anyway, I asked her if she did that recently, all conversational, like. And she said no, it happened when she was a kid and got up against a woodstove. I said that must've hurt, and she said she didn't remember, because it happened when she was real young."

"So it actually could've been from removing a tattoo," I speculated.

"I guess so. I just can't say. I hope it's okay with Martha that I went ahead with the deal. For what it's worth, that lady *really* wanted that saddle."

This seemed like the way this whole case was going. We could get within reach of real proof but never quite get it. The van, the phone records, the transmission replacement, and now the tattoo. What, I asked myself, was it going to take to pin this down?

Bud spoke up just then. "Didn't you say the tattoo was on her left arm? The scar is on her *right* arm."

"Her *right* arm? Are you sure of that?"

"Of course, I'm sure."

So there it was. Michelle wasn't the lady with the tattoo. Not unless Carolyn Gervais was mistaken about which arm the tattoo was on. She could have been, I told myself. If so and if we could prove that Michelle had had a tattoo removed, we might still have a case.

When I called Carolyn, she was adamant that the tattoo had been on the abductor's left arm, not her right. She even described the plain gold wedding band the woman wore on her left hand. And there I was. No suspect.

When Kevin Fox called to say that a judge was ready to sign the order for Grace's phone records, I told him not to bother.

"It's a good idea, Corrigan. Why do you want to just drop it?" Fox asked with some exasperation.

"I got her phone bills. I've already checked it out."

"How the hell did you get her phone bills?"

"My partner knows someone who knows someone," I said evasively.

"So did you find anything?"

"Nothing that proved our suspects were in Pittsburgh when Megan was taken."

Fox knew the drill. "But?"

"But nothing that proved they *weren't there* either. At least not for sure. We did find that Grace accepted a couple of collect calls from a pay phone in Ogden, Utah, two days after the abduction."

"You think it was them on their way back to Pittsburgh?"

"I checked where the pay phone was. It was in a restaurant—right across from a transmission shop. So I figured their van broke down, and they had to call Michelle's mom to borrow money for the repair."

"That's possible."

"Yeah. The AAMCO shop was able to find a cash invoice for a transmission of the type that would have been in a 1980 Ford van, but it didn't have a name or anything else we could connect to Dayton."

"If Michelle's mom wired money to her, we ought to be able to find a record of that."

I sighed. "Yeah, I guess it's still worth a shot. Will that judge sign the order for that?"

"I'll give him a call."

For the next few days, Martha and I did everything we could think of to keep my case against the Daytons alive. But piece by piece, the case that had seemed so promising fell apart. There was nothing to do but go back and review everything we had—again. Maybe we'd find something we'd overlooked.

Chapter 70

I found myself once again looking at the original witness reports in the feeble hope that I might see something I'd missed in all my previous readings. Word by word, I plodded through the witness statements in search of any connotation or alternate interpretation that could shed a different light on the abduction. And that led me back to omega.

It wasn't just the tattoo. Carolyn Gervais had also described a logo that included the omega symbol on the front door of the old Ford van that the abductors drove. That warranted some more thought. Maybe there was something else in that logo that would help me track down the elusive van. I recalled that Carolyn had said that the lettering spelled out something.

When I went back to reading the detectives' comments regarding the witness statements, I found a notation stating that a sketch artist would be working with Carolyn Gervais to create a replica of the van logo, but I couldn't find any indication that it had actually been done, so I got Carolyn on the phone and asked her if the session with the sketch artist had actually taken place.

"Well, yes. I spent a couple of hours with her. She made about half a dozen different drawings before she got something that looked about right."

"The drawing isn't in the investigation file. Maybe it was lost, or maybe detectives decided that it wasn't any good," I told her.

"Yeah, I don't know why they never used it. It's a pretty good picture," Carolyn said.

"And yet it isn't included in the files," I mused.

"I have a copy of it," she offered. "You'll probably think I'm silly, but I kept a scrapbook of everything about that case. It's the only big news I was ever part of, you know?"

"Could you get me a photo of that drawing?"

"Certainly. I'll have to go to Kinko's, but it's not far away."

Half an hour later, I heard the e-mail alert tone from my computer. I checked and found a message from Carolyn with a photo attachment. I opened the photo and found myself looking at the police sketch of the logo with two lines of type beneath the omega symbol.

**Friendship
Faith Services**

This was the first time I'd seen anything suggesting the name of the church associated with the Omega cult. With an actual name, we stood a much better chance of tracking down the location in Madras where they'd set up shop after splitting from the Sannyasins.

"Martha, here's something for your to-do list. We need to search old business registration records for an organization with a name something like 'Friendship Faith Services.' They used the omega symbol in their logo, and there's a high likelihood that *omega* would've been part of the business name."

"Who's going to have that information?" she asked.

"I'd check the Oregon Corporation Division in the Secretary of State's office. That's where all business names are registered. What's going to make this challenging is that the business is almost certainly no longer active. I think it is likely that the business registration would be of about the time the Rajneeshees split up—1984 or '85. I want to see the names of the people who registered that name.

"Do you think the people in the Corporation Division will actually help me with that kind of a search?"

"If they won't help you, we'll ask Kevin Fox to make the request."

"Okay. I'll get on it."

I went back to staring at the logo. Something about it seemed very odd. Looking back at the interview transcripts, I found no mention whatsoever about "Friendship Faith Services." In her statement, Carolyn had said simply that the name had contained three words, the first of which she believed was something like *Frenchman*. So I was curious how the wording had come to read "Friendship Faith Services." I got Carolyn back on the phone.

"Oh yeah," she said. "That was something we kind of figured out while I was working with the artist. I never actually said that those were the exact words, but they were something like that. I'm sure that the first word started with *F*, and I'm fairly sure that the words below that started with *F* and *S*."

"How did you arrive at those words then?"

"Well, it all had to do with the omega symbol. We talked about what that might mean, and she mentioned that she once saw an omega symbol in some sort of Easter display at her church. So we picked out words that kind of went with that theme."

"You don't sound convinced," I observed.

"No, not really. When I first talked to the police, I told them my impression was that the first word was *Frenchman*. It didn't get changed to *Friendship* until the artist took over. But I never did really think that it was the right word."

That seemed pretty shaky. It was now clear that I'd been putting way too much stock in the artist's rendering without knowing the history behind it. I had another question.

"What about the typeface? Is that what you saw?"

"We worked pretty hard on that, actually. She showed me a whole book full of typefaces, and that's the one that looked like what I saw."

"It's kind of an Old West style," I commented.

"Well, yes. That's what I remember."

Something about that just didn't seem right. I'd been associating the omega symbol with the new age spiritual meditation movement of the eighties. That simply didn't mix with the cowboy theme that the typeface suggested.

Overhearing the conversation, Martha came and looked over my shoulder at the image of the logo. She had the answer almost instantly.

"It's not an *omega*. It's a *horseshoe*. And it's probably a farrier service."

"Farrier service?"

"Yeah. Someone who shoes horses. That's why it has a horseshoe. You wouldn't use a horseshoe for a church, but you would for a farrier service."

I looked again and realized that she was right. So I opened the image in Photoshop and within five minutes had a new logo.

Frenchman's Farrier Service

I fired off an e-mail to Carolyn and got her answer back within five minutes. She agreed that this might be what she saw. Certainly, it was as good as what the sketch artist had produced. She went so far as to confess that she might have been subconsciously led to see the omega symbol because of having seen the tattoo moments before—and she was absolutely certain that the tattoo had been an omega symbol.

I told Martha, "This changes your inquiry at the Corporation Division. You can forget Omega and concentrate on farrier services. You ought to be able to find something."

Martha said, "I'm not so sure we'll find what we're looking for. Farriers are typically one-man operations, and they don't bother registering their business names. They're just guys who do business with their friends in the area."

"We still have to give it a try. We might get lucky."

Unfortunately, this new insight meant that we'd lost the connection between the Omega cult and the van. We were back where we'd started in trying to find the group, its organizers, and the building they'd rented in Madras. All we could do now was hope to trace the van's ownership through farrier businesses. And as Martha had correctly observed, there was a high probability that the business was never registered with the state.

I did a quick Google search for *Frenchman* and immediately came up with Frenchman Mine, Frenchman Camp Trail, Frenchman Falls, Frenchman Springs, and Frenchman Bar. This implied that there might indeed be a lot of businesses with *Frenchman* in their names, but I had no way to sort out businesses from locations.

In a Google search for farriers, I found a website for the American Farrier's Association, which had a "Find a Farrier" search engine. I could enter any state and city, and it would give me the names of AFA farriers nearby. I wasn't optimistic about finding the one I was looking for, because I didn't need the name of someone shoeing horses today—I needed the name of someone who was doing it eighteen years ago.

Still, I had to give it a try. The first step was to enter the name of a city—but *what* city? After a few moments of thought, I decided to go back to my map of sighting reports. Starting with the largest clusters of sightings, I entered the city name and got the names of farriers in the area. I started putting the names on a list without any clear idea what I would do with it.

City by city, I worked my way through the sighting clusters until I got to the smallest clusters—the threes and, finally, the twos. Thus far, I hadn't spent any time at all on the clusters of two. In fact, I wasn't even sure it was fair to call two sightings "a cluster." But I maintained my discipline and forged on.

There were two dots on the map south of Burns, Oregon—maybe about seventy-five miles. While staring at the map, something caught my eye. The town nearest the two dots was a tiny place named Frenchglen.

"I'll be goddamned!" I whispered.

Martha asked, "Did you find something?"

"I found where they came from!"

She hurried over and stared at my map. I put my finger on Frenchglen.

"That's it," she said excitedly. "It *has* to be!"

The Corporation Division was unable to provide any information on the Frenchglen Farrier Service. The business name, not surprisingly, had never been registered with the state.

Chapter 71

Clayton McNary had been the detective in charge of the Megan Moro case from the day of the crime until his retirement from Salem PD late in 2002, so nearly everything in the file had crossed his desk. He, more than anyone else, should know the gritty details of the investigation—including the things that were never put on paper.

It took some effort, but I finally found him in an assisted living facility in Gresham. He seemed lucid when I called, and he agreed to talk with me about the case. I was escorted to McNary's room, where I found him sitting in a wheelchair watching *Judge Judy* on television.

"Why do these morons always think they can go one up on Judge Judy?" he asked.

I couldn't tell if he was talking to me or to the nurse who had ushered me in.

"Clayton, this is the man you spoke to on the phone—Mister Corrigan."

"Yes? What is it?" he demanded impatiently.

"I'm a private investigator. I'm working on the Megan Moro case," I reminded him.

I waited for him to give some kind of acknowledgement, but he remained focused on Judge Judy.

"Megan Moro was a five-year-old abducted in Salem back in '96."

"I know that! Who you working for?"

"Does that matter?"

"I guess not. The girl's dead. Nobody's going to find her."

That seemed like a rather negative way to start the conversation, so I ignored it and said, "I'd like to ask you about some details of the investigation that aren't covered in the files."

"If it isn't in the files, it didn't happen," he said, still staring at the TV.

"I'm not saying that these things aren't in the files. I'm just looking for a little more detail."

Mercifully, at that moment, *Judge Judy* yielded to a commercial break, so for the next four minutes, I'd have McNary's undivided attention.

"Yeah, sure. What's your question?"

"In 1998 and 2000, two different people in a very remote area south of Burns reported seeing a girl who looked like Megan. Do you remember those reports?"

"Of course, I do. I'm not here because my brain doesn't work. I'm here because my balance is all screwed up. Something to do with my ears."

"The files indicate that local authorities investigated the reports."

"That's right. It didn't make sense for us to send our own people all over creation to see what some nearsighted old ladies thought they saw."

"The file just said that the witnesses were found to be in error. Do have any details?"

"It was all done by phone—both times. I put the sheriff's office over there in touch with the witnesses, and they checked out the stories."

"So they never gave you a report?"

"Hell yes, they gave me a report! They did it by phone."

"What did they find when they talked to the witnesses?"

"Nothing! That's what I'm trying to tell you—there was nothing there. The girl those people saw was a kid who lived there and maybe looked something like the Moro kid. That was it."

"Do you remember the names of the officers who did those investigations?"

"Harney County Sheriff's Office. That's all I know. I asked 'em to check out the witness reports, and they did. Wasn't my business to run their show for 'em."

The commercial break ended, and *Judge Judy* came back on. It was just as well. I wasn't getting anything from McNary anyway. I thanked him for his time, but he'd already turned back to the TV. He raised a hand to acknowledge my thanks, and I departed, completely dissatisfied with what I'd learned.

Back in the office, I searched online for the Harney County Sheriff's Office. All I found was a single page on the county's website, containing what amounted to an election campaign statement by the recently appointed interim sheriff. I put in a call to the only phone number on the Web page, which connected me to a courthouse receptionist.

"I'd like to talk with someone in the sheriff's office," I told her. "Preferably someone who was there fifteen years ago."

"Oh. I don't have that kind of information here. But I can transfer your call to the sheriff's dispatcher."

The dispatcher's line was busy, so I left a voice message and silently thanked my lucky stars that I wasn't calling to report an assault in progress. Twenty minutes later, my phone rang.

"My name is Corrigan. I'm investigating a case involving the kidnapping of a girl in Salem in 1996. My notes indicate that two witnesses in your area reported having seen a child who looked like the missing girl."

"1996, did you say? That was a long time ago."

I was aware of that, but I suppressed the urge to say so. "Is there anyone there who has firsthand knowledge of the case?"

"I can't think who that might be. Everyone from that far back is probably retired by now."

"Can you put me in touch with a retired officer who might be familiar with the case?"

"I'm not authorized to give out information like that."

So I went back to Google and resumed my search for Harney County's sheriff. Working my way down the list, I eventually came to the name of the recently retired sheriff. With that, I was able to find a phone number. He sounded grumpy when I called.

"Are you a reporter or what?"

"I'm a private investigator. I'm looking into the—"

"Who gave you this number?" he demanded. "Who the hell are you?"

"My name is Corrigan. I'm investigat—"

"Oh. You're the one who found those girls."

"That's right." And I quickly added, "But there may be more."

I heard a deep and dramatic sigh. "So what do you want?"

"During the first few years after the kidnapping, there were reports that people in your area had seen a girl who looked like the victim."

"That's right. What about it?"

"I'd like to know the details of the investigation into those reports."

"There was nothing to 'em. The kid was someone else."

"So you talked to the witnesses, then?"

"Deputy Lexington talked to 'em. He knew the people whose kid the witnesses saw. That's all there was to it."

When it was obvious that he wasn't going to help me, I thanked the former sheriff and ended the call. I did another directory search and found only one listing for Lexington in the Burns area.

"Is this Deputy Lexington?" I asked the man who answered the phone.

"Used to be. Retired now. What can I do for you?"

I repeated my familiar litany.

"Sure, I talked to those witnesses," he confirmed. "I reported it to Salem PD."

"Your report is missing from their files. Can you tell me what you found?"

"I was able to identify the girl those witnesses saw. In both cases, it was someone I was familiar with."

"Can you give me the details?" I prodded.

"I guess there's no harm in that. I don't remember the girl's name right off, but she was staying with Timothy and Patricia Ranier—kids I'd seen around town for maybe seven or eight years."

"And the girl was their child?"

"Well, not their actual child. She was Patricia's niece as I remember it. They took the girl in when her mother died or something like that."

"How did you determine that?" I pressed.

"Well, I *knew* those people, like I said."

"I know that, but how did you know who the child was?"

"Well, they *told* me who she was! They had no reason to lie about that."

"Can you tell me how to find them?"

"Oh hell. I don't have any idea where they are now. It's been a couple years since the last time I saw 'em. I'm not out and about as much as I used to be when I was on the job."

"So you don't have an address for them?"

"Naw. They were like a lot of folks out here. They live out in the country and come to town to get their mail and groceries."

"Did you ever notice if the woman—Patricia—had a tattoo?"

"Yep. She had some kind of religious symbol on her arm, only it wasn't a cross or anything like that. It was some kind of hieroglyph or something."

"Did the Raniers drive an old Ford van?"

"I don't know what they drove. I only talked to them about the girl."

"Did you actually *see* the girl?"

"Sure. She came to town with Tim and Pat when I talked to them. When I called them, they said they were coming into town anyway, so we just met at the office. The kid confirmed what Pat told me—that her mother was too sick to take care of her."

"So you had a phone number for them?" I asked.

"Oh yeah. It wasn't actually *their* number. They didn't have a phone. But they had left a number for the post office to call when they had mail to pick up. It was a neighbor or something. I left a message, and a while later, they called me back."

"Any idea what became of her—the girl?"

"Grew up, I suppose."

When I hung up the phone, I triumphantly declared, "We got 'em!"

Martha, who had been transcribing the audio track from a witness interview, took off her headphones and asked, "Were you talking to me?"

"We got 'em!" I repeated. "I know their names, and the woman has the tattoo."

August
Saturday 2

Chapter 72

I spent all of Friday trying to figure out where Timothy and Patricia Ranier lived. I contacted the school district, but they had no record that the couple had ever registered a child in public school. The lady at the post office in Burns recalled that she sometimes got mail for the Raniers but not for several years. She knew nothing about a phone number.

What was most important, however, was that we now knew that Megan had survived the abduction and was alive and apparently well several years later. That meant she had developed the survival skills necessary to endure years of captivity. In my mind, I replayed what I'd read in Jaycee Dugard's memoir. I could only hope that Megan hadn't suffered as she had.

But where was she? About all we had was the logo on the van, which had been created more through deduction than observation. Nevertheless, the Frenchman-Frenchglen deduction was good enough to lead us to the identity of the kidnappers, so it was a safe bet that the couple lived—or at least had lived—in that area.

I went to the big public library in Portland and found a 1998 telephone directory for Harney County. There was no listing for anybody named Ranier, but in the Yellow Pages, I found half a dozen listings for farriers. I copied the information and then went outside and dialed each of the numbers. Zero for six. All the numbers returned the same message: "The number you have reached is not in service."

On my way back home, I had another idea. So the first thing I did—after reclaiming my chair from DC, who stubbornly turned limp when I tried to coax him to move—was a search for guides and packers in the Frenchglen area. I found a phone number for Steens Mountain Packers.

"Steens Mountain Packers, this is Cindy. How can I help you?"

"Cindy," I said. "My name is Corrigan. I'm hoping you might be able to help me locate a farrier in your area."

"There are several. But we take care of our own horses, so I don't know much about any of them."

"Actually, I don't need to have any work done. I'm trying to find someone who may not even be doing farrier work anymore. But ten or twenty years ago, he was using the name Frenchglen Farrier Service. Does that ring a bell?"

"Not really. But my husband—John—has lived here all his life. He might know who you're looking for."

"Great. Can I talk to him?"

"Sure. But not today. He's out on the trail. Won't be back 'til tomorrow or maybe the next day."

I left my number with Cindy, but before I had even put down the phone, I knew what I had to do.

"Martha, would you mind feeding DC for the next few days? I'm going to Frenchglen."

"Sure thing, boss."

I was on the road first thing in the morning. The most direct route was via State Highway 22, east out of Salem. I stopped for a quick breakfast at Burger King—the same place where Megan was abducted almost exactly eighteen years before. In my mind, I could see the whole thing—the restroom where Jeffrey Moro had led Tiffany and Megan, the exit where Patricia Ranier had taken Megan out to the parking lot, the curb where Timothy Ranier was waiting in the old van, and the road they had taken upon leaving.

I followed the same route, timing my drive as I went. Later I would coordinate my times with the witness reports from the Minto rest area and the gas station in Sisters. This might help validate the reports and pin down the case against the abductors. I arrived in Burns in time for lunch at a local café, where I asked if anyone knew a couple by the name of Ranier. Nobody did.

Heading south from Burns, I reached the spot on the map identified as Frenchglen, which consists of a small cluster of nineteenth-century buildings, including the historic Frenchglen Hotel. As I pulled into the parking area, a flock of birds circled and landed on the lawn. They were very striking in appearance—pure black with bright yellow heads. I couldn't recall having ever seen birds like that.

I went inside and booked a second-story room, which was authentic to the degree that I had to share a bathroom with all the other guests on the floor. Dinner, the desk clerk told me, would be served promptly at six o'clock.

"What kind of birds are those out on the lawn—the black ones with yellow heads?" I asked.

"Oh, those are yellow-headed blackbirds," she said with a straight face.

I gave her a "ya got me" look and chuckled politely.

"No, really. That's what they are," she insisted.

She poked around under the counter and found an Audubon Society bird-identification book. Sure enough, under a glossy color picture of the bird was its proper name: yellow-headed blackbird.

After we shared a good laugh, I asked, "Can I get a beer here?"

"Not in the hotel, but you can get one next door, at the Mercantile Store."

But my first order of business was to talk with the people at Steens Mountain Packers. I'd intended to phone them, but on arrival in town, I found their headquarters a couple hundred yards from the hotel. So I walked over and knocked on the door. The blond lady who greeted me was, I think, a few years younger than me and quite attractive in a very outdoorsy way. Deeply tanned with her hair pulled back in a sun-bleached ponytail, she showed a raw toughness that said that nobody ever had to carry a saddle for her. She introduced herself as Cindy.

"I talked to you on the phone yesterday—about the Frenchglen Farrier Service."

"You're not going to tell me that you drove all the way out here to talk about horseshoes," she said.

"No. I'm actually conducting a criminal investigation involving missing children."

I may have squinted just a little bit in anticipation of the sudden recognition of me as the person she'd seen on TV. But she didn't comment. Maybe they didn't have television.

"Wow. I haven't heard about any missing children around here."

"It didn't happen here. I'm just looking for a witness who might have some useful information."

"You mean that farrier you asked about on the phone?"

"That's right."

"Well, John got back a little while ago. He's taking a shower right now. Are you staying over at the hotel?"

"That's right."

"How about I send him over when he's done?"

Walking back toward the hotel, I stopped at the Mercantile Store and picked a bottle of Black Butte Porter Ale from the cooler. Sitting in the shade on the porch, I watched a pair of old guys on big full-dress Honda motorcycles pull up to the lone gas pump in front of the store.

"Do we have to pay first?" one of the bikers asked.

I glanced around and realized that he was talking to me. "I don't know," I said apologetically, "I'm just having a beer."

"That sounds like a good idea," the other biker said.

A few minutes later, the three of us introduced ourselves to one another. They were from British Columbia, on their way to Las Vegas to pick up a new motorcycle, and were just passing through Frenchglen.

One of the bikers pointed at the flock of birds on the lawn across the street and commented, "Never seen birds like those. Wonder what they are."

"They're yellow-headed blackbirds," I said authoritatively.

That brought a hearty laugh from both of the Canadians. I was about to say that it really wasn't a joke when a black Chevy Suburban stopped in front of the store. Three middle-aged men got out, all wearing aviator sunglasses and business-casual attire, which looked strangely out of place in Frenchglen. I took note of the Idaho plates on the Suburban.

"You guys look like FBI agents," one of the Canadians blurted.

Two of the men spoke at once, one nodding and the other shaking his head.

"We're from the Minnesota office," one said, receiving a sharp look from the other, who gave a forced laugh.

I was not convinced that it was a joke. There had, for months, been news reports about some rural folks upset about government management of public rangeland in the area. It was entirely feasible that agents might be sent to investigate.

"Hey, I wonder what kind of bird those are," the third agent said, probably less out of curiosity than out of a desire to change the subject.

"You mean the black ones with yellow heads?" one of the bikers asked.

"They're yellow-headed blackbirds," I said.

That brought a fresh round of laughing, but another of the FBI men started tapping on his cell phone screen. After a few seconds, he held up his phone for everyone to see. It looked like the same photo I'd seen in the Audubon book.

"It *really is* a yellow-headed blackbird," he said.

He switched his phone to speaker and touched the screen, and we all heard the call of the yellow-headed blackbird. The birds heard it too and turned to look in our direction. He touched the screen again, repeating the call, and more birds flew in and joined those already congregated on the lawn.

It was starting to resemble an Alfred Hitchcock movie. The agents excused themselves and went inside, returning a few minutes later with sodas and lemonade. I recalled that federal agents aren't allowed to drink alcohol while on duty.

We all sat and sipped our beverages while the lead agent explained that they were just good friends visiting the area to do some hunting and fishing. I couldn't think of any game that was in season, so the hunting story didn't ring true. But there was no point in challenging his claim.

When their gas tanks were full and their beer cans empty, the bikers announced that they'd better get moving if they were going to get to Reno that evening. They started their engines, and the first biker pulled onto the roadway and turned south. Following right behind him, the second biker was dragging his feet to keep his balance until he got out of the gravel parking lot.

But the toe of his boot caught the edge of the pavement, and a fraction of a second later, the foot peg on the bike came up behind his heel. With the bike trying to go forward and with no time to pull the clutch, there was nothing he could do. The bike pivoted hard to the left, the rider's foot acting as a fulcrum, leaving him no choice but to lay it down on top of himself.

The rest of us jumped up as soon as we realized what was happening. Someone got to the ignition switch and shut down the engine, as the bike was still in gear, and the wheel was spinning dangerously close to the rider, whose foot was still painfully twisted and pinned.

It took three of us to lift the motorcycle off of him. Unable to put any weight on his twisted ankle, the biker leaned on one of the agents, who helped him back to the porch. The lead agent helped the biker get his boot off, and with some apparent knowledge of emergency medicine, he determined that no bones had been broken. But that didn't make it feel any better.

The store owner brought out a bag of ice, while the rest of us suggested that it might be a good idea to get a room at the hotel and spend the night. It was a losing argument. The injured man put his boot back on and laced it up tight "to prevent swelling." I didn't think that was such a great idea, but there was no talking him out of it.

By then, the first biker realized that his friend was missing and returned to the store. Together, they checked out the motorcycle and determined that there was only minimal damage—nothing that would stop them from forging on to Reno.

The FBI men got back into their Suburban and headed north, and the Canadians—once the injured biker determined that he could shift gears with his sprained foot—headed south. I went inside and got another beer. Alone once again, I sipped my beer and tried to focus my thoughts on the reason I was there—to find the people who had been seen with the little girl.

The obvious thing to do would be to start asking around until I found someone who could tell me where to find Timothy and Patricia Ranier. Normally, I'd prefer the direct approach, but in a small population, there was a good chance that I might be talking to someone who would feel more loyalty toward a neighbor than interest in helping a stranger.

It would be all too easy for word to get around, and that could set them on the run before I could get to them. So that led me back to the *indirect* approach—tracking down the van. That, I figured, would put me close to the kidnappers before having to reveal my intentions and risk sending my suspects into hiding.

The man who strode across the street to the Mercantile Store looked like he'd just walked out of an old Marlboro cigarette ad. He was tall and rugged, beneath a well-worn cowboy hat with the brim pulled low in the front and back. But for all of his visible toughness, he approached with an outstretched hand and an easy smile.

"I'm John. Cindy said you want to ask me about a local farrier."

"Cindy says you've lived around here a long time," I said.

"All my life."

"Then maybe you'll know who I'm looking for."

I handed him a print of the horseshoe logo. "There's an old van with this painted on the side."

John studied the drawing. "I remember a van like that, but that was a *long time* ago—maybe fifteen or twenty years."

"Do you know who owned it?" I asked, feeling an adrenaline rush.

"As I remember it, the old boy who owned it got kicked by a horse and was never quite right after that. He couldn't work. I don't think he could drive either."

I had to wonder—when he said "old boy," was that just an expression, or was he talking about an elderly man? According to the witnesses, the driver of the van was about thirty years old. He'd be close to fifty now, but by my definition, that didn't exactly make him an "old boy."

"You say 'old boy.' How old was he?"

"He's probably in his eighties now, I guess."

"So he's still alive?"

"Far as I know. The injury left him partly paralyzed on one side, but he gets by okay. Just can't shoe horses, that's all."

This man would have been sixty years old or more when Megan was taken—far too old to be the driver of the van.

"Did someone else take over his business after he got hurt?"

365

"I don't think so. Old Eddie was an independent operator. When he quit, he probably just sent his customers to a friend or something."

"What about the van?"

John shrugged. "Last time I saw it, it looked pretty sad. It's probably long gone by now."

"I think I'd like to talk with Eddie. Do you think that's possible?"

"I don't see why not. You'd have to go out to his place though. He doesn't get out much."

"Where's he live?"

"He has a place out off Krumbo Crick Road, about ten miles north of here."

John scribbled a rough map on a paper napkin. "It's an old farmhouse. Used to be white, but there isn't much paint left on it. There's an old wooden barn next to it—red with a caved-in tin roof. It'll be on your right, a mile or two off the highway."

August 3 Sunday

Chapter 73

After breakfast at the hotel, I drove out of town, back in the direction of Burns. When I got to Diamond Junction, I knew I'd gone too far, so I turned back toward Frenchglen. After about five miles, I spotted a small sign identifying the dry field off to my left as Krumbo Reservoir. Slowing down, I almost missed the narrow gravel road that runs along the southern edge of the dry reservoir. I followed that road until I spotted the old red barn with the caved-in metal roof.

I parked between the house and the barn. An old man appeared in the doorway and watched me get out of my Yukon.

"Hi there. Are you Eddie Florence?" I asked.

"Last time I checked," he said, leaning against the door frame.

"My name's Corrigan. Can we talk a bit?"

"I can probably spare a few seconds in my busy day. You want a cup of coffee?"

"You don't have to go to any trouble on my account," I said.

"Ain't any trouble. It's already made."

"Then I'll take a cup."

He waved me inside, and I followed as he limped to a small wooden table with two chairs in the corner of his kitchen. What he poured into my cup was as black as tar, but it smelled a little bit like coffee.

"Okay, Mr. Corrigan, what brings a city boy all the way out here to talk to a busted-up old bastard like me?"

"Please, it's just Corrigan. *Mr.* Corrigan is my dad. I understand you used to be a farrier."

He shrugged. "Used to be a lot of things."

I showed him the sketch of the logo from the van. His eyes registered recognition, and then he stared at me.

"That you?" I asked.

"What is this? Who *are* you?"

"I'm a private investigator. I'm just wondering if you owned a van with that painted on the door."

"I think you already know that I did. But why the hell do you care?"

It was obvious that I hadn't played this right. I hadn't wanted to tell him that the van was used in a kidnapping, because even though he was too old to have been the driver, it was still entirely possible that the driver was a friend of his or relative whom he'd feel compelled to protect. But I was stuck. I had to risk it.

"The van may have been involved in a crime."

"Well, I haven't seen it in years. I don't have any idea where it is now."

"When did you last see it?"

"Shit. I sold it after I got hurt. Are you telling me that old heap is still running?"

I ignored his question and asked, "When was that?"

"It was in '95. Damned mustang kicked me in the head. My own fault, I guess. They said the horse was tamed, but you can't tame a wild horse. Not really. After that I couldn't work, so I sold all my equipment—including that van—and holed up here to die. Only I didn't die. Hell of a thing, ain't it?

"Do you remember who bought the van?"

"It was just some damn kids—a young couple who didn't have a pot to piss in. They came around offering to do odd jobs. I couldn't afford to pay them, but I let 'em camp out in the barn and gave 'em the van for the work they did. It wasn't worth much. I mean, it ran okay, but it was butt ugly."

I showed him the 1996 police sketches of the couple who abducted Megan.

"Yep. That's them all right," he confirmed.

"How long did they work for you?"

"Oh, probably three or four weeks. The truth is I gave 'em the van mostly just to get rid of 'em. I got tired of all their flower-child crap, ya know what I mean? They wouldn't stop talking about how love made everything right, and the whole world would find peace if everyone would just share everything. It got pretty tiresome."

"Do you remember their names?"

He laughed. "Timothy and Patricia. Not Tim and Patty or Tim and Pat. It had to be Timothy and Patricia. And they were named after a mountain—Ranier. I always figured it was a phony name that they just adopted."

"Where'd they go after they left here?"

"They went squatting."

"How so?"

"They found a vacant house and moved into it. Story I heard is that the property is owned by one of them big California conglomerates that's bought up just about everything out here. They didn't give a shit about the old house, so they never tried to move the kids out."

"You think they're still there?"

"Hell, I don't know. Folks still talk about 'em sometimes, so I guess they must still be out there."

"Where's that?"

"All I know is it's southwest of here a piece. Pretty far out. Out in Catlow Valley, I think. But I can't say exactly where."

"Is there someone who can?"

"I suppose your best bet would be the mailman, who's actually a woman. Malina's her name. Only she ain't the mailman anymore, since they shut down the post office."

"How can I find Malina?"

"She owns the Mercantile Store in Frenchglen. That's the most likely place to find her."

Half an hour later, I parked at the gas pump in front of the Mercantile Store and went inside. The lady behind the counter was older than the one who had served me the day before, and she matched Eddie's description of Malina.

"You need some gas?" she asked.

I nodded and asked, "Are you Malina?"

"That's what my mama told me," she said.

"They say that you used to run the post office here," I said.

"That's right," she said. "But they shut down the Frenchglen post office a while back and moved the whole operation over to New Princeton."

"I'm trying to find some folks who live around here—name of Ranier. I thought maybe you might've delivered mail to them."

"They're squatters, you know," she said flatly.

I shrugged. "So I hear."

"I never delivered any mail to them. They had their mail sent to the post office in Burns—always seemed kind of silly to me. Why'd they want to drive all the way to Burns when they could've had it delivered?"

"Eddie Florence told me that you might know where they live."

"Oh sure. They're a ways out there though," she said.

And then she launched into a long and detailed explanation of how I could find the place. I lost track about three turns into her directions, so I asked her if she could draw a map.

As I pulled out of her driveway to make the hundred-yard trip to the hotel, I spotted a red Mustang convertible parked in the shade next to the hotel. For a fraction of a second, I felt a flash of relief and excitement, before the rational part of my brain reminded me that Kim's was not the only car like that on earth. It was just such a strange thing to encounter one in such an unlikely locale.

As I walked into the hotel, the manager said, "I told your wife to go on up to your room. I hope that's okay."

My heart stopped. "My wife?"

"She said she was—"

I didn't hear the rest as I turned and hurried up the stairs, not trusting myself to believe what was happening. I pushed the door open and felt tears fill my eyes.

"Kim—"

"I'm so sorry, Corrigan—"

There were no more words for a long time, while we simply held onto each other. The familiar scent of her hair and the warmth of her body left me overwhelmed, and even now I am still unable to think of the moment without feeling the tightness in my throat and the wetness in my eyes that I felt then. It is thus impossible for me to put into words what I felt.

"Martha told me where to find you," Kim finally whispered.

She pressed her face against my shoulder. I felt her tears soak through my shirt.

"I thought I'd put it behind me, but when you showed me Brittany's name, it all came back, and I just couldn't—"

"You don't need to explain anything. I know what happened."

"Is it true, what Martha said— that Megan might be alive?"

The uncertainty in her voice was heartbreaking, and I knew it would be devastating if she were to get her hopes up only to be let down again. But I could see that it was already too late. The pleading look in her eyes told me how desperately she was clinging to that hope.

"I just don't know—"

"But Martha said—"

"Kim, all we know for sure is that Megan was seen around here fifteen years ago. That's a long way from proving that she's still alive," I said as gently as I could.

"I know," she whispered. And then she asked, "What's next?"

I couldn't tell if she was asking about the investigation or our relationship. I had the answer to one but not the other. I unfolded Malina's map on the table.

"Here's where they live."

Kim stared at the paper. "If Megan's there—"

"I was just about to go find the place," I said.

"Then let's go!"

We made a quick stop back at the Mercantile to pick up some snacks and bottled water, and then we followed the highway west out of town, up a steep grade to a vast sagebrush prairie. About eight miles out of town, I came to a gravel road marked Rock Creek Road.

We followed the wash-boarded gravel road out onto the open rangeland punctuated only by an occasional juniper tree. Malina's map was all out of scale, and some of the landmarks she'd noted were ambiguous. Several times we had to backtrack when we took wrong turns.

My GPS navigator wasn't much help, because the county roads were identified only by numbers. Most of the crossroads we passed were not marked, so I relied heavily on blind luck, making a right turn after the clump of dead juniper trees and then bearing left where the road split. After a couple of miles, I started looking for a two-story house with blue tarps on the roof.

There, the road I turned onto was a rutted single-track path heading north. A crude sign pointed toward the Miller Place. The road became narrower and rougher. Just about the time I was starting to wonder if I was on the wrong road, we finally found the old homestead where Timothy and Patricia Ranier had been squatting. There was a barn with a rusty corrugated metal roof next to an old house. There was no glass in the windows, and the porch had collapsed. A decrepit double-wide sat on a level patch of land between the road and the barn.

"I don't see a car," Kim said.

"Let's go take a look."

I drove up to the gate that blocked the driveway and parked there. The gate was secured by a loop of barbed wire, but there was no lock. A yellow-and-black metal sign on the gate read "Posted—No Hunting."

Walking toward the double-wide, we noticed fresh tire tracks on the dirt driveway. I called out, but nobody answered. Nor was there any answer when I knocked on the door. Peering through the windows, we could see a vase containing a bouquet of partially wilted daisies on the kitchen counter, a clear sign of recent occupancy.

We walked around looking for anything that might hint that Megan had been there. Parked under a shed roof attached to the side of the old bar, I found a rusting Ford van, most of its original silver paint gone. Kim touched the badly faded horseshoe logo on the passenger side door, and then she paused.

"This is the van that took Megan away, isn't it? I remember someone talking about this."

"Yeah. It's what finally led me here."

"Do you think they might've heard you were looking for them and cleared out?"

"Three days ago, I talked with a former deputy up in Burns—he was the one who vouched for the kidnappers when two different witnesses reported that they had a child who looked like Megan. He didn't ever say that he was *friends* with them, but he did say that he knew them. He may have tipped them off."

"Hold it! Are you saying that people actually *saw* Megan out here?"

"That's right. The reports went to Salem PD, but they relied on Harney County to check them out."

"*Good god!* And they actually *knew* where Megan was?" Kim demanded. "When did all this *happen?*"

"The first report was in 1998. The second was in 2000."

Kim burst into tears. "Are you telling me that she could have been home *sixteen years* ago?"

"*Should* have been," I corrected.

"No, no, *no*," she cried. "And now they're gone again!"

I checked my phone, intending to call Kevin Fox, but there was no service. "Let's get back to town," I said.

We hurried back to my Yukon. I made a K-turn and spun the tires accelerating out onto the road. We'd driven maybe five miles when I started to notice that the big vehicle was becoming difficult to handle. I slowed, thinking it must be my reckless speed that was making it hard to control, but I immediately realized that it was something else.

I pulled into the first wide spot along the road and climbed out to find the left rear tire almost flat. After expressing my frustration in colorful terms, I pulled the jack and spare tire out of the back. Fifteen minutes later, I thought we were ready to go, but as I was getting in, I heard a hissing sound.

The left front was going down. Maybe I'd run over a board with nails sticking out when I turned around to get out of the driveway. It didn't matter. I checked my phone—still no service. The sun had already gone down, and it would be dark in another hour.

"What now?" Kim asked.

"There's no telling how far we'll have to walk before we find a phone. Looks like we'll have to spend the night here and figure something out in the morning."

We climbed into the backseat and did what we could to make ourselves comfortable. During the next couple of hours, we talked. I told her everything I'd done in my investigation after she left. Kim told me a little bit about her travels with Vera.

"We went to Auburn to see Tiffany. You know where Auburn is? East of Sacramento, up toward Donner Pass? Anyway, we stayed there for a week, and I talked with Tiffany. Really, it was the first time since—since it happened—that we talked about it.

"All this time, Tiffany thought that I blamed her for letting Megan get taken. It broke my heart to hear her say that. I *never* blamed her—*never*—not even when I was blaming Jeffrey. We talked and talked. She's married now, you know."

"Yeah, you told me that a while back."

"And she's pregnant. She's going to have a baby—due in January."

We were almost asleep when headlights appeared from behind a rise in the road. I got out and flagged down a dirty pickup truck, which skidded to a stop in a cloud of dust. The driver was a young guy wearing a cowboy hat.

"Looks like you got some trouble there," he said, gesturing at the front tire, which by then was completely flat.

"Yeah."

"You need help changing it?" he asked.

"I already used my spare. I had *two* flats," I explained. "I was hoping maybe you could get us to a telephone."

"Wouldn't do no good. Ain't anybody gonna come all the way out here this time of day."

He climbed out of his pickup and bent over to study the flat tire in the light from his headlights. He seemed to wobble a little bit, and I smelled alcohol.

"Name's Greg," he said, extending his hand.

"I'm Corrigan."

"Corrigan. What kind of name's that?"

"Irish."

"How's the spare look?" he asked. "Any major damage?"

"Not that I could see."

"Let's take a look at it."

I pulled it out and rolled it over in front of his headlights. He turned it slowly, carefully studying it before giving it a slap and standing up.

"Throw it in the back. I can fix it and get you back on the road in half an hour," he declared.

"How're you going to do that?" I asked.

"This is cattle country. You live out here, you have to be ready to fix *anything*. A simple flat tire is no problem. No problem at all."

I looked to Kim for her opinion on the matter, and she simply patted her purse. Of course. She was carrying her Sig. And I had my .45 Colt under my shirt behind my back. We understood each other.

"I'll pay you for the job," I said while rolling the tire toward the back of his pickup.

"I'm not gonna take your money. Come on, let's get going."

So we climbed in, Kim in the middle. While she and I were fishing around for our seat belts, Greg stepped on the gas, and within seconds, we were up on plane, the tires just skimming over the tops of the washboards. We gave up on the seat belts and braced ourselves as we rounded a bend at an impossibly high speed. When the rear tires broke loose and started to kick out, Greg stomped on the gas and accelerated into a barely controlled drift.

Spraying rock in every direction, we careened sideways around the curve. The road straightened out and went up an abrupt rise. We went airborne as the road dropped away beneath us. We landed hard but straight. In the dark, I couldn't see what lay off the edges of the road, but on the drive out there, I'd seen plenty of places where the road was flanked by things you wouldn't want to hit—abrupt ditches or unyielding embankments.

An empty whiskey bottle rattled back and forth under our feet with every turn. I don't know how far we went. It might have been only five miles, but it seemed like fifty. When Greg finally let off the gas and turned up a single-track driveway, the headlights swept across the front of a well-kept ranch house, and Greg skidded to a stop. I got out and helped Kim down, while our driver sat slumped over the wheel.

I walked around and opened his door. He raised his head and looked at me with unfocused eyes. He slid down from the seat and stood for a few seconds, leaning against the pickup. When he took a step, he wobbled and caught himself.

"Ol' Jack Daniel's is sneakin' up on me," he said. "I need to sit down for a minute."

I helped him stagger over to his porch, where he collapsed into a rocking chair. I looked at Kim, and she just rolled her eyes.

"I'll be okay in a minute," he slurred.

"Maybe we should get you inside," Kim suggested.

His chin dropped to his chest. "Prob'ly right."

I tried the door and found it unlocked. Feeling around, I found a switch and turned on the lights. I quickly reconnoitered the house. Everything was neat and clean, but it was obvious that Greg lived alone. I went back out and helped him to his feet and steered him to the only bedroom that contained a bed. He flopped onto the bed and mumbled something.

That was all the help I was going to give him. I closed the door as I backed out of the bedroom. I found Kim thumbing through the thin Harney County phone directory. I handed her my AAA card. Kim picked up the phone and started to dial, but she stopped after the first few numbers.

"Wait. What do I tell them? I don't know where the hell we are."

I poked around, looking for something with an address on it. I found an envelope in a waste basket. It was addressed to Greg Holley, Rural Route 1, Frenchglen OR. That wouldn't help the AAA dispatcher. Kim made the call anyway, and the dispatcher searched for the towing company nearest to Frenchglen, hoping that someone there might know Greg Holley.

But the nearest towing service was in Burns over a hundred miles away. The dispatcher said he'd ask them to call. Fifteen minutes later, the phone rang. I tried to explain to the tow truck driver where we were using Malina's map, but the sleepy man on the other end of the line was unable to correlate anything I said with the county map.

"I can read you the GPS coordinates off my cell phone if that'd help," I said.

He laughed. "Yeah. Then I can call for a UFO to find you."

Kim said, "I guess we're spending the night here."

"You take the couch. I'll take the chair."

Chapter 74

I woke up with a kink in my neck and a bad attitude. As quietly as possible, I went outside to take a look around. There was a barn, and next to it was a cattle chute. A couple of horses grazed in a small irrigated pasture. There was a metal-sided pole building with a concrete slab out front where an old Jeep was parked. I pushed one of the rolling doors open and looked inside.

Greg's shop wasn't nearly as neat and tidy as his house, but it was cleaner than most of the backcountry shops I'd seen. Maybe he actually *would* be able to fix the tire. I went back to the house and found Kim poking around in the kitchen cupboards. She already had coffee started in an old-fashioned electric percolator.

"I hope he doesn't mind," she said. "But those snacks we had yesterday are all I've had to eat since Saturday afternoon."

We didn't find any bread, but there was biscuit mix. With a tray of biscuits in the oven and the smell of fresh coffee filling the house, it wasn't long before our host came out of his room, rubbing his eyes and yawning.

"Good morning, Greg," Kim said happily.

He cocked his head and looked from her to me. "Do I know you?" he finally asked.

"We met last night," I reminded him. "Flat tire—you said you could fix it."

"Oh. Well, I'll take a cup of that coffee, and then I'm gonna take a shower."

He disappeared down the hallway, and a couple of minutes later, we heard the water running. Kim put a cast-iron skillet on the stove and filled it with strips of thick-cut pepper bacon. When the biscuits and bacon were just about done, she started cracking eggs onto the griddle.

"Damn, that smells good," Greg said when he reemerged, dressed in clean clothes, his hair still wet. "I'm sorry. I don't remember your names."

"This is Kim," I said. "And I'm Corrigan."

"Oh yeah—Irish, right?"

Over breakfast, he asked, "Where were you folks heading before your tire went flat?"

"We were heading back to town. The people we came out here to see weren't home," I explained.

"Who was that?"

"Folks named Ranier—down the road a ways. Timothy and Patricia."

"Those squatters? I didn't know they had any friends."

"They're not friends. We've never met them. What do you know about them?"

"Couple of burned-out hippies. I don't know where they came from, but they set up housekeeping on the old Grover ranch—just moved in. They've been there about twenty years now. About once a month, they go up to Burns to get their food stamps and welfare check. They don't even try to earn their own way. You'd think they'd at least weave baskets to sell at craft fairs or something."

"Did you ever see a little girl with them?" Kim asked.

"She ain't so little now. I never understood how those losers ever deserved to have such a cute kid."

"Deserved!" Kim exploded. "I'll tell you what they deserve—"

I interrupted, "The girl is the reason we came out here."

Greg was still wide-eyed over Kim's unexpected outburst.

"You said she's grown up. Is she still living there?" I asked.

"Nope. She ran off a couple of years ago."

"But . . . but where did she go?" Kim begged.

"I heard that she took up with Jake Farmer's kid. Don't know any details."

"Who's Jake Farmer? Where can we find him?" Kim asked urgently.

"If you're heading back to town, you'll go right past his place."

With a renewed sense of urgency, we finished breakfast. Greg led the way out to his shop, where he used a pair of old tire irons to dismount my tire. The puncture was easily repaired in the old-fashioned way—with contact cement and a self-adhesive patch. Once the tire was remounted and inflated, Greg drove us back to my Yukon.

He again refused to take any payment for his trouble, insisting that he still owed more favors to the world than he'd ever be able to pay back. Before parting, he told us how to find Jake Farmer's place, which was less than three miles away.

It was late morning when we found the Farmer ranch. The lady who came out to meet us introduced herself as Sharon. She said that Jake was out checking fence lines.

"Greg—" I suddenly realized I'd forgotten his last name. "—up the road old us that you might know something about a girl who grew up with Timothy and Patricia Ranier."

She gave me an odd look. "You mean Carol? She's our daughter-in-law."

Kim cried out, "Carol? No! Her name is Megan! She's—"

I put my hand on her shoulder. "Maybe you should tell us the whole story," I suggested to Sharon.

"What business is it of yours?"

Kim said, "Megan is my daughter! Those people kidnapped her when she was only six years old."

Sharon stared wide-eyed at Kim, and then she turned to me.

"It's true," I said. "I'm a private investigator. I've been working on this case for the last four months, and there is no question about it."

"You'd better come inside then."

She made a fresh pot of coffee, and when we were all seated in her living room, she told us what she knew.

"Jake and I have lived here for thirty-two years. This ranch has been in Jake's family since 1911. So I guess you could say we're old-timers around here. We watched when Timothy and Patricia showed up driving Eddie Florence's old van. At first we thought they must've stolen it from him, but Eddie told us that he gave it to them. They parked in a little turnout next to Rock Crick and camped there for a few weeks. Then they moved into the old Grover place. Grover had sold out to the consortium maybe five or ten years before. Those people never cared a whit about the old house—it was just an old double-wide—and probably didn't know that Patricia and Timothy had moved in.

"Anyway, they were a strange couple. They never did fit in around here—never talked to anyone, never seemed to *do* anything. They finally managed to get a garden to grow, but that's the only work they ever did. They'd been there a year or two when Carol showed up."

"Megan," Kim corrected.

"Okay. I'm sorry. I've always known her as Carol. Word got around that she was Patricia's niece. Nobody ever questioned that. They seemed to be real strict with her. Never let her go anywhere by herself. They had this peculiar religious belief—actually, it wasn't really even a religion. It was just some spiritual hocus-pocus. But they wouldn't send Ca—I mean Megan—to school. They schooled her themselves at home.

"They made their own clothes, and that poor girl never had a decent thing to wear. Sometimes when we'd drive by, we'd see her out by the road, but she'd turn away if we tried to talk to her. She was real pretty, though, and I always felt sorry for her—the way they always made her do the work that they should've been doing, tending the garden and what not, even when she was little.

"Few years ago, our son—Steven—was out looking for a few of our cattle that wandered off when he ran across Megan. He said that she acted afraid and wouldn't talk to him at first, but after a while, she said her name was Carol. They struck up a friendship. They were still kids—Steven was seventeen, and she was a couple of years younger.

"They met in the same spot several times and got to know each other a little bit. Then one day Steven asked me if Megan could come and live with us. He said that she wanted to get away from Patricia and Timothy. I said, well, if they're her guardians, she might have no choice but to stay there, but Steven was insistent. I guess the kids had talked it over a lot before getting bold enough to ask.

"So one day, Steven rode up with Megan on the horse with him, and we let her stay. I went down to talk with Patricia, but she wouldn't have anything to do with me. They never asked to have Megan back, so she stayed with us. She was such a sweet girl! In many ways, she was incredibly naive and in other ways so mature. We treated her like a member of the family.

"Then last year, in June, Steven announced that he was going to marry Megan and go live in Idaho. I was dumbfounded. He said that Megan would never be comfortable as long as Patricia and Timothy were nearby, and so she had to leave. Steven wouldn't let her go alone, so they answered an ad for jobs over at Sun Valley.

"Of course, Jake and I tried to talk them out of it but—well, you know how kids are. They just up and left. But they seem to be doing okay. They have a little trailer in Ketchum, and their jobs seem to be working out. Above all, they seem to be happy—especially Megan. She's just blossomed."

Sharon looked at Kim. "And you know what? She sure looks a lot like you."

Kim said, "We need to go there. Today. Right now!"

"Should we phone her first?" Sharon asked.

After a brief discussion, we all agreed that it would be better to make the reunion in person rather than by phone.

We hurried back to Frenchglen, where the hotel manager expressed his concern when we didn't show up for dinner the previous evening. I explained about the flat tires and asked where I could get the other one repaired.

"There's a Les Schwab tire store in Burns. That's where I'd go," he told me.

Kim and I hastily packed up and checked out. She followed me up to Burns, where we found the tire shop. It was closed by then, so I parked out front and dropped the keys and a note in the mail slot by the door. It didn't make sense to risk another flat tire without a spare. And it didn't make sense to take both cars to Idaho.

While we waited for our dinner at a nearby restaurant, I called Kevin Fox.

"Their names are Timothy and Patricia Ranier, and they live outside Frenchglen. The van used in the abduction is parked on the property where they live. Three different witnesses have identified them from the police sketches, and they say that she has the omega tattoo."

"I'll need some documentation on all of this before I can get an arrest warrant," Fox said.

"My partner will get everything she has to you in the morning. I'll get you a list of the witnesses around Frenchglen later tonight. Expedite that warrant. Word will get around fast in a small town, and they might take off."

"What about the girl?"

"We're on our way to find her. She's in Ketchum, Idaho. Married and doing okay, we're told."

"You said 'we.' Who's with you?"

"It's Kim. She caught up with me yesterday."

"Okay. I'll be waiting for the stuff from your partner."

Next I called Martha, gave her an update, and asked her to send Fox everything we had first thing in the morning."

"No way, boss. I'm going over to the office right now. I'll get it out tonight."

"Thanks, Martha."

Our dinners arrived, and we hastily put them away, partially out of ravenous hunger, mostly out of the urgent desire to get moving. Still, there was one phone call Kim had to make before hitting the road.

"Hi, Tiffany. This is Mom. We found her. We know where Megan is."

"No. We're on our way to see her. She's in Idaho."

"She doesn't know yet. We'll see her in the morning."

Kim answered a string of additional questions from Tiffany and then concluded, "Tiff, we have to get going. Call your father. See if the two of you can meet us in Ketchum."

I drove Kim's Mustang east out of Burns as the sun went down behind us. I figured we'd get to Ketchum sometime around midnight. Kim phoned ahead to find us a motel room.

August
Tuesday 5

Chapter 75

Kim managed to get us the last available room at the Kentwood Lodge in Ketchum, and we arrived there a little after midnight, exhausted from our long day and the previous night's restless sleep. Still, we were so keyed up that we both had difficulty getting to sleep.

We got up early, hoping to find Megan before she went off to work. Following the instructions that Sharon had given us, we headed northwest until we found Warm Springs Road. Right after we crossed the Wood River Bridge, we spotted a small row of travel trailers.

The second trailer in the row matched the description given by Sharon. The Ford Ranger parked next to it said that Steven and Megan hadn't yet gone to work. As we approached the door, Kim held back and motioned for me to take the lead.

"My god," she said. "I don't know what to say to her."

I gave her hand a reassuring squeeze and rang the bell. It was Megan who came to the door, looking perplexed about the unexpected appearance of two strangers on her doorstep so early in the day. She wasn't as tall as Kim—maybe five three or five four—but there was no question that she was Kim's daughter.

Her eyes shifted from me to Kim and back to me. But then they were drawn again to Kim, where they lingered. "Can I help you?" she asked tentatively.

Kim said, "Megan?"

The girl in the doorway stared at Kim for maybe five seconds. I watched her expression cycle from curiosity to confusion to recognition. Her eyes widened, and her mouth dropped open.

She finally whispered, "Mom?"

Kim was unable to speak. She burst into tears and rushed forward, rapidly nodding her head.

Megan lunged into her mother's arms. "They said that you were dead, but I never believed it," she sobbed. "And they called me Carol, but I always knew my name was Megan."

"Oh, Megan, Megan," was all Kim could say.

A very confused-looking young man came to the door and asked, "Carol? What's going on here?"

I stepped between him and his wife, who was still embracing Kim. "Steven? My name is Corrigan. Can you give them a few seconds? They haven't seen each other in nearly twenty years. This is your wife's mother."

"Her mother? But I thought—"

"It's going to take a while to explain. Maybe you'd better call in and say you won't be going to work today."

He repeated, "Carol? What is this all about?"

Megan turned around, still crying, and quietly said, "Steven, this is my mom. My name is Megan. Not Carol. Megan."

"Megan? But—"

I suggested, "Maybe we can all go someplace where we can sit down and talk."

We took a corner table at Perry's Restaurant and ordered coffees all around. Kim told the story about how Megan had been kidnapped in Salem eighteen years earlier—almost to the day. Megan's memory of that day was very vague. At first, her captors told her that her mother wanted her to go with them. Later they told her that her mother had died of cancer.

Kim told of her years of searching for any clue that might lead her to Megan and her eventual acceptance that she had probably been killed by her abductors and buried somewhere in the forests around Salem.

"They named me Carol. I knew it wasn't my name, but they told me over and over that I had always been Carol, and I should stop pretending I was someone else."

Steven asked how we'd figured out what had happened, so I recounted the whole story, from the discovery of Brittany Harlan's name scratched in the old beam up through our conversation with Sharon the day before.

There was a second reunion late in the afternoon at the airport in Hailey, when Jeffrey Moro arrived with Tiffany. Steven and I stepped aside and let the family have the time to themselves. There were tears and smiles. Stories were exchanged. I took photos of the little family, while strangers around us probably wondered what it was all about.

When my phone rang, I stepped away before answering. "Yeah, Fox. What's happening?"

"I just got the word. State police picked up Timothy and Patricia Ranier about an hour ago. They're bringing them straight to Salem. They'll be here about midnight."

"That's a relief. I was worried that they might end up in Harney County custody, and I suspect that Ranier has friends there."

"After what you told me about the way they handled the old witness reports, I just didn't think it was appropriate to have them taken to Burns."

We all went to Ketchum for dinner, and Steven guided us to a restaurant/bar that he assured us had the best steaks in town. We were seated at a big round table in a corner by the window. In the middle of the table was a stand-up sign reading, "Karaoke Every Night."

"I have to warn you," I said. "I have a black belt in karaoke."

Kim looked skyward.

I continued, "My voice is registered as a deadly weapon. I've been banned in six states. The other forty-four haven't yet heard me sing."

We stayed and talked long after the dinner was over, and I found myself again compelled to tell how I'd figured it out for the benefit of Jeffrey and Tiffany.

Megan, sitting between her parents, quietly told of her years with Patricia and Timothy. It was hard to tell for sure if she was telling us the whole truth, but she never mentioned any kind of sexual abuse. Her captors were stern and strict, and they enforced a harsh regimen. Any infraction against their peculiar rules was punished by her being forced to stand facing a blank wall for hours.

And yet she seemed to know that it could have been a lot worse. In telling the story of my investigation, I'd glossed over the things that had happened to the other girls, but Megan didn't have to be told. Everyone cheered when I related what Kevin Fox had told me—that Patricia and Timothy had been arrested and were on their way to Salem.

Hours later, alone with Kim in our motel room, she came over and gave me a long hug.

"Thank you," she whispered. "Thank you so much."

Chapter 76

While waiting for breakfast, I scanned the Boise newspaper for news of our case. Instead, I found the obligatory front-page article commemorating the anniversary of the bombing of Hiroshima, castigating all Americans, most of whom hadn't even been born at the time, for having used the atomic bomb to incinerate one hundred thousand Japanese civilians—failing to mention that the alternative would have been using thousands of incendiary bombs to do the same job, as had already been done in Tokyo and a dozen other Japanese cities.

I'm not sure how napalm and a million flaming bits of magnesium are more humane than nuclear fission, and I wonder when readers will wake up to the fact that they're reading the same story every year on August 6. Maybe next year, the news media will have interviews with some of the marines who survived Iwo Jima or Okinawa to give some historical perspective. Or not.

I went through the entire paper—twice—finding no mention of the arrests of Timothy and Patricia Ranier. That was just as well, because it allowed Kim and her family to have a day of privacy and anonymity before the inevitable media storm caught up with them.

We spent the rest of that day and half of the next with Kim's family. In most ways, they were strangers, and yet they shared an unbreakable bond—one tempered by pain, distress, sorrow, and sadness that could never completely go away. Things could never be as they were. They all had their separate lives. Inevitably, the conversation went to the topic of what came next.

I looked at Megan and said, "You'll need to give a statement to Salem PD. They'll want to hear the whole story from you."

Steven shook his head. "We can't just take off and go all the way to Salem!"

Kim speculated, "You might not have to. They ought to be able to find someone around here to take your statement. But one thing is certain— you're going to have to be there for the trial."

Steven groaned. "But a trial like that could take weeks! Who's going to pay our expenses?"

"Don't worry about that," Kim said. "You can have my condo for as long as you need it." She looked at me and added, "I'll be staying someplace else."

"But what about our jobs?" Steven asked.

"Just explain the situation to the manager, and they'll hold your jobs 'til you get back. You might even consider checking out the job situation in our area."

Megan was nodding her head, but Steven looked skeptical. I could see that they were going to have to talk this whole thing out.

Late in the afternoon, Fox called to impatiently ask when I'd be able to get to Salem and give my formal statement. I talked it over with Kim, and we decided to start back home the next day. Tiffany and Jeffrey had a morning flight back to Medford, so we offered to drop them off at the airport.

In the parking lot after a group breakfast the next morning, everyone said their goodbyes. After final hugs, Steven and Megan headed off to return to work, and the rest of us crammed ourselves into Kim's Mustang for the trip to Ketchum. We left Jeffrey and Tiffany at the airport and turned toward home.

It had been a dizzying week. Only nine days had passed since I put my finger on Frenchglen and started the snowball rolling. In the days following the arrests of Timothy and Patricia Ranier, the number of missed opportunities became a big part of the news story. There were so many if's.

If the initial bulletin had accurately described the van; if police made public the omega tattoo and the van logo described by Caroline Gervais; if the witness reports in Frenchglen had been properly investigated; if social services had investigated the Raniers.

People encouraged Kim to file suit over the sloppy investigation in Harney County, but when the county attorney offered an out-of-court settlement, she accepted it and put it into an education fund for her future grandchildren.

Contrary to the opinion of Eddie Florence, Ranier was not an alias. Timothy Ranier was the kidnapper's real name. But he and Patricia had never been married. Her real name was Patricia Newberry. She was a runaway from the Bay Area, an emotional basket case who was attracted to Rajneeshpuram by the utopian vision of a society built on love and sharing.

That's where she met Timothy, an immature loser from Portland who had been attracted by the promise of free love at the commune. And somehow Timothy and Patricia together concocted their own fantasy world, where they alone understood right and wrong.

Sitting with Kim in my boat, engine off and drifting lazily on the almost imperceptible current, we talked about all that had happened. The sun went down, and we finished off our bottle of Chardonnay with a toast to our future.

Other novels by Ken Baysinger

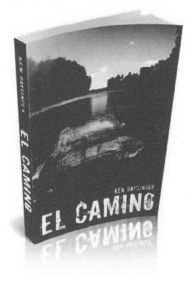

El Camino

The Mendelson-Devonshire case was legendary. It was also political dynamite. In 1980 the disappearance of Jessie Devonshire and Randy Mendelson had been Portland's biggest news story of the year. It remained the region's most notorious unsolved case.

It couldn't even be properly called an unsolved crime, because it had never been proven that a crime had been committed. All that was known was that fifteen-year-old Jessie Devonshire had vanished without a trace and that Randy Mendelson, a twenty-year-old landscaper, had disappeared at the same time.

Everyone had a theory, but nobody had an answer to the mystery. The one fact that everyone knew was that Jessie Devonshire was the stepdaughter of Wilson Landis Devonshire, who was an official in the Portland Mayor's office and a rising star among Oregon's political elite.

The case that lands in the lap of a private investigator named Corrigan had been the biggest hot potato in Clackamas County law enforcement for at least ten years following the disappearances. At least three careers had ended because detectives had been unable to provide the answers that the politically powerful principals in the case demanded.

ISBN: 978-1-02902-079-2 ©2014
Tate Publishing and Enterprises   538 pages $22.99

www.kenbaysinger.com